The Jacobite's Daughter

Lorna Windham

Tyne Bridge Publishing

www.tynebridgepublishing.org.uk

© Lorna Windham, 2018
Published by:
Tyne Bridge Publishing,
City Library, Newcastle upon Tyne, United Kingdom
www.tynebridgepublishing.org.uk

This book is a work of fiction.

I would like to thank everyone who helped me with *The Jacobite's Daughter,* you know who you are. A special thanks to Val Waltl for the spinning lesson. This novel is for Mam and Dad. I must also thank David Hepworth of Tyne Bridge Publishing and his Editor, Vanessa, for having faith in me and the novel.

CHAPTER One
August 1745.

The wind made a final rush over Loch Linnhe and up to Braedrumie's old church in the West Highlands of Scotland. Morag McColl pushed open the oak door. It hit the inner stone wall and the sound echoed in the empty space as light flooded in. Dust motes drifted above the font; dead leaves stirred on the worn flagstones and the stone altar shimmered with jewelled light from arched windows.

Morag curtsied and crossed herself before sitting on a pew. Her fingers drummed on the carved pine. She heard Euan's footsteps and caught her breath. His presence filled the church. She'd loved him since childhood.

"Well done, you managed to evade your maid." She could listen to his deep voice for ever. It took him two strides to be at her side, his grey eyes locked on hers. Her pulse raced. She breathed in the scent of sandalwood aware of the energy that crackled between them.

He held her hands, his touch gentle as always. *Sweet Jesu, I love him for it.*

Euan whispered, "Prince Charles, landed at Eriskay in July. Father's just told me. Only a few trusted chiefs know. There's to be a rising."

She stared at him open mouthed. They'd waited so long for this moment. Euan had vowed to join any rebellions against the hated English. He said no man could prosper under their boot. *Will he be killed?*

With the Irish Sea to the west, mountains to the south and Loch Linnhe to the north, Braedrumie had been a hotbed of Jacobite intrigue for decades. There'd been several unsuccessful risings, the last ended in disaster a year ago. Why should this one be any different? She'd always thought he'd return so, why worry now? *No.*

Euan would come home, he always had. He'd bring their marriage date forward, and she would go with him. She listened as he continued.

"There'll be a gathering tonight and we'll light the Fiery Cross and send out runners. Tomorrow we'll set off for Glenfinnan and the Raising of the Standard."

"So we'll wed and I can go with you?"

"It's no place for a young lass. I thought you'd ken that."

Young lass. The hurt arced deep inside her. She was seventeen and he just three year older.

"I'd like to do something for The Cause." She tried to hide her disappointment.

He rubbed his brow. "You can make bonnets and sew banners at home."

"I want to be with you."

"And I with you, but it's no' possible."

Her stomach lurched. "And our wedding?" She twisted her betrothal ring. "I thought later this month," she plunged on, "but we could be handfasted today if our fathers agreed." Her heart leapt at the thought.

"It wouldna be proper, there'd be no priest."

"It would be a sin," she admitted, "but I wouldna care, I'd be with you."

"I wouldna take you with me."

Her heart missed a beat. "But I want to be your wife and *do* something useful, no' just spin and wield a needle."

"Morag ..."

She sensed his will falter.

"No." He shook his head. "You wouldna be safe."

"I can look after myself." Morag pricked his chest with his own a dirk.

He looked down and blinked. She knew he'd recognised the deer carved in the bog oak handle as it nestled in his hose only seconds before. She smiled up at him.

His voice held a note which teased. "Now where did you learn that trick?" He spread his arms wide and gave her a lopsided grin. "It's no' honourable to draw a toothpick on a poor, defenceless man."

Morag lowered the razor-sharp blade a tad and sliced a portion of expensive lace from the neck of his shirt so it fell like snow on his plaid.

Euan's hand snaked out. "If you dinna mind, I'd prefer my shirts in one piece. It might be useful to remember that if you're no' too fond of sewing." He put the dirk back in its rightful place.

A silence fell between them.

She sighed. "Dougie said it might save my life one day."

Euan sucked in his breath.

Morag knew he'd have words with his father's tacksman and leapt to Dougie's defence. "He was only trying to help."

"You dinna use a weapon against a man who trusts you." His eyes became flint. Seeing her downcast expression he said, "Your attacker would have to be close for you to wield a dirk, too close. One mistake and he'd ravish you before he killed you no doubt." He gathered her in his arms. "And I've every intention of ravishing you once we're married by a priest. And God only knows when we'll find one of those." His lips poised over hers as if he wanted to drink her in.

Sweet Jesu, will he never kiss me? She welcomed his lips as they crushed hers in a joyous rush.

Seconds passed. "That was a very dangerous kiss, Morag McColl." He wagged his forefinger at her.

Her lips hungered for more. She lowered her lashes. "I hadna thought about a priest," she said, "so we wouldna have been able to marry by the end of the month anyway."

His brow became overcast. "Can't you see, Morag, this isna a time for marrying, but for war?"

She almost snapped back, but stopped herself and stirred the dust of the dried leaves with the toe of her shoe. Just as well he couldn't read her mind because she wanted both.

His lips formed a lopsided smile. "How your hair sparks in the light." He lifted a curl. "It's one of the things I love about you."

She turned her head and tugged the strands out of his hand. He knew she hated her hair. His attempt to divert her attention, wouldn't work. Couldn't he understand if they delayed they might never experience married life together?

He held her chin between his thumb and forefinger and turned her face to him. "Morag, my heart, let's have no sulky looks. I've waited years for a Stuart to set foot in Scotland again. When we win there'll be no more famine or want because of the English and their laws. This is a time of celebration and Father expects the whole of Braedrumie at the ceremony tonight. Dougie's waiting outside and there's preparations to make. I'll call for you this evening."

"Our marriage is important too and we need to talk."

He smiled at her and his lips brushed her forehead. "Tonight."

She watched him leave. Did he really think she'd be content to sit at home and sew neat stitches when his life and their country's future were at stake? He'd trained for war since he could walk, whilst she'd managed her widowed father's run-down household, her mother being long dead. Some said her mother, a lady, had married beneath her, but it had been a love match. Her dowry long gone, Morag had even carried out domestic tasks herself when short of money. Euan knew how dull she'd found it.

Fortunately, her father had also ensured she attended the village school until the age of twelve under Braedrumie's enlightened school master, Mr. Drummond. Apart from reading, writing and arithmetic, they'd studied the science of man and talked about equality and rights of African slaves. Morag couldn't see why those ideas shouldn't extend to Highland women.

She rested her head against the ancient pew. She loved this church. The interior, cool after the heat of the day and, as always, a hint of incense and beeswax remained in the air. The memory of a long dead priest and chanting the Latin Mass came to her. A soft smile played on her face.

But no priest dared to cross the threshold now, though the villagers followed the old religion whilst they paid lip service to Presbyterianism. You couldn't wipe away hundreds of years of Catholic faith.

This where she'd been christened and hoped to marry Euan Stewart, second son of the Laird of Braedrumie. She smiled at the thought. She'd grown up with the Stewart brothers and trailed behind them until Euan insisted she joined their group. Involvement in their childhood pranks meant more whippings than she could count, but it had been worth it. She'd been drawn to Euan as he was to her.

She struggled to contain her excitement and imagined how it would be. They'd come from miles for the wedding and the Laird of McColl's free food and whisky. She closed her eyes. There'd be wild rose, mountain thyme and gorse decorating the arched doorway and every pew, so the air would be laden with perfume as she walked down the aisle towards Euan.

She chewed her lip. But they hadn't agreed a date for their marriage and time could run out. She thought of 1715 when her grandfather had been killed and her father badly wounded at the Battle of Sheriffmuir. Could she bear it if this happened to Euan and he needed her and she wasn't there?

The church became dark. There'd be hell to pay at home. Her maid would have reported her absence hours ago. She wrapped her shawl around her. One thought stayed like a persistent midge as she gave a final tug at the door: life without Euan Stewart was unthinkable.

CHAPTER Two

"You told her?" Dougie's chiselled face showed interest as he ran his fingers through his grey beard. As the laird's cousin he acted as the middleman between him and his tenants. He'd been leaning against the church wall and joined Euan as he strode out of the churchyard.

"I told her." Euan didn't slow his stride, his senses full of Morag's heather scent, lithe body and brown hair. He wanted her. It took all of his willpower to put her to one side so he could take part in the Rising.

"From the look on your face she didna take it too well."

"Thanks to you." Euan mentally counted Dougie's attributes: mentor, counsellor and friend he took a deep breath. "She expected a date for our wedding, wanted us to wed without a priest so she could join me. She drew my own knife on me."

"Ha." Dougie wagged an accusing finger at him. "She bested you. You're getting careless."

"And you're testing my patience." Euan jerked to a halt. He'd get a crick in his neck, but still thrust his forehead inches from Dougie's craggy brows. "She's young, she doesna realise what war's like, how could she?"

"Women."

"She'll come round." Euan sounded confident, but Morag could be obstinate. He remembered the time he and his brothers had terrified her father's hens so much that they wouldn't lay for weeks. She'd refused to say it was them and earned a whipping before they could intervene.

"My Isabel birthed our six babes and watched them all die. Says death holds no fears because we'll all be together in the next world. If she ever worried about me, she's kept it to herself. That's how it's always been and I bless the day she said she was mine. She ..."

"And she's never wanted to join you?"

"She's got more sense and likes her own bed to sleep in."

"So why canna Morag be like her?" said Euan.

Dougie looked at him as if he had lost his mind. "Because my Isabel's sixty and Morag's sap's rising. Her father's never been the same since the mother's death. Morag's dutiful enough, but her lady mother had a will of her own. It's as well you're warned now, before you're wed."

"I love her, Dougie. There'll never be another for me."

"That's an end to it then."

CHAPTER Three

Morag's heart performed a jig when Euan called for her as promised an hour before dusk. He looked so handsome. The blue bonnet she'd knitted sat at a jaunty angle on his head. His black woollen jacket and white linen shirt showed off his broad shoulders, slim waist and flanks. Black breeches, white hose and brogues completed his wardrobe.

It was over half an hour's ride to Invererar Falls. A pity Father, furious at her for being 'missing' for hours, had decided to travel with them. For a man in his sixties, he sat upright in the saddle, his grey hair the only sign of age.

"Was it very bad?" asked Euan in a whisper as they set out from the farm, her frowning father jogging behind.

"He dismissed the maid," Morag mouthed and raised her eyes to Heaven. "Euan, tell me again how it'll be."

"Again? Your father might hear."

She sneaked a look at her father's face and sighed. He could be a hard man when he wanted. "He welcomed our match."

"So he did." Euan smiled down at her. "I'll build us a good, stone house on the land my grandfather left me, over there in the lee of the hill, so we're protected from the weather. It'll have two rooms downstairs, a fine scullery and four bedrooms for any ... er ... family that might come along. There'll be a byre and stables. We'll have the best pasture for our cattle and a stream close by. I mean to be a wealthy man so we'll be happy here for the rest of our lives."

"It sounds so wonderful. Euan, about our wedding ...?"

"Not now, Morag." His lips set in a firm line.

She knew that look and nursed resentment at his tone. They rode in silence deep in their own thoughts through Glen Drum towards Braedrumie. Morag had endured a tirade from her father and Euan still refused to listen to what she wanted. *Men are so annoying.*

She fingered her betrothal ring. Father had compared them to Braedrumie Market's dool tree, firmly rooted in the same soil and enduring all weathers. Now Euan was leaving and Morag sensed the ground shifting under her feet.

Invererar Falls towered above them and the air thundered with the roar of cascading water the colour of frothy peat.

Euan leapt from his pony and helped her down.

She enjoyed his closeness and the heat of his body. "Please listen."

Morag turned as he tugged her hair then raced off through the purple heather, waving her blue ribbon as he went.

Her father shook his head at Euan's antics and tethered the ponies.

Morag tucked her hair behind her ears and tried to catch him. "Euan wait." she shouted. "We need to talk."

He clambered up to the great finger of granite where the escarpment came to an abrupt end and overlooked the land and loch below. Pausing, he allowed Morag to reach his side.

She raised her voice again. "About the Rising" She didn't know if he heard her as he pulled her into his arms and stole a kiss. When she responded and closed her eyes, he teased her by flicking icy droplets onto her face and raced away.

"Euan, be serious," she yelled and scrambled after him slipping and sliding over the moss-covered rocks.

Euan crouched down, turned and put a warning finger to his mouth. "Shhh."

Morag poked out her tongue, but he gave her a solemn look and shook his head. She reached his side, looked up and saw a row of men's backs above them.

Euan dangled the ribbon in front of her nose.

"You," hissed Morag grabbing it whilst taming stray curls.

He ruffled her hair and she batted him away.

Morag checked his shirt and plaid, brushed grass from his shoulder and gave a little nod of satisfaction.

"Miss McColl." Euan held out his hand, serious at last.

"Mr. Stewart." Morag slipped her hand into his and allowed him to help her over the lip of rock. Euan had three brothers: Rob, Johnnie and Duncan. Rob left several months ago without a word to anyone. Euan was now the laird's heir and had to act in a responsible manner as did she.

From this sacred place they could see for miles across the green sward of Braedrumie and out beyond to the blue of Loch Linnhe with Cull Bay to their left and Kentallen Bay on the right. Dusk fell, the air filled with bird song and a light breeze sprang up. The sapphire sky slowly darkened as if it knew something they didn't.

Men carrying targes and swords gathered in small groups. The whole clan had come to watch. She knew fourteen-year-old Duncan, would find it hard to accept he wasn't allowed to join the Rising. He stubbed his toe in the earth as if it was the enemy.

Dougie and his men tied horsehair rope round two seasoned yew boughs beside a post hole in the boggy ground.

The clan faced the west and the gold of the setting sun. Euan held Morag so close she could feel his precious heart beating in the rise and fall of his chest.

Johnnie had his arms wrapped round Kirsty Lorne. Her fair head rested on his shoulder. Morag remembered the night of their betrothal and the dreadful argument between Johnnie and his father. She balanced on sharp blades whenever she visited Euan's family.

The last rays of the fiery sun sank and the air cooled. Morag shivered and Euan gathered her even closer so she shared his warmth. Desolation crept over her. *We might never do this again. What if he doesna come home? I canna imagine life without him.*

Her head only reached his chest, but she searched his features with an intensity she hadn't before. She closed her eyes and explored his face with her fingers, "You've a fine strong chin, straight nose, hair like torn autumn leaves; eyes the colour of cloudy skies and lips …"

Euan cut her off with his mouth on hers. The gathering darkness hid them and a fiddler started to play.

At last Morag pulled away. "I'll remember everything about you, how you look, and sound, how you walk… No matter what happens, you'll come back to me, promise?" Her voice quavered. Euan's grip tightened on her hands. She managed to say, "I couldna bear it if … I never saw you again."

"I'll be back. This time we'll win. Prince Charles's promised us French support," Euan whispered, "and when I return I'll build that home we've always planned." He kissed each of her eyelids. "And your father can have a place at the fire so he can play with our bairns."

"Bairns," cackled old Granny Mac, Braedrumie's old midwife, who'd bumped into them.

"Ssshh." Dougie's wife, Isabel, hustled the elderly woman away.

The whole of Braedrumie will know.

Euan led her away from the others. The moon became a pale shadow of itself. He held her hands. "We'll grow old together. I'll work hard, you'll see. We'll live all our days here."

Burying herself in his arms, Morag was sure he didn't want to add to her fears. She knew Euan and his brothers had taken part in skirmishes and worse with clans and redcoats since he could hold a sword. There'd always been the chance he'd not return.

Morag crossed herself as she thought of Euan's mother, Elizabeth, may God keep her. Elizabeth had been clever and insisted the brothers had a tutor at home so they could go to university and become learned gentlemen. Something Rob had endured, Euan loathed and Johnnie, who could handle himself in a fight but just preferred books, longed for. Duncan's older brothers were born fighters and he looked as if he'd take after them.

She'd almost forgotten her gift. Morag stood on her toes, kissed Euan and placed a gold cross round his neck. Her pulse quickened as his skin started at her touch. "It's been in our family for more years than I know."

Euan's lips sought hers again. They clung together. Morag closed her eyes trying to commit all that he was to memory.

"Come home safe to me, Euan Stewart," she whispered.

"Whisht, my beloved darling it's beginning."

Morag sensed the gathering silence as Euan drew her close once more. She sighed relaxing in his embrace and enjoying the strength of his body. Marriage couldn't come soon enough for her at moments like this.

Several couples and families pressed closer together as if seeking reassurance from each other. Darkness descended, a cloak studded with glittering stars.

Dougie lit a brand, which flickered, flared and exploded into a dance of fire. Holding the torch aloft, he faced the points of the compass and finally the laird. Then he set fire to the arms of the wooden cross. A mighty roar came from the throats of all there as ochre flames darted over the dry wood and leapt upward. Crimson sparks leapt into the dark sky. The glow would be seen for miles, the signal calling others to rise for The Cause. Out in the blackness glimmers of light answered, like a string of golden beads across the vastness around them.

Teams of fast runners lit their own small crosses and to yells of encouragement set off in different directions with their message: Charlie had landed and the Stewart clan would meet the others at Glenfinnan on August 19th.

Every man of fighting age held a stone which symbolised his leaving for war. They placed it on the ground to form a cairn. The laird motioned Euan to go first and then Johnnie. Dougie, ever patient, restrained a scowling, kicking Duncan. The mound grew as did the banter and laughter. Each man must have wondered if he'd return to claim his stone, for just a step away stood a substantial cairn from 1715. The die was cast; no going back now.

CHAPTER Four

Euan had a restless night in his own bed. His mind churned and took him back to Johnnie's betrothal dinner some days earlier. They'd been celebrating the *mutual understanding* between Kirsty Lorne and Johnnie. The betrothal ring had just been placed on her finger.

Father had asked, "When are you and Duncan going to enlist? The convivial atmosphere in the dining room descended into one of frayed tempers.

"My intention is to go to university and wee Duncan is too young," stated Johnnie.

"Euan joined the regiment today and by God so will you two. The prince needs you as his father did me in 1715. You'll no' shame me or the clan."

Duncan looked whey-faced as if he'd just escaped from the school room and his eyes flicked round the table.

Euan squeezed Morag's hand. She half smiled at him. Of course she'd seen his father in a temper before.

The serving maids giggled, tucking wisps of hair into grubby caps and rubbing hands on grease spattered aprons. Dougie motioned to them and they poured more wine. Red droplets fell on the white linen cloth. Flickering candles made crystal goblets wink, each engraved with a single rose and six buds, a testament to the loyalty of the Stewarts to the Jacobite cause.

"But Father ..." began Johnnie.

"So I've three worthless sons. Isn't it enough my eldest, that ingrate, skulked off without telling a soul?" He waved a hand at Rob's empty place. "I'll no' have it said you and Duncan are cowards."

Duncan started to rise, but Euan pressed his hand on his brother's shoulder and kept him in his chair. Dougie jerked his head at the maids, sending them fleeing into the night.

Kirsty and her mother sat white faced and strained. Euan and his brothers had known Kirsty from childhood. Her family owned a farm across the glen and valuable land abutting the Stewart holdings. They needed a man, the father having died three years before. Johnnie, a third son, needed a good marriage with prospects. Kirsty appeared a good match.

"I'm no' coward nor is Duncan." Johnnie flung his napkin on the table. "And Rob ..."

"Dinna mention his name in my presence."

Euan felt his father's pain. No one had heard from Rob since he'd left. As Father's favourite his going hurt everyone who knew him. Euan assessed his father's temper. He signalled Dougie who left the room. If they could get the women out and in the coach before his Father erupted, it would be better for everyone.

Johnnie took a couple of deep breaths. "My apologies, ladies."

"Pah," grunted Father.

Johnnie thrust Kirsty and her mother's goblets into their hands as the brothers and Morag snatched up their own. Father's meaty fist slammed down on the oak table making a delft bowl roll onto the flagstone floor and shatter. He paid it no mind, though it had been brought from Holland at great expense in one of the family's ships. Johnnie looked at the ceiling, Duncan stared wide-eyed, Morag bit her lip and the Lornes stared at the table.

"It's your duty to me as sons of my house. I've lost him ... that turncoat, and I'm no' prepared to be shamed again. It's what your mother would have wanted. Do you hear me, or have you gone soft in the head?"

"I'll go if Duncan stays." Johnnie took a nonchalant swig of wine.

Duncan rose in protest, but again Euan pressed him into his seat.

"I'm no' negotiating boy, I'm telling you. It's expected. Told your mother education would stuff your head full of s..." he paused looking at the ladies. "Whig dung."

Kirsty covered her mouth with her handkerchief and her mother looked as if she'd bitten an apple and found a maggot.

It was not the first time Father and Johnnie had crossed swords. Father's jaundiced eyes never left Johnnie's as he grabbed a flagon and poured himself some claret. Johnnie continued to drink his wine.

Father drank and wiped the crimson splashes from his lips with his sleeve. He served himself another drink. "All right Duncan stays, he's just a bairn..."

"I'm no' a bloody bairn..." Euan clamped his hand over Duncan's mouth.

"But you," continued Father staring at Johnnie, "you'll fight for the honour of our family and like it."

"I'll fight, but I'll never like it." Johnnie rose from his seat. "Ladies, it seems it's late, let me escort you to your coach."

Euan and Morag led the way as their guests let Johnnie bundle them out of the door. He shut it behind them as something hit the ancient oak with a thump.

Colour crept up Johnnie's neck and face. "Please accept our apologies. Father's gout I'm afraid."

"What gout?" yelled Father.

Johnnie smiled, "Your cloaks, ladies."

Euan and Morag sighed with relief when they heard the wheels of the coach and saw Dougie in the driving seat.

"Thank you for a most delightful evening." Mrs. Lorne didn't arch a greying eyebrow.

"Most... entertaining." A demure Kirsty gave a sideways glance at Johnnie from beneath fair lashes.

Mrs. Lorne's shrivelled hand clutched Johnnie's shoulder. "You'd oblige me when you're off ... soldiering, by keeping an eye on my dear departed sister's son, Hughie McBean. He's a weak chest. Never could stand the cold. He volunteered yesterday."

Euan could see the barb wasn't lost on Johnnie, but his brother remained at his most civil. "Your servant, Ma'am. Be assured I'll do all I can to bring your nephew safely home." He bowed and kissed her hand.

Euan kept his thoughts to himself. *McBean looks like a slim reed in a bog. A puff of wind will blow him over. What in Hades is he doing going to war?* He watched Johnnie assist the ladies into the coach. *At least Duncan will stay at home, thanks to Johnnie.*

"I dinna care what you all say I'm not bloody staying behind." Duncan stood hands on hips.

Johnnie clouted him. "Don't bloody swear."

"Ow!"

Kirsty's mother gave them a look that should have speared them to the door.

Euan sighed. Morag put her hand in his and Johnnie turned a fierce glance on Duncan.

Euan woke bleary eyed before dawn the following morning.

CHAPTER Five

The waters of Loch Linnhe rippled in the slight breeze. Morag had been waiting by the loch for a good hour before dawn, when the men gathered in the cold morning mist. She'd thought it out before she slept, she'd help The Cause and it wouldn't involve a needle, but she'd a growing dread that her actions might drive Euan from her and she'd lose him anyway.

She loved Euan too much to let him go without her. Part of her plan had been accomplished, now she'd only to complete it, if she could only find Euan and Johnnie.

Morag's gaze wandered up to the old churchyard. *Of course, that is where they'll be: Elizabeth's grave.* Morag ran along the steep path lined with hazel, pine, yew and white heather. She twisted the thick stems of the shrub, pausing to enjoy its fresh scent as she carried sprigs of it up the winding track.

She breathed in the graveyard smell of damp earth as she leant on the wooden gate. The two brothers stood under a pine tree, their bonnets off, in front of their mother's headstone.

She pushed the timbers and winced at the creak.

Euan waved.

Johnnie closed his Bible and mumbled, "Morning." He nodded to her and made off through the gate which creaked again and slammed shut.

The wind whipped across the loch and over the churchyard making huge boughs sway. The pines released their scent into the air. Morag breathed it in and sought warmth. She put her arm in Euan's.

"Johnnie read her the 23rd Psalm." He gave her a half smile.

"She'd have liked that."

"I thought I'd ... say goodbye ... till I come home. She's here I swear it." His voice had a haunting sadness as the wind tugged his blue plaid and rushed through the green ivy covering part of the gravestone.

"She'd understand." Morag stared at the wording. The mason had only just completed it. She laid her white heather beside the purple bunches of Johnnie and Euan. "This is no' right." She pointed at the carved words.

"Father's decision." Euan rubbed his brow.

"Rob..."

"Dinna say his name. He made his choice remember? He didna think fit to tell us why. His leaving killed her."

She took both his hands in hers. "Euan, darling, you ken she was ailing before he left," he made to interrupt, but she continued. "This isna just. I canna excuse Rob for behaving the way he did, but he's your brother and your mother's son. She loved him and his name should be on her gravestone. This is no' right."

"It's Father, he wouldna listen to reason."

Morag had to let it rest at that. Didn't she have enough on her mind with Euan going to war and what she'd decided to do?

As they came down the hillside with its scattered circles of indigo heather and golden gorse, the silver platter of Loch Linnhe lay in front of them. Groups of tearful families held hands and hugged. Some seemed unable to look each other in the face and others held their gaze as if to commit each separate feature to memory. The air filled with lots of joking, banter and forced laughter.

Couples stood in the plum-shadow of the pine trees wanting privacy and time to themselves.

Morag couldn't help, but overhear their whispered words.

Isabel told Dougie, "Dinna be an old fool, come back in one piece." Johnnie and Kirsty clung to each other nearby.

"I'm going to be so bored without you."

Johnnie kissed her. "Why don't you and your mother visit my aunt Munro and her family in Inverness? You can visit your sick cousin at the same time. Look, here's the address." He scribbled on a piece of paper torn from one of his precious books and gave it to her.

Morag watched Kirsty clap her hands.

"Oh Johnnie, you're going to be the best of husbands. I'll write at once. Will you be bored, without me?"

Morag rolled her eyes. *He'll be at war, how will that be boring?*

Johnnie's blue eyes twinkled. He dangled several books, held in a leather strap, in front of Kirsty. "I've these to keep me company."

"Books." Kirsty sounded disappointed.

He dropped them to the ground and cradled her face in his hands. "I'll miss you sweetheart. Wait for me."

"You're so handsome and brave, Johnnie. When you come home you'll be a hero and I'll love you even more. I'll wait for you forever if I have to; you'll be in my heart when I'm sleeping and I'll think of you day and night." Kirsty smothered his face with kisses.

Morag pulled Euan deeper into the leafy forest, so she couldn't be overheard. It was as if Kirsty was on fire, unlike her icicle of a mother. Morag forced the memory of Johnnie's betrothal out of her head, unwilling to waste these precious moments she had with Euan. After what she was going to do, he probably wouldn't want to hold her for a long time.

Morag focused on the steady beat of Euan's heart and nestled her head on his chest. All she wanted was to be with him, breathing the same air and within the protective circle of his arms for the rest of her life. She clung to him till the very last moment, making a good show of holding back tears and mouthed, "I love you," as she handed him food she'd wrapped in muslin for his journey. She knew he'd soon be so angry with her.

The wind whipped a stray brown curl across her face. He caught it, wrapped it round his hand like rope and gently pulled her towards him. She tugged it out of his fingers, must he tease her now?

His hands went to her shoulders, his warm breath caressed her ear lobe, "My heart," he whispered in that deep voice she knew so well, "if I fall ..."

"No." She moved away from him. "You'll come home."

He sighed and took her hand, pulling her to him again. "I'll no' have you part from me out of sorts. I love everything about you and when I come home, I promise the first thing we'll do is marry."

She melted and allowed him to kiss her forehead, cheek bones and the tip of her nose. He eyed her wayward hair with a boyish grin. "I'll miss your unruly thatch."

"Euan." She aimed a swipe at his head, but he ducked and had her in his arms, his mouth on hers, searching, possessing, till her heart pounded and senses reeled. She didn't want him to stop. He broke away with a sudden movement, leaving her with bruised lips and an aching heart. She watched him go with a grim faced Johnnie and gather his men.

McBean, his wife Mary and their children Charlie, Alec and Maggie arrived. Johnnie extended his hand in welcome as McBean had a coughing fit. After all, McBean was Kirsty's uncle and Johnnie had promised his future mother-in-law he'd bring him safe home. Morag started when McBean yelled and charged Johnnie to the ground. McBean scurried behind the nearest bush from which came such grunts and groans that they all looked at each other in alarm. Johnnie drew his claymore.

Mary put her hands over her face as her bairns ran in circles whooping and yelling round everyone.

Some moments later McBean returned belching and rubbing his stomach. "Something I ate last night," he said, oblivious to the grins of those around him.

Johnnie sheathed his blade and hissed to Euan, "An attack of the bloody shite scared more like."

Euan grinned and Morag muffled her laughter.

McBean bent to kiss Mary, who held his lean frame to her as if she wasn't going to let go. Then she gathered her children together and walked away.

Poor Duncan tried to slip into the ranks and hide beside Jamie Moffat. Dougie, knowing the ways of boys, had been looking for him and sent him homeward with a clip of his lugs and a slap of leather whistling round his thin backside.

Duncan stood forlorn and enraged on a hillock behind them. "You're all piss pots!" he shouted as he waved his fist at them. "Do you hear? Bloody piss pots!" Morag couldn't console him.

Dougie used his thumb to point at Duncan. "That brother of yours has a fine, wee voice; he'll make a braw piper one day." Broad grins creased their faces as they marched away.

Kirsty stood beside Morag as they watched Duncan run off. "They need to take that wee devil in hand. Like father like son I suppose if our betrothal is anything to go by."

"He's upset at being left behind and their father's still grieving over Elizabeth's death, as well you ken."

"I can see I'm no' wanted here. I've got better things to do than talk to you, Morag McColl." Kirsty flounced off.

"Please yourself." Morag poked her tongue at Kirsty's back.

Morag saw Euan nudge Johnnie and point up at the Falls. One lone figure stood with his sword raised, the laird. Euan had the whole clan turn and silently answer his salute.

Morag waited, her stomach churning till Euan and his column of men were out of sight and everyone had drifted away. If he thought he was leaving her behind, he'd better think again. She'd hidden a cloth bundle containing clothes, food and her precious, well-thumbed book of simples (her mother's remedies), behind a group of rocks. She grabbed her bundle, placed an old shawl over her head and joined the women at the back of the baggage train.

They greeted her with understanding on their faces. "You canna let him go without you. Come along with us, lass." One of them started to sing in a high sweet voice:

> *Prince Charles it is the hour*
> *When victory's close at hand,*
> *We'll grant you the power*
> *To ensure you win this land.*

The women took up the song and one by one the men's deeper voices joined in filling them with hope for the future.

Morag felt a pang of regret for her poor father who'd return home from collecting rents to find her short note informing him she'd gone with Euan and that she'd return once they'd won. She'd made her choice and now she had to live with it.

CHAPTER Six

Morag found herself with hundreds of Stewarts journeying to Ballacchlulish and the Cona Narrows when they crossed Loch Linnhe in boats to Ardgour. They followed the Cona River. From Cona Glenn they turned north to climb over Meal na Cuarcaige. Below they saw Glenfinnan at the northern edge of snaking Loch Shiel. With indigo mountains at their backs, they descended towards the loch's azure waters.

They rested till they spotted a small boat at the southern end of the loch making its way towards them.

Morag stayed well back, able to distinguish Euan's bobbing head as sailors rowed Prince Charles Edward Stuart, clad in a fine blue coat and white silk stockings, to shore. The boat beached into soft sand and he jumped ashore leading a group of dashing men onto the purple haze of the moor. A couple of Highland chiefs came forward and shook his hand, whilst a shepherd shaded his eyes.

The group settled down some distance away watched by more and more Highlanders on the slopes of the hills. The women kept some distance from him. Those with the best eyesight agreed he was young, tall and charming, everything a leader should be.

So, the prince had arrived, the waiting over. Morag walked faster, pulling her shawl over her head as she left the women in the rear, eager to hear what the Stewart family would make of him.

"It's shameful," said Dougie, "only a few chiefs here to greet him, but I see he's brought the sons of the 'Wild Geese' with him."

Morag looked at the sky for fluttering wings and listened for the familiar honking call. Dougie pointed at a group of men with Irish accents playing cards with the Prince. The *Wild Geese*. How Euan would have laughed at her.

"The prince's taken a huge gamble the clans will rise for him." Johnnie turned a page of Swift's *Battle of the Books*.

She recognised the battered cover; he'd been reading it at home for weeks.

"Can you doubt it?" said Euan.

Johnnie lowered his voice and Morag strained to hear him, "They say the clan chiefs are divided and some advised him to go home."

"Then you have to admire the man," said Euan as a roar interrupted him. It rippled like waves down the hillsides and heralded the arrival of James Kinross with 150 men. "I told you, the clans are rallying."

The strong looking, bearded men made a fine sight as they beat on their targes.

Johnnie shook his head. "Never thought I'd see it."

Dougie found the clan a place to rest on the side of hill overlooking the loch.

Morag squatted some distance away and sipped water from her leather bag as she watched Euan pull out a lump of cheese she'd carved into the shape of two hearts. His ears went pink at the jeers and hoots aimed at him. He swallowed the cheese in two gulps and choked. She started up in alarm, to see Johnnie, thumping him hard on the back. Euan coughed, took a great breath and with eyes watering, motioned he could breathe.

Dougie wagged a crust of bread at Euan. "And that's no' the last time a lassie will be the death of you. I mind the time my Isabel ..."

Morag sank back on the grass, enjoying the warmth of the sun.

***

Euan interrupted Dougie with a question that initiated grateful glances from the others. Much as they all liked and respected Isabel, Euan knew Dougie's eulogies could turn men to stone.

"Isna that William Murray, Marquis of Tullibardine?" Euan asked, winking at the others. "Didna he fight in the 1715? He must be over sixty now." He pointed at a dark, hook-nosed man.

"That's him," said Dougie narrowing his eyes to see clearer. "A bonnie fighter in his time. Now, as I was sayin' about Is ..."

"And who's that?" asked Euan pointing to a portly, rather disgruntled gentleman.

Dougie's eyes followed Euan's finger.

"Aenas Macdonald from Kilochmoidart." Johnnie lifted his head from the book. "Banker, works in Paris. Knew one of his brothers at university, there's five will fight for the prince. Dinna recognise the rest."

"That tall gentleman over there," said Dougie keen not to be out done. He pointed behind him with his thumb. "Looks a bit green round the gills? Colonel Francis Strickland from a Jacobite, Westmorland family." He then went through the backgrounds of several people standing in front of them.

Johnnie whistled at Dougie in amazement.

"How do you ken all this?" Euan asked.

"I use my eyes and ears laddie, eyes and ears." Dougie grinned.

Euan shook his head, Dougie may be the laird's tacksman, but was also a font of information about Jacobites.

James Kinross, the tall, whiskery son of Keith Kinross, approached. "The Macgregors are on their way," he said and moved on to the next group.

Euan joined in the cheer, faltering when he saw Dougie silent and running his long fingers through his bushy beard, a sure sign of deep thought. "Never liked Kinross; dinna trust the man."

But who could you trust in the Highlands? They all knew the Rising would come to nought, unless they trusted each other and clans like the Camerons of Lochiel joined the Cause. He wondered if old Lochiel's son would give his bond. Lochiel still lived in exile in France for his part in 1715, or so Euan's father had said.

The distant skirl of pipes and a runner gasping for breath told the clans, "1800 of Lochiel's Camerons and 300 of Alexander of Keppoch's MacDonalds are on the way."

The clans rose as one man and issued a mighty roar, threw blue bonnets into the air and beat swords against targes. The sound swept up and down the hillsides until the Camerons and MacDonalds arrived.

"How could you doubt it brother?" Euan smiled and slapped Johnnie on the back.

Johnnie shrugged his shoulders.

Pipes played. The aged Duke of Atholl unfurled the white, blue and red silk Royal Standard and placed it in a hole carved in a granite boulder on the hillside. Euan and Dougie bellowed a heady cheer alongside thousands of clansmen confident they'd take the British Crown and restore the rightful king to the throne at last.

Johnnie stifled a yawn and looked around him.

***

With men's shouts ringing in her ears, Morag jerked upright and rubbed her eyes. Damn, she'd been asleep. Had she been discovered? She searched the tops of hundreds of heads till she found Euan's, then ducked behind a tall Highlander and prayed she hadn't been seen. Peeking out from behind the man's targe she saw the Duke raise his hand, demand silence and read out the proclamation which announced the prince as Regent. She squeezed her way to the front of the throng, keeping a constant eye on the Stewart clan as she did so. The prince seemed more suited to court than a Scottish hillside. She glanced at Euan's back, not many as broad as his.

The prince's voice brought her back to the present. "Thank you for your welcome, we are home at last."

Was there just more than a hint of a foreign accent? Startled by the guttural roar that sprang from thousands of throats, she made herself continue to listen.

"This is the start of a momentous journey. We do not stand on our own; France has promised to join us. Our time has come and everything our fathers fought for in the 1715 shall come to pass, this we promise. We will regain our sovereign authority and Scotland will break free of the Hanoverian yoke it has borne for so long."

Morag joined in the rousing cheer at this as men shook each other's hands. A finger and thumb squeezed her backside's tender flesh. "Ow." She dropped her bundle, grabbed the hand, bit down hard on the thumb and drew blood.

Its owner was hidden by the noisy crowd and she struggled with him as he tried to retrieve his wounded digit. He was too strong for her and she had to let the hand go. "Lecher," she yelled at the puzzled faces around her. She rescued her goods realising she'd become the centre of attention.

The prince raised his hand again. "On the morrow we march to Perth, then Edinburgh and freedom, and damned be him who says nay."

Again there was uproar as muskets fired in the air. She looked for Euan and Dougie and saw how they joined in and how Johnnie stood looking in her direction with his arms folded. She tore herself away and melted into the growing shadows. As she stumbled down the hillside she heard her name called and turned, her heart thumping.

"Morag, I thought it was you." Johnnie had followed her, book in hand.

She lifted her chin and wrapped her shawl tighter round her shoulders.

"What are you doing here? Euan willna be happy."

"Phhh, Euan."

"Morag, you canna stay, this is no place for women."

"Whisky?" A young woman smiled at Johnnie. She lifted a leather bottle and then allowed him a glimpse of her ankles.

Morag gave him a wry smile.

"No thank you." He tightened his lips and looked at the darkening sky.

"The women here dinna seem to agree with you," said Morag.

"Euan willna have it. He'll no' let you stay."

"We'll just have to make sure he knows nought about it."

"Would you have me betray my own brother?"

"Sweet Jesu, Johnnie, I need your help ..." She chewed her lip, it hurt her to ask him, but she needed to do it.

"It's no' like you to be short of words."

"If that's how you're going to be, Johnnie Stewart."

He grabbed her hand and his voice softened, "Sit and tell me."

It was like old times when, as mediator, he'd solved childhood squabbles between her and Euan. She sat and then squirmed beside him, put down her bundle, arranged her skirts and began to play with her hair. "You're to promise no' to laugh."

He crossed his heart.

"I want to fight for The Cause but... someone goosed my backside."

"Someone ..." He stared at her not comprehending and then exploded with laughter.

"Stop it, Johnnie," she said, "I dinna want it to happen again."

"Well, no, I don't suppose you would." He laughed some more until he noticed her head droop, "Aye well, I'm always one for saving a damsel in distress. Dinna suppose I can persuade you to go back to the comforts of your own home where you'd be safe?"

"Johnnie."

"No I didna think so. Euan will find out."

"Johnnie."

"Mmm, let me think."

She waited in impatient silence as he lay back on the hillside, closed his eyes and sucked a stalk of grass.

"I think I have it, just the thing. Are you sure this is what you want? When winter comes or the fighting starts it'll be hard enough for men."

"I'm sure. I know you dinna really want to be here. I think it's a noble thing you're doing for Duncan's sake." She put her hand on his arm.

"At least you dinna agree with Father that I'm a coward." He got to his feet.

"I'd never think that Johnnie."

He smiled down at her. "Sit beside the women over there." He indicated a group round a camp fire. "Dinna move; I'll be back."

She watched him stride off up the hill into the gathering dusk, then picked up her bundle and moved closer to the women and the fire. They shuffled along and made room for her and she welcomed their companionship. She warmed her plaid, wrapped it round her and sat enjoying the heat from the jade and turquoise flames. As she watched their hypnotic movement Morag couldn't help but think of Johnnie's betrothal night. What a disaster. When the delft bowl had shattered on the floor she'd thought the Lornes might leave and that would be the end of any wedding plans. They'd been startled and the mother, who looked like an old sporran, had made no comment.

Kirsty seemed to be quite taken with Johnnie and Morag was sure she'd seen her wave something feminine at him out of the coach window when she'd set off home. It surely couldn't have been her garter. Euan had turned scarlet.

Morag remembered Dougie saying, "You'll be led a right dance by that little madam." Johnnie had replied, "I very much hope so," and laughed.

She just hoped he knew what he was doing because Kirsty and her mother did.

Euan had explained to her a long time ago how the Stewart family had ships that sailed to Europe and to the Americas. He'd become excited when he spoke of captains who described lands where you could walk for days and never see a living soul, lands alive with bear and beaver and native Indians.

Johnnie's words brought her back to the present as he sat and warmed his hands beside her. "It's all arranged, I went to see the Crawford's. Heard Lady Amelia's companion left this afternoon; at least she had some sense. You can have the post if you've a mind to sleep there from now on and dinna tell Euan I helped you." He sniffed the air. "Is there some broth?" he asked one of the women who gave him two steaming bowls. The smell of barley too enticing, Johnnie gave one to Morag and passed her a spoon.

Johnnie spoke between gulps, "You shouldna be here. I'm a Jacobite and would kill any man who said different ... but whether the prince can take on the government and win ... Rob met him in France, didna think much of him. I've serious misgivings about the whole bloody enterprise ... How many will die before Charlie wins the throne for the exiled Stuarts, **if** he wins it?"

She didn't have an answer for him. The broth lined her stomach as the night air cooled. In the gathering darkness pinpricks of light flared on the hills as the clans gathered round crackling campfires. McBean brought out a wooden flute. A haunting tune filled the air and Jamie Moffat's strong voice took up the words followed by the rest:

> *We'll sing and dance*
> *Now Charlie's here*
> *To gain the crown for his father…*

The prince solemnly listened and applauded when it finished. Then out came a fiddle and bagpipes and several of the Stewarts danced wild Scottish reels issuing great whoops at every turn.

They listened to the excited chatter and watched the Stewarts hooking arms round each other as the music played. *Surely the smile on Johnnie's lips means he's thinking of Kirsty?* She thought of Euan several campfires away. "You'll no' tell him, Johnnie?"

Johnnie gave a great sigh. "No, but if there's to be any fighting I'll have to, and you'll go home with no arguments. Do you promise?"

"Cross my heart and wish to die." She used their childhood oath, but countered it with crossed fingers behind her back.

He smiled again and lay on his side enjoying the reels. She breathed a sigh of relief. She'd got what she wanted, to be near to Euan so if he became ill or wounded or worse ... better not to dwell on that she decided. She'd think about what use she could be to The Cause with or without Euan's help. She watched a golden eagle soar in the dying rays of the sun and thought it a good omen.

CHAPTER Seven

"Come out, Morag." Euan leant forward and opened the tent flap. "I ken you're in there." He congratulated himself on his even tone, with no hint of the anger he'd experienced when Jamie Moffat told him. How could she? Hadn't he told her? She'd ignored his wishes. Yet most of him ached for the sight of her, her voice, her scent. He stopped himself – such thoughts the way to ruin. *God knows what her father must think.*

"Good morning, Euan."

She looked wonderful with her hair tousled like that, as if he'd roused her from sleep.

"Good morning." He mustn't give in. She had to know of his displeasure and must return home.

"It was nice of Lady Amelia to offer me the position of companion. She wants us to use our first names. What do you think?"

"Think? Think? That's the last thing you did." He raised his voice and realised one or two people had stopped to watch and listen. Dougie shook his grey head and Jamie Moffat looked miserable and pulled his ear.

"Take my arm so we can stroll down to the water's edge." Euan struggled to keep his voice neutral.

"As you wish."

Her closeness acted like a brand. He wanted to take her in his arms, smother her face with kisses and clasp those generous lips to his, but he mustn't give in. No words passed between them until they reached the shore of the loch. He couldn't trust himself to speak, not with her by his side. He moved away from her. "You canna stay here it's no' safe and no' right. This willna do. How can we wed if you ignore the advice of those who know better?"

She stared at him open mouthed.

He couldn't bear the look of pain in her hazel eyes. Pressing her to him, his lips sought hers. Gossamer mouth responded to gossamer mouth. He lost all sense of time and place. His long fingers held her face so she couldn't break away even if she'd wanted to. Struggling for control, his hands gripped her arms as he stepped back. They stared at each other breathless, with only a foot between them.

"How did you find me?" she gasped. "Was it Johnnie?"

"Did you think for one moment that my men wouldna spy you out and tell me?"

"Jamie Moffat always tugs his ear when he's nervous, the little tell-tale."

"You've got to go back."

"Have I now?" She regarded him from beneath lowered lashes.

"Dinna look at me like that Morag, we're not bairns and this is no' a game."

"No?"

"No." He lowered his voice and narrowed his eyes. "You ken very well that this is no place for a woman. You should be home ..."

"Home. Sitting by the fire and sighing over you till you return?"

"I want you to be safe, Morag."

"Safe? So only men are allowed to risk their lives for the Cause then?"

"I dinna want any harm ..."

"Harm?"

"Would you stop repeating everything I say?" He rubbed his brow and ran his fingers through his hair.

"And what about what i want?"

He was confused at that. Hadn't his father always been head of the house? Hadn't his mother always yielded to his will? Though when he thought of it arguments had been held behind closed doors and his smiling father had surfaced hours later, having changed his mind.

"Haven't you seen the women in the baggage train? Their men dinna seem to worry about any harm befalling them," she said.

"Perhaps they dinna understand the hardship that will be inflicted on their womenfolk and on their bairns, I've seen them too."

"Perhaps they do, but their men allow them to make their own choice."

His jaw tightened.

"Lord and Lady Crawford ..." she began.

"Are married."

"Yes." She bit her lip and turned away from him.

He pulled her round to face him. He made his voice soft and low, "I wouldna inflict marriage on you, not before I go off to war. Leave you widowed and perhaps worse, bearing a child without me to look after you. I could no' do it. Surely you can see that? And your father, have you thought of him?"

"Of course I've thought of him." She added, "I left a note."

"Morag, you've got to go home." He put a hand on her shoulder and she shrugged it off.

"No I don't."

He felt anger rise up in him. "Morag."

She twisted his ring off her finger and gave it to him. "You dinna have to concern yourself about me anymore. Good day." She started to walk away.

She canna mean it. "Morag, where are you going?"

She turned to look at him. He took in the fire in her eyes, firm mouth and determined chin. "I'm going back to Amelia and the baggage train," she said as if he meant nothing to her and strode away.

The muscles in his face tightened. "If you stay, I'll have no part in it or you. We'll be friends, but that is all."

He watched her head go up and her shoulders straighten. She kept on walking whilst an aching emptiness opened up inside him.

CHAPTER Eight

Shadows flickered as Morag sat inside the Crawfords' tent at Glenfinnan, an oil lamp by her side. She'd never experienced misery like this. It had been days since her argument with Euan. She regretted how they'd parted, but he needed to understand that she had her own will, her own ideas and the thought of being blindly obedient to anyone was an anathema her.

He'd never been able to tell her what to do. Why should marriage change anything? Was this what he would have been like as a husband? Well, no chance of that now. So, why didn't she feel happy, relieved that she'd escaped a life of being ordered around, like one of his men?

At least the Crawfords acknowledged her worth. They'd been grateful when she'd treated Lord Crawford's hacking cough with ground plantain root as recommended in her mother's simple book.

Morag's mother had died sixteen years ago, before she could pass on all the knowledge she'd learnt. Morag only had her book, bound in calf skin, and her neat writing and drawings to guide her. She had started collecting herbs and drying them, determined to learn more, frustrated that similar simples could work well or be miserable failures. Granny Mac had let her assist her as a midwife, but Morag wanted to know more.

She sighed, Amelia's ripped skirt lay on her lap. Morag tried to thread the needle, licked the silk for the third time, squinted and missed the eye. How Euan would laugh at her now. "Damn and blast." She threw the offending garment away from her.

How could she avoid bumping into him? The pair of them would be the talk of the camp once news got round of their broken betrothal. She'd already experienced speculative eyes lingering on her when she'd put some washing to steep by the stream.

She'd been so grateful when Johnnie discovered Amelia required a companion. Lady Mary McRae had refused to go a foot further on learning that the Jacobites really did mean to fight the redcoats. The Crawfords in their early twenties and often seeking each other out in a crowd and the privacy of their tent had welcomed her. Lord Crawford must think women should play a part in the campaign, a pity Euan didn't agree with him.

A shard of light pierced the gloom of the tent. The Crawfords arrived, arm in arm and with a look on their faces that made Morag make her excuses and leave. They enjoyed the bliss of married life and if Euan hadn't been so obstinate, so could they. *Damn and blast him.* Morag needed to do some work that would make her forget the longing inside her.

What to do on a sultry August day? She wandered down to the river and gazed at the bent backs of the women scrubbing clothes and reached for the bundle she'd left in a pool of lye, fat and plant oils. Not ladies' work, but she needed to do something useful. She gathered the dripping garments in her arms. Catching sight of Jamie Moffat she turned her back. *The little snitch.* At least he'd the grace to blush.

She joined the other women, and copied them by hitching up her skirts so they wouldn't drag in the ice cold water. They stared at her and whispered behind their hands. She ignored them and set to work. She pounded white petticoats and stockings on flat stones, rinsed them in clear water, wrung them out and dried them on the grass. Beads of perspiration trickled between her breasts and her damp clothes clung in the sticky heat of the day. She leant back and let the sun play on her arms and legs.

Men arrived in ones and twos on the opposite bank, outwardly appearing to mend leather, sharpen claymores or talk, but she could see their sideways glances at naked legs and thighs. Morag pulled her own skirts down as far as they would go without getting wet. The younger women elbowed each other, whispered or shyly giggled.

Morag thwacked a shirt against a stone imagining Euan's head. A shadow cast itself across her. She shaded her eyes to see a limp petticoat waved in front of her nose.

"Found it downstream, Morag McColl. James Kinross, at your service." He doffed his cap and bowed, much to the amusement of the other women. "You'll have heard of me?"

"Thank you kindly." She took the petticoat. "I've heard of your father." She remembered Rory Kinross, either a hero or brigand depending on who told the tale.

A nerve twitched on Kinross's whiskery jaw.

"How do you ken my name?" Tall and slim, she thought, perhaps a little narrow in the shoulder, not like Euan. *Do I have to compare everyone to him?*

"I asked." He sat on the bank next to her. "They say you're no longer betrothed to Euan Stewart."

"It's no one's business but ours." She wrung out a shirt and thought of Euan's neck. The news of their quarrel must have raced round the camp.

"Sometimes a man needs to ken where he stands."

"Does he now?" He had a likeable face, light blue eyes and wide grin, but he wasn't for her.

"I'm no' interested in men." She turned her back on him and got on with washing. She imagined him reddening in embarrassment and storming off in anger.

He did none of those things, just bent closer and whispered in her ear, "But I'm interested in you, Morag McColl." His fiery beard scratched her ear and she caught the tang of tobacco drifting from him which tickled her throat.

Morag squirmed at his close proximity, but the sound of a mother's ringing slap as she screeched at her daughter, saved her.

"Dinna hitch up your skirts so high lassie, showin' everythin' you've got. Haven't I enough to think of with your brother and sister?" The woman pointed at laughing children running in and out of the shallows. She tugged at the hem of her daughter's errant skirt. "Keep your mind on your washin'."

***

On the opposite bank, Euan and Johnnie stared at Morag and Kinross. Euan set his lips in a grim smile. Johnnie's eyebrows rose. They'd join other bare-chested boys and men to test their swordplay.

Euan noted Morag's flush of embarrassment with some satisfaction.

"Mr. Kinross," Euan called out.

James Kinross bowed his head. "Gentlemen." He winked at Morag as he walked away.

Euan inwardly cursed Kinross, his mind in turmoil. *What is the man playing at?*

Morag returned to her washing. Wisps of hair escaped from her plait and tumbled around her face. She looked flustered in the fierce heat and very kissable.

Euan raised his claymore and warily circled Johnnie. They practised what Johnnie called 'the art of war'. This involved lots of shouting, yells, banging on shields and sword thrusts, which sometimes drew blood, much to the annoyance of the victim and the teasing laughter of the perpetrator.

Euan tensed as Morag gathered her rebellious hair high on her neck and bound it as tightly as she could before tying a bow and allowing stray tendrils to escape their noose. Her breasts swelled and her waist lengthened and men's eyes widened.

Euan swore.

Unaware of the stir she'd caused, she set to work again.

Johnnie took the opportunity to turn Euan's blade and trip him. A warning shout made Morag jump back in alarm. Euan landed on his backside, in the burn, at her feet. Icy water splashed her from

41

head to foot. "My washing!" she exploded. "For goodness sake ..." she began.

Johnnie's body rocked in laughter as he pointed a finger at both of them.

Euan and Morag sent sheets of water over Johnnie, forcing him to retreat. His hands rose in surrender.

For one fleeting moment Euan forgot his quarrel with Morag. They smiled at each other, sending messages known only to them.

Then he remembered. He rubbed his eyebrow, looked at her, then the ground and muttered, "Sorry ... about the washing."

Johnnie, his shoulders shaking, led him away.

***

Morag was about to give them a piece of her mind when they stopped in their tracks. Lord Crawford strode towards them. Euan and Johnnie's bodies tightened like bow strings. Her stomach lurched.

They sat away from everyone else. Kinross kept others out of earshot.

She could feel Kinross' eyes on her as she laid the clothes over rocks to dry and watched the intensity of the discussion. Johnnie gave a low whistle at one point. Their heads: Crawford's the colour of wheat; Euan's with autumnal tints and Johnnie's like bracken, leant closer together. Their expressions became more earnest and their voices lowered as hours passed. The talk ceased. With a quick nod and handshakes, they rose and gathered their followers together.

Morag's head spun with unspoken questions and her heart thumped with the excitement of it all. She tapped on the Crawford's tent pole and receiving no answer, popped her head in the opening. Where were they? The cool interior invited her in. Amelia had asked her if she would help in little ways. Morag picked up a discarded skirt and bodice. She savoured the velvet texture against her cheek and smoothed out the creases. White petticoats, cream hose and a pair of gaily coloured garters lay scattered in gay abandon as if taken off one ... by ... one .... Perhaps by Amelia's husband? Morag didn't continue the painful thought, just followed the trail of clothes and tried not to make sense of it.

A sliver of light cut across the inside of the tent. "So, dearest ..." Lord Crawford allowed his wife to enter the tent ahead of him. "The prince requested that you help with provisions for our venture. May I tell him you will do it?"

"Of course." Amelia smiled.

He pressed her to him and kissed her for just a few seconds too long.

Morag looked at the ground and coughed as he released his blushing wife.

This could have been Euan and me, damn him.

"Morag, you said you wanted to prove you can be useful to the Cause?" Amelia beamed at her.

"Yes." Morag became alert at once.

"You'll never guess. We're paying a Whig, the Duke of Tolbain a visit. We'll take his cattle and plunder his house for provisions. Now, help me find some riding clothes. I'm sure I've just the outfit for you."

CHAPTER Nine

Before dawn the following morning, Morag stood in the lamplight of her tent trying to ensure her skirt hung in neat folds.

"Ready?" called Amelia from outside.

"Almost." Morag tugged on her boots. "Come away in. This should be interesting. Tolbain kills anyone who gets in his way. His family and ours are old enemies."

Amelia's eyes gleamed with excitement. "You should enjoy this raid then." She smiled. "The outfit suits you."

"As does yours." Amelia wore a sky-blue riding habit the colour of her eyes and Morag one of jade green, a contrast to her brown hair.

Amelia pulled back the tent flap and they walked out into torchlight to be greeted by a group of mounted men. Lord Crawford smiled, Kinross leered, Johnnie gave a low whistle of admiration, Euan glowered and the rest of the Stewart horsemen gawped open mouthed.

Morag saw Amelia draw back her shoulders, but Morag wished the ground would eat her up and stared out into the dark.

"Sir, would it no' be more fitting for the ladies to stay behind?" asked Euan.

Morag scowled at him as Amelia pressed her hand.

"It wouldna'," said Lord Crawford and smiled at his wife and Morag.

Morag knew her face burned and hurried to her pony's side.

Lord Crawford helped his wife mount whilst Euan dismounted to assist Morag, only to find Kinross in the way. Morag ignored both of them and used a boulder as a mounting block.

Euan took a running jump at his pony landing on its back, a trick he'd impressed her with some years ago. She turned away. Kinross chuckled, Euan scowled and the Stewart clan tried to hide their grins.

Darkness still covered the land as they gathered on the hills above Tolbain's cattle and watched a wiry man make his way up the hillside. He swept off his blue bonnet revealing a shock of chestnut hair matching his beard. His voice sounded low and harsh. "Tolbain left at noon, he'll be gone for hours. It'll take the old fox some time before he realises there's no meetin' with the redcoats."

"Well done." Lord Crawford offered him silver.

"I'll no' take payment for servin' our prince."

They watched him stride off into the heather.

Lord Crawford didn't waste time. "Let's hope he can be trusted, gentlemen. Be on your guard. Kinross, track Tolbain. Euan, take your men and gather our cattle. Ladies follow me."

Kinross set off with a wink at Morag which she did her best to ignore.

Euan instructed his men in whispers so the cattle weren't alarmed or Tolbain's men alerted. The Stewarts overcame the herdsmen, encircled the cattle and nudged them up the hill. Euan concentrated on reuniting a calf with its mother.

Morag watched a black grouse start out the heather at the approach of a large bull. It bellowed and charged towards Euan coaxing the calf up the hillside.

"Euan!" She knew it was too late the bull would be on him before he could act.

As his wild eyed pony reared and threw him, Morag urged her mount forward making the bull veer off and rejoin the herd. She scrambled down to kneel beside Euan who was struggling to sit up. He'd hit his head on a stump and blood was pouring from a cut eyebrow.

"Stay still," she ordered as she ripped her petticoat and pressed the material to his wound. "How many fingers?" She waggled two in front of him.

"Two. Go home before you're hurt."

"Looks like you'll have an interesting scar to boast to your friends about." She tied the strip of cloth round his head and finished with a knot. The tight lines on his face told her of his fury, but whether it was with himself for falling or her for ignoring him, she didn't know.

The sky lightened above the sombre peaks and held the promise of a hot day. She wafted away the first of the midges.

Johnnie rescued Euan's pony and held out the reins to him. "If you can pull yourself away from playing pirates with Morag for a wee moment, brother, there's serious business we need to attend to."

Morag stuffed her fist in her mouth. *He did look like a pirate, a very attractive pirate.*

Euan grabbed the reins. "I know." He vaulted onto his pony.

"I've heard of men waving flags, but no' petticoats." Johnnie pointed at a piece of fabric flapping at Euan's head.

Euan pushed the offending cloth back into place.

Johnnie roared with laughter and others joined in when they saw him. Euan just grinned.

"Johnnie look after the beasts," ordered Lord Crawford, "they may be the last meat we'll eat for a long time. If all goes well we'll see you at the foot of Crunnock Falls tonight."

Johnnie waved them goodbye.

It took the rest of the clan half an hour to reach Tolbain's fortified house. The clan left their ponies and wound through thick gorse and heather towards the stark castellated building surrounded by a high stone wall. They crept across fields of rising mist. Morag prayed no one would hear the chink and clink of swords as men clambered over walls or the tread of boots heading towards the house.

With Euan at her side and Amelia the other, they slunk through the open gates to find no guards, the cobbled courtyard empty and windows shuttered. Would the Jacobites surprise them, or could this be a trap?

They waited, nothing stirred. Lord Crawford ordered men to stand guard outside and led the rest into the gloomy scullery, lit by a high window.

Morag shivered. She breathed in a sour mixture of smoke, rancid fat and cooked meat. The floor, paved with large uneven flagstones, led to a huge soot-smeared stone fireplace with a spit and banked fire. She imagined a great haunch of venison cooking there and salivated. Her fingers danced along the oak dresser lined with rows of pewter and stoneware dishes. A stone sink and wooden bench sat against the opposite wall. In the centre, dominating the room, stood a well-scrubbed pine table.

The scullery maid's eyes bulged. She staggered into a terrified boy.

"No sound or ..." Euan mimed cutting his own throat. He looked even more like a pirate as blood seeped through the rakish bandage over his brow. "We want arms and provisions for the prince."

The scullery maid seemed to stop breathing. The boy shook and a light dribble of wet showed on the front of his ragged breeches. He tried to cover the spreading stain with his hands and the men guffawed.

Morag looked at Euan, signalling with her eyes and raised eyebrows. These were bairns after all. With a wave of his hand Euan silenced his men. Turning back to the girl and boy he knelt beside them. "No harm will come to you if you do exactly as I say. Understand?"

They nodded like wooden puppets as they clung to each other.

"Have you names?" Euan asked the bemused girl.

She spoke in a whisper, "Mary and Bruce."

"Show us the armoury, Bruce," said Lord Crawford. "Which way is it?"

Bruce raised a shaking arm and pointed down a dark corridor to the left. Lord Crawford took some men, following the boy's finger.

"Well, now Mary, will you show us the Duke's pantry?" Euan chucked her under the chin and smiled.

This disarmed her and two dimples appeared at the sides of her mouth. "It's here." Holding the scowling Bruce's hand she led them down a dark corridor and pointed at an oak door.

Euan opened it and Morag breathed in. Mouth-watering scents of musky spices mingled with those of salted meats. Tolbain's larder was well stocked with pies, shoulders of ham, sides of beef and venison, butter, duck eggs and stone jars full to the brim with fat, cream, milk and honey. Morag's nose twitched and she licked her lips. From the look of Euan and Amelia the food had the same effect on them.

"Dougie and Jamie come with me," ordered Euan. "Ladies, stay here and guard the servants.

Morag sniffed a haughty nose at Jamie Moffat. She hadn't forgotten his betrayal. He hung his head like a dog and tugged at his ear.

Euan supervised a procession of men loading sacks onto broad shoulders and carrying wooden casks out into the yard.

"The prince has landed." Mary stared at Euan, "He's as handsome as they say."

"But ..." began Amelia when she was nudged by Morag. "I ... suppose so."

Morag whispered in Mary's ear, looked at Euan and nodded.

"Really." Mary's eyes glowed like full moons and her voice became a furtive whisper, "There's lots of us pray he'll win. Look, here's two barrels of his lordship's best brandy hidden under there. You tell him Mary sent it with her best wishes, be quick. Cook will be up soon, he's as sour as milk and isn't friendly to The Cause. Come on, Bruce." She scooped up a haunch of venison, a couple of hares and a bowl of goose fat from under the table and pushed them into Morag's arms. "It's all I can do for the prince." Then she turned to Euan and gave him a bowl. "There's some of cook's best goose grease for your ... affliction, sir." She did an awkward curtsy.

"My affliction?" Euan stopped waving on his burdened men to greater efforts. He eyed Morag.

"Morag?"

She shrugged her shoulders. The joke would keep.

He gave up. After fifteen minutes the larder had empty shelves. "Here's a receipt for the goods we've taken." He pushed the note into Mary's hand and ruffled Bruce's hair.

Mary stared at him open mouthed and Bruce's mouth turned down.

"Tell the Duke he'll receive what he's due when we're successful in our endeavours."

Bruce glowered.

"We need to go." Lord Crawford's voice pierced the gloom, with an urgency they couldn't ignore. He and his men, loaded with claymores, pistols, gunpowder and muskets, clattered past. "There's movement on the upper floors."

"Hurry," said Mary.

"Bless you." Morag held Mary's rough hand for a moment before she went to leave.

"I'll pray you get away," Mary whispered, "but Tolbain never forgets."

Something in her voice made Morag turn. Mary was looking towards the stone staircase. *Bruce?*

"Murder!" Bruce's shrill cry echoed round the house and the sound of running feet filtered down the keystone staircase into the kitchen.

"Everyone out." ordered Lord Crawford.

They ran for the scullery door and Euan slammed it behind them. They sprinted towards the heavily laden carts and horses. Their drivers snapped reins to the creaks and groans of wheels. Euan helped Morag mount beside Amelia and then leapt on his own pony.

Shutters opened above them. A tousled head peered out and yelled, "Here, what's goin' on?"

Euan and his men circled behind the last cart. "Go back to your beds," he shouted. "Tell Tolbain you saw and heard nought. The prince will thank you for it."

Grumbling men and women banged several shutters closed. Then a shout of "Jacobite Jade," rang out and a musket fired from an upper window.

"Aggh."

If Morag had not just moved ahead of Amelia, the shot would have hit her in the back. Amelia clutched a hand to her arm and swayed in the saddle. Lord Crawford took her onto his horse as they spurred out of the gates.

Morag watched Euan order his men to fire their weapons at the hidden marksman.

Euan said, "We leave now. Take Tolbain's ponies." Hooves struck cobbles as neighing ponies were galloped out of the yard and gates.

"Morag get out of here," he shouted and slapped her pony's rump so she was out of the main gates in a trice and able to see the dust of the last wagons in the distance.

Euan caught up with her, his face full of concern as his men raced past. "Are you alright?"

"Of course," she said. In fact her stomach was doing somersaults. Amelia's cry of pain and the blood spurting between her fingers, a sharp reminder they were engaged in a dangerous business.

"Well, now you ken what it's like to be under fire."

"Yes."

They reached the wagons in a flurry of dancing hooves.

"I must report to Lord Crawford," he said.

"I'll follow once I've ... had some water." Her stomach churned. "Amelia's wounded, I must help her."

He grimaced. "It could have been you."

"No' your concern."

His jaw tightened and a muscle quivered in his cheek. "I thought better of you. Make sure you stay with the lead cart."

Morag watched him spur away as she took a drink from a leather bag. She bit her lip as men shouted congratulations to Euan as he rode towards them. They crowed their victory in loud, rough voices.

Did he expect her to follow him all the way back to camp? She'd changed, no longer able to put up with the frustration of being directed by men. If Euan couldn't accept this, then he wasn't the one for her. Yet she yearned for him and made the prospect of life without him, stretch ahead in a miserable eternity.

Her pony stumbled, picked itself up and limped. She dismounted to investigate. He'd lost a shoe and had a bleeding hoof. She'd have to walk him back to camp. Ahead of her the carts continued their slow trundle into the distance, she glanced behind her. No sign of pursuit, just the rear guard some distance off.

Only the thought of poor Amelia made her anxious. She hoped someone knew how to clean a wound.

Damn my pony's lameness. "Come on then," she said rubbing its velvet nose, "we've a long walk till you get some of those oats from Tolbain's stables." She pushed the pony on as fast as she could. Blisters stung her toes and heels as she covered mile after mile following the cart tracks. *Damn these riding boots.*

She thought about her father and those they'd left behind in Braedrumie. Times would be hard with all the young men away.

A shout made her look back. Her mouth went dry. The rear guard raced towards her pursued by a group of men on horseback.

CHAPTER Ten

"It's Tolbain. For God's sake get out of here." The Stewart riders came to a juddering halt at Morag's feet. Where could she hide? She'd a lame horse in a glen with hills and forest on either side.

Morag tried to run and pull her lame horse.

The men formed a defensive wall behind her, whilst one drove his pony at break-neck speed to the front of the winding column.

Within seconds a group of Stewarts spurred towards Morag and the enemy. Euan jerked his mount to a halt and turned back circling her. "I thought I told you to stay with the lead carts."

"My pony's lame."

"Your hand," he snapped, "quickly." He pulled her into the saddle behind him. Her arms clasped his waist as he turned his steed and headed for a thickly wooded incline. The air filled with the distant sound of clashing metal and men's' cries. "You've got my dirk."

"Yes." The blade lay snug against her outer thigh.

He stared at the enemy riders. "Damn it, why didn't Kinross alert us?" He swung her to the ground. "Stay here." I'll come back for you." He galloped off.

She liked the comfort of cold steel in her garter. She hid under the broad green canopy of a fir and watched Euan raise his sword as he joined the hand to hand fighting. A heaving, swaying mass of men, shrieked and shouted oaths at each other. Some fell clutching at themselves to be trampled underfoot and others beat on their shields, oblivious to men in agony on the ground.

She caught her breath as one unfamiliar rider turned and raced towards her. He looked behind him at the fighting and then towards her forest hiding place. Panic rose in her throat as he hauled his pony to a stop, dismounted and tied his reins to an overhanging bough. The stranger was not as tall as Euan, but more powerfully built. He'd a hard face and cruel mouth.

Think. She urged herself. *You wanted to fight for the Cause.*
Think.

She pulled out Euan's dirk, felt the blade with her thumb, hissed
as a bead of blood welled and sucked the wound. *I've skinned hares*
and gutted fish all my life, can I kill a man?

She retreated into the darkness of the forest's ferny floor, step by
frightened step. The ground fell away on an incline as she stumbled
over tangled roots and slipped on moss covered stone. Thorns and
branches tugged at her skirts. She crossed a burn and doubled back,
then scrambled over rocks and fallen trees, desperate to get away.
His steady footfall always there, just a hundred yards behind her.

She re-crossed the burn and watched him from behind emerald
foliage as he tracked her like game. Stone walls rose up through the
trees and she raced towards them. Her breath came in heaving gasps
and perspiration streamed between her breasts. *Can he hear my heart*
hammering against my ribs?

Startled rooks took black-winged flight above her. She stopped.
Her chest heaved as she inhaled the dank smell of the ruined croft,
the thatch long gone. She ran behind it and staggered over a pile of
stacked peat.

"I've always liked hunting," he shouted, his voice honey-sweet,
"but it's the catching makes my blood race."

Her heart almost stopped. *Who is he?* Fighting down fear, she
tried to think. *His voice sounds cultivated, perhaps he'll let me go?* She
peered round the croft's gable end at her pursuer picking his way
out of the trees. He wore an eagle feather in a bonnet perched on
black, wiry hair. His beard curled over his moss green jacket. *A*
noble. She watched him kneel, his eyes tracing the bruised stems of
grass and the imprints of her feet leading to her hiding place.

As he dusted off the knee of his black breeches he looked up. She
pulled back out of sight, but not fast enough as his mouth became a
lascivious smile. *He's seen me.*

Biting her lip she fled to the back of the building. In her panic she'd run from help. Cursing herself, she hugged the crumbling wall and felt her way along its length.

He came at her from behind the rubble either side of the back door. She was free one moment and next imprisoned by a rough arm about her neck and his hand with an iron grip round her wrist. *Damn.* She'd dropped her dirk, which clattered on the step. A cloying stink of stale male sweat and pony almost overpowered her.

"I thought to rape a rebel whore, and instead I'm to bed a woodland elf." His coarse beard grazed her ear. He sniffed at her. "I've a virgin, I'll be bound. You can tell them Tolbain was first." His mouth seized hers and she forced herself not to vomit at the stench.

Tolbain. And I'm powerless or am I? She relaxed and opened her mouth to him. If she fought back he could rape and kill her with no difficulty. She had to outwit this man.

He pulled his lips away surprised at her response.

She almost sagged in relief and thanked God for the arrogance of some men.

He held her in arms of steel. "So it's to be like that is it?" He grinned.

Hiding her horror, she did her best smile and simper in his embrace as his hand encircled her neck and the other explored her bosom at will, gauging her reaction as he did so. She threw back her head closing her eyes as if savouring the moment and hoped his male ego would believe she wanted him. His lips worked at her breasts as he relaxed his grip on her neck and pushed his knee between her legs.

Her groping fingers seized a loose rock from the wall behind them. It fitted neatly in her hand and she used it like a club, bringing it down on his head as hard as she could. Blood flowed from his forehead. He gave a stunned look of surprise, his knees sagged and he collapsed face first on to the ground.

Grabbing her dirk, she ran like a deer, retracing her steps along the path and up the steep gradient of the forest floor. She glanced behind her. *No sign of pursuit, good.* Speeding onwards, through shards of light and dark she expected a shout, or the sound of boots following in her footsteps. She heard nothing, but the sound of her ragged breath as she ran and ran straight into someone's arms.

Tolbain? She lashed out with fists and kicks, unaware of her blows not being returned and her name repeated. A stained head bandage floated in front of her face.

"Morag. Morag. What the devil has got into you? I'm sorry I left you. Didn't I say I'd come back? Did you no' believe me?" Euan's fingers cradled her face as his grey eyes searched hers.

Why didna I finish off Tolbain? Shame flooded over her. *I canna tell Euan. He'd have to kill the man or die in the attempt. He'll say I should have stayed at home.* "I ... thought it ... was..."

"Tolbain's men?"

"Yes."

He wrapped a comforting arm round her. "You've never been frightened of anything. Though I mind the time when we were bairns and some laddies rolled a boulder ..."

"At the entrance to a tiny cave and wouldn't let me out. Yes... I didna like it." She shivered as if something in the forest stirred.

"You must no' let it haunt you so."

He held her close and she enjoyed his warmth.

"I dinna ... usually. I just remember you made them release me and I loved you for it." *Now, what made me say that?*

"Did you?" He turned her to him with that steady gaze she knew so well and held her chin between forefinger and thumb. "And I have loved you Morag McColl since they let me hold you at your christening and you seized my thumb in your firm grip. And ever since you've been nought but trouble." He laughed and she knew he didn't mean it. Her heart lightened as they linked arms and he led her out of the forest and into the light where his pony grazed.

She surveyed the ground behind them littered with bodies.

"Tolbain's men." Euan grimaced.

"The raid?"

"A success."

"That's good. Amelia's wound, has it been dealt with?"

"Her husband saw to it."

She noticed the fresh trickle of blood on his bandage. "You're no' hurt again?"

"No' a scratch. The carts got away and the rest of Tolbain's raiding party rode back with their tails between their legs. We need to leave. They'll be back soon for the wounded and the dead."

She looked at the forest and shuddered. *Is Tolbain dead?* Her teeth chattered as her body shook.

"You're cold darling; have my coat."

She let him untie it from his saddle and wrap her in its woollen warmth, savouring the feeling of him being close.

Stooping, he plucked a flower from a bush. A white rose. "It's as beautiful as you. Let me put it in your hair."

She enjoyed his closeness. He helped her mount and seated himself behind her. She sat upright at first, but tiredness overcame her and his chest became her pillow. She slept in his arms comforted by the scent of sandalwood.

CHAPTER Eleven

"What?" Morag woke with a start on Euan's pony with his arms round her and the sound of cheers ringing out. They'd caught up with the carts. *Everyone's grinning at us as if we were ... well ... How must it look, as if Euan has won and our quarrel over?* She sat erect, her cheeks burning. "Put me down here please."

He stopped the pony allowing her to slip to the ground. She staggered.

"Are you well?" he asked concerned. "You seemed fitful as you slept."

"Of course I'm well," she snapped and instantly regretted the hurt look in his eyes. "I'll ride in one of the carts." A sour taste invaded her mouth and she could smell Tolbain's sweat.

"If you're sure?" He sounded disappointed. "I must thank you, for warding off that bull when I fell."

She nodded, willing him to leave. A sea of nausea threatened to rise up her throat and engulf her. *Why doesna he just go?*

At last he kicked his mount into a trot whilst she ran to the wayside and gave in to her body's need to purge. She vomited into the heather. She could taste Tolbain's tongue inside her, curled, seeking, searching; his rank breath and body odour coming in waves. Her stomach heaved. She vomited again.

Cold shivers and then hot sweats came in succession. A black face and slobbering lips hovered in front of her. His hands on her breasts, touching ... She couldn't rid herself of what he'd done and tried to do. Her cheeks burned. Using the hem of her petticoat to wipe her face clean of sweat and grime, she forced herself to catch up with the last cart.

Grabbing a swaying leather bag she poured water into her mouth and on to her face and throat and ... She couldn't breathe, had to wash, cleanse herself of that man and his touch.

The quick wash would suffice until she checked on Amelia's condition. Lord Crawford sat in the leading cart holding her hand. Amelia looked pale and her eyes remained shut. Her upper arm had a strip of white linen wound round it.

"I'm sorry it took so long for me to reach you," said Morag.

"She's fortunate the ball only grazed her, left her with a sore arm. I poured some of Tolbain's whisky on it," said Lord Crawford, "she's been very brave."

"Good. I'll let her rest while I ride with the driver."

Morag parried all his questions and pretended to listen to the happy banter around her.

They camped at dusk by a river and ignoring calls from Lord Crawford that she should eat, she grabbed a change of clothes and made for a secluded place upstream where the water flowed slowly and formed pools. She'd only one thought in mind to wash Tolbain's stink off her body.

She tore at the soiled bodice and skirt with shaking fingers. Tolbain's stench invaded every seam. She'd never wear these clothes again.

The night air cooled and goose bumps appeared on her bare skin. She studied the circle of shrubs and gathering dusk beyond and threw the last garment into the undergrowth.

The coarse grass scratched the soles of her feet. She caught her breath as she slipped into the ice-cold water until her feet, legs, hips and breasts had been spun into ice crystals. Long strokes took her to the middle of the pool where she dived below the dark surface. She enjoyed the cold rush of water in her ears, until something brushed her ankle, a reed or fish perhaps? Surging upwards, she kicked her way to the starry surface hoping she'd feel re-born, clean and untouched. Water streamed from her hair. Guilt rose up inside her. Instead of fighting back she'd let ... that man ... she punched the water sending droplets winging into the air.

"Morag, is that you?"

Euan.

She crossed her arms over her breasts. Her body tingled from the icy water. She told herself it had nothing to do with him being close. She sank beneath the surface, but had to surface for air.

The gorse parted revealing him. His mouth dropped open, "I... found these." He held up the clothes she'd thrown away. "Mmph ... you look like a water sprite."

"I'm no' decent." A rush of hot blood flooded across her face, throat and breasts.

He turned his back. "You ... er shouldna wander away from camp without telling anyone. Anything could happen to you."

If only he knew. "I wanted to bathe and now I'd like you to go away."

"And I would like to stay," his voice held a teasing note.

"I'm cold."

"Yes, well that's what happens when you swim in a river at night. You'd never catch me doing that."

"That's because you canna swim. He could float on his back, she remembered. He floundered when trying to emulate his brothers, particularly Rob. They'd all wanted to be like Rob.

"Yes, well there is that." He started to turn round.

"Euan."

Laughing he drew out his sword, his back still to her. "I'll stand behind the gorse and defend your maidenly modesty and honour against all comers."

"You'll no' peek?" she asked.

"And I'll no' peek, though I'd like a promise that on our wedding night ... I ... ahem ... see more than your pointy ears."

"Euan." She slapped at the water and he retreated laughing allowing her to clamber out, teeth chattering, but brimming over with happiness. He'd said, 'our wedding night.' *Has he accepted I've a will of my own?* She dried herself and quickly dressed in clan clothes and bundled up the old, remembering a hot summer in their childhood when he'd been trying to swim and nearly drowned. She'd thought her heart would break, but Rob had saved him. Rob whose name must never be mentioned ...

"Are you decent now?" The gorse twitched. "It's no' easy on a man imagining what you're doing back there."

"I'm decent," she said as she dried her hair.

"Oh." He sounded disappointed as he appeared from behind the gorse.

"You said, 'our wedding night'. We're to be more than friends then?"

He crossed the space between them and held her close. "My beautiful lass, I love you so much, never doubt it." He wrapped his fingers in her hair which hung in damp curls down her back. "I'd give my life for you."

"And I mine," she whispered. She fingered his scarred eyebrow. The skin looked healthy with no sign of redness or infection. She decided it enhanced his looks and gave him an air of danger.

His lips hovered over hers, too close. Their bodies clung at breast and hip and thigh, she wanted more, but he held back.

"And Kinross?"

"How can you ask?"

"He's nought to you then?"

"Euan." She rested her head against the steady rise and fall his chest. "No one will ever divide us I swear it. I've hated us no' speaking. Now, perhaps you can see ..."

"Not that you want to stay?"

"I have to stay."

He sighed, rubbed his brow and released her. "We've a hard march to the Correyarrick Pass, then Perth and Edinburgh. Promise me, if I fall ..."

She placed her finger on his mouth, "Shhh ... don't."

"If ought happens," he continued, "you'll go home."

"You know I canna promise that; I wouldna rest till I found you."

He sighed again and slipped the betrothal ring back on her finger. "You are so headstrong. I saw it in you as a wee girl. It's one of the reasons I love you."

She tried to interrupt, but he hushed her.

"I wish to keep you safe at home, but if you dinna want that, then I suppose the safest place is by my side where I can keep an eye on you."

"Oh, Euan." She felt her love for him deepen at that moment. He'd listened and was accepting she'd a will too. "I love you so."

He crushed her to him. "I'll say no more, for the moment, Morag." Then he kissed her long and hard.

CHAPTER Twelve

Morag closed her eyes and smiled. They'd beaten General Cope, the Commander-in-Chief in Scotland and his redcoats in the race to Correyarrick Pass and he'd retreated leaving the way south open for the Jacobites.

They'd pushed on to Perth and to everyone's relief, government troops faded away and the Jacobites entered the city to be joined by Lord George Murray. The prince proclaimed his father as King on September 4th. In a jubilant mood, the Jacobite army marched on and camped outside Edinburgh's walls. A pall of smoke hung above the jumble of buildings. *Old Reekie's well named.*

When she slept Tolbain invaded her dreams so she woke several times in the night.

"You look tired, darling." Euan sat on a boulder facing her.

"And you look less like a wild Highlander now and much more presentable." She wasn't going to share her troubles with Euan; he'd enough to think about. Auburn hair littered the ground. She put her scissors away and kissed his cheek.

"Presentable? But I thought I had an affliction, something about goose grease at Tolbain's? What silly nonsense did you tell that lassie?"

Morag's eyes twinkled in mischief. "She mistook you for the prince."

"Naturally." He lounged back stretching his long limbs in the sunshine. She threw a plaid at his head; he ducked and caught her in his arms. "And?"

"I thought she should ken that this prince has ... some imperfections." She giggled.

"What did you say, you wretch?" He kissed the tip her nose.

She pulled away from him. "I said, you were a bit old ... and had ... and had ..." She ran and yelled, "very small privates!"

He roared in mock anger and set off after her.

She darted under a cart, skirted a horse and tripped over a basket of washing. Euan grabbed her as she fell, twisting and cushioning her with his body. They stopped laughing for a heartbeat and looked at each other. In a flash he turned her and smacked her backside.

"Why you ... " she began. He had a broad hand and it stung.

"Getting to know each other are you?" said Dougie. He squinted down at them. "Now my Isabel ..." He scratched his head as they burst out laughing.

***

"No." Just before dawn Morag awoke with a start, her fingers on Euan's dirk. Perspiration poured off her. She'd been sure Tolbain had been in the tent with her. She'd smelt his fetid breath and the animal stink of him. If she turned her head, she knew he'd be lurking in the shadows. She forced herself to look and saw only darkness. A dull ache began behind her eyes.

Furtive movements came from outside. She drew back the canvas flap. Men had gathered in groups as if waiting. Curious, she pulled a shawl around her and went to look for Euan. She found Johnnie and Dougie deep in conversation, which stopped as she approached.

"Now you're no' to worry yourself ..." began Dougie.

Fear rose in her throat. "Where is he, where's Euan?" Her eyes searched the darkness.

"Now, Morag ..." said Dougie.

Johnnie took her arm and walked her some distance away. He lowered his voice, "He's leading a group seeking a way through Edinburgh's walls. He didna want to worry you. You look exhausted, here, have some of the last of Tolbain's wine."

"I'll never drink anything of that devil's." Her voice cut the air between them like a dirk. She added, "Thank you."

He stared at her. "Very well, I'll see if there's news."

She looked out into the darkness. It had begun to drizzle and a mist rose from the ground. She shivered as the damp seeped into her bones and waited for the sounds of muskets or cannons from Edinburgh. Nothing. First light streaked the sky. Euan and his men must have crept up on the sentries by now. It would only take one to be alert, sound the alarm, kill him and shatter her dreams. Her head throbbed.

Raised voices came from some distance away. Fear grabbed at her throat. *Dear Jesu, has Euan been discovered?* She could hear running feet. Johnnie and Dougie were by her side, claymores ready.

"We're in, we've captured Edinburgh." Jamie Moffat ran towards them out of the murk with a look of wonder on his face, "We didna fire a shot. They've surrendered."

Johnnie came at a run and gave a low whistle. Dougie slapped Morag's back. Euan alive and well and Edinburgh taken. She kissed all three in relief. Johnnie spun her round, Dougie shifted from foot to foot and Jamie went bright pink and tugged his ear.

The men ran off to spread the news. Morag sought out the Crawfords, but the news had gone before her. All over camp scratching fiddles played and jigs and reels were performed. The news of their victory had spread as if on the wind. Bonnets sailed into the air midst the cheers,

"It's grand isn't it?" Jamie's youthful face flushed with excitement.

"Dinna think I've forgiven you for what you did." she said.

His face fell and he looked apologetic. "I've letters from home." He gave one to Dougie and two to her as he pulled at his other ear.

"They willna save you." She stuck out her tongue at him.

"Women have long memories, lad." Dougie put his arm on Jamie's shoulder and looked at her. As he led him away Morag heard Dougie say, "Now my Isabel ..."

Morag scanned the letters for the recipient's name. *Mr. E. Stewart* and *Mr. J. Stewart* stood out on the plain pieces of parchment sealed with red wax. Johnnie's, had a sprig of purple heather tucked into a fashionable white ribbon. She sniffed at the paper, a faint whiff of attar of roses, clung to it. *Kirsty making sure Johnnie didna forget her.* She sighed. There was no letter for her even though she'd written to her father.

Johnnie sat with his back supported by the trunk of a beech tree. It always astonished her how he could read anywhere at any time. His cheeks flushed as he snapped the book closed, grabbed the letter and tore it open. He read it several times, like a man with an unquenchable thirst for news.

"Is there anything you can share?" said Morag.

He looked up. "No letter for you?"

Morag shook her head. "I dinna think Father's forgiven me."

"Give him time. I'm sure he'll send you a letter soon and it will be so long we'll be able to surround the camp with it."

Morag laughed.

"Sit beside me and I'll read you Kirsty's news."

Morag sat and listened to Johnnie's voice.

Dear Johnnie,

How are you? You looked so brave and handsome marching off to war. How is our dear gentleman, the prince? We have heard so much about him. His clothes and manners are said to be exquisite. Is he as handsome as they say?

Thank you for writing to your Aunt Munro requesting that we stay with her in Inverness. It is so exciting! She has invited us for two whole weeks and has arranged for us to go to balls and meet her dearest friends. We have only to inform her when we wish to stay. There will be hardly any time to visit my poor cousin.

Mother and I are having new gowns made as we do not wish to appear countrified. We need it to be known that Braedrumie ladies are up with fashion.

How is dear Hughie? Mother talks of him every day. I send my love.

Kirsty

Morag's heart sank for Johnnie. Kirsty called him *dear* the same endearment she used for Hughie and sent her *love*, but Morag could detect little warmth for Johnnie in her words. She managed to say, "It's a lovely letter, so kind of you to share it with me."

"It is, isn't it?" He grinned at her like a love sick fool, folded the parchment and put it in his plaid. "Next to my heart," he said resting his hand on it.

Kirsty doesna deserve Johnnie. "What book's that?"

He flushed. "Er ... *The Life and Strange Adventures of Robinson Crusoe* by Defoe.

She'd heard the title. "Any good?"

"Yes. It er... first appears to be about travel and adventure, but it's really about the protagonist's attempts to improve his economic circumstances. It's no' really a story for ladies."

"Johnnie," said Dougie, "the prince wants you."

"I have to go." Johnnie leapt up.

He'd left his book behind. She made to shout to him, but thought better of it. Books were expensive and impossible to get hold of when on a march. She picked up the leather bound volume and held it to her nose. It smelt of ink, pulped wood, calf and nights by the fire at home. Tears pricked at her eyes. To hold them back she read the title aloud: "*The Fortunes and Misfortunes of the Famous Moll Flanders ...* What?" Perplexed she read on, "*Who was born in Newgate, and during a Life of continu'd Variety for Three score Years, besides her Childhood, was Twelve Year a Whore ...* No." She continued. "*... five times a Wife (whereof once to her own Brother),*

Twelve Year a Thief, Eight Year a Transported Felon in Virginia, at last grew Rich, liv'd Honest, and died a Penitent. Written from her own Memorandums. By Daniel Defoe. Well!"

CHAPTER Thirteen

By evening Morag had a luxurious apartment in the Palace of Holyroodhouse with the Crawfords and the Stewarts lodged in the stables at White Horse Close, the eastern end of Canongate in Edinburgh.

At the top end of Canongate and the High Street, in the castle, sat the redcoat General Guest, Commander-in-Chief of Hamilton's Dragoons with two companies of foot and some veteran out-pensioners. Morag imagined him to be a spider waiting for prey.

When she'd opened her door to Johnnie, his eyes widened. "That mantelpiece is exquisite, Italian white marble surely?" He'd run his long fingers over the smooth surface. "And the chest of drawers, look at these panels. Whoever carved this fruit was a craftsman, French perhaps? You'll never want to move from here."

She supposed she wouldn't. A huge sash window let in light and air. She'd rubbed her cheek against the gold damask curtains, enjoyed the rich autumnal coloured carpet underfoot and had lain on the four poster's silk sheets. She glanced at him and clasped his book *Moll Flanders* behind her. "Are you here just to admire my apartment, or is there something you wish to say?"

Johnnie faced her and grinned. "I've news from Euan. He wants us to meet him at *Palfrey's Inn* at the head of Canongate."

Morag threw Johnnie's book at him. "*Robinson Crusoe* indeed."

Johnnie caught it with one hand, but had the grace to blush. "You dinna understand, Morag, how else are we men to find about wo ... the world?"

"You are incorrigible," said Morag. "The very idea."

Morag had never been inside an inn, and led the way inside *Palfrey's*. The reek of ale and peaty smoke made her wrinkle her nose as they elbowed their way through a rowdy crowd of Highlanders. Dougie found them a table in a quiet corner while Johnnie bought them some ale.

Morag wriggled with excitement. *When will Euan arrive?* The landlord placed a jug and four glasses on the table. "Wonderful, wasn't it, when the prince entered Edinburgh?" she said.

"Yes." Dougie answered between gulps. "A fine sight. My Isabel would have thought the prince looked well on his bay gelding."

"His tartan coat and blue bonnet made him look the part," agreed Morag.

"More like a gentleman of fashion than conquering hero if you ask me," Johnnie said, "I dinna think ..."

A voice they all knew well came from outside. "We're in old reekie without a fight, we'll send the redcoats packing," sang Euan's tuneful voice. He stopped outside the inn and they heard him say, "An' a good day to you sir."

The door opened with a bang. They watched Euan reel as he hit his head on a low beam. Retreating, he stooped and entered. Morag stared at him through her fingers. He swayed at the top of two stone steps, tottered down, stood upright once again and searched the room till he spotted them in the fug.

To Morag's relief no one appeared to notice him, caught up in their own drunken conversations. She looked at Dougie who stared at the ceiling and Johnnie who shrugged.

Waving one arm at them, Euan made his way stumbling, tripping and apologising through a sea of curses, grumbles and complaints. He flung himself down and sat grinning childlike at them.

"Where've you been?" asked Morag. "We've been waiting hours for you haven't we, Johnnie?"

"Well, ten minutes at least." Johnnie smiled.

Bleary-eyed, Euan misjudged his kiss to Morag. It landed somewhere between her neck and ear. She inhaled whisky fumes and started to cough. Euan thumped her on the back with a hand as heavy as lead, making her cough even more.

Johnnie put a hand on Euan's shoulder and the thumping stopped. "Out with it man, how did you take Edinburgh so quickly and with no bloodshed?"

"Been celebratin' two victories in one month." Euan hiccupped.

"No." Morag's eyes narrowed. "I'd never have guessed. Perhaps if you ..."

Euan slammed his fist on the table and yelled across the room, "A bo'le of your bes' claret, innkeeper and three glashes."

The inn keeper rushed to the table.

Morag assumed he'd scented a drunken customer and money to be made.

Euan poured the claret, inhaled its aroma with a sardonic grin and stood up, glass raised. "A toasht, to The Cause."

The whole room stopped, turned to look at him and raised their glasses.

"To The Cause," they echoed.

Johnnie and Morag sipped the claret whilst Euan threw it down his throat; bowed to everyone; thumped his glass down on the table and fell into his seat.

Grinning, he appeared unaware of Morag's glare. He leant towards her and played with one of her wayward curls. "Love you Morag," he shouted in her ear.

"Well." Her cheeks flushed with embarrassment, she could feel them. "You must have drunk every inn dry Euan Stewart. How could you?" She wanted to strangle him.

"Was eashy." He gave her a lopsided grin.

"Well, let me tell you ..."

"Sshh." Euan put his finger on her lips. "You're very beautiful you ken, ishn't she lads?" He rested his hand on his chin and stared at her, a schoolboy grin creasing his face. A blush burned its way up her neck and face. Not knowing where to look, she settled for the floor.

Johnnie saved her from further embarrassment. "Tell us how you got into Edinburgh, Euan."

Euan tapped his finger against his nose. "Top secret mishion. Well drilled by Murray an' the Duke in Perth. Ah man," he said putting his arm around Johnny's neck, "takin' thish city was so eashy."

"Out with it," said Johnnie, "what happened?"

Euan grinned as he looked at their eager faces. "Lochiel couldna believe it. One minute we're outshide the gate at Nether Bow Port gettin' ready to blow it in and nesht minute we heard voices inside the walls. One said, 'Open the port.' And the sentry anshwered, 'Not without an order from Provost Stewart.' 'Let the coach out as I have the verra order here,' shays another. As the gates opened, Lochiel jumped in and took the mushket off the shentry. You should have sheen his face. We entered unopposed ..."

"And you didna lose a man?" Johnnie whistled in admiration.

"That's righ'. Didn't you hear the pipes and shee the colours flyin'? It was gran' washn't it, Dougie?"

"Yes, grand." Dougie finished his claret with a grimace. "We should have toasted it with Braedrumie whisky, not this muck. No wonder you're drunk."

"An' there's to be a ball at Holyroodhouse tomorrow night," Euan announced to the whole room, "and you're all invited." Then he collapsed in a heap on the table.

"It's the prince's ball," Morag said answering the enquiring faces, "written invitations only. She whispered, "Johnnie, Dougie help me get him back to the stables, before he disgraces himself completely."

CHAPTER Fourteen

Flickering torches illuminated Holyrood's sweeping drive and gates as coach after coach disgorged its chattering passengers at the steps of the main entrance to the building. Morag gazed down at them from a palace window.

"Morag?"

Morag turned to help Amelia dress in an elegant cream gown. Music swelled and filtered through to their apartmen*t*. *Delightful to pick out violins, flutes and double bass on this wonderful evening.* Morag's excitement rose.

"Now my pearl necklace and earbobs," said Amelia, "Crawford's gift on our wedding day." She placed the three strands round her neck and hooked the ear bobs in position. They hung like opulent cream droplets.

Amelia had recovered from her close encounter with a musket ball. If anything, she said, it had made her more determined to stay. The wound had healed, though Morag knew from Amelia's pained expression, it ached on occasion.

"You look ... beautiful."

Amelia laughed. "I will do." She patted her fair hair. "Now let me help so Euan Stewart canna take his eyes off you. We must hurry, there's someone Crawford wants me to meet."

Minutes later, Amelia took Morag's arm as they ran along the draughty corridors until they stood to one side of the grand staircase, looking down on those below. Morag sensed Amelia's excitement in the quick rise and fall of her breast. She tapped her fingers on the balustrade above the Great Gallery which ran the entire length of one wing of the house. It had become a ballroom filled with baroque music, excited chatter and the clink of crystal glasses. Shimmering figures moved backwards and forwards between ceiling-to-floor mirrors, paintings and tapestries lit by a glittering fall of chandeliers.

Morag tugged at her neckline and straightened the bows on her new gown. Her mother had been a lady, but Morag had never experienced luxury such as this. Euan had hired a dressmaker at short notice, not easy in a city agog with news of the ball, but somehow he'd accomplished it. Morag's dress was his gift and she wanted him to think it the most beautiful he'd ever seen.

Morag peered down at the men below. They wore powdered wigs so she ignored them as Euan couldn't abide the itchy headwear. His auburn hair tied with a black bow caught her eye. He'd his back to her, listening to a gaggle of women whose fans fluttered like demented moths.

Euan stood at least a head taller than the other men in the room. *Why wouldna women's eyes be drawn towards him?* Dressed in a white shirt, wine-red coat and ebony breeches it seemed to her at that moment, he'd the most commanding presence in the room.

Dougie looked up at her and nudged Euan. His eyes opened wide in surprise, or was it shock? Her hand went to her décolletage. *Does he think the ruffled neck too low?* She'd snipped off a bow or two when Lady Amelia hadn't been looking. *Or the tartan doesna suit, or my hair?* She pushed a stray wisp back into place, but a dark curl escaped and fell over one ear.

His eyes held hers. Taking the stairs two at a time he stopped, bowed and kissed her hand. His lips brushed her skin, like the fluttering of a small bird's wing. He smiled at her raising an eyebrow. The diagonal cut had gone to the bone and made him look devastatingly handsome. *Surely he can hear my heart pounding?*

His warm breath on her ear and neck sent shivers chasing down her spine.

"That colour suits you, it's like a fine whisky and I could drink you up. My beautiful girl, I'll have to fight the young bucks off; I've this for you." He produced a silk white rose and pinned it to her tartan sash; a symbol of The Cause perhaps, but also their precious reminder of a new beginning.

"You spoil me. Thank you." *Has a fairy creature taken over my body and dressed itself in rich attire?* The ballroom stilled. Enquiring faces stared at the announcement of their names. Amelia gave her a reassuring hug.

"I told you," she whispered. "He canna take his eyes off you." She fluttered her fan and allowed Lord Crawford to lead her down the stairs to a seat.

Sensing her hesitate, Euan took Morag's arm. "I trust I can claim every dance my heart?"

"Of course." She smiled at him.

As they descended the stairs Johnnie joined the throng below. He wore blue tartan and on seeing Morag gave a low whistle.

"So you decided to attend after all," said Euan.

Morag looked at Euan in surprise. *Have the brothers fallen out?*

Johnnie ignored him, stepped forward, bowed and kissed Morag's hand. "My brother doesna deserve you Morag. You put all the ladies in the shade."

"I thought you'd better things to do than attend this ball," Euan hissed. He took Johnnie's arm and led him to an alcove. Morag and Dougie followed. "I'm sure your last words were, 'Dinna wait for me. I'll no' be back till midday tomorrow.'"

"A man can change his mind." Johnnie flushed.

Dougie snorted. "About women waving their handkerchiefs?"

"In their night gowns," suggested a helpful Euan.

Morag looked at them mystified.

"Damn it, I changed my mind!" Johnnie exploded. He looked at Morag. "I noticed some ... er ladies as we marched into Edinburgh."

Morag's eyes narrowed and she folded her arms.

"They waved their wee handkerchiefs at us and laughed and smiled. You must have seen them leaning over that balcony in their night gowns?"

"We noticed," said Euan.

"Well, I didna want to be the last to ... er wish them well."

"It's a mortal sin." Euan bit his lip.

Comprehension dawned on Morag. "Johnnie Stewart. You should be ashamed of yourself."

Euan and Dougie guffawed.

"He should, he should." Dougie grinned and wagged his finger at him. "They probably decided a ... novice ... wasn't to their ... er ... liking."

"An ugly Highland novice at that." teased Euan.

"Dougie! Euan!"

"Close up ..." Johnnie groped for words, "they were... no'... young." His voice sounded as if it had been strangled in his throat.

Euan and Dougie stuffed handkerchiefs in their mouths.

"One had no teeth." Johnnie shuddered. "Her friend had pockmarks and another more blubber than a ... silkie."

Euan and Dougie guffawed again and almost choked. They tugged at their handkerchiefs.

Morag put her hands on her hips. "A good thing Kirsty has the very things in which you appear to be so interested. Teeth, clear skin, a slim waist and I do believe she has a brain. What were you thinking?"

Euan and Dougie slapped each other on the back at that. Tears streamed from their eyes as they tried to dab at them with their handkerchiefs. Morag glared at them till they stopped.

"I only strayed in thought," Johnnie tried to explain. "It's no' easy being a man... with ... thoughts."

"Well, make sure they're sensible ones next time, brother." Euan wiped his streaming eyes. "You wouldna want a dose of c..."

Johnnie poked Euan in the ribs and stuck a glass under his brother's nose. "Perhaps you'd like some refreshment, there's the finest champagne,"

Euan turned green and looked at it in distaste. "I had quite sufficient yesterday evening. I'll no' bother if you dinna mind."

Johnnie grinned at Euan's discomfort. "Morag, a glass?"

For the sake of family peace she agreed and watched Johnnie's broad back disappear behind a throng of twittering ladies. He returned in minutes, a lady on one arm and Morag's champagne in the other. Bowing, he gave her the glass and introduced them all to, "The beautiful Miss Peggie Balfour." He then led her to join the dancers on the floor.

Morag and Euan looked at each other and shook their heads.

Flickering candles in silver and gold candelabra lit the room. Fiddlers played, '*I wake with the dawn, content and filled with hope, now the prince is here to take his own...*'

They tapped their feet to the tune. The women, colourful as butterflies, flocked round the blue-coated Prince who presented them with painted paper fans mounted on ivory sticks.

"I'd much prefer, if you and I were alone on the shore of Loch Linnhe." Euan grinned at Morag

Morag fluttered her fan as his lips brushed just behind her ear sending a rush of delicious excitement through her body.

"Miss McColl, would you do me the honour of dancing with me?" Euan asked bowing, his eyes twinkled at her.

"I'd be delighted sir." He took her hand and led her to the centre of the room to join rows of couples waiting for the minuet.

The music began. She held Euan's gaze as he danced towards her, revelling in the anticipation of his fingers touching hers. A great wantonness swept over her as they danced most of the night. They only stopped so the musicians could rest.

"You'd like some refreshment no doubt?" said Euan. "I'll hunt it out."

He'd only left her for a few seconds when James Kinross bowed in front of her. "Would you dance with me Morag McColl?"

Madness. Doesn't he realise how Euan feels about him? Or doesn't he care? Did she sense a touch of arrogance about his upturned lips as if he was used to getting anything he wanted. She mouthed, "No."

His hand took hers in an iron grip and he led her onto the floor. She could see many ladies eyeing him over fluttering fans. Morag couldn't make a scene, not here and he knew it. She forced herself to allow him to take her in his arms.

For a large man, he was surprisingly graceful and light on his feet, but those hypnotic blue eyes, disconcerting. His hand gripped hers too tightly, pulling her too close. She wrinkled her nose at the stale smell of tobacco.

The music ended and giving a sigh of relief, she curtsied and let him lead her to where Euan stood, in grim silence, with refreshments in his hand.

Kinross didn't appear to be discomfited in the least as he said, "I'm obliged Mr. Stewart, as you can see I've returned Miss McColl quite unharmed."

"Your servant, Mr. Kinross, but you'll note every dance is taken for the rest of the evening."

Kinross smiled, bowed and walked towards a gathering of ladies where he disappeared from sight.

"I'm sorry."

"You should dance with whom you want," said Euan to her, "as long as I'm the one that matters most to you." His voice became like steel, "But that man needs warning off or I can see one day ... we may have a serious falling out."

She kissed his cheek, willing him into good humour. "We'll not spoil tonight because of one man. Now, what have you brought me to eat?"

She dined on oysters and champagne whilst seated in an alcove on what Euan described as, "A very fine French settee." He spent the time teasing her about how such a slender creature could eat so much.

Johnnie joined them and introduced his partner as, "The beautiful Miss Betty Cochrane." Morag raised her eyes to heaven.

Moll Flanders has a lot to answer for. Euan set his mouth in a tight smile.

Within minutes Morag stifled a yawn. Miss Cochran's conversation about red, blue and gold needlepoint held no interest for her. Johnnie smiled an apology.

"Lady Anne Kerr of Kerbilly and Lord Alan of Buick," announced a footman. Morag sat up at the flurry of movement at the main entrance as a woman and her partner arrived at the top of the stairs. Her hair, an un-powdered blaze of red, framed a heart shaped face. A tartan sash lay across a bodice of lilac silk.

A hush descended on the company, followed by turned backs and whispering behind fluttering fans.

Miss Kerr flushed, but drew herself up. Her partner whispered in her ear and they stared at the Stewarts.

Johnnie let out a low whistle. "Kerr, Kerr, wasna that the name of the woman Rob was going to m ...?"

"Yes," said Euan.

"Was he blind?"

"An arranged marriage remember, he never met her."

Morag strained to see this woman she'd heard so much about.

Miss Cochrane's tinted lips became a carmine sneer. She hissed behind her fan, "She's no Jacobite, her father's a Whig. Here for insurance purposes I'm sure. If the prince is victorious he may remember she was at this ball; if he loses then the father can blame a wayward daughter. She's no' welcome."

"She's a beauty," said Johnnie.

The thin nose sniffed, the fan fluttered as she hissed more venom, "Jilted by your brother, Rob, I believe. A pity, no man will have her now she's second-hand goods. I'm sure that's a black taffeta beauty spot above her lip. It's as false as her. I see Sinclair's talking to her. How could he? Didn't he support the Stuarts in 1715 and escape from Newgate with his life? Fled to France so I heard. A hard man, what does he want with her?"

Johnnie turned away and they all sought a more pleasant spot in the room, but not before Morag caught a glimpse of the prince leading Lady Anne Kerr into a small alcove. *Perhaps it's of no matter to him the woman doesna believe in his Cause.* The velvet curtains closed behind them. *Does Miss Kerr think nought of her reputation?*

Amelia hurried towards them. Euan and Johnnie rose and bowed. "Mr. Stewart I'd be most obliged if you'd allow me to borrow Morag for a few minutes, I fear I've lost a favourite earbob and need her help to find it."

"Your servant, Lady Amelia, perhaps my brother and I could also be of some assistance?"

"Thank you, no, only Morag will do, I may have lost it in my chamber." Making her apologies, she took Morag's hand and led her up the red-carpeted stairs and down a long series of dark corridors.

"This isna the way," Morag said, "where are we going?"

"You'll find out, now hush." Amelia stopped and tapped on a door.

"Enter." A man's voice.

Amelia led a bewildered Morag into to a small room, closing the door behind them.

Sinclair rose from behind a table. He bowed, his stiff spine juddering to a halt before he kissed Amelia's hand and hers. Morag shivered as his lips cold and reptilian touched her skin. He beckoned them to sit.

"What have you told her?" He stared at Amelia with unblinking, hooded eyes.

"Nothing," replied Amelia, "as I promised."

He turned to Morag, "I'm Lord Sinclair my dear."

"I know." She'd overheard Dougie talk about him with a look of disdain.

"So you've heard of me," he chuckled. "All good things I trust?" His glance flicked to the rise and fall of her bosom and he licked his thin lips.

Morag snapped her fan open and fluttered it in front of her bodice, delighted to see the corners of his mouth droop. She'd heard he liked women and wasn't particular.

He crossed his bony fingers and tapped his thumbs together. "Lady Amelia has vouched for you, says you want to serve the Cause. There are many ways to serve. Are you willing to work for me, whilst in Edinburgh?"

What is he suggesting? "Work? I'm no' interested in sewing."

"Sewing? Oh no, my dear I dinna see you surrounded by banners and cockades." He leant forward and showed his rotten teeth. His foul breath made her sit back. "I've much more interesting jobs for you and Lady Amelia. She says you're intelligent, brave, with an ability to think on your feet and can be... discreet."

Amelia cocked an eyebrow and smiled at her.

"The work would be highly secretive and you'd be in the midst of the enemy. Lady Amelia seems to think you've something to prove. We need more recruits, to find out enemy numbers, movements, their strengths, weaknesses and intentions. There'd be danger, the risk of being captured or killed." His head moved from side to side. "Are you woman enough for this, Morag McColl, or must I pick someone else?"

Her pulse quickened. She didn't like the man; on the other hand he was offering her the chance to make a difference. She knew what Euan would say, but she'd be helping The Cause, doing something most people would shrink from. What about her father? She knew what he'd say too. *Men. They'd suffocate you if you let them.* "I'm ... willing." At least Sinclair thought she could be of use.

Amelia reassured her with a faint smile.

He nodded, dipped his quill in the ink well and scratched some letters on the paper. He laid down his quill on his desk. "Tell no one of this meeting ..."

Morag tried to explain about Euan, but he waved her attempts away. "Lives are at stake. If captured dinna say you were recruited by me, I will deny it. If you are caught dinna ask for help, it willna be given to you. Realise this: once you have agreed to work for me there is no going back, unless I agree to it. Do you understand?"

"I do." Amelia gave Morag's hand a reassuring squeeze.

He leant forward again. It took all Morag's will power not to shrink into her chair. "You're mine now, with the code name Sword and Lady Amelia's is Shield. We'll contact you with your instructions." Sinclair's brown teeth smiled at her. "You're dismissed." He crossed his fingers again and tapped his thumbs.

They closed the door behind them.

"I feel like I've been eyed as a tasty meal by an adder," said Morag shuddering.

Amelia put her arm inside Morag's. "But you're pleased we're going to be spies?"

Spies? A small noise made Morag turn and peer down the dimly-lit corridor. She sensed something amiss, perhaps a displacement of air. She signalled for Amelia to listen. The music stopped. The sound of running footsteps came from an unlit passage on their right and faded into the distance. Morag's spine tingled. The darkness in the long corridor seemed malevolent.

Morag put a finger to her lips, and swept a silver candelabrum off a table. She used the flickering candlelight to peer into the gloom. The scent of beeswax wafted around her as the musicians struck up another minuet in the gallery. Darkness shifted, hid in corners and clung to edges. The hair on the back of her neck stood to attention. *Is someone watching?* Portraits with liquid eyes jumped out at them. Morag shook her head to clear it. A long shadow loomed and disappeared on the wall some way ahead.

A ripple of fear ran down Morag's back. "I think someone... is spying on us."

"If he listened at the door ..."

They looked at each other in horror. *The game up, even before it's begun?*

They both started at the echo of returning footsteps. Biting her lip, Morag handed the candelabrum to Amelia, lifted her skirts, and grabbed Euan's dirk nestled in the pocket inside. The deer carving on the handle in the palm of her hand gave her some comfort.

Amelia stared at her.

"You can never be too careful." Morag thought of Tolbain.

Amelia's eyes opened wider. "You dinna think ... you cannot possibly think that someone means to ..." Her hand went to her throat.

Morag gripped the dirk; she didn't know what to think. She hid the weapon in the folds of her dress.

A shadow reappeared, larger and more menacing than before. Fighting panic, they watched as a figure emerged in the flickering gloom. Amelia grabbed Morag's arm as the man grew larger and larger, until Morag wanted to scream. *Euan!* Relief flooded over Morag.

He hurried towards them. "Ladies they've announced the last dance. Did you find the earbob?"

"What earbob?" Amelia's, hand clutched at her necklace.

Euan's brow creased. "You lost an earbob, wasna that why...?"

Amelia gave a high, nervous laugh. "I must be quite exhausted, Mr. Stewart, forgive me. Yes, we found it." She opened her palm to reveal a gleaming pearl earbob.

"Euan." Morag passed the dirk behind her to Amelia. "Let's have one last turn about the floor before we leave." *How can I tell him I am a spy? I've given my word.*

Euan's eyes met Morag's. "Ladies, let me escort you both back to the ball."

They smiled and linked arms with his.

CHAPTER Fifteen

Tolbain? Morag's eyes snapped open; a voice had woken her.

She lay in her four poster bed as daylight crept between the curtains and onto the carpet. It was late morning and the rest of Edinburgh seemed to have been up and about for hours.

Distant sounds of shouted orders and marching feet came from outside her window. Morag groaned and turned over. Her pillows lay on the floor and the blankets lay in disarray.

The ball had finally come to a splendid halt at three in the morning, but after Euan had escorted her to her apartment, sleep had deserted her. She'd spent a restless night staving off visions of Tolbain coming at her with a raised sword. She just wanted to rest, but heard more shouts and commands. She prised an eyelid open, it could be redcoats. Springing out of bed, she peered through the window and then went to the door. A chamber maid with a squint mumbled, "The men's doin' drills."

Morag sighed with relief and dressed whilst mulling over what had happened the evening before. It had been wonderful wearing her fine gown and dancing with Euan in the presence of the prince, but had she really been recruited as a secret agent? Had someone been spying on her and Amelia?

No one stirred from the Crawfords' chamber. If they did, they weren't interested in getting out of bed. Envious of their marital bliss, Morag wondered how it would be when she was married to Euan. She went to find him.

Deserted stables greeted her. She knew he wouldn't have marched away without first attempting to contact with her.

A whisp of smoke betrayed Kinross, lounging in a doorway and smoking his clay pipe. "Good day to you Morag McColl, you look tired," he said. He tipped his bonnet and fell into step beside her. Tobacco fumes whirled around her. She coughed.

"My apologies, it's a bad habit, but one I find myself returning to again and again." He put out his pipe and tapped the bowl against his hand to loosen the contents. "Don't you find some people affect you in the same way?" He stared at her with piercing blue eyes.

"What is it you want of me, James Kinross?" she snapped.

"To be ... friends."

That wide grin again. "I canna offer you more than that."

His mouth twitched. "It is enough and as one friend to another, I suppose you could only be looking for Euan Stewart this fine afternoon?"

"Yes."

"The whole army has moved to the lee of Arthur's Seat, they say Cope is marching to Edinburgh."

"Edinburgh? My thanks." She rushed off.

She found Euan in a fever of activity amongst hundreds of tents. The smell of newly greased leather wafted in the air and his sword and dirk lay sharpened and polished. Men came and went like bees in a hive. His brow lifted when he saw her. He dismissed the last of his men, gave her a lopsided grin and put an arm round her waist. "Good afternoon Miss McColl."

"Good afternoon Mr. Stewart." *Can he sense the energy sizzling between us?*

"You've heard the news?"

"Cope's marching to Edinburgh."

"Yes. I was about to send you a message. How did you find me?"

"James Kinross."

His shoulders straightened. "The man likes you, should I warn him off?"

She bit her lip. "No we agreed to be friends. He was being helpful."

His muscular arms held her and she didn't want him to let her go. His lips sought hers and she replied in kind until he pulled away from her. He wagged his finger, "That's a very, very dangerous kiss Morag McColl. I think we'd better talk, don't you?" He sat her down beside him on a low workman's bench. "We mustna let Cope take Edinburgh, there's to be a Council of War tonight." He drew her towards him and kissed her again. "We'll be moving out, you ken?" He ran his fingers through strands, gathering tangles as he went. "I love your hair when it's like this."

"A mess?" She batted his hands away, gathering the waves into some semblance of order.

"No. It's like a sparkling brown waterfall tumbling down your shoulders to your ... breast." He allowed his fingers to follow his thoughts and stopped as if burnt at her body's response. "I want you so much, my heart, but I mustna ..." Taking a deep breath, he took a folded piece of parchment from his saddlebags. "A little bit of home." He showed her the unopened letter.

"You'll share it with me?" Still conscious of the warmth flooding through her, she wished once again that they'd married. "I havena received one." He smelt of clean, male sweat, horses and hay.

"Did your father no' write?"

"No." She looked at her shoes.

He put a comforting arm round her. "Dinna blame him; he'll still be angry..."

"I dinna blame him, but I'd like to ken they're all well in Braedrumie and that he still ... you know..."

"I know." Euan kissed her cheek. "Come share my letter darling." He unfolded it. "It's from my father of course. He says they're all fine." He grinned at her and she grinned back as she snuggled her head on his shirt. "Granny Mac says to tell you that Isabel has some horse liniment that eases her pains. Oh, Duncan has been a little devil and has sworn never to forgive us, but asked to be remembered to all." Euan smiled wryly, "Seems he's got a short memory. Now ... where was I? -The worst news is last. Your father's been to the house and blames me for leading you astray."

"He hasna?" She lifted her head, shocked.

"He has. Morag, my own one, go home, if no' for me, for him."

"I canna..." She buried her nose in his chest, breathing in the smell of him.

Euan sighed. "Morag? You need to listen. We're marching south very soon to meet Cope in battle. I want you home, out of danger. If we lose, you'll no' be safe with the baggage train and if we win we'll be marching into England. Will you no' do this one thing I ask of you?"

"I ... I'll stay in Edinburgh. Amelia will be here, so there'll be no need to worry." *Almost the truth.*

"You will? Do you promise?"

"I will." She couldn't look at his face as he gathered her into his arms and kissed the top of her head. "You dinna ken what a relief it is to know you'll be safe."

Sweet Jesu. He thought she'd be safe. It's a good thing he knew nought of her recruitment to Sinclair's secret world.

"If I fall ..."

"Dinna say that, dinna ever say that. Have you the cross I gave you?" She fumbled at the neck of his shirt. "Good, it'll keep you safe till you come home to me."

"I'll write to you and think of you every night before I sleep." He kissed her nose.

"I'll write and think of you." Guilt pricked at her.

***

On September 20th, Euan watched from his saddle as Morag pushed her way towards him. Crowds lined the torch-lit streets. He just wanted to hold her for one last time. Along the line, tearful women clung to their men as the Jacobites prepared to ride away to meet the redcoats. His ears hummed with heartrending goodbyes. Johnnie grim faced and a resolute Dougie rode to the front.

Morag put out her arms to him and he lifted her onto his horse in one powerful movement. He held her to his chest. "I love you." His eyes took in the concern in her hazel eyes. He didn't want to let her go.

"And I you."

"If I fall ..."

"Dinna say it." She put a finger to his lips. "Be careful, dinna do anything ... rash ... dinna ..."

He kissed her then. His lips didn't skirt hers; he wanted to scorch her mouth, imprinting something of himself on her. He searched her face one more time as if locking her into his memory forever and lowered her protesting to the ground.

She walked several miles with him before he pressed her hand in a last goodbye. He let her go as if a sail boat cast adrift in the sea. He'd never have believed he could have loved her more than when they were in Braedrumie. Leaving her now rent his heart in two.

CHAPTER Sixteen

To Morag's amazement the army returned in triumph on the morning of September 22nd. She ran into the streets with everyone else, looking for Euan.

Morag and Amelia held hands as they scanned the column for faces they knew and loved as the victorious Jacobites entered the city to the skirl of pipes and the beat of drums. Morag bobbed up and down. Could she spot them above the heads of the crowd? She'd never be able to rest until she saw him.

The prince, sat upright in the saddle, leading them all, a broad smile lit his face and he waved as he rode. A grinning Lord Crawford rode behind amongst the chiefs. Morag heard Amelia's sigh of relief as she waved her handkerchief. Where were Euan and the Stewart clan? At last Morag spotted Euan and Johnnie and their men. Dougie driving a fine coach and horses was behind them, followed by the wounded in carts, prisoners and captured guns.

Morag joined the women running beside their men, caught up by the emotions of the day. She loved it when Euan's strong arms lifted her up, so she rode side saddle.

"I missed you, my heart." Euan enfolded Morag in his embrace and kissed the top of her head.

"Missed you too." She leant against him enjoying his closeness and the loping stride of the horse. Blood smeared his torn left sleeve. "You're hurt.'

"It's nothing."

"It'll need cleansing." He didn't look like he'd a fever, but healthy people had been struck down by contagion and died in a day. She resolved to have a look at *nothing* as soon as possible and settled inside his arms once more.

They rode into the stable yard.

"The battle only took ten minutes," crowed Euan as he lowered her to the ground. "Ten minutes and we had them on the run. A

Whitburgh man, Rob Anderson, ensured our victory. He showed us a secret route through the marshes. Johnny Cope and his redcoats were asleep. There's no stopping us now, Charlie's going to win." He dismounted and danced her round the stable yard in front of a grinning Johnnie, Dougie and gawping stable lads.

"This is no' a ballroom," she said at last, tucking her hair in place. "Now, your arm."

"Let me stable my horse first."

"Very well." She spent the time setting out what she needed on the bench, a bowl of hot water, comfrey, and a salve composed of honey and salt, brandy and clean strips of linen.

He reappeared at the stable door.

"At last, sit here." She pointed at an upturned log.

He sat and held out his left arm. Blood had stuck the makeshift bandage to the wound. *A glancing blow* he'd called it.

She tried sponging to no avail. "This will hurt," she said and ripped it off.

He clenched his teeth, but made no sound. She pressed her lips on his cheek before washing the dried blood, pus and grime from his arm. Keeping her thoughts to herself, she noted he'd a bleeding and inflamed sword cut about four inches in length. He smiled at her. She reached for the bottle of brandy.

"Brandy. Now that's what a man needs when he returns home from battle. Find some tankards you two."

Johnnie and Dougie scuttled off to return in minutes holding three aloft in triumph.

She wafted the bottle under their noses.

Euan sniffed at it with reverence. "Nectar of the Gods."

They all grinned.

She smiled at them and poured the precious liquid onto Euan's wound.

"Aaaaagh," he yelled baring his teeth and half rising out of his seat. "Are you trying to kill me?"

"Trying to save you, you ungrateful wretch."

"I was safer on the battlefield."

"Waste of good brandy," muttered Johnnie shaking his head.

"I didna ken womenfolk could be so cruel." added Dougie. "Why my Isabel…"

"I've something that will clean you both out." Morag held up a bottle of foul-smelling medication. "You sound bilious to me."

"Need to see Lord Crawford." Johnnie retreated at speed.

"I'm off." Dougie backed away. "Got to take Cope's carriage with the spoils to the laird. The prince asked that we keep it safe. I'll be back as quickly as I can."

"You'll take our letters? Jamie's done in. Lying like a dead man in the stable, needs to rest," said Euan. "Tell Father I … hmph … you know … and give Isabel a kiss from me."

On hearing his wife's name Dougie grinned, bowed and set off for the Highlands at speed.

Morag advanced on Euan with a horn beaker full of comfrey. "Open wide," she smiled sweetly at him.

He wrinkled his nose. "Johnnie wait for me," he pleaded at his brother's receding back.

"She's only getting the chance to kill one of us today," yelled a grinning Johnnie.

"Now Morag …" began Euan.

She seized the opportunity to toss the mixture down his throat.

"Urgh. Aaagh. Yuuck. You've poisoned me you besom. It tastes like horse piss."

"It's supposed to taste foul so it can heal you from your innards."

He eyed her as she put her finger in the pot of salve. "Now what are you doing?"

"I'm going to put this on your wound and you're going to sit there and let me. It's my best salve and my mother's before me and you're going to stop acting like a … a … a child." Her face hot and flushed, she grabbed his arm. "This may sting a little at first, but it will get rid of the contagion."

Aware of his eyes on her, the hair on her neck stirred as she bent over his wound, rubbed in the salve and wrapped fresh linen round it.

"I didna realise what a practical lassie I'm going to marry. I love you, my heart." He went as if to kiss the tip of her nose, but his tongue licked it instead. She stepped back, but he pulled her to him and his lips found hers. The bowl upended and water cascaded to the floor.

Sinclair had slipped a note under Amelia's door. Morag read it several times.

Shield & Sword,

Go to Cairnpapple Hill, north of Bathgate, Edinburgh, tomorrow. Meet with the clan chiefs camped there. Persuade them to commit to the Cause. If they're still reluctant tell them when we are victorious, I will ensure life will be difficult for those who stay at home.

S.

Fortunately for Morag, Euan was too busy helping Johnnie organising men, checking equipment and training, to puzzle over her absence.

They'd ridden for several miles through forests and glens before Morag's hand in the air stopped them. "Woodsmoke." The women drew rein and surveyed the scene at Cairnpapple. Clouds like torn grey flags streamed across the vast sky towards a mountainous horizon. The hill towered above them with its ancient circular ditch, earth bank and clusters of huge rocks set in a flat, verdant landscape. A swirl of smoke curled upward inside the bank. A group of men sat round a fire whilst their ponies grazed nearby.

"About two dozen by my count," said Morag, "let's hope they'll join us."

Sentries sprang out of the undergrowth and grabbed their reins. "Who are you and what do you want?" snarled one whose hare lip gave him a brutal appearance.

Amelia flinched.

Morag put a calming hand on her friend's shoulder. "You're expecting us. We're from S."

"Dismount here and follow me." He led them towards the dancing flames.

"So, Sinclair sent you, what's in it for us?" A grizzled warrior hawked and spat in the fire.

"The prince willna forget who fought for him ... or who stayed at home." Morag wouldn't be bullied and stared straight at him.

A chief with a pasty face surrounded by flames of red hair spoke up, "We've made our decision. There's not enough to back you. Where's the French?"

"They brought the prince to these shores and have promised men, ships and arms." Amelia answered

A pockmarked chief stepped forward. "Promises mean nothing, it's action we need. No. I'm sorry ladies you can tell S we're not convinced."

A growl of approval circled the fire. Most of the chiefs got up and rode off.

Morag shook her head in disbelief, though several men stayed and asked pointed questions about the French. A few agreed to bring their clans to Edinburgh and join the prince. She knew these men could make the difference between winning and losing, but they'd recruited a pitiful few.

The women rode back to Edinburgh in silence each absorbed with her own thoughts. Morag had lots of questions. Why hadn't the chiefs joined them? Surely the Jacobites had proved themselves at Perth, Edinburgh and Prestonpans? All ventures had an element of risk. *Didna the chiefs realise the more of them who joined The Cause, the more likely the French would fulfil their promises?* She'd always been so certain the Jacobites would be victorious. *Sweet Jesu, what would happen if they lost? No. Think only of Euan, the clan riding home and the prince on the throne.*

Sinclair stared at them with bleak, heavy lidded eyes when they delivered their news. "You're both to visit this house in the Grassmarket tomorrow." He handed Amelia a note. "It would be helpful if you were successful in this endeavour. It should take a week. You can go."

They trudged towards Edinburgh Castle, about a mile away. Morag shivered at seeing the redcoats lining the battlements. If she and Amelia were ever caught, they'd be thrown into the castle's dungeons. Morag forced herself not to think of it.

The Grassmarket, with its gallows, temporary lodgings and taverns lay in a hollow in the castle's shadow. Once in the teaming market square, Morag got her bearings. She knew West Port lay to the west; the King's stables to the north-west and Candlemaker Row and Cow Gate to the east.

She sniffed the air, heavy with the smell of fresh dung and the buzz of circling flies. The cacophony deafened her as drovers guided mooing and neighing animals into pens and hawkers and traders shouted "Come buy!" "Best wares here!"

Morag pulled Amelia past the brightly coloured stalls, greedy customers, grasping beggars and swaying drunks until they stood in front of number 11, a stone house blackened with grime and soot. They studied its four storeys, double front and large black central door before they knocked. A sober-faced servant ushered them into the gloomy ground floor study lined with books from floor to ceiling. Mr. Elliot, a balding and bespectacled man introduced himself. *Not his real name of course.*

"Let us begin, ladies. Pray be seated at the desk."

Mystified, Morag and Amelia sat facing each other with stacks of parchment, several quills, wafers, pots of ink and sealing wax lying between them.

"You are to be trained in the art of disinformation. Naturally we do no' want the enemy to know our positions and strength. We're going to compose letters and notes which contain some truth, but also falsehoods." He waved papers at them. "By this I mean lists of false troop movements, numbers, departures, arrivals and armaments. You will write under various pseudonyms and false addresses to supposed friends and acquaintances. We will ensure your misinformation is intercepted or left in Jacobite meeting places. Here are some examples." He put a wad of papers on the table. "Study them and then begin. I will put you right as we go along."

By late evening a mountain of notes and carefully sealed letters covered every flat surface. By the end of the week they had aching backs, numb, ink spotted fingers, but their writings would be posted all over Scotland and England.

"We did well," said Amelia.

Morag managed fleeting visits to see Euan, always surrounded by men and lists. He had no time to think about her and she didn't want to distract him.

The following week she and Amelia received instructions to attend a number of soirees held by government supporters in Edinburgh and glean as much military information as possible.

Wearing an array of wigs, they arrived escorted by two of Sinclair's men. They all bore false names and played their parts well, though Morag found it difficult to be charming to Whigs who condemned the *mad prince* and his *Jacobite jackals*. However, when the same men or women were in their cups, the conversation often took an interesting turn. Young officers, trying to impress, would comment on the movements of a certain General or regiment. Colonel's wives would state that their husbands were about to leave for Aberdeen, Inverness or Newcastle and how much they'd miss them or not. Ships, armaments and provisions, dates and times were all discussed and everything noted by Morag, Amelia and their escorts.

As more and more useful information came their way, they threw themselves into their roles so admirers of both sexes surrounded them, until the night a drunken Major accosted Morag.

He leant towards her. "Shure I wash introduced to you at Colonel Blandford's last week. Never forget a pretty face, but you shaid you were Lady Mary Scott." His hand grasped her elbow.

Damn the man. "My cousin on my mother's side. You're not the first to say we look remarkably alike." *Does he believe me?* His dull eyes blinked as the lines on his face changed from suspicion to grudging acceptance.

"Two damned attractive ladiesh, by God." He blinked at her again. "Bit of a coinshidence though?" His voice hardened and his fingers dug into her flesh.

Sweet Jesu, how do I get out of this? She tapped him on his forearm with her fan. "Oh, Major and there's only one of you and you're so handsome in that uniform. You quite turn my head."

He swayed as he assessed her. One eyelid drooped, whilst the other regarded her as if through a telescope. He released her at last, and kissed her hand. "Charmed, I'm shure. Perhaps we can get to know each other ... better."

"You are a one." Morag took a champagne bottle and two glasses from the table and led him into a dimly lit alcove. One of her escorts grabbed him, putting a hand over his mouth. Morag ignored the pleading look in his eyes and knocked him out with the bottle. He sagged in the arms of the man who held him. Morag beckoned their other escorts to drag him behind a curtain before they all left.

Amelia looked pale and drawn. Morag could only imagine she presented a mirror image as their escorts led them back to Holyrood by various circuitous routes. If caught they'd be imprisoned and possibly tortured, not something that helped sleep come.

CHAPTER Eighteen

A few days later, Morag, startled by a knock on the door of her apartment, found a piece of folded parchment lying on the floor. She picked it up with trembling fingers. *More intrigue.* A single word 'Sword' written in black ink. *Sinclair's scrawl of course.* She broke the seal, unfolded it and read it several times.

Sword,

We suspect General Guest, the officer commanding Edinburgh Castle, is receiving secret information. Go to his house at 2, Flodden Street. Tell his housekeeper, Mrs. Quin, that the Widow Ross has recommended you for the position of scullery maid.

With our agreement, Mrs. Quin, has been allowed to send the General provisions. Report your suspicions and leave a note addressed to S. behind the stone marked / in the back wall, left of General Guest's back gate. Shield will help. Burn this.

S.

Morag moved across to the marble fireplace and held the paper to the fire. The flames curled round it, but the parchment didn't burn. She'd bury it. *Can I do what Sinclair wants?* Despite her disguise, she'd almost been caught at the last soiree and wasn't sleeping well.

She turned at a light tap at the door and Amelia entered. Putting a finger to her lips she led Morag to the wardrobe. "It appears you're to be a scullery maid. Wear these." She thrust a bundle of clothes at her friend.

Morag hesitated. "This could take weeks. Euan will want to ken where I am."

"Leave a message. Tell him ... an aunt, you have an aunt?"

Morag nodded.

"Very well, your aunt is unwell and has begged you to go to her. Where does she live?"

"Drumnadrochit."

"Perfect."

"But she's an old besom and Euan kens we dinna get on."

Amelia thought and then clicked her fingers. "I have it. You'll take to your bed with a slight fever and receive no visitors until you've recovered."

"But Euan ..."

"If he persists I'll mention smallpox."

Morag's mouth and eyes widened in horror. *So many bear pitted scars and even more die from the disease.* "He'll never forgive me if he finds out I lied about this."

"Then we'll just have to ensure he does not."

"I hate deceiving him. I've never ... oh Jesu." They clung to each other for a time.

"I ken it's difficult, but perhaps what we are about to do might give us victory or prevent him, them ... being ... Come, we must harden our hearts." Amelia lowered her voice, "The game is about to begin."

Morag's heart beat a little faster.

Amelia checked the corridor. Closing the door she said, "From this moment you are Maggie Anderson, an orphan taken in by your aunt, Mrs. Ross, who canna wait for you to get out from under her feet." She laughed, but spoke in hushed tones, "You are to leave here in disguise, so you need to do something with your hair. Sinclair has asked to see me, I'll return in half an hour."

"Would you bury this for me?" Morag handed her Sinclair's letter.

Amelia nodded and tucked it in her bodice.

In a fever of excitement Morag looked in the mirror. Her hair had become a wild bush curling its way over her shoulders and down her back. She set about taming it and grabbed a comb. First she tugged, next pulled and brushed it into submission, then tied and pinned it to the top of her head so little wayward hair could be seen, rather like a conjuring trick.

She laced herself into the rags she'd been given. It was no hardship and though the thin, yellowed bodice gaped a little and the ragged grey skirt was a touch too short, it seemed to Morag as she stood in front of the mirror, it would do. Her outfit was completed by darned grey stockings, frayed cream garters, badly scuffed shoes and a patched grey cloak with a hood

Morag was interrupted by Amelia's faint tap at her door. She'd returned wearing a grey cloak.

"Goodness," she said. She examined Morag's tightly pinned bun. "Where has your hair gone? Hmm, you look far too clean." Amelia gathered a handful of ash from the grate and daubed Morag's hair, face and clothes.

She stopped at last, poured water from a fine china jug into a basin and washed and dried her hands. She looked Morag up and down. "You will do very well, very well indeed. Even Euan wouldna recognise you dressed like that." She flung the towel onto the bed. "Now let us set about this business." She sauntered towards a huge mirror in a gold leaf frame. "Sinclair told me about this."

Morag watched as Amelia, pressed a rose motif on the wall and the mirror swung inwards.

Morag gasped at the icy draught.

"This is a palace of secrets." Cold air swirled around them as Amelia lit a candle with a taper, held one hand round the flickering flame and stepped into the blackness.

Morag took a deep breath to overcome her fear of being trapped in dark places. She remembered Tolbain and the forest and shuddered as she wrapped her cloak tightly around her and followed Amelia into the unknown. Taking deep breaths, she stepped into the narrow tunnel. The ceiling and walls pressed in on Morag, but she fought the urge to run back as she spied steep, stone stairs leading down.

Pulling a lever in the wall, Amelia returned the mirror to its original position. Without the candle they wouldn't have been able to see a hand in front of their faces. Amelia led the way.

Cobwebs brushed against Morag's face. She rubbed at their sticky remnants as she noted pin holes of light at regular intervals along the internal wall. "What are they?" she whispered.

"Spy holes I think," Amelia's voice was low and hushed. "You ken all those portraits, the eyes that seem to follow you?"

"I canna believe ..." Morag stopped unable to resist putting an eye to one. She pulled back quickly, stuttering, "It's ... it's ... "

Amelia had left her own peep hole looking a little flushed. "Oh my."

Morag whispered, "I bet you didna realise the 'beautiful' Miss Peggie Balfour and Miss Betty Cochrane knew the prince *that* well."

CHAPTER Nineteen

Mrs. Quin was as sharp and thin as a quill pen. She'd yanked her feathery hair beneath a starched lace cap and her bony shoulders stood to attention above a flat chest and hand-span waist. She reminded Morag of a bird of prey with a hooked beak and beady eyes.

A miasma of rancid smells, burnt offerings and stale odour from dish cloths rose up from rows of unwashed stoneware jugs, pewter plates, copper pans and wooden bowls and spoons stacked higgedly-piggedly on a pine dresser, table and in the stone sink. Worse, scuttling and squeaking could be heard in the darkest corners of the scullery.

Morag watched as Mrs. Quin strode from one work surface to another wiping the tip of a bony claw here and there. On finding smears of dirt, her mouth turned down and she sniffed.

"Well, Maggie Anderson, you're an orphan and Mrs. Ross recommended you for the position of scullery maid, you say? There's no' much meat on you." She sniffed again. "And you're awful young."

"I'm strong and a hard worker."

"That's for me to judge and you're no' to speak unless asked a question. You'll rise at four and only go to bed when I say the work's done with, one Sunday afternoon off a month from one till four. I'm short staffed, or you'd share a bedroom. If you last, you'll be on board wages: £2.10s a year take it or leave it."

"I'll take it."

Mrs. Quin glared at Morag as if she was something she'd stepped in. "You'll address me as Missus if you please, and I'll call you ..." A malicious look came into her eye. Her crow's feet danced. "Rags...yes, Rags. You're fortunate we have a high opinion of Mrs. Ross. You're on trial for a day. There's Jeannie and you."

"Yes Missus."

"You can start by lighting the fire and collecting the water for the copper from the pump in the yard and no sneaking off with the stable lads. The last lass hid her dead brat in the coal scuttle. They hanged her." She smirked at Morag's sharp intake of breath.

"This is General Guest's house and he expects certain standards from his staff. What must he think, under siege in the castle and this poor city in the hands of those animals?" Mrs. Quin made her point with a knife. "They should be hunted down, wiped out." She made to stab at the butter, but stopped in mid-air as if she'd forgotten something. "And no sneaking into the larder, it's out of bounds to you. Don't stand gawping. The bucket's under the sink. There's the kitchen table to scrub and the floor. Then you can start on the veg." She pointed at sacks of turnips and carrots. "Dinna think I willna be checking what you're doing and dinna raise your head till the last one's done."

"Yes, Missus." Morag wished Mrs. Quin would drown in a barrel of her own acid.

"Jeannie!" Mrs. Quin shouted as she put a parcel of butter and a jug of milk into a wicker basket. "Where's that mopsqueezer? Jean... nie!" she shrieked.

The sound of hurried footsteps came from the backstairs. A pretty little ten year old skidded to a halt in front of the table. She'd pale cheeks, copper hair and deep blue eyes.

"Missus?" Jeannie was out of breath.

"You're to take the basket up to the castle for the general as usual. Dinna forget to smile and remind those Jacobite ... guards, that John Murray, one of their own, agreed to the general having this on account of his age and sensitive stomach. No loitering mind, there and back in fifteen minutes."

"But Missus, I'm scairt," squeaked Jeannie taking up the basket.

"Scairt?" Mrs. Quin cuffed Jeannie's ear.

"Ow."

"I'll go with her if you like Missus. The streets are full of them awful Jacobites, no knowing what might become of her."

Mrs. Quin cuffed Morag's ear. "Get on with your work. I expect your tasks completed in an hour."

"Yes Missus." Morag rubbed her stinging ear. She'd never felt such hate, but kept her head down so Mrs. Quin couldn't see it.

***

Every day was drudgery. Rising before dawn, Morag and Jeannie carried, hauled, scrubbed, dusted, swept, washed, peeled and chopped until dusk. Their backs ached and their hands became chapped.

A week later Morag had learned nothing, other than it was misery working under Mrs. Quin. She'd no visitors and nothing untoward occurred.

That morning Morag overheard Jeannie say, "But I dinna want to go on my own. One of those Jacobites looked like he was going to gobble me up last time. I'm frightened." She rubbed her eyes and tears rolled down her face.

"Ow." The clout on her ear from Mrs. Quin made Jeannie cry even louder.

"They're, vermin, the sooner Edinburgh is rid of them the better." Mrs. Quin patted the butter into shape. "Pull yourself together girl. The general needs his provisions."

"I'll go with her Missus." Morag wiped her wet hands on her coarse apron. "She won't be frightened with me." She steeled herself for the blow which almost knocked her off her feet. Mrs. Quin's hand had landed on Morag's cheek, she could feel it swelling.

"It doesna take two. Didna I say don't speak unless spoken to?" snapped Mrs. Quin.

"I'm sorry Missus, but you did say the Jacobites were animals and vermin."

"They are. They're primitives, only fit to be hunted down." Mrs. Quin spat out.

Jeannie's mouth remained wide open, her eyes spoke of terror and her feet seemed rooted to the ground. "Missus," her voice trembled, "I'm so scairt."

"For goodness sake. Very well, Rags, go with the silly child, but you're to be no longer than fifteen minutes and Jeannie carries the basket. Do you hear?"

'Yes Missus."

Jeannie sighed in relief and once they were some distance from the house, she sang, played with the handle, which went clickety-clack, and swung the basket as she walked. Some of the milk spilt.

"Let me, I willna tell." Morag took charge of the basket and its contents while Jeannie hopped and skipped beside her. They paused to watch some ragged children playing with bone marbles in the dirt. "Jeannie would you like to play for a little while?" she asked.

"We've only got fifteen minutes ... Mrs. Quin would skin me."

"No' if we ran all the way back. I'll sit over there and wait. You've a few minutes."

Jeannie's face broke into a huge smile. "Thanks." She raced away.

Morag sat on the grass. She hadn't seen anything suspicious, but perhaps there was more to the contents of the basket than met the eye. She peered in the jug, just milk, then unwrapped the butter, nothing unusual about its shiny, yellow sheen. An image of Mrs. Quin's knife poised above a slab, made her think. Darting a glance at Jeannie rolling down the slope and shrieking in delight, Morag stuck a finger into the oblong and searched its length. Nothing. She patted it back into shape, wrapped it and popped it back in the basket. What to do with her greasy fingers? Dock leaves, the broad leaves surrounded her. Pulling at one she used it like a cloth and wiped her hands.

But I heard a sound: Clickety-clack. The handle. She tested it and found a gap. The handle slid backwards and forwards. Her fingers grasped a soft, cylindrical object inside. Seizing it, she pulled out a leather tube, and found a folded piece of parchment. *Yes.*

There were more yells and screams from Jeannie who'd landed in a heap of laughter. She sprang up and made her way higher up the slope.

Morag memorised the paper's contents. It detailed Jacobite regiments, positions and armaments and also mentioned a change of plans and a visitor expected at Mrs. Quin's on Thursday at midnight.

Jeannie played on. Morag replaced the note as Jeannie rolled down the bank again.

So, General Guest receives more than provisions. She waved to Jeannie and shouted, "We must go."

Jeannie ran to her. "It was fun, thank you."

"We must be quick." She grabbed Jeannie's hand and ran towards the castle. Morag stopped. She might be recognised by the Jacobite sentries. "I'll ... wait ... here. 'I've ... a ...stitch."

A burly Highlander, Douglas Ross, scowled at Jeannie and Iain Skene growled like a bear making her shrink from them.

Morag knew them well.

Bored with their teasing, they grabbed Jeannie's basket, saw only the jug of milk and pat of butter and waved her through as they did three times a week. She disappeared from sight into the castle.

Minutes later the castle gate opened again and Jeannie came out swinging the empty basket.

Jeannie looked at Morag with imploring eyes. "Just one more roll down the bank," she pleaded.

"Go on then."

Jeannie thrust the basket at her and ran to the bank. Morag gave the handle a tug and it slid open. As Jeannie climbed, Morag's fingers groped and found a tube of parchment. She opened it, read it and put it back. *Sweet Jesu, it was in code and from General Guest. Jeannie?* A scream of delight told her Jeannie had just rolled down the bank. Morag reached inside her pocket for a pencil and paper. She scribbled down the contents of the first note and the code from the second, put the parchment back in its tube and ensured the handle looked as it should.

Morag shouted across at Jeannie, "We have to run. We've only minutes before we're late."

Jeannie's smile turned into a look of alarm. They dashed down the street as if chased. People stopped, stared and looked back at the way they'd come.

Morag paused at the back perimeter wall of the house. "You go ahead," she said, "I've a stone in my shoe."

"Hurry." Jeannie ran through the open gate.

Morag looked up and down the street. *No one.* A dog barked next door. She examined the crumbling wall to the left of the gate searching with frantic fingers for the mark, found the stone, inched it out and felt a hollow. *Anyone watching? No.* She left her note deep within, replaced the stone and prayed.

CHAPTER Twenty

Euan had been in and out of meetings all week, training, helping Johnnie order provisions and sharpening his sword skills. Though Johnnie liked books, he proved a worthy opponent. They stood in the cobbled stable yard, hands resting on their sword pommels, ribs heaving and with perspiration running down their chests, they'd parried, cut and thrust for hours.

"Call it a draw," said Jamie Moffat mending harness. Everything needed to be in working order for their march south.

"I dinna suppose it would do for one brother to kill another," grinned Euan. "You've improved, Johnnie." Euan examined the cut healing on his forearm. It looked pink and healthy. "Morag did a good job with this. I hardly felt a twinge."

"You've reconciled yourself to her being with us then?" Johnnie tossed Euan's shirt to him and they both dried themselves.

"I suppose so, but she's no' going south. I'm pleased the prince's ordered women and children to stay behind."

"It willna stop some of them."

"No, but Morag's promised. She never breaks a promise. I'm surprised she's no' here. I've been so full of soldiering and ..."

A rider clattered into the yard and stopped in front of Johnnie. "The prince has ordered you and your men to oversee the storing of provisions at Leith and stand guard until further orders."

"It will be done," said Euan.

The rider set off at a gallop.

Euan looked at Johnnie. "We'll be in England soon. What do you think of our chances?"

Johnnie didn't speak until they were in the stable. He lowered his voice, "You're asking a reluctant volunteer?"

"Who's my brother and will give an honest answer."

"We're outnumbered by some of the best fighting troops in Europe, they've betters arms ... This rising is ill conceived. We havena even got all the clans with us."

"And the French?"

"In the end, it will be us against the British army. There'll be no help from the French. Rob warned me."

"God you paint a bleak picture. I must write home and tell them we're on top form of course, then find Morag, try and persuade her to go home. She'll be safer there. The garrison willna stay in the castle once we've left. I havena seen hide or hair of her for days and there's been no message. I'll call at the palace tonight."

"We'd better get to the provisions then. Men willna fight on empty stomachs."

***

Euan arrived at the palace in the dark. He didn't arrive in the best of moods. Some of the provisions had been missing and were finally found still in the hold of the ship. Two guards greeted him at the bottom of the corridor leading to Morag's apartment.

"Sorry sir, Lady Crawford's orders, no one's allowed in. Miss McColl's ill."

"Ill? Why havena I been informed?" He'd never known her ill. She'd always had good health, he couldn't imagine her unwell. Why hadn't she sent for him? "Tell Lady Crawford I would like to see her."

Amelia arrived wringing her hands.

"Tell me the worst."

"Pray sit down, Euan." Her face creased into a frown. "Your pacing will no' make a better of it and you'll wear out the carpet. There's no need to worry, Morag has a ... slight fever."

"Then I can see her."

"The physician says she needs rest."

"I would no' disturb her. I just need to see she is alright."

"Her illness must be allowed to run its course. It may be worse than we think."

"Worse? Don't you see I'll go mad if I don't see her, she's my life, I canna live without her. I must see her."

She looked out of the window. "Euan, it may be smallpox."

"God no. Not that." He imagined her sweet features destroyed by that cruel disease. "It doesna matter, I want to see her."

"You canna. You know how contagious it is. It could sweep through whole of Edinburgh and the Jacobite army. We must ensure it's merely a fever."

"Why wasna I sent for?"

Amelai chewed her thumbnail. "She didna want to worry you."

"I'll stay. Sleep here, till she recovers." Lady Amelia fluttered her fan. "It may be days."

"It doesna matter. Tell her I'm close by ... in case she needs me."

Her fan snapped shut. "Of course, if you insist."

"I do. I want be the first to know when she recovers."

CHAPTER Twenty-one

Morag worked like a drudge for the rest of the week, impatient to be free of Mrs. Quin and missing Euan. He must have wondered where she was. She just hoped the story she and Amelia had concocted kept him at bay.

Thursday ticked by, a day of hens not laying and singed linen. The house full of cross words and ruined tempers.

Mrs. Quin had decided Morag could make the bread and cook the meals as well as do her own chores. Morag fell into bed, but didn't change into her nightgown, nor dared sleep. She needed to be awake for Mrs. Quin's visitor and wondered if Sinclair had received her message.

It was well after midnight when Morag heard a dog bark in the back lane followed by a yelp and a skittering stone. She came alert. The gate creaked and footsteps sounded on the flagstones below. A low whistle pierced the night followed by a tap on the kitchen door. Looking through a knot in her shutter she saw a dark, cloaked figure caught in a rectangle of light pass something to an outstretched hand inside the house.

"Freeze or I'll shoot you where you stand." A commanding voice rang out in the dark.

Morag's heart missed a beat. She saw the tall figure duck into the house, heard the door hurled shut and the bolt rammed home as musket balls slammed in and around it. The yard exploded into a whirlwind of noise. Jacobite troops swarmed through the gate. They hammered at doors with their muskets, causing Jeannie to shriek in her bedroom.

Morag expected to hear the fugitive's footsteps pounding up the stairs, perhaps making for the roof. She opened her door, holding a candlestick for a weapon. The stairs seemed one black shadow. From Jeannie's room came the sound of dragging furniture.

Morag crept downstairs, candlestick raised. The external doors splintered and bowed. Windows shattered as the Jacobites sought entrance. She tried to turn the handle of the kitchen door, but it had been locked from the inside. The fugitives couldn't escape. The soldiers crashed into the kitchen and slammed open the internal door. One, a Highlander with straw coloured hair, pressed Morag against a wall with a blade at her throat yelling, "On your life, where's the Whig spies?"

Her candlestick fell to the floor. Words stuck in her throat. She didn't recognise the hoarse rasp coming from her throat. "Get that dirk out of my face and take me to whoever's in charge."

The Jacobite grabbed her shoulder and shouted, "We've got a feisty miss here, thinks she gives the orders."

Morag kicked his shin and grinned at his curse as he manhandled her into the kitchen. A candle made faces look devilish in its flickering light.

"And you're?" asked the captain, his claymore at her breast.

"Maggie Anderson, I'm just the scullery maid sir, I dinna need a ... *sword*."

"Ah." His brown eyes lit up in recognition then became hooded.

A door swung open. "There's no one on this floor," said a blunt nosed Highlander charging in ahead of half a dozen others.

"Take your men and scour upstairs," ordered the captain.

Morag lowered her voice, "You'll only find a young girl, Jeannie. I don't think she knows anything. It's the housekeeper and her visitor you want."

"Everyone will need to be questioned." The captain signalled to two men. "Take the girl, Jeannie, out by the front door."

They pounded upstairs. Crashings, splinterings and the sound of furniture being pushed, could be heard, followed by a child's scream and shouts.

Jeannie. Morag hoped they wouldn't harm her.

"McLean, search the yard."

"But sir ..." he began, indicating Morag.

"Do it."

"Sir." McLean and his men left.

"My compliments Miss. I'm Captain O'Brien. It's a pleasure to ..."

"They're getting away," interjected Morag. She'd noticed the scattered account books on the table; the quill and overturned ink pot. "If they're no' in the main house or upstairs ... where are they?"

The captain followed Morag as she paced the scullery, searched nooks and crannies; tapped wall panels and walked in and out of the larder.

"My men have searched everywhere," the captain said.

"Two people canna just disappear into thin air." Morag took the candlestick. "I wonder." Her eyes narrowed. Mrs. Quin didn't allow anyone in the larder. Morag scanned its shelves holding rows of bottled jams, pots of meat, slabs of butter, cheese and lard, jars of cream, basins of eggs and jugs of milk. A couple of sacks of flour and barley and several barrels had been stacked on the floor. She examined the plaster ceiling, it seemed well constructed with no way to the upper storey and she knocked on the walls listening for a hollow sound. Nothing. The flagstone floor seemed solid, but one barrel wasn't in line with the others. Her candle flame spluttered as she walked towards the cask.

"Here, take this." She shoved the candlestick into the captain's hand. Looking behind the barrel, she knelt and felt wood and a draught. Her fingers explored cracks too straight and square to be accidental.

"Quick, Captain, there's a trapdoor," she cried.

He passed the candlestick to her, sprang forward and lifted it. After one look into the black depths he yelled, "McLean at the double!" In seconds the men scrambled into the darkness below.

Morag couldn't stop shivering with the cold and excitement. Mrs. Quin's woollen cloak hung on the kitchen door, she wrapped it around her. With shaking hands, she placed the candlestick on the table and sat down. She could hear yells and shouts in the distance and the sound of a musket being fired. At whom, she wondered?

Through the smashed pane of glass she saw Mrs. Quin struggling in the grasp of two Jacobite soldiers and Captain O' Brien arguing with James Kinross, but no sign of Mrs. Quin's visitor.

Jesu! Kinross will recognise me and tell Euan. My spying days will be over before they've begun. She snuffed out the candle, pulled the hood over her face and watched from the darkness inside the scullery.

Captain O'Brien walked towards the house and Kinross started to follow him.

"Stay in the yard," ordered O'Brien.

Kinross retreated running his hands through his hair and brushing the shoulders of his cloak.

Opening the door, Captain O'Brien whispered, "Miss Anderson?"

"Come in captain and shut the door. I must leave before I'm recognised. Can you get me away from here?"

"Certainly."

He raised his voice, "Disperse the crowd, release Jeannie after questioning and return to your billets. Kinross take two soldiers and put Mrs. Quin in the Tolbooth." "What? No!" she shrieked

"Gag her," ordered O' Brien.

Silence.

Morag and the captain waited for five minutes until bored watchers snuffed out their lamps and candles in the houses opposite. Morag closed the back door behind her and the captain. They stepped into silent blackness. As they picked their way through a labyrinth of wynds, with tall, overhanging tenements on either side, she asked, "No sign of Mrs. Quin's guest?"

"None, we just missed the b...... begging your pardon, Miss."

"Where did you catch Mrs. Quin?"

"Climbing out of next door's well." They both grinned.

Morag stopped at a familiar corner. "My thanks captain, I can find my way safely from here."

"I don't doubt it. You're a brave woman," he said, bowed and kissed her hand.

They both started at the clink of metal on brick from further down the street.

Morag lowered her voice, "We've been followed."

"Get on your way, I'll hold them here. Go." He drew his sword.

She'd only Euan's dirk - not much good in a sword fight.

"Good luck," she hissed, as he stood legs apart, sword in the air, "I'll get help if I can." She kept to the shadows and ran. A shout and a shot rang out behind her. A musket ball whistled past her head. Raised voices and the sound of clashing swords filled the night air.

Her heart thundered against her ribcage. Ahead, in the distance, she could hear drunken singing. A lit torch illuminated a patch of wet cobbles. *An inn.* She raced towards it, her breath coming in hard pants now, knowing every second counted, that a man's life was in her hands.

Skidding to a halt outside the *The Grey Mare*, she found a stone and hurled it at a window shattering it.

Uproar. Men surged into the street, "Who the hell did that?" one demanded.

Morag lounged against the wall like a doxy and pointed down the street saying, "They went that way, towards where poor Captain O'Brien is fighting redcoats."

"Redcoats! Why didn't you rouse us earlier woman?" They ran off claymores at the ready, shouting as they went.

Morag wrapped her cloak around her and trudged on. The abbey containing the tunnel entrance loomed in front of her and she checked behind her in case she'd been followed. She could see no one. This time she didn't pause at the eye holes in the secret passage, but entered her bedroom and pulled a desk in front of the mirror.

She didn't need any unwanted visitors. She fell fully clothed and exhausted onto the bed as dawn peeped through the curtains.

CHAPTER Twenty-two

"Wake up Morag, you must wake."

Amelia? She could also hear the battering of fists and an insistent male voice that sounded like Euan. *Am I dreaming?*

"Morag."

This female voice was close and persistent. Morag opened her eyes to see Lady Amelia's worried face in front of her.

"It's late morning. Euan is insisting on seeing you. He's worried to death. He's been here for three nights. We told him you'd a fever that you needed to rest, but... Crawford is reassuring him as we speak. Come dear, you must get up."

"Captain O'Brien, is he all right?"

"Who? Let me help you bathe. I'll send for hot water while you get out of those dreadful rags. Then you can tell me about this captain."

Lady Amelia left for a few minutes returning with a servant carrying a steaming basin and towels. Amelia waited till the servant closed the door behind him. "Euan calmed down when I told him you are well enough to see him. Crawford has invited him to play cards. Tell me what happened. I want to know everything."

An hour later, Morag was led into Euan's presence. The Crawfords smiled at each other. "We'll be next door if you need anything," Amelia said as they left the couple alone.

Euan kissed Morag's cheek, led her to a seat by the fire and sat opposite her. "You look pale, my heart." He took her hands in his. How she'd longed for his touch.

"I've no' been well," she lied feeling stirrings of guilt. She couldn't look at him. "Thank you for being here."

"They said you had a fever, I've been out of my mind with worry. Poor Johnnie's been doing my military tasks. He sent his regards." Euan pursed his lips on the palm of her right hand and rolled her fingers over it. "You can keep that kiss forever."

116

She managed a weak smile. He racked her with guilt.

"You're never ill, darling."

"There's always a first time." She smiled at him. "What's been happening?"

"Well, the French have made lots of promises, but there's no sign of them joining us as yet." Euan's brow creased.

"No I meant, what's ... what's been happening ... in Edinburgh?" asked Morag.

"The prince has decreed all the women and bairns must stay behind when the army moves out. Edinburgh will become a dangerous place once we leave. I wish you'd go home." Euan kissed her cheek. "And something's annoyed old General Guest in the castle. He's been aiming cannonballs at Highlanders most of the morning, listen."

Morag heard a distant roar followed by a dull thud. *How did I sleep through that?* She swallowed hard. "No casualties I trust?"

"A few, and not just from cannonballs. They found a Captain O'Brien early this morning in one of the wynds off the High Street. Looked like he'd been outnumbered in a sword fight; not expected to pull through."

She swayed slightly in her seat, trying not to think of O'Brien lying wounded on the cobblestones all night.

Euan put his arm round her. "You've gone pale again." He called Amelia into the room. "If you permit, I'll visit again this evening when my duties allow." He turned to Morag. "Unfortunately because of military commitments, I'll no' be able to attend any balls or receptions. There's a ball in a few days. If you wish, and you're recovered, I'll ask Johnnie to accompany you."

"Thank you."

He kissed her hand before Amelia packed her off to bed again. She sank into the feather mattress and slept.

***

Johnnie escorted her to the ball. Euan had insisted he buy her a new dress. She chose jade silk. Johnnie danced with her throughout the evening, allowing himself to be swallowed up by a gaggle of insistent females every now and then.

She smiled, some things never changed.

The music struck up. "Miss McColl, may I ask you for the honour of this dance?" Kinross took her hand, her acceptance as read yet again.

He had something about him, an air of mystery, perhaps, which intrigued her, but she said, "No."

He grabbed her hand and tugged. She found herself in his arms pretending she enjoyed the music and fluid movement of the dance.

"You've been ill, I was sorry to hear it," said Kinross.

"It was nought but a slight fever. I'm quite recovered. I'd like to sit down."

"And I'd like you to take a turn with me, though it's obvious your Mr. Stewart and his brother," he indicated Johnnie's grim face watching their every movement, "dinna like me." Kinross' face relaxed into a wide grin, as if the thought amused him.

Morag glanced at Johnnie. *Sweet Jesu. I hope he doesna think I'm enjoying this.* "Euan's good enough to trust me," she said.

"Does he now? I notice he's not here. And do you trust yourself Miss McColl?" Kinross's whiskery lips brushed her ear. His eyes held hers captive and his hand grasped hers a moment too long. She floundered in a rush of senses. Did she trust herself with this overpowering man? It would have been easy to be overcome by the sheer force of his presence, but he wasn't Euan and not for her. The music stopped.

Johnnie had his back to them, his arm in the clutches of Miss Balfour.

"Thank you, if you'll excuse me..." Morag made to walk away, but Kinross took her arm in a firm grip and led her to a quiet corner saying, "Dinna make a scene. I want you to understand that it's because I... care for you..."

Morag tried to interrupt.

"No. Hear me out. It's because I care for your welfare that I warn you not to become involved in ... things you dinna fully understand."

"Your words make no sense sir." She tried to go, but he grabbed her right shoulder.

"You little fool. The redcoats ken women are involved. One's even been given the nickname the Jacobite Jade."

She blanched. Hadn't she heard it shouted at Tolbain's?

He motioned towards her gown. "Look at the colour of your dress, have you no sense? Miss McColl, this is a friendly warning. Dinna get involved." Then he let her go with a smile and a bow and walked away as the music started up once more.

Some minutes later Johnnie joined her. She'd hidden the red marks left by Kinross' fingers under her shawl.

***

The following morning Euan with a face like granite came to see her, a concerned looking Johnnie in tow. "We need to talk."

He took her out on the windswept moors, whilst Johnnie held the ponies. "Kinross was bothering you last night."

"It was nothing."

"You danced with him." *Sweet Jesu, Euan's code of honour will not let this go.*

"Did Johnnie tell you this?"

"Dinna think your actions are not observed by others. There are no secrets in the palace."

"He made me dance, I ..."

"Made?" Euan's brows drew together.

Her shawl slipped down her arm. Too late, she remembered the marks left by Kinross' fingers.

"What are those marks?"

"Kinross ..."

"My God, he laid hands on you."

She remained silent. Everything she said seemed to make things worse.

Euan glowered as he strode up and down. Then he stopped. "I'll kill the bastard."

"No, Euan you canna." She tugged at his sleeve, but he shrugged her off.

"He's besmirched my honour. No man does that and lives."

Morag chewed her lip. The authorities took a dim view of duels. Even if Euan survived he could be hanged.

That afternoon Morag breathed a sigh of relief when Amelia told her Kinross had been seen spurring his horse out of Edinburgh. Perhaps he'd heard Euan wanted to call him out. There was always the risk Euan would be killed. *Dinna think this.* Even if he survived they'd be the centre of a scandal, the last thing she needed.

Morag sensed an estrangement between her and Euan. He'd become distant and tight lipped. Surely he didn't think she cared for Kinross? The days passed and she wished their former closeness and easy relationship would return.

When Euan came to Holyrood for her she knew from his sombre expression their lives would never be the same again. *What's he going to tell me? Damn Kinross for driving us apart.* Her stomach seemed hollow as he helped her onto her pony. No Johnnie this time. They rode out into the country and cantered along a ridge which overlooked the Firth of Forth. An east wind blew into their faces from the sea, untangling Morag's hair so it streamed like a banner.

He helped her dismount. His hands either side of her waist, let her slide down the length of his body, her bosom brushing his chest. She loved him so much. Their bodies tautened and their lips met. She couldn't help responding to his kiss.

He stroked her hair and kissed the top of her head. "We're marching south tomorrow."

She looped her arms around his neck, nestled her face on his chest and could not, would not let him go. She burrowed her face deeper as he made to pull away.

"Morag? Morag? My heart let me look at you."

She held him tighter, her voice muffled, "I canna let you go, I canna do it, not again."

He kissed the top of her head, lifted her off her feet and carried her to a slab of granite stretched out across the ridge from where he could see the Firth of Forth in the distance. Sitting on this lovers' seat, he cradled her on his lap. "Listen to me my own one, you're my heart and I need you to hear what I want to say." He brushed away her tears with his thumb. "This time you must listen to me. If I fall ..."

"No ..."

He stopped her, his lips crushing her mouth. Then said, "If I fall ... in battle I want you to forget me, marry a good man and have children."

"No ..." Her tears started again.

He kissed them away saying, "Hush my beloved darling. I promise you, if I'm captured, I'll escape and come to you in Braedrumie. Whilst my heart beats in my breast, nothing and no one will stop me seeing you again. I swear it on your cross." He kissed it and cradled her tear-stained face in his hands. "Come, my beautiful girl, let me remember your smile, so it warms my heart wherever I am."

Guilt swept over her. She turned away, got off his lap and walked a few steps from him. She twisted her betrothal ring. This man she'd known all of her life had always been honest with her and she'd deceived him. She battled with her conscience and looked out at the horizon as if entranced.

"Tell me," he said wrapping his arms round her waist and burying his face into her neck. "Something has been troubling you for some time, I can tell, but I've been so busy ... tell me what it is, my heart."

She loved him so much. The words spurted like water in a flood, "I've lied to you. I've been working for The Cause in Edinburgh. I'm one of Sinclair's spies. When you thought I had a fever, that's what I was doing. I'm sorry. Sinclair made me promise to tell no one. I couldn't let you go and not know the truth of it. "

"You lied ... to me?" He let her go.

She turned hating the hurt on his face. "I'm sorry. I couldna bear you to leave ... to find out ... I didna want you to think I've no' been honest with you. I gave my word I wouldna tell what I've been doing, but I did it for The Cause and for us and because I had to.

Can you ... find it in your heart to forgive me?" She reached out and touched his arm as he stared at her. Unable to help herself she held him. He buried his face in her hair. She couldn't bear his silence. "Euan, please ... please say you forgive me ..." Her voice cracked.

He sighed and at last, looked at her and said, "Ah Morag, you've the determination of a man twice your size." He took her hands and kissed her palms and then her betrothal ring. "I love you so much sometimes it hurts to breathe."

She let relief flood over her and closed her eyes.

He gathered her to him and held her close. "You're so dear to me." He stroked her hair. "And so brave. You mean to stay in Edinburgh, don't you?"

"Yes with Amelia."

"She works for Sinclair too?"

Morag nodded.

"I'll no' spoil our last hours together with an argument. I'm proud of you for joining the baggage train and working for The Cause. I didn't realise how brave you could be, but be very careful my own one, you're precious to me and I mean to make you my wife when I return."

It was then she realised the true depths of Euan's love. That he could forgive her deception. "You're the best of men and my heart's breaking," she said, "I'll no' rest till you're beside me again."

"Nor I my beloved darling."

He smothered her face in kisses and her neck and traced her collarbone with his fingers. His lips pushed her bodice down to the point at which her breasts parted. "I love you so much." He kissed her at the sweet cleft.

She could have surrendered to him then, but he stopped himself and held her close.

She whispered, "Just come safely home to me."

He crushed her to him. They held each other for hours, counting the minutes and seconds as they ticked away and watching the sun in its western course.

"We must leave," he said at last as the light faded.

They walked to where their ponies cropped the grass. He helped her onto her mount and they rode hand in hand back to Holyrood. Nudging his pony closer he leant across and kissed her making her senses reel. "I'll look for you in Braedrumie," he said.

"Yes." Her throat tightened as she strove to hold back tears. "Come home to me there."

"Keep safe, my beautiful girl." He caressed her face with his fingers exploring each curve and plane. "I'll come safe home to you."

"Write."

"I'll write," he said. "I love you."

"Lo ... ve you ... too."

Then he rode away.

"Tell Jamie Moffat he's forgiven," she shouted.

He turned, grinned and gave one last wave.

Her life, her first and only love, she couldn't bear the thought of life without him.

Next morning, just before the sky flushed with light, Morag and Amelia climbed to the top of King Arthur's Seat and watched with other weeping women as the army moved out. They heard the shouted orders; the skirl of bagpipes the stamp of feet and hooves; the jingle of bridles and the creak of wheels. The first slivers of dawn touched dirks and sword hilts so they shone like silver as the procession wound south. They watched with their arms wrapped round each other until the untidy carts of the baggage train became tiny dots on the horizon swallowed by dust. Morag prayed in silence: *Sweet Jesu keep him safe.*

CHAPTER Twenty-four

The Jacobite army left Edinburgh in November and within hours Morag watched the redcoat garrison march out of the castle. They took up defensive positions in the city, ransacked Holyrood and any house where they thought Jacobites might be hiding.

Morag, Amelia and Sinclair had already moved to new premises with pseudonyms. Sinclair now lived in an unassuming house in the fashionable part of town. Amelia had become Ailis Hammond and Morag, Morven Boyd, her sister. They were assistants in Mrs. Scott's milliners shop in the High Street, lived in the flat above and served in the shop below, in a city that had become a cauldron of rumours, counter-rumours and discontent.

Mrs. Scott had black teeth which she hid in an unsmiling face. A widow and ardent Jacobite, she professed again and again, 'I'd die for The Cause.'

Morag thought Amelia looked wan since the army had left, not helped by the insipid white wig she was forced to wear or the padding that gave her a crook-back. Morag knew she did not look much better under her mouse-brown wig, which had seen better days.

Mrs. Scott stacked bolts of velvet, taffeta, damask and silks in all shades in neat rows on wooden shelves. Ribbons, plumes, flounces and lace spilled over the counter and several beautiful hats sat in the window.

Morag and Amelia hadn't expected to work in a shop, never mind one that served as a Jacobite Receiving Office where *innocent customers* delivered and collected coded messages about redcoat plans and troop movements.

Edinburgh seethed with redcoats and Hanoverian supporters who betrayed Jacobites foolish enough to have remained. Ranting voices full of anti-Jacobite sentiment fed by that *government rag* as Amelia called *The Courant* could often be heard now.

It was as if the stakes rose as weeks passed. What had begun as an exciting game had become a deadly enterprise. The women knew their customers could be government spies or loyal to the prince. All brought danger that increased every day and played on their emotions. Morag chewed her lip and Amelia wrung her hands.

Amelia exploded first. "Morag, have you read the *Evening Courant*?" Amelia stabbed her forefinger at a sentence. *That well known Jacobite, Lady Crawford dresses and behaves like a highland savage and has bedded every man in the army, including a certain gentleman.* "They can only mean the prince. Look," she said. Her finger stabbed again. "They've called me, *the Jacobite Whore*, how dare they." She thrust the paper at Morag. "My God, what kind of gentleman hides behind a quill whilst ruining a woman's reputation?"

Mrs. Scott sniffed. "A scoundrel, that's who."

Morag scanned the paper to see Jacobite women who rode with the army described as *bitches* and *whores*. Sweet Jesu and a description of the *Jacobite Jade*, which fitted her. It went on to say that *the Jade has slept with at least one high ranking Jacobite officer.* Morag tore the paper into shreds much to Amelia's delight

Morag had a nagging feeling the redcoats knew about the shop's clandestine activities and from their countenances so did Amelia and Mrs. Scott. Soldiers had peered in the window and Mrs. Scott had been questioned in the street. Sinclair couldn't be contacted. He was always out. Should they leave?

The shop bell jangled. Morag slowed her breathing and rested one hand on another to stop them trembling. Amelia fluttered around, repositioning bolts of cloth and ribbons and creating disorder. Mrs. Scott found something important to do below the counter.

A crane-necked Miss Menzie and plump, pop-eyed Miss Webster peered round the door. They liked picking over lace and ruffles and leaving a mess in their wake.

Mrs. Scott's head appeared above the counter. "Good morning ladies. What can we do for you this fine morning?"

"We heard you'd a new shipment of ribbons." Miss Menzie's mouth snapped shut and then opened again. "Have you heard the latest news?" She launched forth before they could reply, "*The Courant* says the rebels are still marching south, much good will it do them. It'll be like the 1715 all over again, mark my words. Cumberland's in charge, he willna stand any nonsense from treacherous rabble and the fact that ... females are with them ... like this Jacobite Jade creature is unnatural, don't you agree Mrs. Scott?"

Mrs. Scott pushed a basket of ribbons across the counter. "We've every colour."

Morag bent her head over a book of accounts. She wished she was with the army.

Amelia turned paler than usual. "We ... we ... ken little of these matters, dealing only in fripperies and trust in those with better understanding, like you, to guide us."

Miss Menzie and Miss Webster sniffed in haughty approval, made their purchases of ribbon and left. Morag and Amelia sagged into each other's arms. Mrs. Scott scowled. "Good riddance."

"Were they sounding us out? Do you think they suspected?" asked Morag scratching beneath her brown wig.

The doorbell jangled making the women jump apart.

"Miss Menzie says to remind you about her dress fitting tomorrow at 3 o'clock." Miss Webster studied Morag before closing the door behind her.

"Something wrong?" asked Morag.

"Your wig is slightly askew," said Lady Margaret.

"Bother!" Morag had another scratch and adjusted it.

"You must be more careful," said Mrs. Scott wagging her bony finger.

"Should we stay?" said Morag.

"Just one more day, to help The Cause," begged Amelia.

The next afternoon Mrs. Cruikshank arrived, built like a comfortable bolster. Miss Menzie and Miss Webster entered behind her.

Mrs. Scott's face became a mask.

"This material is too dark, this too light, this too patterned and this too plain," said Mrs. Cruikshank.

A flustered Amelia kept trying to please her whilst Mrs. Scott took Miss Menzie for her dress fitting, Morag served Miss Webster. Morag watched her eyes dart everywhere as she dithered lifting and disregarding material as they went. She finally bought a yard of French lace. Miss Menzie returned with Mrs. Scott who thanked them for their custom, opened the door to speed them on their way and closed it with a sigh.

Mrs. Cruikshank went from difficult to sweet in the twinkling of an eye. She whispered her code name, "Jacobus".

Relief made Morag's knees give way and Amelia held onto the counter with white knuckles.

Mrs. Scott's eye's gleamed. "You've information?"

"Some of our messengers have been caught, so take care, and our lads have crossed the Esk," said Mrs. Cruikshank.

Who'd have thought Mrs. Cruikshank worked for The Cause? Morag knew the Esk flowed into the Solway Firth so Euan and Lord Crawford were in England. They'd heard nothing since the army left, this was sweet to hear. Morag and Lady Amelia hugged each other.

"You've messages for me to deliver I've no doubt?"

They handed a bundle to her which she hid beneath her shawl as she ordered several swathes of material. Her manservant loaded these onto her carriage. "Goodbye," she lowered her voice, "and good luck."

Morag closed the door behind her. *My first news of Euan. In England.*

"It's so wonderful to know where the army is, let's hope their luck holds." Amelia clasped her hands together. "I'll write home and pass it on."

"Pray God they come ... safe home."

"Pray God for victory then," said Mrs. Scott. "My dear, are you well?"

Amelia put her hand to her brow and swayed. Morag took one look at her friend's pale features and put an arm round her waist. "Sit."

Amelia sank back on the settee. "I'm so sorry, one minute I was fine and the next ... I've had the same thought for weeks." She blushed. "I'm sure I'm with child."

"Oh, my dear," said Mrs. Scott.

"That's wonderful. Does Lord Crawford know?"

"If I'd told him he wouldna have left."

"You must tell Sinclair."

"Do you not see it's an even better disguise? The redcoats would never suspect."

"So brave," said Mrs. Scott. "You need to rest and put up your feet. There you are." She took off Amelia's shoes and placed her feet on a cushion.

Morag kissed her friend on the forehead. "Here." She plumped a cushion and put it behind Amelia's back. "Now is there anything I can get you?"

"No. Thank you. I'm sure rest is just the thing."

Morag could see from her determined look, there'd be no changing her view. "Do you mind if I go out for a breath of air? I'll close the shop."

"Of course not, my dear, I'll look after her," said Mrs. Scott.

"Go while you have the chance," said Amelia.

The day had patches of sun and rain. Morag didn't care. She climbed up to Arthur's Seat, looked out to the blue of the Pentland Hills in the south, closed her eyes and thought of Euan, willing him to come to her in some shape or form at that moment. The sun came out from behind a slate cloud.

She remembered their last moments together, the light sensual touch of his fingers, and lips; the warmth of his arms and the sound of his voice, like a caress, 'I love you.'

"Dear God, bring him safe home," she whispered, then said louder, "I love you Euan Stewart."

In her imagination the wind carried her words over the distant hills; the deep valleys and flowing rivers, to him, always to him and her feelings wrapped around his broad shoulders like a protective cloak. It seemed as if the wind carried his words, "I'll come safe home to you." He would return and they'd marry and live all their lives together because she willed it so.

She stayed for hours because she felt closer to Euan there and turned towards Edinburgh when storm clouds threatened rain. She clambered down the hillside with the walled city stretched out in front of her and could just make out the crown spire of St. Giles and its golden cockerel in the smoky haze.

The rain started in earnest as she made her way up the High Street. Thunder rolled in the distance. Water ran down the cobblestones and gurgled into the fouled Closes that clung to the sides of the High Street like ghastly terraced- ribs. At least it would give the occupants some relief from the noxious mix of rubbish and raw sewage that sluiced down to Nor Loch.

Soaked through and shivering, she reached the shop. The door stood ajar. She drew her dirk. The closed sign lay dejected on the floor, a muddy boot print on it. The street: empty. She ventured inside her mouth dry and heart thudding. "Amelia, Mrs. Scott?" she called. No reply. Morag stood in shock. Shelves had been pulled down and bolts of brightly coloured cloth looked like splashes of blood on the floor. She had to force her breath in and out. Dreading what she might find she followed the trail of ribbon and lace upstairs.

Furniture had been overturned, the bed upended, Amelia's white wig lay on the floor, but of her and Mrs. Scott there was no sign.

CHAPTER Twenty-five

Morag said a silent prayer for Amelia and Mrs. Scott as she scanned the High Street with its blackened tenements eight stories high on either side. Nothing stirred. Yet the hairs on the back of her neck prickled. A flash of colour at a window opposite made her aware of hidden watchers. She needed to get away from this place, find Sinclair and get help.

She gathered her cloak around her, covered most of her face with her hood, and ducked into the gloom of King's Close. Its low ceiling and soot blackened walls pressed in on her as she raced down the narrow lane. Lanterns flickered outside skinners, saddlers, tanners and butcher's premises which spewed human and animal waste with all its odours.

Morag slipped and regained her balance as she heard loud oaths, laughter and children whining as she passed rotting doors and windows. She dipped her head under ragged clothes strung on sagging washing lines and neatly avoided clucking hens, stray cats, and dogs barking at her ankles. Behind her came a shout and running feet as she continued down into the bowels of Edinburgh.

A huge head with horns poked over a gate making her jerk to one side. She bumped into someone and the tang of old tobacco filled her nostrils. "Sorry," she said without thinking.

"What the hell?" A hand grabbed her. "Morag McColl, is that you?"

Kinross. No' him again. Thank goodness Euan's left the city. She tried to step past him, but he moved quicker than her.

"What are you doing here? This is no place for a lass on her own." He examined her face. "You're frightened. What happened?"

"I must go." A dog yelped as her redcoat pursuers stumbled over it. She tried to pull away from Kinross, but he dragged her against the wall. He held her to him in an iron grip as she strained to get away. His warm lips sank on hers and his moist tongue searched her mouth, whilst she struggled to breathe. Heavy footsteps raced past and down towards Nor Loch.

He released his hold at last and her hand whipped across his face and left a livid mark. "How dare you."

He fingered his cheek. "A fine thank you for saving your life, they were redcoats."

"You didna have to kiss me."

"Oh, but I did." He glanced around as curious heads peered out of ramshackle doors and windows. "This is nought but a den for thieves. What possessed you to come here? We need to leave this place, now." He drew his sword. "I'll escort you."

"She's a beauty, what's 'er price?" A gruff voice came from a shop doorway.

Kinross wheeled and thrust Morag away from him. The breath was forced from her lungs as she crashed against the wall. "She's no' for sale, she's mine."

Two men yelling as if their lungs would burst came at him in a rush from two directions. Morag stuck out her foot. The leading man tripped and the second stumbled over him. "Oh dear," she said.

"Run." Kinross shouted at her, too late. The men had picked themselves up. Her dirk flashed in her hand and her back was to his. Kinross slashed downwards as his adversary attacked. The man groaned, crumpled to the ground, a crimson stain spreading across his stomach. At the same time a grimy arm lunged at her, but she gave its owner a deep razor-cut on his forearm. Blood welled. He screamed and his sword fell with a clatter on the cobblestones.

"Bitch." Her victim spat the words at her from between two stumps of rotting teeth. He clutched his arm as blood seeped between his fingers. Kinross's blade cut into him, he groaned and slid down the wall leaving a bloody smear. Blood spread like scarlet ink over his shirt.

"We're getting out of here." Kinross grabbed her wrist. He led her through warren-like rooms, up stairs, through doorways and trapdoors until they surfaced in a cellar and exited through the side door of a hovel.

"Now explain yourself. Why were you in the close?" His brow furrowed and his fiery hair bristled with anger.

She breathed in lungfuls of fresh air. "I dinna need to explain anything to you." She made to walk away, but he seized her wrist and pulled her back.

"I risked my bloody life for you." He bared his teeth. "Stewart should have had more sense than to leave you here to fend for yourself."

This fool was stopping her getting help for Amelia. "Take your hand off me." She raised her dirk. "I have urgent business elsewhere." *Kinross has caused enough trouble between me and Euan.* He released her.

"What business?" He loomed over her.

"My own." She hurried away from him. *So, the damned man's returned. Why isna he with our army? Coward.*

She ignored his shout which followed her down the street, "You dinna suit that bloody wig."

She wound her way through streets and markets, doubling back, stopping and checking that she hadn't been followed. Sinclair's house had a coach loaded with valises waiting outside it. She watched the street for some time before deciding it was safe to call on him. His door opened as she went to knock and out he came. He sidestepped her and headed for the coach.

"Lord Sinclair, I must speak with you."

"Get in the coach." His gaze swept the area as he joined her. "Were you followed?"

"I lost them."

He tapped on the roof with his walking stick and the carriage set off at a pace.

"You're leaving?" she said.

"Edinburgh has become too dangerous."

"Then you need to know Mrs. Scott's shop has been ransacked and there's no sign of Amelia or her."

"Amelia's been taken to the castle for questioning. Mrs. Scott escaped and left the city." Sinclair flicked lint off his breeches.

"You know?"

"Did you think you're the only spies in Edinburgh? I've informants in every close and wynd. Those redcoats cannot ... spit without me knowing, too fast this time."

"Can we rescue Amelia?"

"You're known," said Sinclair. "None of you are of any use to The Cause now."

"You'll no' help her?"

"Individuals are ... expendable. It's The Cause that matters."

"Jesu. You've used us. We've got to get her out, she's in no state to ... she's having a bairn. Lord Crawford will expect you to help her."

"She's breeding, eh? Go to this safe house and wait." He scrawled down an address and flung it at her. "I must be off." He tapped on the coach roof and the horses slowed to a stop as he motioned her to get out.

Morag couldn't resist saying, "Don't make me wait too long, Sinclair or I'll ensure Lord Crawford knows who's responsible for Amelia being left in redcoat custody." She dismounted and slammed the coach door.

CHAPTER Twenty-six

The rain drummed off the roof of the safe house, a rat-infested tenement flat with water seeping through the dank ceiling. Floorboards protested at every step and the stench of human waste hung in the air. As Morag tried to sleep, she longed for home and Braedrumie, for purple mountains, heather-scented moors and the thrumming of Invererar Falls. Most of all she wanted Euan by her side and her father's forgiveness.

The following morning the rain ceased and weak light, filtered by sooty window panes, streamed into the room. Cryptic instructions came in the form of a note under her door: *Midnight and White Cockade. S*

Her mind swirled. *What's it mean?* She thought of Euan so far away and poor Amelia imprisoned in the castle. Everything seemed to lie in its grim shadow and who knew what went on inside its walls? Morag shivered and clutched her shawl about her. *My poor friend.*

Unable to settle, she paced up and down and listened to the sound of carriage wheels and calls from the traders below: "Silver herrings!" "Second hand clothes for ladies!" "Barley, peas and flour!"

Instead of Jacobite plaids, crimson coats wove amongst the crowds. Morag chewed her lip. She missed Euan, his voice, his arms, his love. *Will it always be like this before we see each other again?*

She sat in the only chair as night fell and waited as traders locked their shops and the streets cleared. She waited as the shadows lengthened and candles glowed at windows. She waited whilst lanterns flickered and a half moon sailed across the spangled night sky. Most of all she waited for a furtive footstep and a knock.

Some hours later, she heard the sound of glass breaking and a loud curse.

The tat-a-tat at her door made her start. She opened it to a man with bleary eyes, rumpled clothes and a bottle in his hand. *Kinross.*

Jesu. What's he doing here? I've no chaperone, if this got out, I'm ruined.

"Ligsht of my lishe." He smiled as he swayed. Alcohol and tobacco mingled in the air.

"Light of your ...You reek of wine. How dare you come here at this hour, when Euan hears of this your life ..."

He closed the door behind him and stood steady on his feet, his eyes alert. "Won't be worth a bawbee, I ken that, but then we live in dangerous times don't we?"

He looks and sounds like a sober man.

"Here, put these on." He flung a bundle of coarse, grey clothes containing a sword at her.

"You're no' drunk."

"The White Cockade, at your service."

"You canna be." She stared at him aghast. *Sinclair couldn't have sent **him**.*

"I assure you I am. We've little time if you wish to rescue your friend. I'd be obliged if you'd hurry."

He wanted her to undress here, in front of him. "You'll turn your back."

"I will."

Kinross, a spy? She struggled with that fact as much as she struggled into the breeches, shirt and stout shoes. She tied her hair into a pony tail with a strip of leather.

He lowered his voice. "You look uncommonly fetching. I do hope breeches for women become the fashion."

My reflection in the window. The shirt leaves little to the imagination. She grabbed a cloak and wrapped it round her. "You sir, are no gentleman."

He threw his head back and laughed. "I did as I promised; I didna turn round. Can I help it if the fates decreed a window well placed?"

She held the tip of her sword at his throat. *How dare he.*

"My, my ..." He moved the sword away from him with one finger. "I never imagined a tigress with claws beneath such beauty."

Teasing me. She couldn't bear it and pricked him enough for a trickle of blood to run down his neck.

He dabbed at it with his scarred thumb. "My God, you bloody mean it. No wonder Sinclair hired you. You've quite ruined my shirt. It's as well we're on the same side. We'll use the back door. We're going by way of Loch Nor. I do hope you're no' squeamish."

CHAPTER Twenty-seven

Squeamish? Morag couldn't help Amelia escape on her own. *Can Kinross be trusted? Sweet Jesu, he's my friend's only hope.* She set her lips, raised her chin and followed him. He took her hand, but she twisted it out of his grasp once they were in the gloom of the back yard,

He hissed in her ear. "Dinna be a bloody fool. I could lose you in the dark and where we're going you'd sink without a trace."

That stopped her. She let him take her hand and unsheathed her sword. The moon played hide and seek as he led her down by towering black tenements lit by pinpricks of light. Children's cries, women's screams, shouts, laughter, a fiddler's jig and raucous singing came from behind shuttered windows and bolted doors. The noise billowed like a cloud, died and rose again.

She smelt Loch Nor long before they came to its banks, its stench overpowering. Dark shapes scavenged, whether human or animal was difficult to tell. The ground squelched under foot as Kinross pulled her onward through marsh grass and reeds until the castle loomed above them. They stopped by a ruined tower on the north bank of Castle Hill. The tower once, perhaps, three stories in height.

The moon came out bathing them in light. "Damn." Kinross cursed under his breath and he pulled her against the tower's crumbling walls.

She felt the prickles of his beard as he whispered, "This is the Well House Tower, used to supply the castle. Stay quiet and keep close. Sound carries at night and the sentries will be alert."

A shiver sliced through her. *Cold or fear?*

He waited till the moon hid behind a cloud, then plunged into the tower pulling her behind him. They descended spiral stone steps and stopped at the bottom. He let go of her. She could make out his breathing and the methodical sound of metal tapping on the wall, searching for something. Hinges grated as rock scraped against rock.

He grabbed her hand. "Duck."

She lowered her head to step into the inky blackness of a low, narrow tunnel with a steep incline, her worst nightmare. She staggered, could feel the walls closing in on her. Her mind went back to childhood, of being trapped, unable to breathe, her chest squeezed. She closed her eyes. Her breathing slowed as she fought for control. She had to do this.

"Come on," he urged.

She steeled herself, every nerve tingling, as she followed him up the path and deeper into the volcanic rock. Water dripped from the ceiling and the walls oozed damp. After thirty yards he stopped and put an eye to a chink of light in the wall ahead. He watched and listened for some time. Again she heard the chink-chink on the stone. Morag sucked in foul smelling air as dim light flooded into the tunnel. A corridor lit by torches stretched ahead of them with several iron doors and barred windows on either side. On the right, she spied steps leading upward.

"We're in the dungeons. Stay here, I'll get her."

She put a hand on his arm. "Two will be quicker than one."

He stared at her hand and then at her, as if he'd learned a little more about her. With a nod he motioned her towards one set of cells. They met minutes later. Nothing.

"One corridor in this hell hole looks much like another, a pity to return empty handed." Kinross' mouth formed a grim line.

"She has to be here."

Above their heads came the sounds of several boots, something being dragged across a floor and Sassenach voices raised in complaint.

Morag and Kinross froze.

"Shouldn't have taken the king's bleedin' shillin'. Must have been ravin."

"Dead drunk more like."

Laughter filtered towards the listeners.

A commanding voice with a Scottish burr brought silence. "Enough of that. Carry her and be gentle or I'll have you on a charge."

A grunt, the clank of swords against stone and then footsteps getting nearer.

Morag's gut twisted. A bead of sweat stood out on Kinross' brow.

A woman being carried down steps towards them? Jesu.

"Bloody run," hissed Kinross.

They raced for the tunnel entrance and closed the door behind them, a tomb, except for the presence of Kinross. Morag's nose wrinkled. He stood too close, his breath on the back of her neck. The darkness wrapped round her. She imagined festoons of silvery cobwebs overhead and the skittering of rats' claws underfoot. *I need to get out.*

She put her eye to a sliver of light between the tunnel door and solid rock. The boots and voices became louder as the redcoats turned the stair. Two privates carried a lolling woman, one at her head and the other at her feet.

Morag couldn't make out the woman's face. *Who is she?*

"Careful with her I said or I'll have your hides."

Morag froze. This time she recognised the commanding voice with its timbre of surf on sand. *It couldn't be **him**.*

"She's as light as a fevver, pretty for a Jacobite whore. That Duke of Tolbain treated her bad, he..."

"Shut your mouth, or I'll shut it for you, private."

It was him. What was he doing here?

The rattle of keys in lock, squeaking hinges and a woman's moan came to them.

"Leave her. Go about your other duties."

"Sir."

"Madam," he spoke in the soft Highland burr Morag knew so well, "I sincerely regret... I didna ken the Duke would... Damn it. Drink this, that's it. I'll leave it by you. I'm sorry I canna do more... What he made you do is against all honour."

"Thank ... you ... for ... your ... kindness."

Amelia.

The cell door squeaked shut and a key turned. Morag peered at him striding away from her. She knew him. At 6 foot 4 inches he'd be difficult to forget. *Rob, Euan's eldest brother, and wearing a redcoat uniform.* Open mouthed she heard his boots ascend the steps. Kinross' warm breath played on the back of her neck. *Does he have to stand so close?* He squeezed her shoulder making her jump.

"Has he gone?"

"Yes. They returned Amelia to her cell."

They clambered out of their hiding place and raced back along the corridor. Amelia lay in the flickering torchlight on a bed of straw in a dank cell no bigger than a broom cupboard with a jug of ale and a half full tankard beside her.

Morag grasped the bars and whispered, "Amelia, can you hear me? We're going to get you out."

Amelia didn't stir.

Does Kinross know? "She's with child."

"So Sinclair said."

"How are we going to open this door?" She rattled it.

Kinross fished inside his sporran, "With this." He held up a key. His lips curled into a grin.

"You have your uses, Kinross."

"Thank you." The lock turned and the cell door protested as it opened. Amelia's pale form lay still.

He put one arm beneath Amelia's thin shoulders and another beneath her knees and lifted her. "We need to leave, now."

Morag strained her eyes and ears for the least hint they'd been discovered. No sound. She closed the tunnel door behind them and stepped into black, coal black. She had to fight her demons again. She could hear Amelia's soft moans and the sound of Kinross' curse as he stumbled and recovered. She followed the sound of his harsh breathing as he trudged down the path. She forced one foot in front of the other, thinking only of escape and not the terrors of her imagination.

He surprised her again as he'd ponies waiting, stabled in the tower ruins. He led them by a circuitous route to one of the city gates lit by two torches.

"Halt! Who goes there?"

We've been caught. They'll put us all in the dungeons. Morag held her breath as sentry strode forward out of the shadows. He stood in their path, feet apart and musket at the ready.

Kinross spoke in murmurs and she heard the chink of money change hands.

Relief flooded through her.

Without a word to her he spurred his pony forward. She rode after him into the pitch blackness of the countryside beyond.

CHAPTER Twenty-eight

Morag looked out of a window at the thin veil of the early morning mist; she could just make out faraway turrets and rooftops. Kinross had taken them to a house several miles to the west of Edinburgh.

She helped herself to woollen stockings from the pile of clothing left for her and Amelia by the kind house owners. She'd just begun to pull them on in the early morning light, when the faint roar of the castle cannon made her stop. *Of course the redcoats have discovered Amelia's empty cell.* Morag glanced at her sleeping friend, cheeks flushed and fair hair strewn across the pillow. *We're safe now, but for how long? There'd be house-to-house searches.*

Morag's heart beat faster. Her pony had galloped behind Kinross' mount for hours as they'd travelled west. He'd held Amelia in front of him and hadn't checked his pony the whole journey. The house had been in darkness. It had remained so whilst the inhabitants, loyal Jacobites, spoke in whispers, "Hurry, we'll see to the ponies. Go inside."

Kinross had carried Amelia with Morag plodding behind him. Her bones ached for rest.

An elderly woman in a nightdress and shawl pointed the way upstairs. Amelia didn't open her eyes as Kinross laid her on one of two beds. A candle flickered on the stone mantlepiece. A battered chair with an oak leaf embroidered cushion stood to one side of the fire roaring away in the hearth. Opposite, water steamed in a blue and white bowl beside a pile of snowy linen on an apple wood table. *The servants have been busy.* Morag rubbed her friend's icy hands. *The sheets warm, thank goodness.*

Morag covered Amelia with the woollen blankets. "She needs rest and good food. Thank you for helping her."

Kinross stood close, too close. "You're brave." His voice hissed in the dark, "I admire that." His whiskers scratched her ear and his hand brushed her breast.

"No." She jerked back. Her shout echoed through the house.

She held her breath. Mice scratched and scuttled in the wainscoting.

"Ssh. Silly little girl, what did you do that for?"

"Get out," she snarled.

She heard his laugh, then the door closed and she rushed to bolt it. *A dangerous man addicted to risk just as much as to his foul smelling tobacco.* She sank into the warmth of the feather mattress, snuggled under the blankets and allowed her restless mind full rein.

She could only imagine the frantic scenes inside the castle, the opening of the cell, the search for the prisoner and guards being charged. The Duke of Tolbain would be furious. Morag smiled with satisfaction.

Then she remembered Rob, the laird's eldest son and Euan's brother. She chewed her lip. *The turncoat.* Her shock at seeing him in redcoat uniform had almost overpowered her. *Was a wish to join the British army why Rob had left? If word got out it would kill his father and the clan. They'd never forgive him.*

She thought back to July 1st, the day of Euan's proposal and her acceptance. They'd been lost in their love for each other, unaware of Rob by the garden gate. *Did a faint shadow cross his face before he'd congratulated us? Did he care for me? Next day he'd gone. A matter of honour I suppose. Surely Rob must have known I could only ever love Euan.* She prayed Rob would never meet his brothers in battle. She closed her eyes and let sleep overtake her.

Hours later a faint moan came from the other bed. She ran to Amelia, wishing away the bruised shadows beneath her friend's eyes.

"Where ... am ... I?"

"Safe. We got you out of the castle last night."

Amelia's eyes flickered and then opened wide. She looked wan with tousled hair. "Not in ... that dreadful dungeon? I'm free?" The words came out in a croak.

Morag rushed to her side and placed a supportive arm behind her friend's shoulders. She propped her up and put a wine goblet to her lips. Amelia took small sips. Morag lowered her friend's head back onto the pillow.

She rubbed Amelia's cold hand in hers and said, "You're free. I asked Sinclair for help. He sent Kinross, apparently he's also a Jacobite spy."

"Kinross? Never liked the man. I've misjudged him and must thank him." She made to rise, but sank down again. "I feel so weak."

"Would you like something to eat?"

Amelia nodded. As Morag made to go Amelia's words stopped her. "Mrs. Scott left soon after you, said she'd fetch me a tonic. I think she realised we were about to be raided. She couldna leave fast enough. Her and her talk about dying for The Cause. I thought I'd die in that dungeon. Tolbain made me stand all day. I told him I was with child, it made no difference. He seemed to enjoy it and all the time he asked me the same questions over and over about Jacobite plans and you, the Jacobite Jade. He seemed very interested in you."

Sweet Jesu, Tolbain remembers me. She tried to concentrate on Amelia's voice.

"He went on and on, wanting to know the Jade's identity and where she was from. I didna tell him. All I wanted to do was sleep, but I told him nothing." Tears streamed down her cheeks.

Morag squeezed her hand. "Dinna weep Amelia. You're safe now. You must rest for the sake of your babe."

Amelia turned her face to the pillow and cried in great gulping sobs.

Poor Amelia at least she's free and out of Tobain's clutches.

The clang of pans and crash of breaking pottery greeted Morag as she went downstairs.

"Drat. That's my best jug." Her hostess picked up the broken shards and put them on the table. She swept back tendrils of grey hair from her wrinkled face.

"Morning, my dear. Better we dinna use names. Sleep well?"

"Good morning. Yes, thank you."

"And your poor friend?"

"Upset. May we have something to eat and drink please? My friend's with child." Morag sat on one of the long benches at the oak table as flames from the kitchen fire licked up the chimney.

Her hostess nodded as she stirred the spluttering contents of the kettle hanging over the fire. "I've porridge and ale. The gentleman looked out of sorts." She wiped her nose with a clean rag. "Didna say where he was going, just left this for you."

So, he's left, good riddance.

She handed Morag a water-stained letter.

The faded black ink allowed her to read the shaky letters which spelt 'Morag'. Her heart lurched. She recognised her father's handwriting and held the parchment to her breast.

The woman banged a slopping tankard on the table in front of Morag's nose and followed it with the clatter of a bowl of porridge and clash of a spoon.

Morag had longed for a letter from her father, but needed to read it in a quieter place than this.

"The redcoats will be combing the neighbourhood for you," said her hostess. "You're known. Best you're on your way as soon as your friend's recovered."

Morag ate hers before taking up a tray for Amelia. "Kinross has gone." Morag put the breakfast on a side table and helped her friend sit up by plumping her pillows. "I hope you've an appetite."

Amelia gave a sad smile. Whilst Amelia picked at her food, Morag sat down in the chair by the sunlit window in their bedroom.

She broke the seal with trembling hands, read the contents and stared out of the window.

Amelia put down her knife and fork. "Trouble?"

Morag sighed as she folded the letter. "My father's very ill. He wants me to come home."

"Ah, then you must go at once."

"But The Cause ..."

"Will go on without you. You said yourself, Sinclair has left Edinburgh. We're known, better we leave. I'll go home too, wait for news from Crawford."

"You'll write to me in Braedrumie."

"If I can."

A few days later Morag waved goodbye to Amelia whose coach was heading for Crawford Hall, north-west of Inverness. Morag then set off to Fort William which lay in the opposite direction. She shut out thoughts of Tolbain and Kinross as the monotonous sway of the carriage sent her into a disturbed sleep.

CHAPTER Twenty-nine

Morag shaded her eyes. The November sun had reached its zenith in the cobalt sky. Rock giants dwarfed Braedrumie village. Mountain peaks glistened with ice bonnets. The lower slopes glowed cinnamon and russet. She tracked the flight of a heron soaring over skeins of tawny gorse, bracken and heather in the valley below. The bird flew on and landed with a splash in shimmering Loch Linnhe. Diamond light danced on the loch's surface reflecting the cliffs above.

She paused on the brow of the hill and breathed in peaty smoke drifting from the rooves and the tang of salt, seaweed and baking bread. Nothing had changed. *Home.* She trudged on, down the cart track to the village, the market cross and the old dool tree. As always she missed Euan's comforting presence. *Where is he? And Father, will I be able to help him?*

"It's Morag, Morag McColl." Children shouted and shrieked with delight as she trudged to meet them. Villagers peeked out of croft doors and ran to greet her. White haired Isabel led the throng with Granny Mac tottering behind, leaning on a stick.

"You look different," said Isabel, "more self-assured somehow. Dougie told us such stories. When he arrived driving Cope's carriage we couldna believe it."

"Looks just like her mother." Granny Mac squinted at Morag. "Now who was she?"

Her memory's fading. "And you look ... as I expected." Morag laughed.

"How's, Hughie?" Kirsty's mother, the old sporran, elbowed her way to the front.

"Fine, apart from a heavy cold."

"Dougie and our men, they're well?" asked Isabel.

"Yes, they made a bonny sight when they set out from Edinburgh," said Morag.

"Do you think we'll win?"

"Yes."

"Were you at any of the battles?"

"No."

"Was anyone wounded?"

"A few, I have a list."

Isabel put an arm round Morag's waist and took her bag. "She'll answer your questions in her own good time. Can you no' see she's weary from her journey? She's come to see her father. Isn't that right, Morag?" She held the younger woman's hand for a moment and squeezed it.

Morag gave a grateful nod. "He's... well?"

"He's... improved."

***

Morag had a pang of guilt when Father opened the door. *He looks haunted and much older.* His wizened face stared at her through tired, pale blue eyes. He'd a stoop. His frame was slighter and his grey hair thinner.

He wheezed and patted his chest. "So you're home at last."

She noted a cobbled patch on his shirt sleeve. "You wrote you were ill."

"I'm much better, thanks to, Isabel." A cough rattled out of his lungs.

"I'm sorry I left the way I did, but I'm no' sorry for helping The Cause."

"I can see that. You've grown up, there's more of your mother about you I see. She wouldn't do as she was told either." A fit of coughing made him stop.

"Father." Morag ran and hugged him and felt his bony frame. "You sit down." Morag put a rug round him and put more peat on the fire. "I'll make some soup, you need feeding up." *I should have been here, looking after him, but how could I have helped The Cause?*

In the pale morning light her spinning wheel and bag of wool fibres stood covered in dust under the window. Her sewing basket, overflowing with rent seams, torn cuffs and holed socks lay overturned and her wooden knitting needles transfixed a grey ball of wool on the sill. She'd thought she could leave these tasks behind. After the life she'd led in Edinburgh, knitting her Father and Euan warm bonnets seemed comforting.

She'd make cock-a leekie soup with chicken, leeks and onions. As she chopped the onions, eyes watering, she shared her life with the baggage train, the raid and Jacobite victories. Her last news came out in a rush. "And Amelia was imprisoned in Edinburgh Castle."

He lowered his brows. "Did you think war would be easy on women?"

"I didna ken what I thought. We got her out."

"Did you now?" He coughed again. "Are you no' sorry for all the worry you caused? I blame, Euan."

"It wasna him. He tried to send me back. I wouldna go."

"Well, perhaps the poor fellow's had a narrow escape, him thinking you were biddable." He rose from his chair and gathered her in his arms. "If you'd been a pony I'd have sold you long since. Thank God you're home." He kissed the top of her head.

She relaxed. She was precious to him and had been forgiven. However, she could feel his ribs and the torturous breath being squeezed in and out of his lungs. *Would his cough have been as bad as this if I'd stayed at home?* She'd make up one of her honey drinks for him; it might make both of them feel better.

CHAPTER Thirty

Euan staggered on his way to his room. It had been a hard slog keeping men, ponies and carts moving south into England. Highlanders could march perhaps 30-40 miles a day, but carts carrying precious provisions broke down.

He'd spent the morning mending a broken axle and the afternoon and evening catching up with the main party. On November 15th, after a five-day siege, Carlisle had finally capitulated. A few of the English welcomed them. Some threw rotten vegetables, but most stood in solemn silence when they passed.

Having seen to his men, horses and provisions, at last he could rest. Jamie Moffat, acting as postie again, had just arrived. Euan lay back on a feather mattress in a well to do house in Carlisle and imagined Morag beside him. He broke the seal on her letter, hungry to read her words.

My darling Euan,

I love you so and hope you are well. I miss you more each day and need you by me.

You will be pleased to hear I am home and cannot wait till you return. Darling, I think about when we will be man and wife; that is all I can think about. Father has been unwell, but is much improved. He says I am heartsick as I almost forgot to milk the cow the other day.

Braedrumie is not the same without you. I will put a candle in the old church and pray for you till you come safe home. I never want to say goodbye to you again.

Your father and Duncan are well and send their blessings and good wishes. Duncan is still keen to fight for The Cause. Your father is holding to his agreement with Johnnie and will not let him go.

Granny Mac has lost her last tooth. She says Braedrumie is not the same without you and for you to hurry home.

Give my love to Johnnie, Dougie and all the clan.
God keep you safe,

Morag

The report of a shot came from outside, followed by shouting voices. *What the hell?* There'd been no mention of redcoats in the vicinity and as far as Euan knew the British army had retreated south.

He grabbed his sword and ran to see a snarling group of men wrestling with Rory Graham, a handsome young Highlander. In a glance Euan saw the defiance in Rory's brown eyes and a man lying dead at his feet, a bloody bullet wound in his chest. *What's gone on here?*

"He's shot Red McIntyre." The McIntyre chief brandished a fired musket in his hand. Tendrils of grey smoke curled from the barrel.

"An accident. My musket went off. I didna mean to kill him."

Euan's heart sank. Rory, Angus Graham's eldest son and heir had killed a McIntyre. Both clans had been at each other's throats for centuries. *God.* Euan couldn't believe it. It was hard enough keeping the clans focused on The Cause and not their differences. If this wasn't dealt with in a manner agreeable to all, it could cause a rift that would lead to blood feuds. It would mean the end of Jacobite hopes.

"You heard him. It was an accident," said Euan.

"Doesna change the outcome, a McIntyre is dead."

"I'm sorry." Rory hung his head.

"He's apologised." Johnnie, a book in hand, stood at Euan's side.

"It's no' enough."

"I'm sure his father will offer gold in reparation," said Euan.

"A life for a life."

"For God's sake, we need every man. Take the gold," said Euan.

"I want him dead, blood for blood. That's the old way. We canna fight beside a man who's killed one of our own, even a Stewart must see that?"

Euan saw it for what it was, folly. *The man's spoiling for a fight. He willna be satisfied until young Rory's dead.*

Johnnie stared at Euan willing him to do something. "Euan?"

Euan shook his head. He knew the McIntyres would leave if the death sentence wasn't carried out, despite the fact they were in enemy territory; despite the fact that they might be killed by redcoats and despite the fact it would deplete the Jacobite army.

Rory looked at him and then Johnnie.

A fine, honest lad. Bile gathered in Euan's stomach. "Send for his father," he said.

Old Graham arrived and barged his way through the gathering crowd. The men formed into two groups facing each other, their hands on sword pommels. Two burly McIntyres held Rory by either arm.

"What's going on?" asked old Graham, never taking his eyes off his son.

Euan told him.

"I'll pay gold."

"He willna accept it. Angus, you ken what this means?" said Euan.

"Yes. He's my eldest. God, he's... have pity McIntyre... take the gold."

"No." McIntyre aimed a great gob of spit at Angus Graham's feet.

Old Graham seemed to sag and then recover. "Let it be by my hand then and no other." He walked to Rory, put his arm round him and kissed his cheek. The boy let his father lead him away behind a stone barn, followed by the baying McIntyres.

"Euan, can't you stop this?" said Johnnie.

"I tried. We need the McIntyres and they want him executed. There's nothing more I can do."

Euan couldn't look at Johnnie. He trudged back to his quarters, dreading what would come next. He imagined Rory standing against the barn wall, his father raising his musket to his shoulder, aiming for his son's heart; the shot and the boy falling as a crimson stain spread across his white shirt.

Euan steeled himself and when the shot and the McIntyres ululation came cursed the air around him. *Damn the clans and their old ways.* If he was ever laird there'd be changes. No one would die for the sake of a mistake when he was clan chief.

He broke the ice in a bucket of water at the house door, plunged his hands in and soaked his face. He'd tried to save the lad and so had Johnnie, but they were deep inside enemy territory. Rory had to be sacrificed to save the rest. It didn't make Euan feel any better. Nothing would. He caught sight of Morag's letter lying on his mattress where he'd left it.

He held the parchment to his nose and breathed in the faint trace of heather and wood smoke and longed to hold her. *Thank God she's home and safe.* He found his bundle containing quill, ink and parchment in his saddle bags and leaning on his saddle wrote:

November 1745

My heart,

I long to be with you and miss your dear face so much. It is good to hear you are safe at home.

We have taken Carlisle and are marching south soon. Do not worry. We are all in good health.

I thank you for the candle and miss you more than I imagined possible. You are in my dreams, my heart, and I too, long for our wedding day. I think only of you and when we will be together again.

Tell my father and Duncan I love them and the campaign is going well and not to worry. Give my regards to your father also and say I am pleased his health has improved. Send my best wishes to Isabel, and tell Granny Mac she will always be a beauty with or without her teeth.

Johnnie and Dougie send their love. My love is with you always.

Euan

He couldn't tell her about poor Rory Graham. He wished he could have done more. The boy's death would be on his conscience till his dying day.

CHAPTER Thirty-one
December 1745

Thick falls of snow covered the lower slopes of the mountains and the valley. The air seemed muffled, the snow crisp as Morag's boots disappeared under its white crust. She had to work hard to lift each leg as she trudged down to the village to Granny Mac's croft.

Morag had assisted Granny Mac for years. With Mary McBean due in April and Granny Mac failing, Morag wanted to know everything she could about delivering babies, so she could cope alone. She'd just reached the outskirts of Braedrumie when a shout came behind her.

"Morag, Morag McColl."

A ragged group of Stewart men, thin as whipcord, their faces hard and lined, half ran to catch up with her.

"Left the army in Manchester," Douglas Ross said, "struggled through mountain passes, snow up to our haunches. Come to help on our farms and crofts for a bit."

Villagers came to their doors and ran towards Morag and the men.

Johnnie's fiancé, Kirsty Lorne and her mother shoved villagers aside as they plied the men with questions about loved ones.

Morag felt for the Highlanders when they couldn't meet a questioner's searching eyes.

"Hughie, ask about, Hughie," said Kirsty's mother.

"He's fine, a bit of a cough, but fine," answered Iain Skene.

Dinna the Lornes care about Johnnie?

Douglas handed out letters. "We're giving Jamie Moffat a rest."

Morag chewed her lip until given a water stained packet which she hugged to her bosom. She said a silent thank you and hurried home to read it by the fireside.

My heart,

I miss you so much. Sometimes I think I can hear your voice on the wind and your dear face in everything I see.

Our march continues and we have some of the English in our ranks now. We are so close to London and everything we've hoped for, it's as if I can taste it.

We're all in good health and spirits. Johnnie and Dougie send their love. I've no time to write more, forgive me.

I love you.

Euan

The door opened bringing an icy wind with it and a flurry of snow. Morag held onto to Euan's letter and tugged her shawl round her.

"Any news about where they are?" asked her father as he dropped a stack of peat into the basket.

"Close," said Morag, "close to London and victory."

"That's good." His lips curved into a smile as he blew on his blue fingers.

Morag settled at a table with an ink pot and pen and wrote:

December 1745

My darling Euan,

I wish you were beside me now, I miss you so much. I never realised how beautiful the Highlands are or how fresh the air is here until Edinburgh, but it is not the same without you. The thought of Christmas makes me appreciate all those happy times we had when we were carefree.

How the men struggled through the passes we will never know, but are so grateful they did. Your news heartens everyone.

Braedrumie is covered in snow and the streams are iced over. Remember how Loch Linnhe shimmers like silver?

Your father and Duncan are well. Duncan is taller and asking after you all. Isabel misses Dougie, but keeps herself busy caring for Granny Mac who complains about her joints, though a dram of whisky seems to cure most of her pains.

My father is much better and sends his best wishes. Despite my protests, he still blames you for my leaving. Give my love to Johnnie, Dougie and all the Stewarts as always.

Till we meet again. I love you more than words can say.

Morag

With a sigh, Morag picked up a sock, threaded a needle with a strand of blue wool, and using a piece of wood shaped like a toadstool, inserted it beneath the hole on the heel and began to darn.

The men repaired leaking thatches, broken fence poles, stone walls, all the odd jobs that needed doing on crofts whose inhabitants lived on the edge of survival and left soon after to rejoin the army in the south carrying good wishes and villagers' letters with them.

The months passed. Morag had gone back to rising at cock crow and her early morning tasks of milking, collecting warm eggs from under hens' feathered backsides and making porridge for breakfast. Her father carried in buckets of water from the burn, checked the pregnant cattle and sheep in the byre and those in the infield so they hadn't trampled the first shoots of his precious barley, oats, vegetables or Morag's herbs.

There'd been no letter from Euan since December. Morag hadn't dared write any of her troubles in her letters: her nickname the *Jacobite Jade*, her part in Amelia's escape or Tolbain's' interest in her. Euan had enough to worry about.

Christmas had been miserable without Euan and the other men. The villagers had kept to their own crofts and the church remained abandoned, still without a priest. They'd been hunted for many years by British Governments terrified by the thought of a return to Catholicism, a Catholic monarch and the divisions it would cause.

Month after lonely month without Euan seemed forever. Winter eased its grip for a while and mountain springs began to spurt water again. Morag became as restless as a hungry cat.

She'd kept herself busy churning milk into butter and crowdie, a cream cheese, helped her father cutting and stacking peat and visited the laird and Isabel, examined pregnant Mary McBean, a fourth cousin twice removed from Euan, and chatted to Granny Mac.

"She's due in April as you ken, but I'm sure the babe's the wrong way round," Morag told Granny Mac. "It doesna feel right. Would you have a look?"

"You've spent years assisting me with delivering babies, Morag McColl. You'll have to turn it. Is she carrying it high or has its bottom engaged in her pelvis?"

"High I think," said Morag. "Please come and look. I'd value your opinion."

"Help me to her, I'll tell you what to do," said Granny Mac.

When they arrived at Mary's croft, Morag shooed away the children. The fire burned in the central hearth and Mary, with a look of concern, stirred from her low stool.

"No need to worry, Mary. Morag just wants me to check something. We've done this before haven't we with Charlie, Alec and little Maggie? Just lie on your bed."

Granny Mac's expert hands examined Mary's distended tummy. "You're right Morag, but the babe's high which is good. Dinna fret, Mary, we'll sort this out. Morag place your hands here, see you massage like this, gentle, gentle... and again, there you are... feel."

Morag felt. The baby had flipped over with the head downwards. Mary put a hand on her womb. "What have you done?"

"We've turned your baby, Mary. He's in the best position for birth now," said Granny Mac pressing Mary's hand. "It'll no' be long, you'll soon have another bairn to show Hughie."

"Thank you, thank you both," said Mary.

On the way back to her croft Granny Mac said to Morag, "You've got healing hands, I've always known it, but sometimes babies turn back again. You'll do well by Mary when her time comes. Get her walking like you've seen me do with lots of mothers, it seems to help.

Morag hadn't even had bairns, most of the women in the village were more experienced in giving birth than her and she just hoped Mary McBean wouldn't have any problems this time. Mary had lost two babies in the past.

When Morag heard Jamie Moffat, the clan's postman, had been sighted, she put her concerns about midwifery to one side and flocked with others to meet him as he limped towards the village. He pulled at his bonnet, but couldn't disguise the livid scar running from his forehead to his cheek.

Behind him icy veins scored the flanks of grey mountains topped with snow. The gloomy sky hung low and heavy like a wet blanket. Morag pulled her shawl round her. "Jamie man, what happened to you?" Her breath frosted. His wound had healed, so she couldn't do any more. Her eyes darted to the worn leather bag over his chest.

Jamie's eyelids seemed heavy and words stumbled out of his mouth. "A redcoat got in my way, the weather's been very bad and the rivers are flooded. I've never known a winter like it, fortunate to get through the passes."

He looked thinner than in Edinburgh. "And your news, man?"

"I left Derby with the army on December 6th. There'd been talk of them marching on London. Came to nought, they're retreating."

"Retreating?" The word caused consternation.

"Morag's heart dropped and then leapt thinking that Euan was closer, perhaps in Scotland and she hadn't known. *How could I not have known? Is he ... are they ... well?*" She scanned his face noting his gaunt look and the new angles to his face. Poor Jamie.

"Yes. Euan sent his ... you know." He tugged at his ear, blue with cold. "And Lady Crawford's home and sends her best wishes."

"Sweet Jesu, that's good news."

He held out two battered letters.

She stood on her toes and kissed him. "I thank you, Jamie Moffat."

He put a red chapped hand on his scarred cheek. She skipped away clasping her letters to her breast. She'd read Amelia's first. It had taken two months to reach her.

December, 1745
Dear Morag,

I hope you have a restful Christmas, this letter finds you safe, well and your father much recovered.

As you will have gathered I am safe home, though I worry about the baby. All the time I wait for news from my darling Crawford. I cannot bear not knowing what is happening to him. I know you will understand when I say I am going on a journey and you may not hear from me for some time.

The redcoats continually harass us. Winter is biting here and we are all but cut off by deep snow drifts. It is dreadful underfoot and we sit huddled round our fires.

It is a wonder to be able to write a letter to you and hand it to a reliable postman.

My thoughts are with you and yours in these dreadful times. Till we meet again.

Your friend,
Lady Amelia Crawford.

Does Amelia mean to go south and join her husband? The journey would be fraught with difficulty for anyone, never mind a woman expecting a child. Morag wished she could join Euan, but her father needed her help and she couldn't leave him. *Poor Amelia hounded by redcoats. Thank goodness there's no sign of their lobster coats in Braedrumie.*

Morag wanted to savour the moment when she opened Euan's letter: the tang of sandalwood as she unfolded parchment; his dear sloping hand; reading precious words meant only for her and dwelling on the meaning of every line... until she could recite them by heart.

She went up to the Falls where she always sensed him close. She blew on her frozen fingers and raised the packet to breathe in his scent. He could have been sitting next to her. She opened his letter dated December. It was now February two months had passed since his dear hand had written it. *Where is he?*

December 1745

My heart,

Wish everyone a happy Christmas from me and say that I miss them. Remember always we are meant to be together; I long to hold you. My life is worth nought without you.

I kiss your dear cross each night before I sleep. Sometimes in my dreams I hear your sweet voice calling to me across the miles and am heart sore when I wake.

Know this: nothing, not redcoats, rivers or mountains will stop me coming home to you. I promise I will be home soon. Trust in our love and faith in God and this will come to pass.

We left Derby to head north on December 6th. We could have been in London in a few days. It was not to be. God willing, Prince Charles will soon be victorious and we will come safe home.

Tell Father I am well and to move the cattle, he'll know where. In times like this you cannot be too careful. Give my regards to your father, Isabel and Granny Mac.

All the Stewart men are well. Duncan and Father are in our thoughts and prayers. Johnnie and Dougie send their love to all.

My love is with you always,

Euan

She read it again and again.

Some hours later Morag made her way down the hillside, her mind full of Euan and her body full of wanting. *Why have they retreated?*

Every night, torn between tears and hope, she filled a crusie lamp with mutton fat and lit it in the window facing south, as if it would guide Euan home. She prayed that Our Lady would keep him safe and he'd return soon.

She'd called on Euan's father most days, shared any news with him and Duncan and grasped at anything Johnnie wrote to them. The laird's housekeeper sometimes sent her away and at others she welcomed her indoors. She dared not mention Rob, could never tell them he'd joined the British army.

Today the laird had skin and eyes like yellow parchment, as he lounged in an armchair by the fire, hard to find anything of Euan in him. Perhaps a movement of his head or a gesture, an echo, with no hint of the person she really longed to see.

"I've news from Euan," she said. "Jamie Moffat arrived this morning. The army's retreating. They left Derby on December 6th."

"Retreating? The laird growled at her. "Why? They need to stand and fight."

"I'm sure they'll do that when the time is right. They've probably been in Scotland for some time. Oh, and Euan said to remind you to move your cattle, you'd know where. I'm sure he's just being cautious. He also sent his best wishes."

"After our victory they'll all come safe home, dinna worry." The laird swallowed his brandy in one gulp. "You'll join me?" He lifted the bottle at his elbow and looked at her, dull-eyed.

"No thank you."

Duncan ran into the room. "Morag, it's good to see you. Have you news of my brothers?"

He'd grown since August with longer limbs and the promise of muscle to come. In a few years he'd be tall like his brothers. He gazed at her with his mother's black lashed brown eyes. Morag struggled to answer. *Elizabeth would have been proud of him.*

"They're fine, Duncan, and back in Scotland again. Euan mentions you and your father in his letter. See." She allowed him to read a few lines.

Duncan's face broke into a wide grin showing strong, white teeth. "That's good to hear. Remember in his last letter, November I think, Johnnie said they were marching to Derby and he made it sound bloody s... as if it wasna a good thing."

Morag remembered. *Derby.* She thought back to her school books, about 100 miles from London, so, why had they turned back?

"Take no notice of Johnnie." The laird polished off another brandy. "He always sees the worst, thinks too much."

"Oh, Father." Duncan ran a hand through his hair so its brown waves rippled in the light.

He's a feverish look about him, but he'll play no part in this rebellion, still so very young, so very vulnerable.

"Duncan, you need to move the cattle to the up pasture," ordered the laird.

Did she mistake the flicker of rebellion flare and die in Duncan's eyes?

"Father." Duncan gave Morag a half smile which reminded her of Rob as he went to do his father's bidding.

If only Euan were home. She longed to shelter in his arms; to hear his voice and the beat of his heart. She wished, just wished him here, now, this minute. She'd rush to him and nestle in his arms and never leave so she could tell him all the things she hadn't said. He'd guide Duncan. Everything would be like before.

Morag dismissed her last thought. People changed, and not only those who fought, she saw that now, the laird, Duncan, Rob, those Stewart men who'd come and gone. The naive young lass who'd joined the baggage train had become less trusting, more aware of danger.

CHAPTER Thirty-three
Late February 1746

Snow fell in soft tufts from a grey-sheet sky as Morag picked her way between the pine trees and tramped down to the village to see Isabel. Smoke belched over snow-covered roof tops.

Market day had always been a noisy affair, Morag thought, but less so since the young men had gone to war. Cattle flicked their tails. Women bartered over prices near the market cross. Ponies neighed as knowing hands ran over their backs and flanks. Old men, sucked at their pipes as they huddled round the bonfire. A gaggle of women warmed their skirts as they gossiped. Children shrieked with delight as they wove in and out of legs chasing squawking geese and fluttering hens round the old dool tree. Stall holders hopped from one freezing foot to the other behind rough wooden benches with wizened apples, fish, rabbit, woven cloth and lace.

Morag scratched at her red hands as her thoughts wandered to Rob. She wrestled with the idea he'd left Braedrumie because of her. She'd suspected something and felt ... she didn't know what. She'd ignored it, too full of her love for Euan. An icy breeze snaked round her neck and ankles making her pull her shawl tighter round her body. The snowflakes fell like goose down.

"Ow."

"I'm sorry." Morag had been so lost in her thoughts she hadn't noticed Kirsty Lorne and her mother, the old sporran, near the dool tree.

Kirsty rubbed her foot. "You need to look where you're going. I'll have a bruise."

"I'm sorry I was thinking about Euan and ... well, I didna see you."

"Obviously. They'll be home soon enough and then we'll be sisters when I wed Johnnie."

Sisters. Morag didn't know whether she could bear it.

Kirsty twittered on and on about new fashions and fripperies until Morag's head spun with her silly talk. *What a feather-head. Has she no idea of the dangers for Johnnie? Her mother never stops going on about the fine wedding Kirsty will have.* Their talk finally turned to their visit to Inverness.

"We stayed with the Stewart's aunt again you ken, didn't we, Mother? That's once last year and once this. The Munros wouldna have it any other way, of course. They realised we expected certain ... refinements. Wonderful. We had invitations to the finest parties and balls in the area, such gallants, youngest sons of course. I'm sure I don't know how my head didn't turn. I'm quite worn out from all the dancing. The Munros introduced us to the most important families didna they, Mother?"

Has Kirsty always been this selfish?

"The most important," said the sporran nodding her head.

"I thought you went to visit your sick cousin again and your stay would be longer."

"Mother felt ... unwell. We didna want to risk her health and the Munros are still recovering from their son's death, of course."

"Jack's dead?" Morag's mouth went dry. *Euan will be upset – they were the same age.*

"Didna you know? The post is so haphazard these days. It was sudden, a fever I believe. She begged us to stay."

"Begged," repeated the sporran, "begged and begged."

"Have you heard from Johnnie?" Morag asked. "I had a letter from Euan dated December saying the army was retreating."

"You'd think they'd fight, not go backwards. Johnnie's letter took three months. I bet Jamie Moffat stayed at inns on the way."

"That's unfair, Kirsty, the poor lad's been wounded and is exhausted."

"If you say so, I just think Johnnie could have found the time to write more." She sniffed. "He said they'd be coming home and that he'd see me soon. Of course he'll probably think I'm still in

Inverness and send some letters there." She sighed. "The redcoats will follow them. King George willna forgive an invasion of England. The Jacobites have tweaked the lion's tail and run away."

"They wouldna do that. They'll have been ordered to retreat."

"It's of no matter, we left Inverness as soon as we could, we'd no wish to be in the middle of a war with redcoats rampaging all over Scotland and of course Mother unwell. It's hard when your sole protector is gallivanting all over the countryside."

"Gallivanting," agreed the sporran.

Gallivanting. Have they no sense in their heads? Morag bit back a cutting reply, remembering they'd be family one day and said, "Excuse me, but I must find Isabel. She may have more news from Dougie." As she strode away, a market stall with a piece of handmade white lace, gossamer and fine as a spider's web caught her eye. She lifted it to the light.

Kirsty and her mother sidled up beside her. "What a pity the colour doesna suit your skin." Kirsty smiled at Morag with feline eyes.

The sporran nodded sagely in agreement. "Dinna suppose you can do much about it, helping your poor father in all weathers. That must be why your hands are in such a state, my dear."

Morag hid her chapped hands behind her back.

"French lace is all the fashion now you ken." The sporran added. "You really should keep up." They smiled like cats relishing cream and went on their way.

Tears pricked at the corner of Morag's eyes. *They spread nastiness as they go with no thought of the hurt they leave behind.* She thought of Euan and their wedding and bought the lace from Mary McBean whose clothes stretched tight over the roundness of her womb.

Her tired face lit up at the coins Morag gave her. "You'll be buyin' it for a special occasion, I'm thinkin'?" Mary beamed at Morag as she grappled with Charlie and cleaned his face with the hem of her skirt.

Morag noted Mary's brown hair had a spattering of grey now.

"Yes. How are you and the babe?"

Mary smiled at her and put a hand over the mound of her belly. "Just waitin' for Hughie to come home. How do you get so dirty, Charlie? Go and find wee Alec and Maggie." She shook her head at her smallest son and patted his bottom lightly as he waddled off. "Euan will be very proud of his bonny bride. Dinna suppose you've heard ought of my Hughie? Johnnie sent word to Kirsty that he's well, but it's not the same as Hughie writin' it is it? But, as he canna write and I canna read, we have to make do with what friends and family tell us. The Lornes dinna say a lot."

Morag's heart went out to her. "Euan's letter said ..." She looked at Mary's peaked face. "All the clan's well and they're on their way back. I'm sure Hughie's alright. Dinna worry."

"It's good news you've given me." She rubbed her lower back. "Hughie will be so proud. I canna wait to see him again."

"That's lovely." Morag kissed Mary's pale cheek, concerned that her skin seemed to be drawn tight over her cheekbones and her arms looked like twigs. "I've made a pan of stew. I'll bring some over for the bairns and you."

"That's kind, thank you."

"Well, I'll say goodbye. I must see Isabel and call on Granny Mac." *Mary's last two babies were stillborn, what if something happens to Hughie? Have I given her false hope?* The thought hung over Morag like a damp rag. She searched the market for Isabel, but couldn't see her. She'd look in on Granny Mac instead.

A number of single storey crofts sat some distance from the market cross. The low walls made of large boulders, the spaces between plugged with earth and peat. Thatches were formed from branches, turf and heather and covered with fishing net held down by stones hanging from lengths of rope.

Granny Mac's was the last dwelling on the left. Morag took a deep breath, preparing for the peat smoke fug swirling from ceiling to knee height, till it found its way out through the hole in the roof. She bent her head and pushed open the wooden door. A couple of low, battered stools, a footlocker and a single box bed with curtains stood on the uneven stone flagged floor. Dried herbs hung like dead bouquets from a series of wooden A-frame roof trusses resting on the walls.

The old woman, smoke-dried and dressed in a belted striped plaid, huddled by a central hearth surrounded by a circle of stones. An iron kettle, its contents bubbling over the flames, hung from the rafters on the end of a thick iron chain.

A wicker screen divided the room into two, behind which Granny Mac's cow and calf stood lowing in hunger on a sloping earth floor. Little food for Highlanders, never mind animals, in winter. Morag took a breath and coughed.

"Shut the door before I freeze to death." Granny Mac shifted her bony backside and a malodorous fart hung in the air.

Morag secured the latch as her nose wrinkled. *Damn, there's no fresh air and the only light is the fire.*

"It's going to be a bad harvest." Granny Mac prophesied as her toothless gums smiled at Morag.

No mention of any battles of course. "You silly old devil." Morag instantly regretted her words and kissed Granny Mac's wrinkled cheek. She pulled a blue and yellow rug off the bed and tucked it round the old woman's bony knees. "Mary says she and her babe are well and Euan sends his best wishes. Now, what stories can you tell me about Euan and Johnnie?" Morag asked.

"Who?"

Morag gave her a sad smile. Granny Mac had always been known for her prodigious memory. She'd known the brothers all her life. Now she was failing and her knowledge would be lost to the village. Her family were all gone now, her children having died when they were little and her man in the 1715.

Every day since Morag's return, she'd fed the old woman soup, asked her questions about herbs and how they helped certain conditions, wrapped Granny Mac's warmest shawl around her and stoked up the fire. Then Morag left when Dougie's Isabel arrived. Isabel would make Granny Mac something to eat and listen to her tales until night fell.

Morag spooned the soup out of the cauldron. She'd feed the old woman and then seek Isabel and find out Dougie's news

CHAPTER Thirty-four

An hour later, having fed Granny Mac, Morag found Isabel by the market cross looking at samples of woollen cloth in all hues. The snow had settled like white eiderdown on trees, over rooves on hills and mountains. Mary McBean and her children had packed up and left with most of the villagers as icicles formed on rooves and water butts. Most of the cattle and ponies had been sold and the geese and hens loaded onto carts.

"I called on Granny Mac," said Morag.

"That's good. I'll see to her after I'm done here."

"Have you heard the news? Our army's retreating north. They're probably in Scotland now."

"Yes. Dougie said the prince wanted to press on to London, but General Murray and the Council wouldna have it. I've tried getting more out of Jamie, but the lad's exhausted, just wants to eat and sleep all the time." Isabel's voice dropped. -"I've heard some of our local men have captured Fort Augustus and they're going to lay siege to ... Fort ... William." Her mouth opened and shut like a landed fish. She crossed herself. "My God, look who's here."

Morag's heart missed a beat and then raced. Tolbain's towering figure stood talking to Kirsty and her mother across the market square. Morag hadn't dreamt of Tolbain for months. She led Isabel into the shadows of crofts and watched as he turned. He'd a patch of white in his black hair and grey in his beard; deep lines ran from his nose to the sides of his mouth and his cold eyes swept the square. *He looks even more brutal than I remember.*

She chewed her lip as she watched him deep in conversation with Kirsty and her mother on the opposite side of the market place. *Why? There's been bad blood between him and the clan for centuries, never mind their recent raid.* A Whig, unwelcome and extremely powerful, he made Morag sick to the stomach. *To think he might be fighting Euan. With the Stewart men away, no one will dare upset him. What's he doing here?*

Isabel's comforting hand patted hers. "You know him then?"

"I thought him dead. He's a devil."

Isabel's eyes narrowed, but she didn't ask any questions. "His reputation goes before him. He's a nerve showing his face here. I'll find out what he wants." She skirted the square stopping to talk to crofters as she went.

Unbidden images of Tolbain's attempted rape swept over Morag. She shrank into the shadows. *What business has he with the Lornes?* She watched as he kissed their hands and they replied with simpering smiles and low curtsies.

Of course Tolbain hadn't come alone. Morag watched his men spread out. They worked their way round the market threatening and questioning stall holders and customers.

They're coming closer. Morag backed away until she stood under boughs, heavy with snow. She scanned the forest's virgin snowy floor. *I daren't go this way, my tracks will stand out.* She whirled at a woman's shriek. One man had shoved over a water barrel. The ice cracked sending freezing water over feet.

No.

A young girl howled as men tipped over her wicker basket and trampled ribbons and lace underfoot in the slush.

Why?

"Here, what do you think you're doing?" yelled a middle-aged stall holder. A fist slammed into her face, breaking her nose and sending a spray of blood over two girls as she was sent sprawling into them. One of the girls screamed when Tolbain's men drew their swords.

Jesu.

The villagers ran, streaming away in all directions and grabbing crying children as they went.

They're too close. Where's Isabel?

174

A hand tugged at Morag's shawl.

"What?" Morag whirled round.

Isabel hissed, "Let's get out of here." She took Morag's arm as they used the cover of the trees to skirt Braedrumie. "Tolbain's men are scouring the area for a comely, brown haired woman about your age and build." Her brow creased. "He called her the Jacobite Jade."

Sweet Jesus, it's me he's after. He hunted me in the forest and tracked me to Braedrumie. Can't he forget I bested him? If Euan ever finds out he'll kill Tolbain with no thought to his own safety, the Highlanders' code of honour. She gnawed at her lip trying to blot it all out with pain, but the scenes in her head wouldn't go away.

"Morag, I'd not come to Braedrumie for a while." Isabel's words brought Morag to her senses. "We'll take the river road. He's looking for one woman, not two."

CHAPTER Thirty-five

April arrived, but the nights had grown even colder. Morag's mind churned making sleep impossible. She dreamt of Euan's smiling face and their lives when he came home.

A fist hammered at the door. *Tolbain. He's found me.* She grabbed her dirk to kill him before he put one foot in their croft. "Father, your sword."

"What now?" He grabbed the weapon from its place above the fire. "Who is it?" he growled at the locked planks.

'The Laird of Braedrumie."

Euan's father. Morag opened the door. He swayed in front of them, bottle in hand.

Morag braced herself for the worst and her imagination took flight: a battle had taken place; Euan and Johnnie were dead; there'd be no marriage and she'd die an old maid with no bairns. She'd never marry another, Euan was her life.

Saliva dribbled down the laird's whiskers. "Have you seen Duncan? He's been missing all day."

Morag steadied her breathing, but wrinkled her nose at the waves of alcohol. "He hasn't been near has he, Father?"

Her father shook his head.

"He'll have joined the men going to attack Fort William." The laird sounded proud and smiled at them.

"You'll be strutting around like a bantam cock now I suppose, boasting that all your sons fight for The Cause. Duncan's just a boy," said Morag.

The laird gave her a beatific smile, waved the bottle at her and lurched away.

Her father shook his head at her. "It's no' your place, he's a laird."

"Then he should act like one," she snapped. "Poor Johnnie only agreed to fight if Duncan stayed at home."

"It's not our business." Her father stomped to his bed, leaving her to wrestle with her thoughts.

Will he try to join his brothers? She couldn't warn Euan, Jamie Moffat had left with his pockets stuffed with post a few weeks ago.

Blinding rain drove in Euan's face on Drumossie Moor, just south of Inverness. He held Morag's crumpled letter in his hand. Jamie Moffat had intercepted their army on Scotland's east coast.

Why had they retreated? He remembered the Council of War meeting in Derby. Prince Charles had been adamant he wanted to march on London and General Murray and the others had refused to do so. They'd only been about 100 miles from London and their leaders wavered and then capitulated. The Jacobite army had risked everything and for what?

Johnnie had shrugged. "And our ally?"

They both knew from reports that the French fleet had not sailed. *Damn them. Promised English support hasn't materialised either, just a few thousand men.*

Euan thought of poor Rory Graham and his father, Angus, whose ghost-like figure had trudged by Euan's side as they'd retreated north harassed by redcoats. *Does Angus think it's all been for nought, now he's shot his eldest son? I daren't ask him.*

The prince had been drunk most of the time and despite his orders in Edinburgh that women and children stay behind, some had carried on to Derby. When they'd retreated, the baggage train had been left to its own devices. *Thank God Morag's in Braedrumie.* The women, and worse, the bairns had been in a dreadful state. Their hardships and what he and his men endured on the long march north at Asbourne, Leek, Macclesfield, Stockport, Manchester, Wiggon, Preston, Lancaster, Kendal, Penrith, Shap, the Battle of Clifton and Carlisle had etched themselves on Euan's mind.

They'd entered Carlisle, left wounded and able-bodied men behind to defend the castle and made it to the Esk which had been in spate. Crossing upstream had taken all the strength of a chain of men linked arm to arm and even then some had been swept to their deaths.

Once in Scotland, they'd trudged to Glasgow and demanded shoes, clothes and food. Half of the army headed north over mountains and the other half headed east. They'd fought shrieking blizzards, snow up to their thighs, gales and slanting rain, which cut into the bone.

On January 17th Euan, Johnnie and Dougie together with the Jacobites who laid siege to Stirling Castle, won at Falkirk. They later marched north in April and assembled at Culloden

They'd even tried to mount a surprise attack on Cumberland at Nairn last night, lost their way and had to return, exhausted and hungry, before dawn. Now over 5000 exhausted and starving Jacobites readied to do battle on windswept Drumossie Moor, eight months since the Rising.

Why in God's name has the prince chosen to make his stand here? Euan went over and over it in his head. *This is a wild, bleak, boggy place with black-shroud hills to the west and the Moray Firth, a silver winding sheet in the distance. No' a place for Highlanders to do battle. We like to come down on the enemy from above and rely on speed and strength to see us through.*

Euan shivered as if someone had walked over his grave. The Stewart clan huddled together for warmth. "No' too close, lads," Euan joked. "No offence, but our cows smell sweeter than you." They jeered and laughed at that.

The rain turned to sleet and Euan's hands and feet froze. A bitter wind blew into his face. Light-headed from hunger, he stood in battle order with the clan again. He didn't think it could get worse until he heard raised voices. Dougie had his huge fist wrapped round some miscreant's neck as he marched a small, familiar figure towards them.

His victim repeatedly shouted, "Let me go. Get your bloody hands off me." He lashed out with his feet at Dougie.

"I found this stray beast." Dougie shook him. "He says he's Duncan Stewart, your brother." Dougie pushed him towards them. "But he canna be because I remember chasing him with my leather belt to the laird and telling him to stay at home."

Euan's mouth opened and closed a couple of times and he rubbed his brow.

Johnnie let out a low whistle.

Do I beat or hug the little beggar? Euan looked over at Johnnie who shook his head.

Duncan's grimy face grinned cheekily at them. "There's nothing you can bloody do is there?"

Johnnie clouted him. "Don't bloody swear."

"Ow!"

Euan ran his hand through his hair. They didn't dare leave their positions as hunger had driven too many to do that. Mist swirled and a biting wind drove sleet and freezing rain into their faces. It seemed the blackening sky grieved.

Duncan rubbed his reddening ear.

"You wee devil, you should have bided at home." Johnnie's voice softened. "It's what we wanted." He ruffled Duncan's hair. "Father didna send you?"

"No."

"Are you sure because ...."

"I bloody ran away."

Johnnie cuffed him again on the other ear.

"Ow!"

They stared at each other. Duncan held his red ears with dirty hands and Johnnie looked fit to kill him before he grabbed Duncan's thin arm and pulled him to his chest. He held him there till Duncan squeaked, "I canna breathe."

Locking eyes with him, Johnnie relaxed his grip. "Listen well, you wee fiend, if you're to be with us you'll obey orders, right?"

"Yes Johnnie, anything you say."

"Good because the battle's about to start. You stay behind us … to … to …" Johnnie faltered.

"Guard our backs," Euan suggested. He raised an eyebrow.

Johnnie nodded and looked at Duncan again. "Yes, to protect our backs. You can be with McBean here." He put his arm round the thin shoulders of the man in the middle of a coughing fit. "And if we fall, stay close to Dougie. Understand?"

"Yes." Duncan's face lit up. "And what if Dougie falls? What should I do then?"

"Run like hell," Johnnie said and they all laughed.

Duncan bunched up his nose just as he'd done when a babe and smiled.

Euan cursed his father for not keeping Duncan on a tighter leash.

"You wee devil." Dougie shook his grey head at him. "Keep your head down."

Not being able to make a better of it they welcomed him and kept their worries to themselves. Hour after hour they itched to do battle. Bone weary and ravenous as wolves, they'd had nothing but water and a scraping of a meal for days and still, Cumberland, the Hanoverian commander, didn't come.

Thoughts of Morag filled Euan's head. He read her letter again.

February, 1746
My darling Euan,

I'm so pleased you are in Scotland, nearer to me and home. I know we will win because right is on our side. I am sure it will all be over soon and we will be together again. I cannot wait for the house you will build for us and our wedding day. I miss you so. I long to hear your voice and feel your arms round me.

Sometimes I fancy you are standing beside me, especially when I am at the falls. I envy the birds their flight, for if I could, I would fly to your side.

Your father and Duncan are fine and send their love. Granny Mac
says to come home soon, she misses your handsome face.
Jamie is in a rush to leave, so I will end my letter now.
I love you, always and forever.

Morag

Her words of love and home gave him comfort. He tucked the
letter in his plaid. He longed to hold her close so he could hear the
beating of her heart and feel her sweet head just one more time on
his chest. He turned away and spent his time looking at the distant
hills. He never thought war would be like this, the waiting hard.

Mist swirled over the moor and in the distance came the trudge
of marching feet, the creak of lumbering cannon and the rat-a-tat-
tat of drums.

Jacobite officers yelled orders sending men racing in all
directions over the moor, others stumbled to their positions half
asleep. Horsemen spurred towards Inverness to chivvy Jacobite
troops who'd left the field to forage for food

Then Cumberland and regiment after regiment of redcoats
arrived with colours flying, drums beating and bayonets fixed.
Guttural orders pierced the air as they marched into position,
behind their cannon, with dragoons at the rear and one side, facing
the Jacobite army.

A muscle twitched in Euan's cheek as he estimated they faced
over 7000 soldiers. He pointed at a green and yellow banner. "I see
Tolbain's brought his men to fight against us." There'd been bad
blood between the families for centuries and talk of cheating at cards
with lost land never regained.

Johnnie checked his musket and Dougie stared at the horizon.

The Jacobite cannon fired first, sending government troops
reeling. The spaces in their front line filled with more redcoats. The
repetitive roar of the Hanoverian field guns accompanied the
screams of the dying on both sides. Smoke drifted across the moor

and brought with it the stink of gunpowder. Fear stalked the battlefield. Euan put a steadying hand on Duncan's thin shoulder and nodded to Johnnie and Dougie. He kissed Morag's cross and muttered a silent prayer for them all.

The Jacobite line wavered, shrank and then surged forward with a roar. They stumbled in the boggy ground, men on the left being forced to veer to the right to avoid the sucking mud. The air hummed with musket balls and boomed with mortars. Above all the cries of desperate men clashing blades, stabbing, thrusting and slashing ... anything to get through the bristling redcoat ranks. The Stewart clan clambered over the dead of both armies.

Eaun looked for Duncan and Dougie in the melee, to no avail. He tried to get to Johnnie by cutting his way through a redcoat. A shot whistled past his right ear. His blood ran cold. From behind stone walls on the right fusillade after fusillade thundered into the backs of the Jacobites whilst Tolbain's dragoons massed at the walls urging more and more mounts to jump over them.

"They've outflanked us. Follow me." Euan yelled rallying those left of the clan. They raced over and around bodies and stood shoulder to shoulder with others in the breach. Hand-to-hand fighting at its most desperate, devilish faces loomed up in front of him to be cut down, shot and hacked at. In the background men shrieked, groaned and the guns roared. Then a faint ripple ran through their line, it fell back, rallied, fell back again and broke.

Euan, aware of Johnnie to his left slashing his way through the sea of redcoats, parried bayonet thrusts to gut and throat. A mortar exploded overhead and Johnnie disappeared behind a row of Highlanders.

No. A horse and its rider lunged towards Euan. *Tolbain.* Sidestepping the blade, Euan cut into his opponent's arm.

"Aggh." Tolbain fell back holding his bloodied limb.

Euan's cross whispered its way to the ground. He faltered and reached for it before a vicious blow from a musket felled him. The battle raged on.

CHAPTER Thirty-seven
April 16th 1746

Morag still hadn't heard from Euan since his December letter. A nightmare woke her just before light. Tolbain's face, so real, so believable, had loomed at her in the darkness. He'd boasted he'd killed Euan. *Sweet Jesu, no.* She'd wiped away tears, but sensed something wrong for the rest of the day.

The overcast sky pressed down on her. A frisson in the air made her hair worse than normal to handle, always the first sign of a storm. She wetted and plaited it so it lay down her back under some sort of control.

A cow kicked over her milking pail and a white puddle formed at her feet. She didn't notice as her mind seethed, wondering about Euan.

Father waved the cow's horsehair rope at her. "What are you thinking? You should have tied her leg. That's good milk wasted." He stamped off.

The early morning breeze became a gale and rattled round the house. They moved indoors. Her father tended the fire and she cobbled a shirt seam here, a hem there. She sewed as if her life depended on it until she pricked her finger and crimson drops fell on the linen. Each drop reminding her of all the blood spilt in the last months. Tears welled, never far off these days. They'd no news for weeks. Why did she have the feeling something dreadful had happened?

***

A few days later, Morag woke again from a fitful sleep. The light of the silver moon streamed between the gaps in her shutters and played hide and seek on her bed. The wind shrieked through the eaves and rain lashed against the farm rattling shutters and the door. The storm, threatening to come in from the sea the evening before, had arrived.

What is that pounding? Someone at the door. Dirk in hand, she wrapped her shawl around her, but held back and let her armed father go first. *Has Tolbain discovered where I live?*

"Who is it?" hissed her father.

"Dougie. Open the door, man."

Morag's heart leapt as she lit the cruisie lamp.

Dougie and about twenty of the clan looked haggard in the light of the lamp. Some had claymores out, others empty scabbards. Their heaving chests and dull eyes told her they'd had little rest. Rain dripped down their lined faces. She searched the dark behind them. "Where's Euan and Johnnie?"

They looked at the ground.

She knew before Dougie spoke, she knew, but could not accept what her brain reasoned.

"There's been a battle. We lost. We havena seen Euan since he fought." Dougie's voice flat and low, struck her like a mailed fist.

She staggered. *Battle?* Morag's throat tightened. "No." Her father put a strong arm around her; without it she'd have fallen. "I'd ken ... I'd ken if ..." She struggled to make sense of what she'd been told. "He could still be alive." She looked at her father begging him to agree.

"I saw him fall, lass," said Dougie with sombre finality, his eyes on the ground, "Cumberland ordered no quarter."

The redcoat commander. She couldn't breathe. 'If I fall ...' How many times had Euan said that to her? 'If I fall ...' A strange numbness crept over her. *Has someone else crept inside my skin?*

"And Johnnie?" asked her father.

"Headed for Inverness after the battle, said he wanted to know Kirsty and her mother were safe."

"They've been in Braedrumie for weeks," growled her father. "And Duncan?"

"We tried to protect him but..." Dougie shook his weathered head.

Morag's hand went to her throat. "Duncan? Poor wee Duncan?" She knew his brothers would have done everything to protect him. "And Hughie McBean? Mary's been asking about him."

Dougie shook his head.

Poor Mary, the bairn's due any day. "And the Crawfords? Were they at the battle?"

"Got away, I think," said Dougie, "as did the prince."

"They escaped?" *Jesu, what am I thinking? These men need food and warmth. They've been kept on the doorstep as if strangers.* "Come away in, when Euan comes, he'll ... he'll ..." The words twisted and caught in her throat and her father held her tighter.

"We thank you for your news, bad as it is," he said.

Dougie nodded. "We'll away. There's no rest for us till we've told all those in Braedrumie." His brow had new furrows and his cheeks sagged.

The men looked dead on their on their feet, but determined to do their duty moved off in the growing light, the mist swirling round them. Her father closed the door. He said nothing, just patted her shoulder and put more peat on the fire. She crouched on a chair near the hearth and let her father put a thick plaid round her, when she wished only for Euan's arms.

She thought of Duncan... From the age of two, he'd fished with them in Loch Linnhe. He'd still had the chubbiness of childhood round his cheeks and innocent mischief in his eyes. She'd shared his delight when he'd caught a salmon; his horror when his brothers stove its head in with a stone and enjoyment when they'd cooked and eaten it.

Euan would ... *I'd know, surely I'd somehow know if he'd ... died.* 'If I fall ...' She ached for the sound of his voice. To never hear it again, or see him or feel his presence beside her seemed like a death sentence. She crooned and rocked her body to and fro in grief. She couldn't weep.

Morag prayed to Our Lady. She tried to think. *I would have felt it, kenned if Euan was lost to me, wouldn't I? I would know that half of me had died. He had to be alive.*

***

That morning she couldn't work or eat for thought of him. *He could be wounded or sick out on the hills struggling to come home, might need me.* Her father brought her broth and ale, she forced herself to swallow and drink.

She paced the room like a caged animal, up and down up and down. A thought came to her. *The laird must be sick with grief.* She made up her mind flung her shawl around her, kissed Father and told him she was going to see the laird. *Perhaps he knew more.*

"Go, if you think it'll help."

Her father understood.

The laird did not. He refused to come to the door. A sluttish servant wrung her hands and said, "Ever since Dougie talked in private with him," she lowered her voice, "he's done nothin', but sit in the dark, cradlin' the clan's bloody banner. They say they found it wrapped round Duncan when he died. And the laird willna suffer a fire to be lit. Said he couldn't be warm whilst his sons are cold. The housekeeper's up and left. No food's passed his lips, only whisky since Dougie broke the news."

"Jesu. If he willna see me I'm seeing him."

"He said no visitors." The servant barred her way and folded her arms.

"Out of my way, I'm family." Morag thrust the servant to one side.

"Here."

Morag strode into the hallway and then the laird's study. He sat sprawled in a chair by the cold fireplace. He'd wrapped the bloody banner round him like a shawl and had a half empty brandy bottle in his hand. Piles of parchment, books and empty bottles littered the carpet at his feet. The room was dark and smelt stale.

What would Euan think? She dragged open the curtains and windows allowing fresh air and light to flood in.

"What the hell? What are you doing here?" The laird shaded his bloodshot eyes and squinted at her.

"Ensuring you're comfortable."

"I couldna stop her, sir, she insisted," said the slovenly servant at the door, wiping her hands on her greasy apron.

"It's a good thing I did," said Morag. "You'll get your master something to eat and I'll sit here till he's eaten it. Then you'll clean up this mess or I'll ensure his sons know that you didn't carry out your duties."

The servant stared at her, dipped a curtsey and said, "Yes, Miss." She scurried off.

The laird let out a bellow of a laugh. "So, Morag McColl, you've some fire about you. I like that."

"And I'd like you to be well for when your sons return."

"Ah, but will they? There's many a one never returned in 1715."

"You have to hope. I know Duncan's ... gone, but the others will be home soon."

"You sound so sure, but what if they dinna?" His face twisted into a malicious smile. "What if they're lying out there dead without a proper grave and no one to mourn their passing? What then Morag McColl?"

It was as if he'd a dirk and was working it into her heart with each word he spoke. *I won't let him see his words have hurt me.* "Then a part of me will die too, but I won't mourn living men. Now I'll find out where that servant is with your soup because if you dinna eat, you'll be no good for man nor beast."

"Jesu." Morag's legs almost gave way when she closed the main door behind her some time later. She'd spooned soup into the laird, ensured the servant lit a fire and threatened her with Euan and Johnnie's wrath if she didn't keep it lit. Then she'd persuaded the laird to go to bed and rescued the bloody flag as it slid off his shoulders onto the floor. She tried not to think about whose blood stained the silk as she folded it and placed it on a chair. Once he'd fallen asleep she'd left. Her heart ached for him, Euan, Johnnie and Duncan and every croft where they'd lost someone.

A few hours later Isabel rapped on the door. "Morag, you're needed. Mary McBean's in labour. She's asking for you."

So many deaths and now a birth. With a heavy heart, Morag collected her kit, wool, a dirk, scissors and whisky, wrapping them in clean linen just as Granny Mac used to do. *I have to help the living.*

She heard Mary's moans before she saw her. Isabel took charge of pale faced Charlie, Alec and Maggie and shoed away concerned neighbours. "There's hot and cold water in buckets by the bed," she said to Morag. The fire had been banked and lightened the gloom. Mary scrunched up her face and lay in her shift, knees apart, on the only bed in her croft as a contraction shook her whole frame.

Morag washed her hands and dried them. "Hello Mary, looks as if the bairn's coming today. How long have you been in labour?"

"A few hours. You'll have heard ... about Hughie ... I ..." Another contraction and her belly tightened. Sweat made her brown hair lank as her mouth contorted in pain.

"I heard. I'm so sorry, Mary. Let me examine you." Morag' rolled up Mary's shift and felt for the baby's head engaged in the pelvis, instead she felt its bottom. Morag's heart sank. The baby had turned again and lay lower, ready for birth in a breech position. *I mustna panic. What had Granny Mac said? Births such as these are usually quicker, but dangerous for the baby.*

Another contraction shook Mary. "I have to push. I have to push," she shrieked.

Amniotic fluid spurted onto the linen on the bed. Mary hunched up over bent knees, groaned and then screamed, a few seconds later she did the same again and again. Morag stood back letting Mary push the baby's legs and bottom onto the sheet, then supported the head and neck as they slipped into the world.

Mary sank back with a grateful sigh. "Is it alright?"

"It's a boy, Mary."

Jesu. Why doesn't he cry? Morag, tied wool in two places around the cord and waited for it to stop pulsing. She placed a small wad of linen beneath it, cut the cord with a knife, wrapped the bloody lifeless baby in linen and rubbed his body. Nothing.

"Is he alright?" asked Mary from the bed.

Morag rubbed some more. Still nothing. *Breathe.*

Morag dunked the naked baby in a bucket of cold water used for drinking and then in the hot water a couple of times. *Please breathe.*

"Mo... rag?" Mary's voice came from behind her.

Sweet Jesu, let him live. Mary's lost two babies and Hughie, she canna bear any more. Morag dunked the baby again. The infant's chest heaved and he wailed. She wrapped it in clean linen saying, "Hush, sweetheart."

"Thank God," said Mary as she took the baby in her arms and Morag dealt with the afterbirth letting it plop into the bucket, ready for burying.

"What will you call him?" asked Morag.

"Hughie," said Mary, Hughie McBean. Her next words cut into Morag like a dirk, "I heard about Euan, I'm sorry for your loss."

***

Euan. Days dragged by when Morag spun, pulling wool fibres from their cloth bag, breathing in the scent of cedar wood that staved off moths. *My darling man.* She placed the fibres on one of her wooden carding combs. *I mustna think the worst.* Using her right hand she stroked the right comb over the left five or six times transferring the wool to the right comb. *He'll be home soon.* By flipping over the comb's teeth nearest the handle to catch the last hairs, she rolled the wool into a sausage shape on her knee. *We'll be together again.*

Her foot moved rhythmically on the treadle whilst her hands teased the wool from the rolag allowing it to twist and wind onto the bobbin. *He'll build the house we planned.* Whilst she spun wool, she went over her dreams about how married life with Euan would be and spun them into fact. *We'll wed and have bairns.* Only when she stopped, did she remember Dougie had seen him fall.

A trickle of terrified crofters arrived in Braedrumie fleeing from Fort Augustus. Morag shared some soup with a lone woman, Flora Gordon, and her four children. In between spoonfuls Flora told her story. "Butcher Cumberland and his redcoats found we'd blown up the fort and he'd to sleep in a turf hut. He ordered his devils to steal our cattle and burn our crofts. They took some poor men away in chains and hanged others for having weapons. My man ... " A tear trickled down her cheek. She let it fall.

Morag put a comforting arm round her. *This couldn't be true, men couldna be so cruel.* The old ones shook their heads and talked about the 1715.

She couldn't rest. *How can I sit or work knowing that somewhere out there Euan might have escaped, might be calling for me?* She paced up and down, up and down. *Sometimes I think I'm going mad.*

Father made her go with him whilst he took their milk cow and her calf up to their shieling, built of turf and timber with a stone roof, high up in the hills and a difficult climb. She trudged behind with sacks of cheese and bread.

"It'll be the same as after the 1715," he said. "They'll burn steal, kill people out of hand and hunt any fighting men to extinction. If we're lucky, they willna bother coming up here. We've milk and food until the hue and cry dies down."

She itched to be elsewhere with Euan. His words swam into her head. 'If I fall ...' She slept through sheer exhaustion.

CHAPTER Thirty-eight
April 17th 1746

His eyelids fluttered. Euan heard a moan. It was him. His mouth dry, he struggled to focus as he followed a crack running the length of the yellowed ceiling and ending at the central rose. Flies circled, their drone added to the low conversational sounds in the room. He took a deep breath and regretted it. The dank smell of latrines infiltrated his nostrils. His head pounded. He lay on a straw pallet and a rough, grey horse blanket had been thrown over him.

He willed himself to move, touched his head and detected dried blood. Hazy, grotesque images of battle and Rob's face danced in front of him. Holding his head in a hand, he looked around to see rows of men lying on straw pallets and red jackets hanging over a rickety stool. *Where am I?* He had a vague memory of being stripped, so cold, dressed again and Rob's voice. *Did Rob dress me as a redcoat and put me with the government wounded? What sort of nightmare is this?*

Men wept, spat blood and vomited and no one tended to their needs. The floor was the latrine. *Good God, I **am** with the enemy wounded. I have to get out of here, get back to Morag.* He struggled to sit up.

"'Ere, soldier take it easy why don't you? You've been out cold since yesterday."

Euan felt his head and shoulders supported. *Yesterday?* "Who won?"

"Why us of course. Cumberland saw to that. 'Ave a drink." A mouse-haired man with freckles handed Euan a flagon of luke-warm wine.

We lost. What about Johnnie, Duncan, Dougie and the rest of the Stewarts? Lost? Euan drank his fill and stared into the wiry face of a hated Sassenach. Euan made himself smile and the man smiled back.

"Cat got your tongue?"

Euan shook his head and wished he hadn't.

"Sore head, is that it, old son? Don't worry. There's worse fings 'ere. You and me'll get back home, not like the rest of these poor devils. See that one, stomach wound. 'E'll be gone by the end of day. And 'im, they'll 'ave to amputate, wound stinks. Red streaks, nasty business. I 'ope I'm back with my company before they starts on 'im. Don't want to be the one holdin' 'im down. The quack's due soon. He'll be pleased you've come to your senses."

"Where... where am I?"

"*Balnain House*, on the other side of the Ness. You're Lowland Scots if I'm not mistaken. I'm Alfie Smith, private, from Barrell's regiment. Lost two fingers, holdin' on to the Regimental Colours, got the bugger who done it."

Euan's wounded friend extended his right hand. His left was bound in a filthy rag encrusted with blood and pus. Euan did the unthinkable and shook hands. Surrounded by redcoats, he'd no choice. He noticed a louse run up Alfie's filthy cuff.

"And you're ...?" said Alfie scratching his arm.

What had Rob said? Think. Alfie looked at him full of expectation. *Bloody hell, what had Rob said?* "John, John Maxwell, Wolfe's regiment."

The door in the middle of the room swung open to admit a man into the gloom. Euan noted the muddy shoes, tarnished buckles, dirty silk stockings, worn breeches, filthy linen and the battered pig skin leather bag he carried. He didn't flinch at the fetid stench.

Alfie mouthed the word, "Quack."

The man took a swig from a small bottle and knelt beside a soldier beaded with sweat and mumbling. "He's got a fever," he said to no one in particular. His hand shook as he took a bowl and silver case from his bag and placed them on the filthy straw. He drew a lancet from the case and made a swift cut across a vein in the soldier's forearm.

"Aagh." The soldier moaned as his blood trickled into the bowl held by the quack.

Euan struggled to his feet. *I'll take my chances outside.* His head swam and he sank back onto the pallet.

"I'll bleed you." The quack stood over him.

Euan shook his head. "No," he mumbled, "I'll fend for myself..."

"He's ravin', sir, don't mean anythin' by it," said Alfie. "Once 'e's well I'm sure 'e'll be beggin' for your potions."

The quack stared at Alfie a muscle worked in his cheek. He gave Euan and Alfie a disparaging look and checked the patient he'd just bled. "Dead, weak heart." He pulled a dirty blanket over the corpse's head, burbled something about urgent patients elsewhere, grabbed his bag and left.

"How do I get out of this place?" said Euan.

"Through that door and down the stairs. It's not like we're prisoners." Alfie opened a window. "Cor can you 'ear that noise?"

"Trouble?"

"Celebratin', been goin' on all mornin', listen."

Euan became aware of a growing hubbub some distance away.

"Look." Alfie helped him stand and pointed out of the ground floor window. Euan stared at a front garden, railings, the grey Ness and then on and up to the town. Huge plumes of grey smoke rose over the rooves of buildings. Then they heard the musket shot.

Euan leant on Alfie and they hobbled outside as fast as they could. They stood wide eyed with the rest of the walking wounded. The sounds came from the other side of the bridge.

"What do you think it is?" asked one with a broken arm.

"Bloody Jacobites," said another.

"You don't fink they've come back do you? To finish us off like?"

"No, there's only been one shot. One's escaped I reckon. Anyone want to bet on the beggar's chances?"

Odds were shouted and with a spit and a handshake deals were made. *Little do they know,* thought Euan, *they've another escaped Jacobite in their midst. What would be the odds for me?*

And my brothers? What of them? Have they survived the carnage and its aftermath? He thought of Rob and how he could have been executed for what he had done. *Would I have helped him if our positions had been reversed? I daren't think of that. Mother's death has been hard on those left behind and I blamed Rob. Please God, let me get back to Morag and sanity. I have to escape.*

He wished the Jacobite escapee God Speed. His pounding head told him he needed to lie down. A fetid hole appeared to be the only place on offer and he prepared to return. He leant on Alfie and breathed in a precious lungful of fresh air, then fainted.

CHAPTER Thirty-nine

Every wisp of smoke on the horizon brought fresh streams of frightened crofters needing shelter and food to Braedrumie. They spoke in whispers of redcoat atrocities. The maelstrom of war edged closer as Morag waited for the redcoats to arrive.

As if in answer to a prayer Dougie came to Morag and her father's farmhouse a week after his return. "Tolbain's looking for men to take supplies to Inverness. I've volunteered. He's been given a few soldiers to guard the wagons. Once there I'll look for Euan and Johnnie."

Morag kissed him on his grizzled cheek. "I'm going with you."

"Are you mad? The roads are dangerous for men, never mind a woman," growled Dougie. Her father agreed with him. Morag said nothing, just disappeared inside. Sometime later she reappeared dressed in her father's shirt, waistcoat and breeches.

"You look ... It's a ...well ... it's a disgrace," blustered Dougie. "There must be a law against it."

"There's no law, because every other woman knows her place and that's in a skirt and no' my britches," snapped her father. "Good, honest women stay at home and look after their men folk, not roam the Highlands like a ... like a..."

"Bad, dishonest man?" she suggested.

Her father exploded. "I dinna approve, dinna approve at all. This is the second time you've defied me. Bad things will come of this, mark my words." He tapped his favourite clay pipe against the fence post and it broke into two pieces. "This will give you away." He plucked off her hat as she lifted a saddle on her pony. "Morag, your lovely hair, what have you done?"

They stared at her in horror.

"What I had to, to find Euan and Johnnie," she said mounting her pony. She'd used sheep shears and knew her hair looked like ragged stalks of brown hay. She didn't tell them she'd bound her breasts as well.

Dougie gave her father a questioning look, shrugged and followed her.

"Father, tell Granny Mac I'm sorry I willna be there this morning. Would you ask Isabel see to her and check that Mary McBean and her baby are well?"

"I suppose so," muttered her disgruntled Father as they trotted down the muddy track to Fort William. He shouted, "I'll move to the shieling, take more of the cows. We've a chance up there."

Morag scanned the peaceful valley and the loch beyond. *How long before the redcoats arrive?* She shivered then looked behind her. "May God protect you lass, for I canna," yelled her father. He went into the house and slammed the door.

"I think I've broken his heart." Morag sniffed using her hand to brush away the tears.

"I've known your father all my life. We were together in the 1715. He doesna want any harm to come to you. None of that weeping, I dinna want to be swimming all the way to Inverness."

The journey took hours. Maryburgh, the town that had nestled beside Fort William, had been burnt to the ground. The fort looked battered, though it still stood despite the Jacobite siege and teamed with redcoats.

"Dinna look them in the eye. Walk like me or they'll guess," muttered Dougie. She copied his confident stride, hands in belt. He showed a paper to one of the sentries who pointed them in the direction of a group of men heaving hessian bags full of loaves over their shoulders onto a dozen carts. Morag and Dougie joined them. After several hours they harnessed the horses, climbed aboard and joined a line of patient carters waiting to set off with a full military escort to Inverness.

Wade's military road made the journey easier and faster, but the mountains had ice caps and the air made them shiver with cold. She saw swirls of smoke in the distance as they passed burnt out cottages with stunned, sad-eyed people squatting on the ground. They tore at Morag's emotions because she could do nothing to help. She had to concentrate on Euan and their future together.

After travelling most of the morning one of their redcoat guard stopped them with a wave of a hand and said, "We'll rest here for half an hour."

Morag quenched her thirst and ate Dougie's warming soup.

"I'm going to water the horses," Dougie said.

She made to hand him a bucket.

He swept it aside saying, "I dinna need that. Follow me." He walked behind some undergrowth. "Turn your back," he said, "I willna look if you dinna." Then he pissed into the heather.

They camped that night beneath the stars at Laggan and she dreamt of finding Euan in Inverness or on the road and taking him home to Braedrumie and saying to her father, "There, this is what your daughter did. Now tell me I couldna do it because I'm no' a man." She woke with tears on her face and had to brush them away so none could see.

The journey continued until she wondered if her shaken bones could take any more. A sudden groaning from the swaying cart in front alerted them to a problem as the front wheel collapsed with a crack. The carter jerked forwards. The horses neighed, rearing in panic as they tangled themselves in their leather traces. Hundreds of loaves rolled and spun onto the earth. The soldiers cursed, but ordered the carters to help by stuffing the bread back in the sacks as well as unhitching and unloading the cart. Then the redcoats set about the task of taking the wheel off its axle and replacing the broken parts.

Dougie calmed the horses, whilst Morag gave them water and itched to get to Inverness and find Euan. She glanced across at a little church surrounded by a low stone wall. The doors creaked open and several ragged, barefoot children shot out. They ran round the gravestones whooping and hollering and charged through the wooden gate. They stopped, bug-eyed when they saw the sweating soldiers in their shirt sleeves trying to mend the wheel.

A laughing thin faced man with his arm around a slender, smiling woman stepped out of the church into the bright sunlight. She'd a baby in her arms.

Perhaps she'd just been churched or the babe had been christened Morag mused. The rest of the church community came behind them. They froze and stared at the redcoats.

A red haired boy moved like lightning and grabbed a loaf of bread which had rolled behind a nettle patch.

The mother shouted, "Conall, no."

He threw it and it hit a redcoat's shoulder.

Another dark haired boy grabbed a stone.

"No, James," yelled his father, too late. James hurled it. A soldier held his cheek as blood welled.

The soldiers shouted, the mother shrieked and her baby cried. The father stepped forward to protect his sons, but two burly redcoats who'd been mending the wheel held him fast. The boys screamed as angry soldiers grabbed them. The mother, white faced, shielded her remaining children.

"They're only bairns, they dinna ken what they're doing. Let them go," shouted the father. The baby cried louder.

"Taylor, Sanderson, Miller, load muskets."

The father struggled to be free.

Morag watched with the others, not quite comprehending.

"Oh no, God no. They're only bairns. They meant nothing by it," shrieked their mother. The baby howled with her.

"Present. Aim..."

They couldna shoot bairns? No one could be that cruel. Morag was about to shout, but Dougie clasped his hand over her mouth.

The redcoats aimed their muskets at the two quivering boys.

"They're only bairns," sobbed their mother on her knees. She clutched the scarlet faced babe to her breasts, trying to stifle its cries.

"We canna do anything," hissed Dougie as Morag struggled in his iron grip. She closed her eyes and prayed for the boy's souls.

The sergeant yelled, "Fire!"

The fusillade of shots sent ravens fluttering out of trees. The mother sagged and the boys shrieked in fright.

"Let that be a lesson to you. Next time we will shoot 'em," said the sergeant. "You need to teach your brats better manners." The soldiers laughed as the tearful boys ran to their mother.

They let the father go. Grim faced he put his arm round his weeping wife and screeching baby, gathered the rest of his family around him and walked away. He ignored the redcoats and looked into the distance as if he could see something there that no one else could. Morag thought he looked a noble figure. His neighbours hurried behind.

A few of the soldiers sniggered.

"Shut up and get on with it. We haven't got all day," bellowed the sergeant and then he winked at Dougie who winked back.

"What's that about?" Morag asked.

"They could have shot those boys, or the whole family for that matter. There's worse happening around here every day."

"Cruel."

"But those bairns lived. That sergeant gave them a warning and showed them mercy. I never thought I'd live to see the day. Those boys will tread softly around redcoats in the future and that might just keep them alive."

The father must have agreed with him, or perhaps just wanted them on their way. He returned a few minutes later with his tools and helped the soldiers mend the wooden spokes. The men worked together in silence and it was his strong back that lifted the cart so the wheel slotted into place. The father gathered up his implements and strode off.

CHAPTER Forty

Euan came to with a scream in his throat, his clothes soaked in sweat and Alfie's hand clasped over his mouth.

Alfie said, "You had a fever. The surgeon cupped you."

So that's why my chest hurts. He looked at the lanced blisters. "If that bloody quack comes near me again, I'll spear him with his own knife."

"Said your blood was too 'ot, and the 'umours needed to be properly balanced."

How the hell can I get away from this place, if I can hardly walk? What about Morag and Braedrumie? The redcoats will plunder and maraud. I need to get home, but how? Alfie even has to help me piss. Euan never thought he'd have an Englishman as a friend.

Alfie talked about the south and the flat lands of Essex; the Thames marshes and the rolling hills of Hertfordshire. "I've been to London once, too many folks intent on their business. No time for anyone else. And the noise. Give me my quiet village, Royston, any day and the smell of malt brewin'. I was an apprentice farrier by trade, the recruitin' sergeant got me drunk in the *Old Bull* and by the time I'd woken up next mornin', I'd taken the King's shillin'. I'd no one to care about so 'ere I am. And your family?"

"Canna remember; it's the knock on my head."

Alfie gave him an odd look then talked of the battle and his eyes glinted. "It were gut wrenchin' watchin' them Jacobites get a poundin'. When they ran at the line with those swords, I swear my stomach stuck to my backbone. Remember before the battle when we celebrated Cumberland's birthday and filled our bellies?"

Euan grimaced, the Jacobites had been ravenous.

"And it's Cumberland who supplies us glorious wounded with the cheese and wine you like. He ordered that the poor, bloody Jacobites had to be left on the moor to die, or shot out of hand. Good thing we won."

"There must be some prisoners."

"They're held in churches, ships or marched south to await trial."

Euan thought about his brothers and Dougie. How many Stewarts survived the battle? He'd saved cheese and wine from his rations for the trek home. He had to escape, every morning they carried the dead out of this place.

One afternoon after the quack's ministrations, Alfie looked glum. "Says I'm fit for duty." He packed and gave Euan a searching glance. "Looks like your fever's gone. Take care, old son, I'll come back and visit." He shook Euan's hand and rejoined his regiment.

Euan missed him and his cheerful talk of home. *Perhaps not all Englishmen are bad.*

Euan had taken to walking a little further every day. If he overdid it, he'd a cold sweat and felt as weak as a child.

The quack tut-tutted. "Fresh air is contrary to the humours, young man. We need you fit for duty. I'll purge you tomorrow. Fortunate you're a British soldier. They captured that Jacobite who escaped, threw him in with the wounded in the old church. Dead meat."

A bayonet thrust of despair stabbed at Euan.

"Thanks, sir." The redcoat wounded slapped each other on the back and money changed hands.

Strange to think that without Rob's help, that Jacobite prisoner could have been him, thought Euan.

"Who's volunteerin' for the firin' squad? Nothin' Captain Hartlass likes better than killin' unarmed men," said one wounded redcoat.

Euan suppressed a shudder. *To think those Jacobites, my family, friends came through the battle to die defenceless in a churchyard and I canna help them. Poor devils.*

"Who's Morag?" asked the quack.

Euan's heart missed a beat and he mumbled, "Just a lass." What had he said when unconscious or sleeping? Had he given anything away when he woke screaming? It was like living with a bayonet at his back. One wrong word and he'd be a dead man.

He dreamt of the blue waters of Loch Linnhe and the green pastures of Braedrumie. He knew Morag would be his forever. God how he missed her.

He looked at his hands and tried to still their trembling. He'd been on a constant state of alert for weeks, surrounded by redcoats who spoke in English, Hanoverian, and Dutch. He couldn't take much more. He'd a plan, just a few more days to gain strength, then home.

CHAPTER Forty-one

"It's beautiful," said Morag as she sat in on the rickety cart with Dougie heading for Inverness. She looked out to the ripple of indigo mountains and then turned her gaze to slopes covered in purple heather where crows wheeled over a distant castle. She caught the flash of bridle and the small shape of a rider winding along a track that disappeared into the hills.

Dougie's attention was elsewhere watching a cloud of dust on the road ahead. He pointed. "Your eyes are better than mine. What do you see?"

"Redcoats riding fast as if they're after someone."

The redcoats hauled their lathered horses to a halt and an officer shouted, "Seen riders on the road, anyone who could be the prince?" They shook their heads, but one of the soldiers pointed to the hills.

So, he's spotted the horseman too.

Dougie clasped her arm in warning. Sensing someone beside her, Morag turned and stared at a familiar face in a redcoat uniform. She'd forgotten his ocean-blue eyes. Her look of stunned horror met Rob's look of astonishment. He recovered, his face a mask of unconcern. She looked away and chewed her lip. *Was he at Culloden? Rob and Dougie were close, did the tacksman know Rob had enlisted? Will Rob betray us? He knows we'd never work for the redcoats, unless forced.*

Rob looked as if he was going to say something when a commanding figure on a grey horse issued an order to a long jawed officer, "Captain Hartlass, take your men and capture that damned rider."

"Sir. Come, Romsey." Captain Hartlass beckoned his dog, a curly coated retriever, and ordered a group of soldiers to break off from the main body and follow him.

"Captain Stewart, you're to accompany me to the castle. Let's see if our princely fox is there."

"Sir." Without a glance at Dougie or Morag, Rob followed the grey horse and rode off.

Morag sighed with relief. *He recognised us, but said nothing.* For that she'd always be grateful. He must be wondering what two Jacobites were doing taking bread to Inverness to feed redcoats. *How could he join the British army?*

"Never thought I'd see the day," said Dougie and spat into the grass.

The sun beat down on Morag, insects droned in the bracken and Loch Ness shimmered as some hours later Captain Hartlass caught up with their carts again.

"They've a captive," Morag said nudging Dougie to look at the woman prisoner whose hands were tied behind her back. Dirt and dust clung to her bodice and skirts, as if she'd been wrestled to the ground. Morag took pity on her. *Jesu only knows what she's done.* Rob was nowhere to be seen.

Morag watched in mounting horror as a sergeant hauled his prisoner from her saddle. "A fancy piece, she helped Charlie escape." The woman kicked him and he slapped her across the face sending her sprawling onto the road. "Tie her to the last cart, she can walk to Inverness," he ordered as he limped away.

Morag elbowed Dougie. Morag waited. When the sentries moved away, she whispered to Dougie, "Distract them."

Dougie strolled up to them, pipe in mouth and a bulging leather pouch in his hand. "Tobacco, lads?" He used his broad back to shield Morag and the woman from view.

"Thank you." The woman gulped at the water and chewed the bread with small, white teeth. Her green eyes blazed from under fronds of auburn hair. A livid bruise had appeared on one cheek.

Morag peered at the woman. *Do I know her?*

A redcoat shoved Morag away at bayonet point. "Clear off, she's gaol bait."

Morag moved. *The woman wears the dress of a washer woman, yet speaks like a high born Scottish lady. I've seen those eyes and that hair before, but where? In Braedrumie – no. The baggage train – no.* She cast her mind back to the first Holyrood ball and the entrance of red haired Lady Anne Kerr in a lilac gown. She'd been met with disparaging looks and malicious talk of her being a Whig. Realisation came to Morag in a flash. *Of course, **this is Lady Anne**, the woman Rob jilted and I last saw with the Prince. Why's she tied to a cart and bound for Inverness Gaol?*

She'd no time to ponder more, as much as she wanted to help Anne Kerr, she'd Euan to think about. *Where is he? Lying wounded or dying on some Godforsaken moor with no one to ease his pains or his passing? We have to get to Inverness and find him.*

CHAPTER Forty-two

Several shots roused Euan just after midnight. Sweat poured out of him. *Have the redcoats realised who I am?* He summoned his strength to sit up on his pallet when some minutes later one of the guards clattered in. "A bloody Jacobite's escaped from the church."

Euan let out his breath, prayed for the man and envied his bid for freedom. One day it would be him.

The following morning, despite his disturbed night Euan was stronger and the headaches had lessened. "Having trouble with my eyes, everything's a bit blurred," he lied to the quack.

The quack's face hardened. "Dear me, and I wanted you fit for active service today. I could use leeches or hot poultices made up of cow dung. A cart for the wounded is going south in a couple of days. Let's see if your vision clears for that."

Not south.

The other soldiers muttered amongst themselves. Euan heard the word *malingerer* and saw the quack fumble with some probes. He dropped them on the dirty straw, wiped them on his jacket sleeve and threw them in his bag. Most of his patients died, but he seemed to view Euan as one of his successes. "Without the blood-letting," he told the wounded, "he'd have been dead within the week." He looked sideways at Euan and tapped the side of his nose.

Did the quack suspect? Prickles of concern ran up and down Euan's spine. He'd been walking further each day and the sentries joked with him as he passed now. Euan didn't want to be shot as a deserter and needed a change of clothes. Then it came to him, his Uncle and Aunt Munro and Cousin Jack. Why hadn't he thought of them before? The dull ache of his head reminded him why. The Munro's had a house in Inverness. If his memory served him well, he just had to cross Ness Bridge, walk along Bridge Street and turn into Church Street. He'd escape tomorrow.

He'd been mulling this over, when Alfie arrived full of news, pulled up the stool and sat beside him. "You know that prisoner who escaped? 'E 'asn't been caught. Someone got the sentries roaring drunk, tied 'em up and unlocked the door. They found a couple of whisky bottles beside 'em. Where would privates find the money to buy them I'd like to know? Captain 'artlass' is a laughin' stock, boasted no one could get past **his** sentries. 'Es 'ad 'em whipped senseless."

Euan silently wished the escaped Jacobite safe home.

Alfie lowered his voice. "The captain's not popular cos he made us watch the deserters' 'angings. Reckon he's lousy too, never stops scratchin'. Must be desperate if they wants his blood." Alfie paused and looked thoughtfully at Euan and then away as if he was in another place. "My pal deserted. When he run, he took 'artlass' best breeches and shirt with him. When he was caught 'artlass made 'im wear 'em. It were a rum thing watchin' 'im 'ang. Bein' made to watch your mates kickin' at the end of a rope does somethin' to you, deep down. It's like somethin' in you dies with them. I hates that 'artlass along with the rest. He oughta watch out, cos talk is it ain't only them Jacobites he's got to worry about now." Alfie looked gloomy then brightened. "I'm 'opin' the regiment will march back to England soon. Pity these missing fingers weren't on my right 'and 'cos I wouldn't be able to fire a musket and they'd have to send me 'ome."

"I hope you get home, Alfie," Euan said and meant it. He'd been a good friend for a Sassenach.

Alfie lowered his voice again. "I think you should go 'ome too, John, soon. That's why I come. You talked wild some nights, what I heard made me think. Wouldn't want to go to another 'angin', John, if you catch my drift?" He held out his right hand and Euan shook it. "Don't suppose we'll meet again in this world. I wish you all the best."

"You're a good man, Alfie Smith," Euan said. "I wish you the same." Then Alfie left.

Euan gathered what little he had: some cheese and several oatmeal biscuits and stuffed them in a dirty neck cloth. Euan knew the hills round Bradrumie would be covered in heather and gorse in April, though the mountain peaks would be topped with ice. He had to leave now, before the redcoats reached the village.

"Play a hand?" asked one soldier waving a grubby deck of cards at him.

"No thanks."

The soldier spat on the straw and shrugged. "Your choice."

Euan walked on, feeling every eye on him and stealing himself for a shout or a hand on his shoulder. He tripped. *Damn.*

"Mind what you're doin'," said a soldier, moving his bandaged foot out of Euan's way.

"Sorry."

"It's alright, mate," the soldier said between brown teeth. "This should get me 'ome, back on the farm." He indicated his bloody bandage. "No more soldiering for me, more's the pity, it's a good life. Just 'opes it don't slow me down so I can pay me way. Don't want to end up beggin'. Name's Bill, Bill Townsend, you?"

God. "John Maxwell. We'll talk when I come back, alright? Quack says I need exercise."

"See you when you get back, John."

Euan breathed a sigh of relief as he headed out the door.

The sun shone, but a cool breeze rippled the River Ness. He forced himself to stroll like a soldier with no cares and within ten minutes he reached Aunt Munro's. No one answered his knocks, so he ventured round the back. Someone had barred the doorway with a splintered dresser, wobbly table and broken chairs. He pulled them away to find the lock on the door broken and the house ransacked. His uncle a Whig, his aunt a Jacobite and their son Jack, the same age as Euan, had been caught in the middle of this rebellion. Euan searched the premises, but found no sign of the Munros.

Safe? Euan hoped so. His head spun. The walk had exhausted him and shards of pain stabbed behind his eyes. He crawled up the stairs and into his aunt's bedroom. Then staggered to the four poster bed and lay on one of his aunt's torn sheets. *Why torn?* His eyelids closed and he slept.

He woke in the dark, used water from a pail in the kitchen and washed. He found half a stale loaf and a small chunk of mouldy cheese on a low shelf in the pantry. He needed a change of clothes so went upstairs and raided Jack's wardrobe.

Downstairs a floorboard protested. He opened the bedroom door and listened to the furtive footsteps and whispers filtering up from below. *More than one.*

"Bet we'll get a pretty price for the valuables. 'Er 'usband might be a Whig, but she's a damned Jacobite. Got it comin' to 'er," hissed one voice.

"Sssh. We'll 'ang if we're caught," said another.

"Just fetch that bag 'ere. Coo look at this! Bet the best stuff's upstairs." A stair squeaked.

Looters. Euan didn't wait to hear any more. He couldn't afford to be caught in the house and didn't want to disturb them. The noise would rouse every redcoat for miles. He thanked God for well-oiled runners when he slid open the sash window. The ground loomed about 15ft below. He just remembered to grab the cheese and biscuits before he jumped.

It didn't take him long to discover that all the roads out of Inverness were guarded, the sentries alert and asking for passes. He found a wynd littered with discarded rubbish where he sat and waited for dawn. He had to get home.

CHAPTER Forty-three

The provision carts carrying Morag and Dougie arrived on the outskirts of Inverness just as the first crimson streaks lit the sky. The castle had been blown up by the Jacobites so the government army had been forced to camp on the moor. Morag stood in front of an ocean of redcoat tents.

Anne Kerr leant on the cart. She lifted her head like a flower on a slender stalk when they manacled her and held her shoulders back as two huge redcoats bundled her away.

Morag watched her go. She wanted to help, but her priority had to be finding Euan and Johnnie. Sighing, she joined Dougie unloading and stacking the bread. They finished at midday, trudged to Inverness and found lodgings in the *Crooked Billet*.

"A pint of your good ale, landlord and one yourself." Dougie slapped coins on the bar. He leant forward. "Must have been terrible having a battle so close."

"Aye." The landlord put his bulbous nose close to Dougie's and quirked an eyebrow at him.

Dougie slapped more coins on the bar.

The landlord looked at the coins, then Dougie and scooped them up.

"The redcoats' blood was up. They were shootin' and cuttin' the Jacobites to pieces as they ran away. The dead and wounded stretched from the moor to here and there was fightin' in the streets and on the bridge, never seen anythin' like it, hackin' and cuttin' at each other like demons. Sensible folk stayed indoors."

Morag turned her face away. *Poor Euan and Johnnie.*

The landlord put Dougie's ale on the counter. "Where you from?"

"North of here. We're helping the army bring in bread. Don't get much excitement on a farm."

"I dinna suppose you do. I saw Cumberland ride into Inverness waving his sword about."

"Really? Did many escape?" Dougie asked.

"A few, I know of one from the old church. The bridges and roads are well guarded, he willna get far. Shot the rest yesterday."

Morag's knees sagged as hope seeped out of her.

"There's prisoners held on ships at the quay. They're to be shipped to London for trial. Poor beggars."

"Thank you." Dougie finished his ale and took Morag's arm. "I think we'll take a wee stroll. We've never been to Inverness before."

Morag let Dougie lead her down to the cobbled quayside, past rowdy taverns heaving with redcoats and British sailors. She quailed at the number of sentries lining the quay. The stink and moans emanating from several ships' holds did nothing to reassure her. They couldn't get close without arousing suspicion.

Dougie spent the afternoon and evening scouring taverns, whilst she searched wynds, under arches, in barns and doorways. Nothing.

Morag's hope of finding Euan receded as darkness fell, candles twinkled through chinks in shutters and torch flames did fevered jigs. Still nothing. They'd wasted their time.

"It's no good, lass," said Dougie at last. "We'd best get back to the inn."

"There must be something we can do, someone who could help. Who do you ken in Inverness?"

"Why would I ken anyone here? It's full of strangers who dinna speak properly."

"Dougie." *Can he no see we mustna give up now?*

"I'm thinking." He paused and ran his fingers through his beard. "The family's got an aunt ... Muir ... no ... Murray ... no ... Munro ... that's it."

"Kirsty Lorne and her mother were going to stay with her. Do you ken the street?"

Dougie scratched his beard. "It begins with ..."

"Dougie." Morag jumped up and down in frustration.

"Church Street, Munro House, Church Street. I'm sure that's it."

"Well done." She tugged his hand. "We must hurry, it's our last chance. He might be there."

They arrived to see that broken stools, tables and chairs littered the street. The doors and windows hung open at drunken angles. A cat screeched in a wynd nearby and someone swore.

"Oh, no." *He couldna be here, could he?*

"Stand inside the door. I'll search the house." Dougie disappeared into the gloom as someone sawed at an out of tune fiddle down the street.

Morag wished Dougie would hurry. Within minutes he joined her and shook his head.

Desperation clawed at her throat. *We have to be ready to return to Fort William with the carts at dawn tomorrow. If we dinna find Euan tonight, we'll have to leave without him. He could be lying out on the moors wounded or dead. What a fruitless task we've set ourselves.*

They padded back through the shadows to the *Crooked Billet* when Morag saw a tall, lone figure singing to himself. He tripped, righted himself and staggered on in front of them. His auburn hair, broad shoulders and low, rich voice reminded her of Euan. It hit her like an iron fist. *It is Euan and he's approaching two sentries. Why head south? He must realise redcoats guard every road. Breathe, just breathe.*

Dougie put a restraining arm on hers.

"Even' sofficers, it'sh a lovely night."

Her stomach coiled into a tight ball. *If the redcoats suspect, he'll be shot.*

"Get home to your bed, you're drunk." The sentry gestured at Euan with his bayonet.

"That's what I wanna do, go home." Euan staggered round them.

Their muskets rose. "Halt! You're not crossing this bridge. Not without a pass."

"Haven't go' a pash."

"Then go home." The sentry jabbed his bayonet at him.

"It'sh over there." Euan grinned. His forefinger pointed behind the sentry to the distant hills.

Morag couldn't let them arrest him, not when she'd found him again. Struggling free of Dougie, she shouted, "Father, are you drunk again?" She stood arms akimbo in an oversized shirt, brown breeches, holed hose and worn shoes.

Dougie, the sentries and Euan stared at her.

"I'm sorry, sirs." She indicated Euan with her thumb. "But he thinks mother's still alive and we live in Edinburgh. When he's drinking there's no doing with him. Isna that right, Grandfather?" She looked at Dougie.

Dougie gulped and managed a strangled, "Yes."

"Come away with me, Father." Morag took Euan's hand. "And we'll go home."

"That's it, Mister let the lad take you home," a sentry agreed.

Euan looked bewildered. Morag pulled his hand. Euan stared at Dougie, her and Dougie again. A spurt of recognition and his jaw dropped.

Why didna he move?

Speechless, Euan let Morag lead him away.

"That's it lad, go and sleep it off," the second sentry shouted.

As soon as they were over the brow of the hill, she hissed, "Euan Stewart, how can you be drunk? Why ..."

"I'm as sober as a priest." Euan straightened up and rubbed his brow. "If you hadna stopped me I'd have been through the sentry post."

"I saved you, you thankless loon, they were going to throw you in gaol."

"Loon." His brows lowered.

Morag couldn't help herself as she flung herself at him. "Euan, I missed you so. We've been so worried about you with no word whether you were alive or dead. Why, you're just skin and bone."

"Morag, my heart, is it really you?" He peered under her bonnet and searched her face. "I was wounded and ... I lost your cross."

"As if I care. Are you alright?" She searched him for some sign of injury.

"My head's fine now. There's some benefit to having a thick skull. Dougie, how could you bring her to Inverness, man? You of all people know the dangers."

"Ah, hush, Euan. Dinna blame Dougie, he couldna stop me." Morag snuggled up to him.

"Wild bullocks wouldna have stopped her," agreed Dougie.

Euan held her at a distance. "Let me look at you. You're still as beautiful as I remember, but you shouldna have come to Inverness." Euan stood back from her. "Those breeches are no' proper."

"We tried to tell her." Dougie shook his head. "She's more headstrong than ever."

Morag's eyes blazed at them both. "No I'm not. Euan, how did you get away?"

Euan laughed and kissed her. "Someone, Rob I think, saved me after the battle." His words tumbled out. "Made it look like I was a redcoat and put me amongst their wounded. Thank God for him, I took a blow to the head and wasna thinking straight at the time. He's joined their army, unless I dreamt it."

Morag stared, mouthing air, the image of Rob in his red uniform searing her brain. She shivered, a cold wind had picked up. The dark streets, overhanging buildings and narrow wynds seemed menacing. "We need to get back to the inn."

She clung to Euan as they walked, enjoying his closeness and warmth. She never wanted to be parted from him again.

Dougie said, "We met Rob on the road, one of a group of redcoats after the prince. He could have given us away, he didna."

"What about Johnnie and Duncan?"

"Duncan died at Culloden." Dougie squeezed Euan's shoulder.

Euan rubbed his brow and looked at the ground. "Poor Duncan."

"After... the battle, Johnnie said he'd head for here. He was worried about Kirsty," said Dougie. "Didna realise she's back in Braedrumie."

"How's Father and everyone?" asked Euan.

"Braedrumie's fine, your father is ... as well as can be expected considering ..." Morag began.

"He's no' well in the head," Dougie said blunt as usual. "The drink."

"He's not taken the news well then. And the prince?"

"Still on the run." Dougie grimaced.

"So The Cause is dead." Euan hung his head. "All those lives, for a prince full of empty promises."

"Oh Euan," Morag linked arms as they took him back to the twinkling lights and raucous sounds in the *Crooked Billet*. The heat and noise of the inn were a stark contrast to the cold outside. A blanket of stale ale, sweat and tobacco enveloped them.

To Morag's horror, Euan insisted on pushing his way through the throng of uniforms to the dimly lit bar to get them some ale and beds for the night. He'd accepted coins from Dougie, clinked them in his hand and had disappeared into the fug where every mouth held a clay pipe. Dougie took Morag by the arm and led her to a place by the fire where they sat on the settle, warmed their hands and waited.

Morag chewed her lip. *Will Euan be arrested? Thank goodness the soldiers seem too fuddled by drink to notice him.*

After a time, Morag's finger drew a circle in a puddle of ale on the table. "Dougie ... you and Isabel ... did you ... miss each other when you were away all those months?"

Dougie sighed and turned to her. "I've known my Isabel all my life. You see her now as an old woman. In her youth she was a beauty, had all the men after her. But she chose me, Lord knows why. And there's no' been a day in my life I havena loved her and been grateful that my love's been returned."

"So you'll know how I feel about Euan. I've missed him so for all these months, I just want …"

"I know what you want lass. That's why the good Lord, in his infinite wisdom, created wedlock." They sat in studied silence until Euan arrived with tankards of spiced ale. He stared from one to the other, perhaps sensing an atmosphere.

"Problem?" Euan asked.

"No." Morag raised her tankard and drank.

"Nothing a good night's sleep won't solve. Sup up, man, we're going home tomorrow." Dougie gulped his ale down without taking a breath.

CHAPTER Forty-four

The following morning, Morag tried to calm herself as they greeted the other carters blowing on their hands and stamping their feet because of the cold. A rim of light appeared above the distant hills as rain drizzled down turning roads into muddy lakes. Damp hung in the air. Even the redcoat tents seemed to shiver in the stiff breeze blowing over the encampment outside Inverness.

Morag tried to appear unconcerned as Dougie winked at Euan. They'd passed several sentries and as soon as Dougie put Tolbain's paper under their noses, had been waved through.

Thank goodness the redcoats ignored them as they loaded barrels onto the carts.

Euan slipped towards the back of the cart as Dougie sidled up to the nearest guard. "It's a cold morning. Fancy a swig, laddie? It's fine whisky and will warm you."

The sentry sniffed the flask and scanned the area.

"No one's about. Go on." Dougie urged.

The sentry closed his lips round the flask as Euan slid between the barrels on their cart and lay flat. Morag covered him and their cargo with a canvas.

The sentry smacked his lips. "Uncommon fine whisky, I thank you." He took up his position again.

Dougie winked at Morag, she gave an answering nod. *Is it going to be this easy?* With a snap of the reins and rumbling wheels they set off for Inverness as light streamed down on them from behind pendulous clouds.

Reveille sounded behind them, the signal for the redcoat encampment to wake.

Sometime later Morag and Dougie turned into Friar's Lane in Inverness, bordered by double fronted houses and single storey dwellings. A mongrel, his ribs showing, stopped his search for food in stinking offal and stared at them. A mangy ginger cat hissed, arched its back and shot off down a wynd.

"Halt!" barked a grim faced redcoat who ran in front of them whilst another held the horses' bridles.

Sweet Jesu, to be caught now and still over sixty miles from home.

"Whoa!" said Dougie.

Had Euan been spotted clambering into the cart? She could see Dougie's brow furrow with worry. *If caught we'll all be executed.* She gnawed her fingernails as the horses snorted, stamping their hooves. Theirs was the last cart in a convoy of twelve.

By the time they heard the sound of marching boots Dougie's face had turned ashen and Morag's nails were bitten to the quick. *Why have we been stopped?* A red tide of uniforms flooded into the street. Musket butts hammered on doors and families were dragged out of their homes and herded round the corner into Bridge Street, their protests ignored.

Shouted orders filled the air and drums began a funereal beat.

"What are they doing?" Morag's knuckles were white from gripping the cart as a woman shrieked, a man growled and a child cried.

"I dinna ken." Dougie spoke between tight lips. "Dinna like the look of this."

Redcoats waved them on. Dougie snapped the reins, the horses strained, but the cart wheels refused to move in the glutinous mud. *Will Euan be discovered?* A command rang out and soldiers put their shoulders to the wheels and the cart surged forward. Morag clutched at Dougie's arm. The redcoats cursed as brown mud splattered their uniforms.

After 400 yards they turned into Bridge Street. Nothing prepared Morag for what she saw. The silence hit her first. The crowd remained still. One man clenched his jaw, a second his fists and another stared at the ground. A woman wept, another shed silent tears and hid her children's heads as soldiers stood to attention in two ranks across Ness Bridge. Two lines of wounded Jacobites sprawled inside their bristling cordon. Some wore only shirts and others held their hands over their privates, trying to conceal their nakedness. Blood and dirt encased them all. *Jesu, they've received scant food or treatment of wounds.*

"They're being humiliated."

"Not a word more. We can do nothing. Keep your eyes on the road." Dougie clenched his teeth. "They're proud men treated worse than animals. It's the perpetrators of this foul deed who are shamed this day."

Morag could only imagine Euan's thoughts under the canvas in the cart. Dougie urged the horses on. She couldn't speak. She'd a lump like a thistle in her throat. One tear escaped.

"Dinna cry, don't you dare," Dougie snarled at her. "They dinna want your pity. They want you to be strong, so you can tell their families they fought bravely for The Cause they believed in."

Morag and Dougie sat upright in the cart, like two statues looking nowhere but forwards. The grey clouds which had gathered over the grey hills descended on Inverness and the storm broke over them in a torrential downpour.

CHAPTER Forty-five

Morag, Dougie and Euan, their secret passenger, had travelled several miles along the Great Glen. By late afternoon the sun came out from behind layers of clouds and dried the clothes on their backs. Moorland gleamed with sage and jade and smudges of maroon and ochre, washed by the storm.

Their horses pulled the laden carts up the track as sinew and muscle worked together. Sunlight flooded the glen below them. A dog barked and Dougie nudged Morag and pointed at the scene.

"Watch Hartlass," said a guard, "he's the very devil."

Oh God, no.

Hartlass directed a group of redcoats to circle the croft and line a quaking woman and man against its stone wall. Morag saw the sparks and little puffs of smoke from the muskets and heard the shots as the couple crumpled to the ground.

No.

Dougie snapped at the reins urging the cart horses to pull harder up the incline.

Morag had to sit and watch as another party, led again by Hartlass, went inside the dwelling as others gathered the lowing black cattle. Hens clucked and fluttered as soldiers made grabs at them. One redcoat flung himself headlong in the dirt, the dust exploding around him and his empty outstretched hands. He picked himself up and sneezed as his friends jeered. Their meaty fists were full of fluttering birds suspended by their feet.

High pitched screams came from the croft and made them turn. Dougie put a hand on Morag's shoulder. His eyes warned: nothing we can do. The door of the croft flew open.

"Mother! Father!" A girl, perhaps fourteen, raced out, clothes in disarray and hair like black ribbons. Blood trickled down her bare legs onto her feet as a dog nipped at her heels. A few minutes later sniggering soldiers adjusting their breeches, followed her and thumped each other's backs.

Hartlass gave an order; torches were lit and flung onto the thatch. It caught immediately and a stream of yellow flames rippled along the roof.

Morag's hand went to her mouth. With mounting horror, she watched the girl, tripping and stumbling arrive at the base of a cliff face. She scrambled upwards as the dog barked and then leapt with open jaws at her bare legs. Her feet kept stepping on her skirt hem on the way to the top.

Please let her escape.

"Bring the bitch back," ordered Hartlass.

A couple of redcoats set out after her, gesturing and shouting ribald comments from below. She clung to the rock, but her fingers slipped.

The soldiers moved back as her body broke on the jagged rocks beside them. Silence.

The dog kept barking. Someone made a joke. The redcoats laughed and strolled away.

Dougie spat on the ground and Morag wiped hot tears away with her jacket sleeve. *Have we to sit here and watch such cruelty and do nothing?*

Crimson and turquoise flames spurted out of windows and the thatched roof. Black smoke engulfed the croft, curled in columns into the sky and drifted across the glen, signalling the death knell of its inhabitants.

Morag overheard the tight-lipped soldiers escorting them muttering amongst themselves.

"God curse Hartlass."

"If ever a man was well named, it's 'im."

"The devil took 'is 'eart and threw away the key," said another and spat a stream of brown tobacco on the road.

Morag wanted to cry, but tears didn't come.

The redcoats spurred ahead. The carts trundled in their wake, like a funeral procession following the windings and undulations of the road. The farmyard animals, destined for markets in the south, had been driven away by soldiers. No clucking, no hooves rattling, no smoke from crofts, no hum of human activity, no chatter and no laughter remained. Nothing stirred.

Morag struggled to speak and then gave up. *How can men do such things to others?* The acrid stink of burning was their constant companion now. She turned her head away from any habitation. Their journey became a road of sighs.

***

"Euan's not in the cart," Morag whispered to Dougie. They'd stopped for the night and she'd taken Euan something to eat and drink.

"Perhaps he thought it better to leave us now and head for Braedrumie over the hills."

"But why didna he tell us, why didna he tell me?" asked Morag.

"I dinna ken, lass."

"Dougie, I dinna like it. It's no' like him. I feel … I feel he's in danger. How could he do that, put himself in harm's way again when we've risked our lives to save him? Hasna he had enough of killing and fighting?"

"Calm down lass, you'll make the sentries suspicious." Dougie nodded to one in the distance who nodded back. "He couldna have stayed with us all the way to Fort William. Better he slips away in the countryside."

"But it's full of redcoats and he's still no' well. If he's captured …" began Morag.

"No point in worrying. We canna make a better of it, but kenning Euan he'll have a good reason for making his move now," hissed Dougie.

***

The reason sat on a horse about 50 yards away. Euan lay concealed behind bracken, staring at a redcoat officer, but was he the one Euan wanted? The man became lost in the gloom and fires of the redcoat camp, the same soldiers who'd raped an innocent girl and murdered her family.

A burning hate welled up in Euan as he watched the soldiers chatting and eating. *Devils incarnate.* He'd watched them through the narrow chinks of the planking of the cart. He saw men with civilisation and humanity stripped from them; they would do anything. *No discipline in their ranks just lust, avarice and cruelty.*

Whilst everyone had watched the young girl fall to her death, Euan had left the cart without a word. He knew Morag would have tried to stop him, there'd have been a fuss and the soldiers alerted.

Better I slip away, into the long grass, behind the gorse and granite rock. The image of Hartlass' face burned in his brain. Euan's hate coloured his thoughts. He longed for revenge for the mistreatment of the wounded; for the humiliation of the prisoners on the bridge; for every family who'd lost their homes or their lives and most of all for losing the battle. *I'll kill the bastard.*

Euan waited till they made camp and posted sentries. He knocked one out, took his musket and got an officer in his sights. Euan tested the wind, blowing to his left. He squeezed the trigger, aiming for the backbone. The officer turned. *Rob!*

CHAPTER Forty-six

"We must go to *Braedrumie House* first," said Morag.

"He willna be there," said Dougie. "If he's any sense, he'll be hiding in the heather."

Morag bit her lip in frustration. They'd heard a shot, then been delayed by a lame horse, flash floods and patrols looking for Prince Charlie. It had taken them days to return the carts to Fort William. Then they'd walked to Ballachulish, waited for a boat to cross Loch Leven and then walked to Braedrumie along hidden paths, fearful of redcoats, even though Dougie had a document decreeing their safe passage. Tired and impatient, she didn't want to listen to reason.

"Get down." Dougie put out a warning hand and drew his sword. "Someone's coming." They hid behind the gorse, pressing their bodies into the cold earth. Morag's heart raced.

Before Dougie could move a dirk pricked his throat. "I taught you well."

Morag saw Dougie look into Euan's twinkling grey eyes and sighed with relief.

"Or you're slowing down." Euan grinned at him. "Thought you were redcoats, they're sending out patrols all the time now."

Flinging herself at him, Morag cried, "Why did you go Euan? Why didna you tell me?" She beat his chest with her fists and then hung onto him and buried her head in his shirt in a fit of tears. "I love you so."

"I wish you well of her lad." Dougie shook his head. "She's so impatient I thought she'd throw herself off the ferry and swim with the silkies. There's been no living with her since you disappeared from the cart. How's the laird?"

"As you'd expect," Euan said holding Morag. "You were right he's no' taken Duncan's death well. Johnnie's back, he's hardly said a word, apart from saying cousin Jack died some months ago."

"Oh Euan I forgot to tell you." Morag held him tighter.

"I'm sorry to hear about Jack, but pleased Johnnie got home." Dougie put a comforting hand on Euan's shoulder.

Morag's tear stained face looked up at Euan. "I thought I might never see you again." She sniffed.

He kissed her and she gave herself up to his lips and eager mouth.

Dougie grinned. "Well, lad I can see you have your hands full. I'm away home, my Isabel will be worried."

"Dougie?" said Euan making him pause mid-stride.

"Yes?"

"Thank you, man." Euan shook his hand.

"Just doing my job." Dougie gave a half smile, waved and left.

Euan wrapped his arms around Morag's waist and his warm lips crushed hers again. Her body quivered.

He drew back and looked at her. "I dreamed of this day and night."

"I did too." She clung to his shirt trying to breathe all of him in. "Why did you leave the cart?"

"I wanted to kill Hartlass, but when he turned, it wasn't him, it was ... Rob."

"You didna ... you didna kill him?"

Euan laughed. "I let the musket discharge in the air and then ran. Morag, you didna think I'd kill my own brother, my own flesh and blood? Besides saving my life, Johnnie says Rob helped him too."

"Then I'll love him like a brother, redcoat or not because you've come back to me." *Dare I tell him I saw Rob in Edinburgh Castle? Perhaps no', Euan would know the danger I'd been in. He'd be furious.*

His lips brushed hers, seeking, nibbling, burning. Her head tilted back and her blue bonnet fell to the ground.

"Morag, what have you done?"

She ran her hand through the spikes. "It's getting longer every day. I did it for you, so I looked like a boy, so we'd have no ... problems with redcoats. Dinna look at me that way."

"My heart." He held her close. "I love you despite you looking like a half plucked hen." He ruffled her hair and ran.

"Euan Stewart. You come here." She set off in hot pursuit. He lay in wait and caught her so they arrived laughing and teasing each other in front of her deserted home. She'd forgotten her father was up at the shieling.

Euan waited till she'd changed into a bodice and skirt. She wrapped a shawl around her head and shoulders.

"Have you something to wear you could give to a woman?" he asked.

"A woman?" She squared up to him her eyes sparking. "What woman?"

"She's called Alais and there's two bairns as well."

"Two?" She marched up to him, a besom in her hands, demanding answers.

"Calm down." He took the broom from her and pulled her to him. "Johnnie brought her and two orphans back with him. She's called Alais and she doesna speak, no' a word. Johnnie says she's been like it since redcoats killed her family."

"Kirsty, willna like the idea of this Alais," said Morag.

"She hasna a choice. The house isna safe, so we're all up at the den. You'll mind it's where we used to play in the hot summers?"

She remembered the den, a cave high up in the mountains, with a pool fed by a stream.

"I'll look for some clothes." She bundled up some and they went to seek her father.

***

Morag heard the thud of his spade and the slap of the cut peat from some distance away. Her father stood up to his knees in muddy water clearing the ditch that ran between the sheiling and Benn a

Beithoir. Planting his wooden spade in the boggy peat, he shook Euan's outstretched hand. "You've had a bad time of it so they say, though there's hardly a mark on you. I've forgiven you for taking her away."

"Father, it was my decision." Morag pouted at him.

"Morag..." He hugged her. "You've your mother's strength. You said you'd bring Euan back and you have. I thought the redcoats would spy you out." Her shawl slipped revealing her shorn hair. His voice became waspish. -"I see you still look like a lad."

"Whisht, Father, it'll grow." She struggled free to cover her hair. "You'll see. I'm safe home because of it and so is Euan."

"It's the truth, sir."

"You must have some tales to tell round a fire at night. It's good to have you and Johnnie back, sorry to hear about Duncan."

"Thank you, sir."

"I know you've been busy fighting a war, but have you given any thought to the wedding?"

"Father."

"Of course, but I've just returned home, sir, as you know. We're grieving over... Duncan and there's family business I must attend to. You understand of course?"

Morag looked at her feet.

"I understand, but she's always been biddable in the past. Take my word for it, I know females, she needs a gentle, but firm hand."

A firm hand. Morag stormed off. She was her own person and didn't need a man's 'firm hand'. She climbed up Ben Uir and cooled her temper. Euan caught up with her when she flopped down exhausted on a worm eaten log beside a fast running stream. Crack! Half the log lurched towards the water. He grabbed her hand as she hung over the edge, put his arms round her waist and reeled her in.

"Just ..." she began.

"Just ...?"

"Just love me," she pleaded.

She knew he could have taken her then.

"I've thought of nothing but you for months, your voice, heather scent ... your body," he said. He smothered her in kisses, her lips, an ear, the nape of her neck...

She surrendered to each caress. *He can do this forever.*

Euan held her at arms' length, and let his breathing steady. "Do you no' think we'd better wed soon?" He grinned at her.

Jesu, at last. She grinned back.

CHAPTER Forty-seven
June 1746

The hot day buzzed with bees and the flutter of butterflies as Morag dumped her wicker washing basket on the ground. Every day the black smoke came nearer and streams of despairing crofters continually arrived in Braedrumie, but the hated redcoats did not.

"Only a matter of time," said Morag's father before he went off to dig peat to fuel the fire.

Morag gazed at the far mountains imagining soldiers swarming towards them and then resented the thought. It would ruin her morning if she thought about what the redcoats could do to Braedrumie. No. She'd think of Euan and their life together. She hummed as she draped washing over the heather bunched round the shieling. *Euan hasna mentioned our wedding again. How can it be accomplished with him a hunted man and no priest?*

A puce faced Isabel shouted and waved at her as she climbed up to the hillside.

"I swear … that hill's … steeper." Isabel took a few moments to catch her breath. "Have you heard about the falling out between Kirsty and Johnnie?"

Morag shook her head. *More trouble.*

"She's gone through a handfasting ceremony with Tolbain of all people."

Morag shook out a sheet. "No. How could she? Poor Johnnie, what happened?"

"Tolbain insisted on a grand ceremony in Fort William. Braedrumie's buzzing with it. Stuck up madam. He'll have wed her for the farm." Isabel lowered her voice. "They say there were terrible screams … on her bridal night. She got more than she bargained for if you ask me."

"Sweet Jesu." Morag stared at Isabel. *Tolbain could be cruel. Kirsty will spend the rest of her life regretting marrying him.* She let the sheet fall over clumps of heather.

"Yes. And now he's brought the village slut into their house."

"The man's depraved." Morag hung up a petticoat.

"Kirsty's made her bed ... think of Johnnie."

"Poor Johnnie." Morag shook her head as she sorted out pairs of woollen stockings.

"Lucky Johnnie, if you ask me. I never cared for Kirsty and her mother has a face like old boot leather. They're living in *Toll House* of course."

Morag pictured Tolbain's ancestral home sitting like a decaying tooth on the western edge of Loch Linnhe and wished it would tumble into the water.

***

Later that afternoon, Morag took a pack horse laden with supplies up to the den. The cave was big enough to shelter several people, had hidden entrances and lay deep in the mountains. She had to hide behind rock outcrops, shelter in woods, huddle beneath gorse and travel miles out of her way to avoid redcoat patrols.

Rocks clattered in the glen below her. She dismounted, hearing the tinkle of bridles, clatter of hooves and low English voices. *More redcoats.* Tying her pack horse to a fir tree she knelt on one knee and watched from behind the purple heather. A few officers on horseback commanded a crimson line of men sweeping the heather with bayonets fixed.

"Well, well. What have I here?" The familiar honey-sweet voice came from behind her.

Her skin crawled. *Tolbain.* She half covered her face with her shawl as she turned. Panic clawed its way up her spine as he and several bearded Highlanders came towards her.

He pushed her onto her back and waved his men away. "She's mine." His face had sagged into deeply carved lines since she'd last seen him.

Has he recognised me? She made to go, but he held her arm in a cruel grasp. "I thought ... do I know you?" He tugged at her shawl.

"No." She struggled with him.

Her hand caught his left arm and he grimaced. She guessed he nursed a wound. He shoved her back onto the grass and her shawl fell to the ground. "What the devil happened to your hair?"

"It ... it ... I was ill and it fell out," she lied.

"Never mind, I'm no' interested in your head." He ripped her bodice and squeezed her breast. Humiliation and pain shot through her.

"Please sir, I must be goin'." She tried to rise. "My father's ill and expectin' me. I'm late already."

He pressed his hand on her shoulder, forcing her to remain seated. "Your father?" He sneered. "He'd have been a Jacobite in the 1715. They all were round here, treacherous dogs." He hawked and spat in the heather. "These are bad times and the government has a long memory. Why, I think I've a letter on my desk suggesting sequestration of known Jacobite lands." He stroked her cheek.

It took an effort not to shudder. "Sir, I beg you, he's an old man and played no part in this rebellion. If he lost his land it would kill him."

"So we understand each other then. You want something from me and I desire something from you." He took her hand and put it to his britches so she was under no illusion as to his 'need'.

"But sir, you're recently married, you have a wife."

'A harpy, a self-willed harridan with a raving mother to boot." He ripped at Morag's laces. "I deserve a wife who knows her place; serves her husband properly and doesna put her mad mother first. She'll learn." He showed Morag his fist. 'Madness begets madness. If I'd known, I'd never have ... it's a handfast marriage, I like to test the goods first. I'll be rid of her in a year. I'll father no sons from that bitch." Spittle formed round his lips. "But you my beauty, I bet you'll drop many a fine litter." His hands were under her petticoat and making their way towards her thigh.

This man is insufferable. She thought fast. "Sir, I'm to be married."

"What of it? It shouldna make any difference, no' if you care about your father and want to eat." His fingers scrabbled at her garters. "I've always preferred virgin flesh, so ripe for plucking."

Desperate now she lied again. "I'm with child." She forced herself to blush as if in shame. "I've been so sick." A man strode towards them. *James Kinross. What's he doing here?*

"She's telling the truth," said Kinross.

Morag closed her eyes. *I never thought I'd be thankful to see him.*

"Could I have a word, my lord?"

Morag struggled to contain her shock. *My lord? Is Kinross a friend of Tolbain's?*

"Is it important?" Tolbain feverishly eyed Morag's bosom.

She covered herself.

"Yes."

"It had better be." Tolbain rose. "Dinna move," he ordered.

Kinross stared at her spread-eagled on the ground like a doll with no shame.

She pulled down the hem of her skirt until it covered her ankles.

The men stood a distance away from her in deep conversation, both stared at her. Morag looked for a way to escape, but Tolbain and Kinross would be on her in minutes. The tone of their conversation changed. She heard a note of disparagement in Kinross' voice and smirks in their glances at her.

Tolbain broke away and growled. "Slut. You should be whipped through the village." He strode off taking his men with him, leaving her and Kinross alone on the hillside.

She scrambled up. "What did you say?"

"That despite your undisputed charms ..." Kinross bowed to her. "I knew for a fact you're a well-known whore ..."

"Oh!" Morag's cheeks burned.

"... and riddled with the pox." Kinross's face broke into a grin.

"No." Morag's hands covered her face.

"I suggested he leave you to infect the Highlands and do his job for him."

"I canna believe ... how could you? You're the most insulting man I've ever met."

"And the most ... inventive. I've just saved your virtue."

"And lost my reputation," hissed Morag.

"You lost your 'reputation' in Edinburgh. I dinna believe you can lose it twice. If you can, it's very careless of you."

She glowered at him.

"And your hair?" His hand brushed across her shorn head. "Your idea?"

Morag pulled her shawl in place and said nothing.

"Now, why would you cut it? Somehow it suits you." His eyes roamed freely over her breasts and hips. His lips broke into a knowing smile. "I heard a whisper that Euan Stewart survived. You wouldna ken where he is, now would you?"

"He's dead." Morag lowered her eyes under his scrutiny and said, "Who are you working for?"

He put a finger on his lips. "I work for ... James Kinross." His eyes burnt into hers as he towered over her. She gathered saliva in her mouth and spat at him. She watched the spittle trickle down his chin.

"My God, you'll pay for that." He wiped his face with his hand. "Wild cats need to be tamed."

"Kinross, are you coming, man?" Tolbain shouted from the glen below.

He blew her a kiss. "I'll be back, Morag McColl."

Morag poked her tongue at him and stamped her foot. She could hear him laughing as he walked away, making her even more cross.

She waited whilst Tolbain's line of skirmishers disappeared. Her mind churned as she collected the packhorse. *Kinross didna betray me, why? Why?*

CHAPTER Forty-eight

That evening Euan found Morag and her pack horse a few miles from the den when the warm night released the heady scent from the heather. A huge golden moon and silver stars lit up the sky. "I was worried for you, my heart." He clasped her to him, his lips searching hers for a welcome. He found it as her mouth gave way to his in a rush of heat. "I expected you hours ago."

"I had to be careful because of patrols. I think Kinross has changed sides, he and Tolbain are scouring the glens for you," said Morag.

"I never trusted him, Dougie didna either. Should have killed the bastard in Edinburgh."

She looked tired, he thought. She clasped her cloak round her as he guided her up to the den and untied the knots binding the supplies onto the pack horse.

"Apart from food and ale, I brought more plaids and warm clothes for the bairns. I thought they'd be cold up here at night. Where are they?" she asked.

"At the pool," said Euan. "Here's Johnnie."

Euan wished he could do something for his brother. A gaunt Johnnie with troubled eyes walked towards them. *Perhaps Morag can help him.*

"I'm pleased you're back safe and sound." Morag gave Johnnie a hug. "You must have had a terrible time."

"I don't talk about it."

Euan saw her bewilderment as she blinked at Johnnie's dull tone. "I'm sorry about Duncan and ... Kirsty," she said.

"Yes."

Couldn't Johnnie summon up more than that?

Morag took a small package from a bundle she brought with her. "I've something for you, a book from your library at home."

Surely Johnnie would spark into life with this gift?

Johnnie took it from her and unwrapped it.

"It's *A tour thro' the whole island of Great Britain* by Defoe," said Morag.

"Thanks." Johnnie put it to one side.

Morag looked at Euan.

Euan shrugged his shoulders. *War and women affect men in different ways. Some brag about what they've done, others stay silent or go mad. He has to handle his demons in his own way.*

Dark figures moved behind Johnnie. Euan recognised them at once. Johnnie motioned towards a slender brown haired girl with light brown eyes. "This is Alais Murray. She doesna speak."

"Euan told me." Morag turned to Alais. "I'm pleased to meet you and sorry for your loss."

Alais gave a wan smile and put a hand on her heart.

"She's got lots of signals she uses. I can understand some of them now."

Alais smiled at Johnnie.

Morag gave Euan a knowing look. She nudged him with her elbow.

"What?" said Euan. *Why does she seem to know something I dinna?*

Morag watched as Johnnie whistled and two small children dressed in rags made their way hand in hand through the ferns, their wet hair clinging to pinched faces.

"Why, they're thin as besom handles," Morag lowered her voice so only Euan and Johnnie could hear. "You can see their ribs."

Johnnie whispered back, "Orphans, starving when we found them." He raised his voice and gave the children an encouraging smile, "Morag, this is Neill and Comrie Douglas."

"I'm pleased to meet you." Morag held the children's hands. "Now, who'd like some milk and oatcakes?"

"Please," said Comrie.

"Thank you," said Neill.

Euan studied the bairns for the first time. They both had dark hair and large brown eyes. Comrie sucked her thumb and looked no more than four. Neill seemed about ten years old and reminded Euan of Duncan. A great wave of sadness swept over him. *I should have kept Duncan safe, something else to feel guilty about.*

When Neill finished the last crumb and Alais wiped the milky moustache from Comrie's face, Morag gave Alais a bundle of clothing.

Euan could see Morag fighting back tears. *She's probably never seen bairns so hungry.*

Alais signed and Johnnie translated. Alais says, "Thank you for your kindness." Alais gathered the children to her and took them into the den.

"Poor wee bairns." Morag set out more oatcakes. "Help yourselves." The men sat down and she poured the ale and asked, "So, Johnnie how did you get away?"

He didn't reply, just picked at his food. Morag raised her eyebrows at Euan and he shrugged. *Johnnie has to find his own path.*

Later, Euan steeled himself to tell her what he and Johnnie had been planning. They'd waited long enough. He hoped to God she'd understand and took her in his arms. "Johnnie and I are going to visit our Uncle John in Port Glasgow."

"What? When?" She drew back from his embrace.

"Tonight."

Her eyes widened.

"We must. He owes us money, an amount that should see us through any hardships to come."

"And our wedding?"

"We'll be wed when I return. It'll only take a month at most."

His heart ached when he saw tears well in her eyes. "Will there ever be a time when you put our wedding first?"

"That's unfair," he said. "You know we havena a priest. I aim to find one."

"You do?" She nestled her head against his chest and he enclosed her with his arms. How he loved her. "I do."

"Then go with my blessing."

***

Evening came all too quickly when Morag forced herself to smile to speed Euan and Johnnie on their way. "Be careful."

They'd all heard rumours of the government's latest decree that they weren't allowed to carry arms on pain of death. So, Johnnie exchanged his sword for a dirk from Alais and Euan followed suit with Morag. Johnnie hid his dirk in his sleeve whilst Euan thrust his in a belt under his jacket.

They have to defend themselves, thought Morag.

It was a long journey and they'd decided to travel at night, hiding from redcoat patrols during the day.

Alais and the bairns crowded around Johnnie. Neill shook his hand and Comrie clung like a squirrel to his knees. "Now, Alais will look after you, won't you?" Johnnie looked at her.

Alais nodded her head and smiled at him. And Morag thought her smile full of longing, but Johnnie didn't respond to it.

"I'll be back before you know it. What would you like me to bring you?"

"Just you," croaked Neill.

"Loves you, Dada," said Comrie taking her thumb out of her mouth as he swung her up and kissed her.

Dada. It brought a lump to Morag's throat.

"Right," said Johnnie looking at Euan, Morag and finally Alais. Alais wiped the children's tears with her apron and took their hands. Johnnie held her gaze and laid his palm on her cheek. Then he mounted and mumbled, "Let's away, Euan."

Morag saw the anguish in Alais' eyes as she watched till Johnnie and his horse disappeared behind some trees.

"Not a word of goodbye to her," Morag whispered in Euan's ear, "we've had weeks of his silences. He goes off for hours. How Alais puts up with him I dinna ken. Doesna he realise she loves him? Can you no' do something?"

"I could lose him on the way back," teased Euan.

She elbowed him in the ribs.

"Oomph! Did you see that Neill and Comrie? Your Aunty Morag is beating me to a pulp. Why, I'll have bruises for months." He lifted his shirt to show them and they giggled. "The poor man who weds her doesna ken what he's getting for a wife. I'll have to tell him."

Morag stayed silent and looked at the ground.

Alais led the children away.

"I'll miss you, my heart." Euan lifted her chin with his finger. "Once we return in July with a priest and the gold owed by my uncle, we'll wed."

Morag flung her arms around him. "I promised myself I wasna going to weep." She sniffed into his sleeve as he held her.

CHAPTER Forty-nine
July 1746

Euan and Johnnie had been gone three weeks, when Morag had two visitors at the shieling. They'd ridden and then been forced to lead their ponies up the hillside.

"You'll have heard I'm wed?" Kirsty Lorne ignored the strands of fair hair falling from her badly tied bun and twisted the fine lace handkerchief in her hands.

The skin under her eyes looks bruised. "I heard handfasted."

"We're cousins."

Morag tried not to feel sorry for her. "Well, why are you here?"

"It wouldna have worked with Johnnie you know, I wanted more." She moistened her lips with her tongue. "I need your help."

"What? After you jilted Johnnie for Tolbain. "

Kirsty looked at her groom and lowered her voice, "Please, Morag. Is there somewhere we can talk, in private?"

After Kirsty's visit, Morag couldn't weave, make bread or sew and went from burnt milk to singed clothes in a daze.

"What's wrong with you?" grumbled her father. "Can't a man have rest in his own home?"

Morag silently prayed and made up her mind. "I'm going out."

"It's to be hoped you'll return in a better mood." He bent his head and went back to mending his leather belt.

Morag held on to her shawl as the wind whipped across the loch. She went to see the only person she thought could help, Isabel.

"I canna talk here." Morag pointed up the hill. "Would you come to the old church with me?"

Once inside its stone walls, Morag told her what Kirsty had said. "She knows about my knowledge of plants and simples and asked me to help her ... poison Tolbain."

"She'd commit murder?"

"I told her it'd be a mortal sin. That's when she threatened me, said she'd tell Euan some nonsense about Edinburgh. Said she'd tell the whole village."

Isabel stared at her.

"It's just malicious gossip. Apparently her friend Miss Balfour wrote to say I'd been dancing with James Kinross, had intimate talks with him and he'd visited me late at night when I was unchaperoned. "

"No."

"If anything it's Miss Balfour's morals that should be in question. What's worse Kinross told her I'm expecting a child."

"It's no' true?"

"Of course not. He only said it because I'll have nought to do with him. Euan was jealous, warned him off and then threatened to kill him in Edinburgh. What can I do? My reputation will be in tatters," said Morag wiping tears away.

"Euan loves you."

"I know, but there's a semblance of truth in Kinross' story. Everyone saw me dance with him at a ball when Euan was absent. They didna ken it was against my wishes. I didna want to make a scene. Euan even commented on the impression of his fingers on my arm."

"He touched you?" Isabel said shocked.

Worse, Kinross and I were unchaperoned at one point when he helped me rescue Amelia. The Whig broadsheets called me a 'Jacobite Jade' and now Kinross is blackening my reputation even more. Euan willna want me after this."

"Oh my dear, dinna let them win. It's quite a conundrum. Let me think. Dougie says the lads are visiting their uncle in Port Glasgow?"

"Yes."

"For how long?"

"They left three weeks ago and should be back next week."

Isabel's brow wrinkled with concentration. Morag fingered her betrothal ring in frustration.

"It's a matter of your honour and Euan's. Euan has to marry you." Isabel put her arm round Morag's shoulder.

"Euan willna like it."

"He'll have no choice and the village will insist."

"That's what concerns me." Morag chewed her lip.

That night as the wind moaned round the sheiling, Morag struggled to get to sleep. Kirsty, Kinross and Tolbain's faces seemed to taunt her. *It's just as well, Euan and Johnnie are doing business in Glasgow. At least Johnnie willna have to endure any glances or smirks about Kirsty and Euan willna have heard any scandal about me yet.* She thanked Isabel in her prayers.

***

The storm broke when her father overheard a conversation in the market place.

His face was crimson with fury. "So is it true?"

"No."

"You shouldna have joined the baggage train. I kenned something like this would happen, bringing disgrace on us."

I said it's no' true. It's gossip. Nothing happened between me, Euan or Kinross."

"The damage's done. No one's going to believe you. Can you no see you're ruined? I'll see the laird. Euan's put off marrying you for far too long." He stomped off to *Braedrumie House.*

***

"They were at each other like two wounded bears." Dougie told Morag later. "Only the whisky calmed them down. They've agreed on a wedding date, but the servants must have heard. The whole village will ken."

Morag hid her face in her hands. Then she squared her shoulders. *Now I have to face Euan.*

An uneasy peace descended on Braedrumie, as if the villagers had sucked in a communal death whilst they waited for Euan's return.

A week later, in the early hush of morning, Euan reached for his dirk before he realised Kirsty Lorne stood in front of him. *Not another delay.* Johnnie and the priest jerked their ponies to a halt. They'd only a few miles before they reached the den. Johnnie turned his face away.

Kirsty looked at Johnnie, the priest and then Euan. "It's private."

"We'll ride on," said Johnnie giving no hint of their troubled past.

Euan sighed and led his pony some distance from the others. He'd never liked her and by the end of their heated conversation Euan loathed her. *Had he heard what was being said about Morag and Kinross? Did he ken about the baby? What bloody baby?* He sought solace in telling Johnnie and the priest.

"She's handfasted to a madman" said Johnnie, as if this excused Kirsty.

What the priest said turned Euan white hot with fury. He kneed his tired pony up to the den where he found two fathers waiting for him.

At Dougie's suggestion, Johnnie took a concerned Alais, the goggle-eyed children and reluctant priest to Isabel's.

"You've brought a priest I see?" said Morag's father, a hopeful glint in his eyes. "A little late, but at least you'll wed her."

Euan's eyes narrowed. "Will I?"

"You *have* to marry her," said Morag's father.

Bloody hell. "Have to?" He loved Morag, had brought a priest so they could marry, but this gossip had shocked him. "I swear on my honour, sir, nothing happened between Morag and me."

"And Kinross?" asked his father.

"He sniffed around her, I warned him off, threatened to kill him in Edinburgh. He'd better say his prayers because he's no' got long on this Earth."

"Could you wed and bring up another man's bairn?" asked his father.

"She's no' carrying his bairn," Euan growled. "I'd never believe it of her." Rage bubbled up his throat. "I'm off to find her and get this sorted out."

"The wedding's tomorrow before noon. Be there," said her father.

Euan spoke between gritted teeth. "It'll be three weeks because the priest insists I confess and spend time in the sinners' pew."
Her father's mouth shut like a trap.

Euan stormed off to find Morag at the shieling milking one of her father's cows, the morning light washed over her. She'd her head buried in its black flank as she worked at the udder.

"Morag, what in damnation is this all about?" His words made her turn and knock over the bucket. They both ignored the milk puddling on the floor. "I brought a priest so we could be wed properly."

She jerked upright. "You dinna believe it? When I danced with Kinross, when we met ... I'd no choice."

"No choice?" It sounds like you had plenty of choice while I was away."

"Euan, you dinna think that I ... that I ... you dinna think it's true?"

"According to Kirsty Lorne, everyone thinks it's true." He raised his voice, folded his arms and glared at her. "You met him."

"Please believe me. I'm no' having a bairn. I've no' lain with any man."

"Is that it?"

"Yes." She jutted out her chin.

Euan recognised the signs. *She's telling the truth and she's no' going to budge an inch.* Even when she was little with two of his brothers dangling a dead frog in her face, the movement of her chin had been the same and she hadn't run away. "I told you no' to join the baggage train. You realise the position you've placed me in?"

"Yes."

"The whole village kens either Kinross or me are the father of this imaginary bairn?"

"Yes."

"To save your bloody honour, I'm to confess and sit in the sinners' pew for everyone to gawp at for the next three Sundays whilst the Banns are read. The priest insists on it. What about my honour? They'll think I've lain with you before we're wed and I've fathered a bastard."

"I forgot about ..." began Morag.

"They'll make us wed in shame instead of joy."

"I'm sorry," said Morag.

"Sorry?"

He stomped away from her. He'd marry her, but the way he felt at the moment, he'd never forgive her for this. She should have listened to him. A girl on her own in a baggage train. And Kinross, he wanted to spit roast the man, destroying Morag's reputation with his behaviour. Playing the gentleman when all the time he was nothing, but a lying whoremonger. He'd better pray he never saw Euan again.

CHAPTER Fifty-one

The bridal day arrived. Euan ensured the clan stood guard outside the church and on the surrounding hills, in case of redcoats.

Inside, Morag's father sat on a pew, face as thunderous as the skies above. Euan drew his dark brows over his eyes and glowered at everyone. He tried to look as dignified as a man over six feet can who'd sat in the sinners' pew for the past three Sundays. No villagers' glances lingered as they scurried to their seats.

Johnnie propped up their father. Alais had an arm round Neill and Comrie who wriggled beside her. A stoic Dougie and smug Isabel were to Johnnie's left. Jamie Moffat sat upright in the pew in front. Behind them, Mary McBean, Hughie's widow and Euan's distant cousin, sat dressed in mourning, rocking her five-month-old baby whilst crying silent tears. She struggled to control her restless brood whilst ignoring Granny Mac's advice. "Skelp the little fiends within an inch of their lives."

The rest of the village squeezed in like tattered mice standing at the back of the church. Even the ne'er do wells, faces washed and dressed in their Sunday best, had to be there. Word had also got around about the priest and many had overdue confessions that needed to be made. Euan knew the juicy gossip about him and Morag would give folk lots to talk about in the coming year, judging by the sly nudges and whisperings.

Some fool has dressed the old stone in white, wild roses. Dougie winked at him and grinned. Euan inwardly groaned. *I might have guessed.* Flowers decorated the old arched door, drooped over the altar and twined round the font. *Why the bloody font?* An arm waved at him from the door. An expectant hush descended on the congregation.

Johnnie, Euan's best man, nudged him as Morag's father rushed her up the aisle. She wore a fitted yellow jacket, with a white lace kerchief at her throat, a white apron, striped skirt with a glimpse of blue petticoat and yellow shoes. She stared at the floor when she stood beside him.

The priest lambasted them with a sermon about chastity, fallen women and unseemly doings by men. He seemed to forget Euan had just paid him a goodly sum. Euan saw Morag's cheeks flush with embarrassment.

"Do you take this woman ...?" droned the priest.

There was a long silence as Euan made as if he had to think about it ... "If I must."

Morag flinched. The priest's jaw dropped like a stone, the audience gasped and a nervous titter ran the length of the church.

"What did Euan say Mammy?" asked Comrie in a loud voice, hushed by Alais.

The priest rushed on. "Do you take this man ...?"

There was a long silence from Morag ... "If I have to."

The onlookers guffawed.

"If she had to," roared Dougie. His breath exhaled in an 'Umph' as Isabel nudged a hard elbow into his ribs. Neill and Comrie giggled despite Alais' attempts to quieten them. The congregation rocked with laughter.

"If you ..." began the priest staring at Morag. He scowled at Morag who scowled back with fire in her eyes. He glanced at Euan who knew his face was black with fury.

"Get on with it, man," Euan hissed.

The priest took the wedding by the reins as he spurred them into a canter as Euan shoved the ring on Morag's finger, and finished at a gallop. "You may kiss the bride." The priest wiped his crimson and sweating face.

Euan saw the congregation lean forward in anticipation. From their wide grins, they'd loved it. This hasty wedding would be the talk of the parish for years to come. He showed Morag off to them, much to her embarrassment. She'd never looked more innocent or more beautiful. He pulled her to him and kissed her for a long time.

So long, that bemused mutterings from watchers about how unseemly it all was, made him release her. He liked to think some of the women were a little jealous too.

Morag looked as if she wanted to spit in his eye, but he held her in an iron grip. Then he paraded her down the aisle so she had to greet and curtsey to everyone in the pews. Pink faced, she forced a smile.

She's humiliated me, why should she escape scot free? As they reached the door, a loud fart reverberated behind them. Granny Mac. Such, thought Euan, was his wedding to Morag.

The bridal feast, a sombre affair, had a meagre amount of food. It seemed wrong to celebrate when almost every family in the valley had lost loved ones. So, their guests sat and picked at the scraps in front of them, whilst Euan and Morag kept their thoughts to themselves about their wedding night.

CHAPTER Fifty-two

Will he forgive me? This thought troubled Morag as they rode deep in the mountains above Braedrumie and said little to each other. Darkness surrounded them.

The weather deteriorated. Dark shapes swayed backwards and forwards, battered by the wild gusts. Huge storm clouds gathered and jagged zigzags of lightning lit the mountain track. Rain fell, drove into her face and soaked her to the bone.

They pushed on, knowing Euan's safety depended upon it. Word of their wedding would get out, particularly when drink loosened men's tongues. He'd told her he didn't want to spend their wedding night feeling like a hunted man.

The rain stopped as Euan dismounted and pushed the reins of his fractious stallion into Morag's cold hands. 'Wait!' he commanded. "Hold the reins." He talked at her the way he commanded his men.

She dismounted. Her clothes stuck to her, sodden from the rain. She watched him creep to a cliff face shielded by boulders and waving, spiky silhouettes. His dark shape melted into it and disappeared. She loved him so much. *Will he ever forgive me?*

She moved from foot to foot in an agony of tiredness and damp. He kept her waiting for a long time. The dark and the wind combined to make moving shadows out of everything. Morag stood beside the horses, stroking their necks and talking to them to cover her own fear. *Is he punishing me?*

"You can go in now." Euan's voice sounded taut and close making Morag jump. A roll of thunder startled the ponies, which reared and plunged in a sudden frenzy to escape. He took the reins from her and calmed the animals with gentle commands. She longed to hear that warmth in his voice when he spoke to her. "Go in," he ordered, "I'll see to the horses, put them in another cave further up, it'll do as a stable." His manner cold, his voice like steel, he'd never forgive her.

Morag walked towards the cliff. Had he forgotten her childhood fear of enclosed spaces? Brief flashes of lightning lit her way. She searched behind black stubs of prickly gorse determined to scratch her. Ahead lay a black fissure in the cliff face. She stooped and met a rock wall with an opening on the right. She slipped into the cleft and gasped in amazement. Flickering light revealed a series of caves each bigger than the other until she came to a huge cavern lit by hundreds of candles. Golden flames played on the walls and floor revealing a bed of bracken, green plaids and peat gathered for a fire. *He's done all of this for me.*

The dull shriek of the wind announced the storm rising in fury outside. *Where is he?* They hadn't spoken much since their wedding earlier that day. She'd endured his silence for the whole journey. If it had been any other night she'd have enjoyed the adventure of being alone with him. Instead she'd hated the loneliness of it and longed for the easy camaraderie of the past.

She ran her fingers over her spiky head. The rain had wet her hair to the scalp and she wished it was long and how it used to be. She'd always hated the tangle of curls, but he'd loved it. Now it was as if he'd become a stranger and wasn't the man she loved. Would he think her ugly and awkward and that she'd trapped him into this marriage.

She could have wept when she thought of her wedding. It should have been the happiest day of her life instead of something she wanted to forget.

She sensed Euan's physical presence at her side. He towered over her charging flickers of want in her breast.

"I should have told you," he said. "I bought you something." He handed her a small oilskin packet tied with string. "It came from France on one of our ships."

She glanced at him, uncertain and untied his gift. "Oh." A shimmer of silk, light as goose down cascaded onto her hands. She held it against her. The nightgown fell in soft creamy folds to the floor, the neck, cuffs and hem embroidered with gold thread.

"Do you like it?"

"Euan ... we've been so mean ... our wedding was ... awful ... I ... I ..." Tears coursed down her face as her voice broke.

His arms encircled her like a soft cocoon. "I thought I'd never forgive you, my beautiful lass, but we love each other and that's all that matters." She made to speak, but he put a finger on her mouth. "I will love you until death and beyond. Now, do you like your gift?"

"I love my gift, it's the most... I love my gift, but I have nothing for you."

He kissed her forehead. "You are all I need, my beloved darling. Come let me show you. I've been waiting for this night all my life." He led her behind a rock fall to a hidden opening, into an area the size of a large room. The air filled with the thrum of water as it tumbled down one wall and into a frothy pool around which he'd lit more candles.

He held her face in his hands. His lips lingered on her forehead, the tip of her nose and brushed, then crushed her welcoming mouth. He rained kisses like shooting stars along her jaw. Her head went back and he traced the veins in her slender neck till he reached the sweet hollow of her collarbone. His lips flicked down into the warm valley of her breasts and up their rising peaks.

Her head spun all senses alert. She too had been waiting. Her skin on fire, she followed where he led. With each caress he or she peeled an item of clothing off the other. A shirt, a bodice, breeches and skirt lay in disarray on the ground. They meandered, kissing, nibbling and biting across the valley of his muscular chest or up the peaks of her breasts. Naked skin throbbed against skin until she thought she could stand no more. Her eyes closed as he smothered her face and neck with hot kisses, scooped her up and sent her sailing into the air and down into the icy water of the pool.

"Why you ..." She spluttered as she surfaced, but he'd jumped in after her, had entwined her in the circle of his arms and legs and would not let go. His mouth covered hers, his tongue explored, wanted more as if drawing her into him. Heat coursed through her. *I want more, want it to never end.* When his manhood took her with a rhythm older than time, she welcomed the pain as she welcomed each thrust. They were one at last.

CHAPTER Fifty-three

Euan came down from the cobalt haze of the mountains riding on one pony with Morag on his lap, whilst he held the reins of her mare. He enjoyed her physical closeness as she leant against him, her skirts up to her knees and teased his ear with a stalk of grass. Wild flower scent, bird song and the thrum of insects surrounded them.

After two weeks alone, they'd forgiven each other, though she hadn't spoken of their quarrel since their first night together. He held his peace, believing she'd a good reason for what she'd done and would tell him one day.

His fingers rubbed his brow as he pushed a faint shadow of concern away.

"What is it, darling?"

"Nothing, my heart." She was his wife, in his blood and this marriage what he'd always wanted. *Surely even a hunted man deserves happiness?*

Her head bumped against his chin as he brought his pony to a sudden stop. His keen eyes scanned the horizon and he sniffed the air. "Something's wrong, look." He pointed at the grey smoke billowing over a distant hill. "That's Braedrumie. Morag, ride your own pony. We need to find out what's happened."

Morag's face creased into a frown of concern. "I must check Father is safe first."

They rode hard to find him in a lean-to beside the shieling. He'd two hands on a calf's hooves as he brought it into the world. The lowing mother seemed grateful for his presence. He cleared the birth sack from the calf and ensured it could breathe.

Morag ran to him and wrapped her arms round her father's neck. "He's so small."

"He'll make a fine bull." He cleaned the calf with straw before pushing him towards his mother's udder. The calf scented milk and his nose disappeared under his mother's stomach.

Euan itched to get to Braedrumie. He rubbed his brow. Before he could speak, Morag's father turned a fierce gaze on him.

"You've had a fine time the two of you, I see. Made it up then?"

"Father." Morag flushed.

Euan put out his hand. "Good to see you, sir."

Her father's stern face turned into a smile and they shook hands.

Morag sighed with relief. She didn't need enmity between those she loved most.

"There's trouble in the village, we must go." She kissed the top of her father's head. "We came to see that you were alright."

"Redcoats? You take care, do you hear? Now stop squeezing and kissing me to death." Morag gave his head a final kiss and let him go.

Euan saw that age had caught up with Morag's father. His pink scalp showed through white hair, his shoulders had rounded and his back humped.

"Keep her safe. I'll follow you." It took her father time to rise from his creaking knees.

Euan felt for him. "I will, sir."

They set off at a mad gallop down the hillside, urging their ponies through the glen till they came to the edge of the cliff overhanging the village, the smoke stronger and denser here.

"Wait," Euan hissed at her. Dismounting, he crawled through the heather to the top of a crag. The woody smell of burning timbers hit his nostrils.

Down below, crackling flames engulfed Braedrumie. Thatches had been stoved in. Several fired crofts spewed smoke. Glowing embers swirled upwards, tossed here and there by the rising wind.

Euan waved for Morag to creep forward through the grass and then his body stilled. Hartlass sat twenty yards away on a chestnut thoroughbred, one hand on his hip and a smirk on his brutal face. His growling brown dog sat nearby. They heard raised voices coming from the figures below.

"Have you no control of your men, no sense of right and wrong?" Johnnie shouted. "I only killed a MacNair because he tried to take her by force." He pointed at Alais weeping at his feet. "And you'd no need to murder Dougie."

Euan's jaw tightened and Morag gripped his arm. Isabel was bent over Dougie's motionless body lying at Johnnie's feet.

A grinning Highlander stepped forward and felled Johnnie with a vicious punch. "You'll no' have such a pretty face now. I say we want a dead Stewart for a dead MacNair." The MacNairs bayed at that; the dog joined in and the crofters stood in silence.

"Sweet Jesu ..." began Morag in a whisper.

Johnnie wiped the blood from his torn mouth and spat out a back tooth. "You're a dead man, MacNair." He turned to Hartlass. "You've murdered men surrendering arms." He pointed up at three men hanging from a branch. "Are you mad dogs that you treat us so?"

"Oh no," said Morag clutching at Euan as they watched the scene below.

"Hang him with the other vermin," Hartlass ordered two burly privates. "It'll serve as a warning to others. Corporal, read out the proclamation."

Johnnie struggled as they dragged him to the old dool tree.

A corporal stepped forward, unravelled some parchment, coughed and allowed his voice to ring out:

"*By order of his majesty's government, all men suspected of carrying arms must make the following oath: I swear as I shall answer to God at the great day of judgement I have not and I shall not have in my possession any gun, sword or arms whatsoever or never use tartan, plaid or any part of Highland garb ...*" A groan came from the crowd. "*... and if I do so may I be accursed in my undertakings, family and property, may I never see my wife nor children, nor father, nor mother or relations, may I be killed in battle as a fugitive coward and lie without Christian burial in a foreign land, far from the graves of my* *forefathers and kindred; may all this come upon me if I break this oath."*

Wheeling his horse around, Hartlass sneered. "I think you'll find I'm on the winning side and you count as nothing."

"Those that are left count and will never forget," snarled Johnnie fighting the noose being slung round his neck. "They'll serve as witness to what you and the MacNairs have done this day. Your name will go down in infamy."

The crofters became one and roared him on.

The snarling dog had white foam round curled lips. "Down, Romsey," said Hartlass.

Redcoat bayonets lowered as a soldier placed the knot behind one of Johnnie's ears and the noose tightened.

Euan turned to Morag. "I must help him."

"I ken it."

"He's my brother. I canna just sit here and watch."

"Do it." She pressed his hand. The silence below became howls of outrage as Hartlass raised his hand.

Morag placed her head on Euan's chest. "I love you."

Euan kissed her and made to go.

"Wait!" she hissed. "They've stopped. Someone's come, he's … Euan, it's Rob. I swear it's Rob."

Euan stared. *What's he doing here?* Euan, dirk in mouth, wriggled on his belly through thistles, bracken and heather towards the village.

CHAPTER Fifty-four

Sweet Jesu, I've only had Euan to myself for a few weeks and I've let him go into danger again. Morag chewed her lip as Euan snaked between gorse bushes towards the crowd below.

She leant forward and watched Johnnie gape at Rob.

Rob ignored him and dismounted. "Sir, I have orders for you."

"They can wait till I hang this rebel."

"Sir, General Witt instructed me to tell you they're of the utmost urgency." Rob persisted.

A grinning redcoat sergeant gave a brutal tug on Johnnie's noose. Johnnie danced on his toes and fought for breath.

Alais screamed.

Morag's hands covered her mouth.

"General Witt? So, he's been promoted, very well." Hartlass clicked his fingers and held out his hand.

Rob gave the letter to him. Hartlass tore the seal. He read the orders. "I've been recalled to London." He sounded disappointed. "After the hanging, you're in charge here, Captain Stewart."

"With respect, sir ..." Rob lowered his voice.

Hartlass looked at him in surprise. "Did he by God? Witt said that? Name's on a promotion list you say? Always knew Witt could judge a good man." Hartlass scanned the letter again his humour restored. "Well, Stewart, I've done most of the dirty work here. I'm sure I can leave you to conduct a simple hanging."

"Sir."

"Dangerous times. I'll take most of my men and leave a platoon with you."

"Sir," said Rob.

"Come, Romsey." Hartlass spurred his horse into activity. The dog leapt up and followed him. They all watched until he and his men rode out of sight.

"Sergeant!" ordered Rob.

"Sir." The sergeant dropped the rope and snapped to attention, much to the relief of Johnnie, who sagged at the knees as the tension of the rope eased.

"Round up your men and head for Fort William," ordered Rob.

"Sir. And you, sir?"

"Me? I'm staying to hang this rebel, Sergeant."

"On your own, sir? Beggin' your pardon, but they'll kill you, sir."

"Major Hartlass has ensured they know who's master ... unless you're suggesting otherwise?"

"No, sir."

"Do as you're ordered, at the double!" snarled Rob.

"Sir." The sergeant sprinted to the others and they ran back to their picket lines.

Morag saw Euan wait till the last redcoats disappeared into the trees and then he sprang up behind Rob.

CHAPTER Fifty-five

Morag rose to her feet. She'd go down to the village, help, perhaps calm the situation. James Kinross' familiar voice came from behind her, "I think you'd better stay here."

She froze, but a shout from the crowd below diverted her attention. "Rob Stewart, you're a dirty traitor."

Morag watched in horror. A clod of mud hurled at Rob, made his horse shy away.

Rob tightened his grip on the reins. "Stand back," he yelled his sword in one hand. "This is no' my doing."

The crowd jeered at that and shook their fists at him.

"For God's sake," shouted Euan pointing at the hanging men. "Cut them down."

"So the prodigal's returned." Johnnie sneered staring at Rob. "Your precious redcoats have hanged good men and bayoneted Dougie. He had no weapons; he was defenceless."

Isabel knelt over Dougie and cushioned his head in her lap.

Rob went white, but jerked on the rope so Johnnie was gasping for breath and standing on his toes once more. "You'll be respectful when you speak to me brother or I'll hang you where you stand. I've helped you all, redcoat or no' and I wish I could have helped Dougie; he was like a father to all of us. Now, are we going to do what needs to be done or are you going to let Hartlass get away?" He stared at Euan.

Rob had changed, more hardened than Morag remembered.

Johnnie nodded. "Let's do what needs to be done." Rob cut the cords round Johnnie's wrists and took the noose from his neck as the crowd moved forward with a roar to grab Rob.

Morag rose to her feet. She had to help.

Kinross' arm wrapped round her throat, constricting her breathing. "I heard you married Stewart."

She'd forgotten his presence. "What ... are you ... doing here?"

Kinross ignored her question. "Pity about your marriage." He stroked her cheek and relaxed his hold.

"You lied and ruined my reputation. There could never have been anything between us. You're a turncoat, you've been spying for both sides."

"Not quite. The redcoats offered a lot more incentive, shall we say, than the Jacobites. If Mrs. Quin had handled it better ..."

"Mrs. Quin? Morag had a vision of General Guest's acidic housekeeper in Edinburgh and a tall figure brushing his hair and shoulders in the dark, cobwebs that would have betrayed his presence in the well. "Was it you, the man in the cloak at Mrs. Quin's?"

"Of course. I thought perhaps you might care for me."

"Never."

"No, as you say preposterous idea." Kinross smiled at her. "Wouldna have worked." Before she realised, he covered her mouth with his. She struggled in his embrace, hitting him with her fists and kicking his legs.

How dare he?

"Thought I'd put it to the test. Your lips are sweeter than honey. I want you, Morag McColl. You can see The Cause is dead and your village in flames. Use your head. Tolbain's moved into the Stewart's house and ..."

"What?" Morag's brain reeled. *Tolbain's taken possession of Euan's home.*

"The Stewarts are ruined; they'll be hunted down like dogs." Kinross said, "You'll always be poor, living from hand to mouth, old before your time if you stay here with bloody Stewart." He pressed her to him. "Leave with me, I've gold hidden away that will take us anywhere we want to go."

"Gold?" Morag's eyes narrowed.

"Yes, French gold, gold meant for The Cause." Kinross grinned at her as if he expected her to be pleased. "The gold goes with me as do you." He swept her into his arms.

"What? No." She clawed at Kinross scratching his arms and face.

He grabbed her and held her to him. "I've wanted you for a long time."

"Sweet Jesu, will you stop at nothing? Look at what the redcoats are doing, the Highlands need that gold." A livid scar on his right thumb triggered a distant memory of her biting someone and holding on, leaving her mark. Realisation swept over her. *I've underestimated this man. It had been him in the crowd at Glenfinnan all that time ago; he must have betrayed us on the raid and he's lied to Tolbain, he doesna want to save me, he wants me for himself.* Morag managed to scream one last word, "Euan!" Kinross's punch silenced her.

CHAPTER Fifty-six

Rubbing his brow, Euan scanned the crag where he'd left Morag. *Did she scream his name?* He found it difficult to make out individual voices because of the maddened crowd. Then he saw them, Kinross with a lifeless Morag thrown over his saddle and heading west. *What the hell does he think he's doing?*

'Leave him.' Euan ordered the villagers and pointed at Rob.

"But Euan ...?" began one crofter as Rob mounted his horse.

"Rob, Johnnie," Euan snarled. "Morag's in trouble," he shouted as he ran.

"And we'll kill anyone who interferes," Johnnie told the baying crowd.

"Take Dougie's ponies, Johnnie, they're in the meadow under the trees," yelled Isabel.

Euan led Rob to a bog and reached down into the thick, black mud and produced three filthy oblong packages wrapped in animal skins. A musket, ramrod, two leather pouches and two broad swords fell to the ground.

Rob shook his head as they armed themselves.

Euan checked the musket. "No offence, but we'll move the rest after this."

"No offence taken," Rob hissed softly, "but after this, I'll keep looking for them."

The brothers stared at each other in silence, acknowledging the family bond that held them together and the chasm lying between them.

"Duncan's ..." began Euan.

"Dead. Johnnie told me about him and Jack in Inverness."

Euan nodded and lowered his voice. "Johnnie hardly speaks and never mentioned you."

"Long story," said Rob.

Euan concentrated on the task in hand. After assuring the musket worked, he opened a leather pouch and checked the cartridges. Satisfied, he bit off the end of a paper cartridge, spat out the residue and primed the pan with gunpowder.

Johnnie arrived with the ponies.

"Kinross has got Morag," said Euan.

Johnnie let out a low whistle of surprise.

"Who's Kinross?" asked Rob.

"Later," said Euan as he poured the rest of the powder and the ball down the barrel and tapped it into place with the ramrod.

"Dougie never trusted the bastard." Johnnie's jaw tightened. "Let's go."

Euan took the reins from Johnnie's hands and leapt onto the pony. "They're up on the crag. He's heading for the coast."

The brothers set off at breakneck speed with Rob in the lead as he always had been when younger.

CHAPTER Fifty-seven

All Euan could think of was losing Morag. His head full of her scent, her voice, her touch, more precious than ever to him now. Kinross had her and only God knew what he'd do to her if they didn't catch him. Euan had nightmare visions of Morag, cast off and whoring in a far city. He couldn't conceive of her being dead.

Euan assured himself that they'd find her. When they reached the crag, they turned west and followed Kinross' tracks. Down the hillside they went, galloping along Loch Linnhe and turning into the dark forest. They doggedly tracked Kinross and Morag for hours when a whooshing sound came from nowhere and a bough thwacked Rob's chest sweeping him backwards over his horse's tail. "Umph!"

Euan rolled into the undergrowth followed by Johnnie.

The ponies trotted off for a distance and stopped to crop the juicy grass by a burn. Nothing stirred on the forest floor.

"Rob, you alright?" Euan hissed from the deepest shadow of a birch. "Rob? Brother, answer me."

"He canna, he's got my dirk at his throat." Kinross spat. "Captain Stewart, undo your sword and be very, very careful. I dinna want to spill blood on that nice, clean linen."

Euan heard Rob's sword clatter against a tree root.

"Now get up and your brothers had better come out from hiding or I'll kill you where you stand."

Euan stepped out of the undergrowth with his musket raised and Johnnie beside him. "Where's my wife, Kinross? What have you done with her?" he snarled.

Rob looked at Euan in surprise. "Wife?"

"Drop the musket and swords, or I'll kill the captain." Kinross tightened his hold and pressed the razor sharp blade against Rob, just under his ear, raising a bead of blood.

Euan flung his sword and belt into the green undergrowth. Johnnie undid his belt and let his claymore slide to the ground.

"Stand still lads so I can admire the family resemblance." Kinross' mouth curved into a smile. "Captain, you seem familiar, have we met before?'

"I'd have remembered meeting a mad dog like you," growled Rob.

Kinross increased the pressure on his neck making Rob struggle to breathe.

"Let him go, you treacherous ..." Euan said as he and Johnnie advanced.

"Get back, lads, I'd hate this dirk to slip. It's interesting you mention treachery. What will the army say about a redcoat officer helping his Jacobite brothers? It'll be a good day when you hang together and I collect the reward."

Bastard, thought Euan.

Rob stamped his heel on Kinross' right foot simultaneously pulling Kinross' right hand and dirk away from his throat.

Enraged, Kinross grasped the dirk in two hands and lunged at Rob's chest.

"Look out, Rob," shouted Euan as Rob sidestepped the lethal blade. Euan watched the fight with bated breath.

Johnnie put a hand on Euan's shoulder and went to retrieve the muskets and swords.

"Dinna kill him, Rob. He's mine," said Euan.

Rob's shoulder muscles bunched as he grabbed Kinross' wrists and squeezed.

Kinross clenched his teeth in agony and beads of sweat appeared on his brow.

"Stop playing with him, Rob," said Johnnie sitting on the trunk of a fallen tree.

Rob and Kinross grappled backwards and forwards for supremacy. Rob increased the pressure forcing Kinross to release his weapon and it dropped to the ground. Rob knocked Kinross' hands aside and punched him in the solar plexus.

Kinross staggered and dropped to his knees as the air flew from his lungs and Rob stood over him with clenched fists.

Johnnie picked up the dirk and threw two swords to Euan.

Rob grabbed Kinross' collar and drew back his fist.

"Stay out of it Rob, this is personal," said Euan. "I sent him a challenge in Edinburgh and the coward ran."

Kinross jerked upright. "How dare you, Stewart. You'll take that back."

Euan hurled a sword at Kinross' feet. "Make me."

Kinross rubbed his wrists, picked up the sword and licked his lips. Pound for pound, Euan knew they were evenly matched. Kinross smiled. They circled each other looking for an opening, Kinross taller by an inch, but Euan had the broader chest and shoulders.

Rob made himself comfortable on the tree trunk beside Johnnie and shouted to Kinross, "I'd play to his left; he's always weak on that side."

"No, no it's his right." Johnnie joined in.

"Lads," said Euan not daring to take his eyes off Kinross as he parried a stroke to his left. Metal rang against metal and the two men parted.

Rob roared with laughter. "Just trying to even the odds, give the man a fair chance. We know how good you are, Euan."

"He's improved," said Johnnie.

Euan grimaced and wiped the sweat from his brow.

"What's wrong, Stewart?" sneered Kinross. "Frightened your wife went with me willingly? Did she no' tell you about me and her in Edinburgh, after you left?"

"Shut your filthy mouth." Euan circled him looking for a weakness.

Kinross launched himself at Euan and brought thirty nine inches of tempered steel hissing through the air. Euan nimbly side-stepped to the left, Kinross' claymore missed his right shoulder by a hair, a second later and he'd have been cut in two. Euan attempted a slice to Kinross' head, but Kinross' sword slashed downwards and caught Euan's thigh. Rob grimaced and Johnnie winced as blood welled. The air filled with the sound of heavy breathing.

"Finish him," Rob said. "We've more important business than this gaol bait." Euan feinted and Kinross went for the opening. Euan knocked his blade aside and hacked at Kinross' stomach muscles and as he dropped, sliced across his neck. Blood spurted. Kinross lay still.

Euan stood over him, chest heaving.

"You took your time." Johnnie collected their musket and swords. He threw Rob's weapon to him.

"I'll get the ponies shall I, while you find your wife?" Rob disappeared into the forest.

Euan found Morag tied up and groaning in the undergrowth. He wiped the blood from her split lip with his thumb and untied her. She turned white when she saw Kinross' body. Euan bundled her onto his pony and mounted behind her.

Rob and Johnnie noted her cut lip, but said nothing.

Euan waited for his brothers to mount their ponies.

"I've a bone to pick with a redcoat officer." Johnnie set his lips in a line.

Rob sighed. "Thought so, Hartlass?"

Euan nodded in agreement.

"Dinna suppose I could persuade you otherwise?" Rob tightened his reins.

"No," said Johnnie. "He bloody deserves it."

"I watched a young lass die because of him," said Euan as Morag's hand gripped his.

Rob's jaw tightened. "She's no' the first. Let's do it."

Without further discussion they headed east, to get between Hartlass and Fort William.

CHAPTER Fifty-eight

Euan knew Morag's wrists and ankles had been rubbed raw by Kinross' ropes, but she didn't complain. After a couple of hours of hard riding, curling smoke indicated the army encampment at Druimaruin.

"Stay with the ponies." Euan's tone meant there'd be trouble if she didn't.

The brothers crawled between fir trees, then bracken and fern closing in on their quarry. They settled in shadow beneath a low bough.

"This man's mine." Johnnie's voice was flat and cold.

"But..." began Euan.

"Dinna argue. You're bleeding like a stuck pig." Johnnie pointed at Euan's thigh.

His blood soaked plaid had a rent in it and a six inch gash needed tending. *Damn.*

"He's mine." Rob took the musket off Johnnie. "I've watched him murder and pillage throughout the Highlands. It'll be a good day when he's judged by his Maker and I want to be the man to send him there."

"Agreed," said Euan.

"He's yours," said Johnnie. "Dinna miss."

"Whoever aims at this bastard can't afford to miss."

Euan watched Rob raise the barrel, rest the butt comfortably into his shoulder, then note the direction and speed of the wind. He heard Hartlass 50 yards away issuing orders. "At the double." Soldiers scurried to and fro. Dusk had fallen, making the shot more difficult, but a lantern illuminated him. Euan held his breath with Rob and let it out slowly as Rob squeezed the trigger, but someone beat him to it. A shot rang out across the glen. Euan saw the puff of grey smoke and the motionless Hartlass below, his dog running in

272

circles and barking. Soldiers shouted, but pointed away from where the shot had come and returned fire.

What the hell had happened?

A sergeant knelt to check for signs of life. "Dinna bother boys," he shouted, "the poor officer's dead."

The redcoats waved their hats and cheered.

Hartlass' dog howled.

Euan couldn't believe what he'd seen and heard.

"My God. Who shot him?" Johnnie asked. A light breeze stirred the leaves above their hiding place and rippled the forest grasses.

A grinning redcoat strode into the camp holding his musket in the air. His friends slapped him on the back.

Alfie Smith. Euan recognised him at once. *So, he didna get his wish to go home then, but he's done the world a favour by taking Hartlass out of it.*

"Give me the musket," said Johnnie.

Rob stared at him.

"We'll be blamed for his death, so we may as well be blamed for another." He pointed at the redcoat camp. "I've another score to settle."

Euan looked at MacNair standing smoking a pipe beside the dead Hartlass. Rob handed over the musket and they waited. Johnnie raised it so the butt nestled into his shoulder, sighted down the barrel and pulled the trigger. MacNair fell in a crumpled heap.

No loss, thought Euan.

The camp erupted into chaos. Men dived for cover and shouted orders.

The brothers didn't wait for returning shots and ran towards Morag waiting on her pony. Euan didn't say a word, just took the reins and mounted behind her. They galloped in silence towards Braedrumie.

CHAPTER Fifty-nine

Some hours later Morag had drifted to sleep in Euan's arms. Euan's words to Rob made her start.

"Take off the red jacket, the colour's not too popular round here."

Surely Euan isna going to fight with Rob? She rubbed her eyes and tugged Euan's sleeve. He ignored her.

"Giving orders suits you." Rob shrugged off his uniform and laid it over the saddle in front of him.

"I've had time to adjust to it," said Euan. "I'd a fine role model, till he slunk off without a word."

"Euan." She needed to stop this.

Rob bowed his head. "You're right, my actions were inexcusable. I'm sorry, I ... I'd personal reasons ... the arranged wedding ... someone I ... cared for ... I had to leave."

Morag stared at Rob. *Was it **me** he'd 'cared for'? If so, he did the honourable thing, he left.*

"And what about us? What about Mother?" Johnnie spurred his pony beside Rob's.

Jesu, no' Johnnie as well.

"I've said I'm sorry."

"And the British army?" asked Euan. "How could you?"

"Johnnie, Euan, can we no' talk about this another time?" Morag looked from one grim face to another.

"They've a right to know," said Rob. "Fighting's what I ken best. Joining the redcoats made sense. I never agreed with The Cause, doomed from the start, but how I left ... unforgivable."

"And Mother?" said Johnnie his jaw set for an argument.

Jesu. Morag hissed in a breath. *They're brothers.*

"Believe me when I say I'll regret her death till my dying day."

"Father blames you," said Euan.

"Euan, stop this," said Morag worried they'd be at each other's throats.

They both ignored her.

"He would. How is he?" said Rob.

Euan shook his head. "No' the man he was, but then none of us are, are we? I never heard you apologise before."

"I've learnt a lot. War does that to a man. None of us are perfect, least of all me. I caused my family pain and I regret that."

Euan put out his hand. "Brother, you risked your life to save mine and Johnnie's. Despite your red coat, we can never thank you enough. Isn't that right, Johnnie?"

Morag sighed with relief. She might have known the blood that flowed through these brothers bound them together tighter than most.

"Yes."

Rob stretched out his hand to Johnnie.

Johnnie stared at him. "I forgive you for leaving us, but you were at bloody Culloden and poor wee Duncan ... died because of you. I'll no' shake your hand, there's blood on it."

Morag put her hand to her throat.

"I'll no' fight you, Johnnie."

The words came out of Johnnie in a rush. "Never wanted to go to war, tried to keep Duncan out of it, but it was no good. Gut shot. He had me with him ... at the last."

Morag chewed her lip. *I didna ken that.*

Rob winced. "Poor Duncan, I'll pray for him."

"Say a prayer for me while you're at it."

Morag watched in dismay as Johnnie spurred forward and was soon out of sight and heading in the direction of Braedrumie.

Rob and Euan stared at each other.

"Give him time," said Euan as they followed Johnnie.

***

That afternoon Morag's first glimpse of Braedrumie was of curling smoke and smouldering embers falling like petals over the village. The stink of burnt timber and thatch hung in the air.

Granny Mac sat on a flat stone, her head in her hands. Isabel knelt with Dougie's head on her lap. Huddled family groups stared at the ruined crofts as one after another the blackened roof arches collapsed with a groan into the billowing smoke.

What will the crofters do now?

"Thank God." said Morag's father who'd an arm round Isabel. He helped Morag dismount and held her to him. "I've been worried sick. They said you'd been taken."

"Kinross is dead," said Morag.

"Dougie never trusted him. Same as his father, he said."

Isabel hugged her.

Morag put her cheek against her friend's. "We're so sorry for your loss."

Tears streamed down Isabel's lined face. "He was... a good man." She wiped her eyes with her hands. "Do you ken Tolbain's seized *Braedrumie House* and brought that slut, Kirsty, with him?"

Morag gasped, Rob's eyes narrowed and Johnnie cursed.

A muscle in Euan's jaw twitched. "They willna be there long."

Isabel seemed to notice Rob for the first time. "You've come home."

"I have ... for a few hours."

"Dougie thought a lot of you. You broke his heart."

Oh Isabel, thought Morag. *No you too.*

"It wasna my intention. Sometimes a man has no choice."

"You're a redcoat."

"I'm still a Stewart."

"I can see that. Blood will out. It's good you saved your brothers."

"I wish I'd been in time to save Dougie."

"He tried to stop them. It would have been different in his youth." Her eyes glistened, but her voice remained steady. "The laird couldna do anything, hasn't been right since Duncan was killed. I told Jamie Moffat to take him to the den, so he'd be safe with the priest. Johnnie and Alais had been visiting the laird at *Braedrumie House.* One of the MacNairs grabbed Alais and Johnnie killed him."

So, that was the way of it.

"A dead MacNair is no loss," said Euan, "but to think of Tolbain eating at our table, sticks in my craw. He'll have no' joy in it."

Rob nodded. "It's no' right, and you say you have a priest?"

"Yes. We found him in one of Uncle John's ships. He married Morag and me. I need to get him back ..."

"Oh no, you don't." Morag took Euan's arm. She'd had enough of Euan gallivanting all over the place. "I want to look at that leg. Sit down."

Euan did as he was told much to Rob and Isabel's amusement.

"I'll take the priest back tomorrow." Johnnie looked miserable. "After Dougie's ... you ken."

"That's good of you, man." Euan put a hand on Johnnie's shoulder.

'I wish we could have buried Duncan beside him," said Johnnie.

Euan nodded and Rob sighed.

Poor Dougie and Isabel and no wonder Johnnie's changed, he's still grieving over Duncan.

"It'll be good to get the priest out of our hair," said Johnnie. "I've never kenned anyone complain so much. I'd better find Alais, see how the bairns are." He went to where she waited for him in the shadows.

Morag watched them walk away together and smiled to herself. She rummaged in her bag of simples, found what she wanted and examined Euan's wound. Her fingers prodded round the nasty gash across the top of his thigh.

He grimaced.

"Here, put this on your lip." Isabel handed Morag a wet cloth. "It's boiled yarrow, healed Dougie's cuts many a time."

"Thank you." Morag held it to her mouth. She didn't look at Euan. They'd a lot to discuss. Kinross' lying words had cut her to the quick. Goodness knows what Euan thought. "Your wound needs stitching."

"But you dinna like sewing." He held her gaze.

Morag arched an eyebrow at him. "Isabel put this needle and silk in boiling water please. It seems to help wounds heal." Isabel dropped them into a bubbling pot.

Euan grimaced.

"And have you whisky?" asked Morag.

Isabel reached for a jug and horn tumblers.

"Drink?" Morag offered Euan and Rob.

Rob thanked her and sighed after he drank it. "It's as good as I remembered. No one makes whisky like Braedrumie's best."

Euan studied Morag and the whisky, then downed it in one gulp and grinned.

Morag grinned back, took Rob's tumbler, filled it and whispered in his ear.

Rob grabbed Euan and Morag poured whisky over the wound. Euan bucked and half rose on his stool. Rob's grip on him tightened, groaning, Euan sank back clenching his teeth.

"That'll teach you to play with swords," Morag said and Rob chuckled.

Euan glared at Rob and then Morag. "I didna ken when I married that my brother and wife would torture me."

She offered him a piece of wood to bite down on. He shook his head and she tutted. She threaded the needle and pulled the gaping wound together with a row of neat stitches. His body tensed each time she pierced his skin and eased the silk through the raw flesh.

Beads of sweat peppered his brow, but he sat like a statue staring at Rob as if in a contest of wills.

Several minutes later, Morag tied a knot, bit off the thread and brushed Euan's thigh with her lips. His knee jerked as if she'd burnt him. Covering her embarrassment, she sat back on her heels and said, "They're very neat stitches, very neat indeed."

"Well, now I look like a piece of embroidery, can I have another dram? I'm very badly wounded and that needle makes a fine weapon."

She gave him a rueful smile and poured him more whisky. "I'm sorry I hurt you."

"Are you now?"

She flicked a look at him and dropped her eyes.

"I'd sooner it was you, than someone else."

She watched him swallow the whisky and manage a grin as she cleaned the dried blood off his leg with hot water. Her nose wrinkled as she applied a mixture containing turpentine, myrrh and vinegar to his thigh. Using her fingers and thumb she gently massaged it over his wound. She stopped, aware his breathing had stilled.

Rob fingered his neck cloth as if it had become too tight.

She sensed Euan watching her every movement. Her face grew hot as her fingers bound his wound with strips of linen from her petticoat, difficult to do it and not touch him. After a couple of false starts she tied the two ends of cloth into a large bow and sat back to admire her handiwork. Euan hadn't made a sound, but she could have sworn he enjoyed the experience.

"Very pretty," he said.

"Very," said Rob, "I'd go so far as to say that bow wouldna look amiss on a lady's hat."

Morag threw a wet rag at Rob. He withdrew laughing.

Self-conscious under Euan's gaze, she dropped the ointment, recovered it and dropped it again. He picked it up and gave it to her, then turned away as if a sheet of ice had fallen between them.

She blamed Kinross.

CHAPTER Sixty

Later that afternoon, Euan led Rob to the den, the air fresh as always higher up the mountain. Their view encompassed 360 degrees. Misty hills to the north, at their feet the pewter salver of Loch Linnhe, to the west the shimmering coast and more mountains to the south and east. Eagles wheeled overhead as they tramped round rock spills and knots of spiky undergrowth.

Their father sat outside the den, wrapped in the bloody saltire, while Jamie Moffat fed him broth by the fire. The cave's dark interior concealed heather beds, woollen rugs stacked in neat piles and bundles of clothes. A couple of leather bags drooped from broken boughs making it more difficult for mice and other vermin to raid the paltry amount of food.

Euan heard Rob's sharp intake of breath at their father's appearance.

"My thanks." Euan shook Jamie Moffat's hand. "I'd be grateful if you stayed with him." He indicated his father. "Till tomorrow morning."

Jamie nodded. His mouth relaxed into a smile and his pink scar puckered.

Rob knelt beside his father counting the threads in the saltire. "Father?"

"Do I ken you?" He peered at Rob and shook his head. "Euan, who's this? Who's this man?"

Oh, God.

"It's Rob, Father, don't you ken me?" Rob asked.

"He died some time ago I ken that."

Rob stared at him. Euan squeezed Rob's shoulder. *What a homecoming.*

"Have you a drink for me?" asked Father.

Euan offered him one. His father took a gulp and spluttered. "It's water."

"It's all we have." Euan lied and stroked his father's back.

The old man crooned to himself as Rob shook his head.

"I know, he's worse than you kenned," whispered Euan not knowing what else to say. "Now, where's the priest?"

"When he heard your footsteps, he bolted like a deer into the heather," said Jamie.

"I'll get him," said Rob venturing forwards.

"Don't shoot. Don't shoot." The priest came out with his hands raised.

Jamie laughed and Rob grinned.

"It's all right Father, we dinna shoot priests on Sunday," said Euan.

Jamie hooted at that.

Euan stood with folded arms as the priest put down his hands and flushed. "Your father's raving, should be in the mad house." He pointed at the laird. "I've lived with him long enough, I should know. Now take me to the coast as you promised and put me on a ship for France. I daren't stay ... if I'd known redcoats would be here..."

Euan looked at him with distaste. "We've dead to bury, Father. I'm sure you'll want to say prayers over them..."

"Prayers? Bury the dead? I want to leave the Highlands. Take me to the coast."

Euan eyed the priest. "Johnnie's agreed to take you tomorrow, after the funerals. You'll understand that our people need us at this time."

The priest glared at them and his mouth curled into a sneer, until he noticed the look on Euan's face.

"Go in peace, my son." He made the sign of the cross. "I'll be ready."

As they left Euan hissed, "Keep an eye on the priest, Jamie lad." Their father's weeping followed them down the hillside.

"I didna realise Father... like that." The words seemed to stick in Rob's throat.

Euan eyed his eldest brother. "It's the drink. It'll help if we're back in our own home before winter. Can you no' do anything for us, Rob?"

"I can try, but you fought for the Jacobites. The government willna forget that. Only luck Witt sent me with orders for Hartlass. When I discovered that bastard had been sent to Braedrumie I feared the worst."

They'd arrived at the outskirts of the village now and could see small fires ahead of them through the trees.

Euan limped favouring his aching leg. "You ken, the prince wasna worth dying for. He left us to fend for ourselves on that moor. We were damned fools."

"Not fools, you fought for a Cause you believed in. Another time, another place you might have won and I'd be the fool. Scotland needs to out think the British Government; the battlefield isna the only way to defeat an enemy."

CHAPTER Sixty-one

The sun sank behind the mountains to the west. Euan watched storm clouds cradle the silver moon to the west as night fell and the air cooled.

"I need to make my peace with Mother." Rob motioned towards the old church.

Euan had been dreading this moment. "Rob, Father wouldna ..." began Euan.

"Just take me to her."

Euan held a bracken torch to light their way as he limped up to the graveyard with Rob at his side.

Euan opened the creaking wooden gate, pointed out the grave to him and handed over the torch. He watched Rob stride away, take off his hat and kneel on the hard ground beside her resting place with his head bowed. *Dear God what will he do when he sees his name's missing from her gravestone?*

Euan saw Rob's back stiffen and sensed his pain. He watched him draw out his dirk and carve something in the stone. Rob's chin was set and his eyes fired blue ice chips as he closed the churchyard gate. He said nothing, just replaced his dirk in his boot.

"I'm sorry about the gravestone. Father ..." Euan mumbled.

"I put it right," said Rob in the clipped way he had, when he didn't want to discuss something. "You're the heir now and you must both do your duty by Dougie and the others. My presence isna welcome here and questions may be asked if I delay my return to the regiment any longer."

"Where are they?"

"Inverness."

"Stay, a little while longer Rob, don't go." Morag slipped between them. "You missed our wedding."

Rob paused for a heartbeat. "I canna, I've got to report back to Witt. I'm pleased you're married. You're right for each other."

"Look after Father," continued Rob, "and write, promise me you'll write."

"We'll all write," muttered Johnnie moving beside them. He put out his hand. "I've been a bloody fool. I canna let my eldest brother go without saying goodbye again and thank you."

Rob clasped his hand and a muscle twitched in his jaw. "That means more than I can say. Tell Father I'll always be part of this family, always, even if we're thousands of miles apart. Will you tell him?"

Eaun rubbed his eyebrow. "I'll tell him, brother."

"We'll all tell him," added Johnnie.

"Look after that wound, Euan. Stay safe all of you." Rob shook their hands and hugged them all. "I'll do what I can about *Braedrumie House*, but I dinna hold out much hope." Mounting his horse, he galloped away, but this time he looked back and waved.

CHAPTER Sixty-two

The following morning Morag and Alais helped Isabel wash Dougie and the three hanged men: Hamish, Callum and Alan and dressed them in clean plaids, whilst Euan collected his father and led him like a child down to the village. The solemn faced villagers waited for them.

They buried the dead Stewarts on a slight rise in the graveyard facing east.

Morag thought Isabel looked bereft. She put her arm round her.

Isabel gave a wistful smile. "He'll feel the sun on his face each dawn and he'll never be alone."

They piled the earth on top of the graves and the women placed freshly picked gorse and heather on them until the mounds were a mass of gold, purple and white.

Euan stepped forward and looked up at the overcast sky. "Lord, it is loyal Stewarts we bury this day. They didna deserve to die. We ask that they sit by your side on the Throne of Justice.

Dougie Stewart was the laird's tacksman, cut down when unarmed. No man could have done that if he'd had a sword or dirk in his hand. He taught us what it meant to be a Highlander: honour, bravery and kinship, he lived up to them all. We'll never forget the man or his teachings.

Lord, look after them all as they looked after us in life. May they have eternal rest. Amen."

"Amen," the sad crowd repeated.

Isabel embraced the mourners one by one. She bade them go and help the others who grieved. They left her sitting in tears beside his grave.

Morag saw Johnnie with his arm round Alais and her comforting him.

The grim lines of Euan's face pierced her soul. *Is it poor Duncan, Dougie and the dead clan or Kinross' lies eating away at him? Nothing*

I say or do eases his pain. Will we ever feel comfortable with each other again?

***

They took Isabel to the den and Morag found her a place where she could rest before she returned to stand beside Euan to say goodbye to Johnnie.

Morag watched the priest mount his pony before the others.

"Can we go now?"

She thought the priest's thin lips and face mirrored his mean ways. *Damn the man, has he no soul?*

"A moment." Giving the reins of his pony to Euan, Johnnie hugged Morag, then knelt and kissed Comrie and Neill who clung to him. "I expect you to be good and look after your ... mother." He glanced at tearful Alais. "I'll be back soon."

She nodded and swept her fingers under both her eyes. Morag put her arm round her friend as Johnnie said his goodbyes to the children.

"I love you, Dada. More than all the ponies in the world." Comrie smothered his face in kisses. "Come back soon."

Neill put his small hand on Johnnie's shoulder. "I'll look after Mother and Comrie, Father."

Johnnie patted their heads. Alais joined them and his arms held them all for a long time. Eventually, he and Alais prised themselves away whilst Morag took the children's hands and watched Johnnie lead Alais to one side and embrace her. He stared into her eyes, whispered something, bent his head low and kissed her.

Morag's heart ached for them all as Johnnie shook Euan's hand and left for Port Glasgow with the priest.

***

Johnnie had been away for three weeks when to Morag's delight, Jamie Moffat came up to the den with two visitors on dust covered ponies. "I've brought friends on the way to France."

Morag ran towards the Crawfords with her arms outstretched. She'd never expected to see them again.

Amelia's wan face lit up at the sight of Morag.

Morag greeted her with tears and hugs. "I'm so pleased you're here. So much has happened since we last met."

"Yes." Amelia bit her lip at Morag's questioning look.

Ah, she's lost the baby. Morag wished she could give Euan a bairn, then he'd forget Kinross' words, but there were no hopes of that at the moment. They hardly spoke and led a frugal existence, supported by Euan's hunting ability, the goodwill of villagers and her father supplying them with a few vegetables, cheese and milk. This was not the time to bring another hungry mouth into the world, but she longed for Euan's arms to be around her once again and a kind word. Since the redcoat attack on Braedrumie, they'd drifted apart.

Euan shook hands with Lord Crawford and nodded to his wife. "It's good to see you're both safe and well. You're welcome to stay and rest with us. We've little, but can share some broth." Euan led them by the fire.

Pushing her painful thoughts to one side, Morag did her best to make her friends comfortable. It made her heartsick to see Amelia so travel stained, weary and with such a restless look in her eyes.

"So what happened after you returned home, your letter mentioned a journey?" asked Morag.

"I went to Inverness and found Crawford." Amelia's eyes glistened.

Morag squeezed her friend's hand. "Some broth, it'll warm you."

"Thank you." She worked her spoon till the last was gone, then ran her finger round the rim and sucked it. "It tastes so good."

"There's more," said Morag knowing she'd have to do without.

Amelia shook her head. "It's good enough for you to share what you have. Being hunted is wearing, isn't it?"

"Were you at Culloden?"

Amelia nodded. "We agreed I'd wait at a distance with a spare horse in case the battle went against us. The prince left the field and the dragoons almost ran Crawford down." Her voice became a whisper, "I canna tell you how awful it was. So many lives lost. There's been little mercy in the aftermath, we've heard of the dreadful executions of friends. Cumberland has a lot to answer for." She sighed. "We escaped with the prince, but he encouraged us to disperse or we'd have all been captured. We've been hunted from place to place all these months. There's nothing for us in Scotland now, our land and properties have been sequestered. Crawford says we'll rally again in France, The Cause will never die."

"You think so?" Morag was stunned.

"I have to, dinna you? Or everything we've done and sacrificed will have been in vain."

Morag thought of the decimated clans and the sheer numbers of redcoats in the Highlands. She thought of Sinclair, who but for her, would have deserted Amelia in her hour of need, and she thought of the feckless prince who'd ridden from Culloden leaving behind those who'd fought for him. The Cause lay dead on the battlefield.

Amelia smoothed her muddy skirts. "We'll start a new life in France, Crawford has cousins there. And you?"

"Euan and I are married now."

"I'm so pleased for you." Amelia kissed Morag's cheek. "But you look unhappy."

Morag bit her lip. "I have lots to tell you, but all bad news I'm afraid. Tolbain's taken our house and lands and Kinross tried to kidnap me, he worked for both sides.

"A traitor," gasped Amelia.

"And a liar, Euan killed him, but not before he hinted we were more than friends in Edinburgh. Things haven't been the same between Euan and me since."

"I'm so sorry, Morag. Do you think Euan believes you ... cared for Kinross?"

"I ... yes ... I dinna ken." Morag's head drooped.

Amelia pressed her hand. "Does he ken nought of what we accomplished in Edinburgh?"

"No."

"You've not told him?"

Morag shook her head. "Only a little, I let him think I was safe."

"Then I will tell him all of it and the truth about Kinross."

"But Amelia ..."

"I canna make it worse. He'll listen to me. You're no' to worry anymore."

Morag wrung her hands as she watched Amelia call Euan from the fire and walk for some distance from the others, talking to him as she went. He lowered his head and listened.

That evening, the Crawfords were on their way to the coast with Jamie Moffat leading them, but not before Amelia whispered to Morag, "I told Euan everything and he thanked me. Dearest Morag, I hope all will be well between you now." Amelia kissed her. "Write won't you?"

"Yes." Morag tried to hold back tears. "Let us know when you're safe - and thank you."

"Of course. It was nothing." Amelia dabbed at her eyes. "It's so difficult to say goodbye to friends." She embraced Morag for a final time.

Euan put his arm round Morag's shoulders. She gave a deep sigh and leant her head on his shoulder. *He understands.*

"Jamie will see you safe through the patrols, God speed and a safe journey." Euan shook Lord Crawford's hand. Euan and Morag waved till their friends were out of sight.

"Forgive me my heart," he said once they were alone, "I should have trusted you. What you did for The Cause was brave and bold. I see that now. My beautiful lass has become a woman."

Sweet Jesu, he really understands. "A woman who loves you very much." Morag lifted her parched lips to the tender heat of his.

Where's Johnnie? The leaves had turned into a tapestry of red and gold and the moors bracken brown. Johnnie hadn't returned from his journey with the priest to Port Glasgow well over a month ago. Morag kept herself busy in the den by folding woollen rugs and picking up a besom. *Hooves?*

Jamie Moffat dismounted from his pony and beamed at her. "Your friends got away on a French ship. I've cousins who do a bit of smuggling and they took them out in their boat. The Crawfords should be in France by now."

"Oh that's wonderful." Morag kissed his rough cheek. *Jamie Moffat has whiskers.*

"I've other news from the village." Jamie tugged his ear, "Kirsty's mother's dead and Tolbain's broken his leg, fell downstairs. Pity it wasna his neck. They say the bone came through the skin. Any other man would be dead by now, but no' that devil. They say, though it's no love match, Kirsty's never left his bedside since his accident. She's very tender towards him, too tender some say. Oh, and the village would like to know when your babe's expected."

"Babe? Morag had forgotten she was supposed to be pregnant. "Tell them there was no babe."

"They'll be very disappointed." Jamie tugged his ear.

Disappointed? The irony of it.

"Oh and I've letters for the laird."

"Thank you."

As Morag held the letters her thoughts turned to how convenient that broken leg must be for Kirsty. She patted the laird's shoulder as he drooled and rocked backwards and forwards in the shadow of the den near the hearth.

"I'll show them to Euan first," she said to Jamie. "You can see how it is?"

"Yes. He's no' getting any better." Jamie tugged his ear.

"Sit yourself down," she said. "Alais. Alais. Jamie Moffat's here."

Alais arrived with the laughing children in either hand. Their wet hair stuck to their heads. "Johnnie?" she signed.

Morag shook her head. "No, not Johnnie. Oh, Alais, Jamie says my friends are safe in France." Morag grabbed hold of them all and danced with them in circles. "Give Jamie some whisky from our last keg and there's porridge you can share. I'm away to take these to Euan." She waved the letters in the air and went off enjoying the beautiful day full of the fertile scents of the warm peaty earth, gorse and heather. Euan had gone fishing. She knew the spot, about a mile from the den. He'd found a place where the water pooled before making its downward rush to meet the loch below.

She sank into the heather. Several silver fish lay on the bank, whilst Euan, stripped to the waist, had his back to her. She enjoyed his muscles playing on his broad back as his arms let the rest of the plaid fall down to reveal lean flanks and long legs. This was the first time she was able to view him rather like, well, like a painting or a statue, like those she'd seen in Holyrood, but they'd been, pale, unmoving creatures; he was flesh and blood and very much alive.

My beautiful man. Not that he'd like that description. Wading out further, he hummed to himself oblivious to the icy touch of the water as he washed.

Perhaps that's why she threw the first small stone. She watched it sail over his head and land with a plop in front of him.

He raced out of the stream with a warlike yell that frightened the devil out of her, straight at her hiding place in the heather. She scrambled to her feet and ran, weaved, dodged, to get away, but she felt his hands on her waist. They slipped away as he roared like a rutting stag behind her.

"Aaaargh." A red faced Euan hopped round in circles nursing one foot in his hand.

She started to giggle and then laugh and couldn't stop.

"It's no' funny I thought you were a redcoat." He limped off hardly allowing his foot to touch the ground.

"Let me see." She followed him.

"I think you've done enough seeing," said Euan with an air of injured dignity. She struggled not to smile as he covered his private parts with his plaid, sat on a tree stump, examined his foot and shook his head. "It hurts a lot." He sounded like the little boy she'd known so well.

"Let me." She lifted his foot and squinted at his sole for some time. "Why it's just a tiny thorn." Gripping the tip of it between her thumb and forefinger, she pulled it out.

"Ow." He howled grabbing at his foot. "You do realise I've had two terrible injuries now? Both caused by..."

"Me?" She felt guilty.

"Yes. I need something..."

"A salve." She studied the pink scar on his thigh. It looked healthy, with no ominous red streaks. "I'll just... Euan, what are you doing?"

His hand had strayed and cupped her breast and the other had made its way up towards her knee.

"Well." He planted burning kisses on her neck. "I may be terribly wounded,"- Kiss, "but I'm not dying"- Kiss. "And part of me"- Kiss. "Wants to remember"- Kiss. "What it's like"- Kiss. "To be a married man."- Kiss. "Now let me see, if my memory serves me well -"

"Euan Stewart."

"Yes." His mouth moved lower to the valley of her bosom. "I thought I was right." He gave her a lopsided grin. "Now, I just need to check..."

Sometime later, a lot later, they emerged from the heather and bathed in the cool mountain waters of the stream.

"You know, if we carry on at this rate, I dinna think I'll reach old age, but I'll have led a very happy life."

She giggled and teased him by flicking his ear with a grass stalk and smiled as he tried to waft the supposed fly away. She struggled to dress as Euan kept pulling her skirt and stole one of her garters.

"Oh." She stopped and looked on the ground all round her.

"What?" He jerked upright with a start, looking for his dirk.

"I'd letters for you, well, the laird really. But he's no'... Jamie Moffat brought them. Where are they?" She looked under the gorse and heather widening her search.

"Got them," she yelled waving them above her head.

He put out his hand and she gave them to him. She snuggled under his arm, pleased they were back to how they used to be with each other.

Euan examined the packets, but didn't recognise the handwriting. He quickly broke the first seal and unfolded the parchment. As he read his brow creased. "It's from Uncle John, dated September 10th, over a week ago. Oh no, it's about Johnnie..."

She closed her eyes, put her head on his shoulder resigned to hear the worst.

He read her the letter:

Port Glasgow, September 10th, 1746

My dear James,

Steel yourself for I have bad news. Johnnie has been arrested and taken to Carlisle Castle.

I am sure he is innocent of any misdeed and will do all I can to inform the authorities of this fact before he is taken to York later this week for trial. I have taken it upon myself to write to your Uncle Munro requesting his assistance as he has more influence with the government than me. Rest assured that I will do all within my power to help the poor boy.

Your loving brother, John

"Sweet Jesu, no."

Euan held her face in his hands and kissed her forehead. "My uncles will do their utmost to get him back."

His words steadied her. "And your other letter?"

Euan examined the writing. "It's from Aunt Munro." His eyebrows lowered as they read it together:

Inverness, September 20th, 1746

My dears,

We were quite distraught at hearing the dreadful news from your Uncle John about poor Johnnie's incarceration in Carlisle and then York. Rest assured your Uncle Munro will use what influence he has to help. He has despatched a letter this very day, begging for clemency and verifying Johnnie's good character and his Whig background on this side of the family.

Your uncles are meeting in York to see what they can do to better aid him there. I am so sorry that I cannot convey better news, but be assured they will not rest until he is safe.

My thoughts and prayers are all for Johnnie and you. We have heard the most dreadful tales of what has occurred in the Highlands and hope you have been spared the worst of it.

You'll have heard, whilst your uncle was absent doing government business, I was arrested for being a known Jacobite supporter, sorely mistreated and my poor home ransacked.

Rest assured that I am quite recovered and if I receive any news about Johnnie, I will inform you at once. Please let me know if we can be of any more assistance.

Dearest regards, Aunt Munro"

Morag wrapped her arms round Euan and nestled her head on his shirt. "It was kind of her to write to us. Poor Johnnie didna even want to fight. At least he has the assistance of his uncles, but will they be able to do anything?"

I dinna ken." Euan's gaze turned to the mountain-peaked horizon as if seeking an answer there.

CHAPTER Sixty-four

Morag made Alais sit down and held her hand whilst sharing the letter about Johnnie with her, the laird and the children. Alais looked shocked, then pensive. The laird smiled and nodded. Morag wondered if Neil and Comrie fully understood either. They'd already had trauma in their young lives, how would they cope with this? The children walked off hand in hand and sat in the cool shadow of the rock face. They played in the dust.

The sun shone like a gold coin and a gentle breeze rippled through the grass and shrubs. Thoughts about poor Johnnie seemed easier to bear as she wrung water out of Euan's plaid and shirts.

Neill played a game in the dirt throwing a stone in the air and trying to catch it on the back of his hand. Comrie sucked her thumb and watched.

Alais tugged at Morag's sleeve. She signed, her hands and fingers moving like quicksilver, "I ... have ... to ... go ... village. You ... look ... after ... children? She made a rocking movement with her arms.

"Of course," said Morag and before she could ask why, Alais had gone.

Towards evening when the air cooled and the sun sank, Alais returned, her eyes shining. She swung Morag round by her waist and took her to a quiet spot and signed, "Kirsty ... she ... help ... Johnnie."

"You went to Kirsty Tolbain for help?"

"I gave her ... note. She ... loved ... once. I asked ... testify ... good character."

"What did she say?"

"She ... couldna ... abide ... fools. Asked ... had ... I ... written ... note? She ... will ... help ... asked ... for ... £50."

"You'd better tell Euan." Morag chewed her lip.

Euan strode up and down in fury. "Dear God, Alais? You've asked Tolbain's wh... **her** to help us? What have you done?"

Morag translated as Alais signed, "She ... influence ... cares ... about ... Johnnie. We ... need ... money ... pay ... her."

"We dinna need her help, we'll look after our own." Euan glowered at her.

Alais signed again, "How? You ... hunted... rebels. She... married ... powerful... man, a ... Whig..."

"All the more likely he'll make matters worse, for God's sake."

"She's ... pregnant," Alais signed again, "Tolbain ... thinks ... it's ... a ... son."

Morag felt a pang, she wished she was carrying Euan's child.

"It might change matters," Euan mused.

"Better ... suggestion? Johnnie ... hang ... without ... her ... help. You ... have ... money, use ... buy ... his ... life." She put her arms round Comrie and Neill. Their faces pressed into her apron.

"Euan, Alais is right, it's a good idea."

Euan frowned at her and Alais signed, "I'll ... take ... children ... to ... play."

Morag and Euan watched them go.

"Alais is right, Euan." Morag repeated, putting her arms round his neck. "We've no powerful friends that could come to Johnnie's aid. You said yourself Carlisle's a fortress and York impossible. As much as I dinna like Kirsty, she's Johnnie's only real hope. We have the money. I'll take it to her.

At least we know your uncles are trying to help and perhaps Kirsty will have some influence too. One of the servants told Isabel that Tolbain doesna beat her so much now she's carrying his bairn. They say he thinks it's a son. He'll be in a good mood. This might help Johnnie. God help her if it's a girl."

"And God help Johnnie." Euan held Morag close.

CHAPTER Sixty-five

This waiting tore at Euan's soul. *Just like Culloden, only now we need news of poor Johnnie and with the laird as he is*, the *clan will look to me for decisions. This winter's going to be hard.*

The October wind moaned through the pine trees when Jamie brought Euan's uncles to the den. They'd ridden as fast as they could from Johnnie's trial in York, they said, their faces grim and etched with weariness.

"It's good to see you, Uncles," said Euan. "The laird's sleeping. A dram? We've bread and cheese, thanks to Morag's father."

Alais signed, "Neill ... Comrie ... firewood."

"Must we?" moaned Neill.

"Go ... "

Euan's uncles accepted a dram and Uncle Munro said, "You have my sympathy. You know I worked for the government, saw no sense in your Cause, but they mean to grind you underfoot. Despite all our pleas, Johnnie has been convicted as a Jacobite rebel."

Alais gasped as Euan felt a gaping hole open up inside him and Morag squeezed his hand.

Uncle Munro sniffed and waved a piece of parchment at them. "However, much to our surprise the Duke of er ... Tolbain gave ... er... Johnnie a glowing character reference that convinced the court he was a gentleman of means. God knows how he did it. Johnnie's sentence has been commuted from death to transportation to er ... the Americas for life."

Alais stared open eyed at him. She signed, "He ... will ... live?"

Euan hugged Morag. "Yes."

Morag sagged with relief, then grabbed Euan's hands and danced round the room saying, "Sweet Jesu, she did it, Kirsty did it."

Alais stood as if not knowing whether to laugh or cry and the laird stroked the bloody saltire and stared at all of them.

"Kirsty?" asked Uncle Munro looking mystified.

"It's better you dinna ken, Uncle," said Euan. "Thank you for your part in this."

"He has his life at least," muttered Uncle John.

"But we'll never see Johnnie again, he's lost to us." Euan sighed. "We canna even see him before he sails."

"He's already embarked," said Uncle John.

Alais' mouth sagged open.

Euan and Morag stared open mouthed.

Uncle John adjusted his spectacles. "What I can tell you, is he looked well and asked us to give you all his love and this." He handed a letter to Euan who broke the seal and read it aloud to them:

October 19th, 1746

My dear family,

Rest assured that I am fit and well. You will have learned by now that I have been sentenced to transportation to the Americas. Thank you for doing all you could for me. Our uncles risked much, not least their own characters and livelihood to come to my aid. I thank them for it.

When you think of me, don't say: he's a young man and can withstand many things, but that he's a Stewart and will withstand them.

It only grieves me that I cannot see your dear faces or hear your voices once again or walk along Loch Linnhe or on the hills as I did when I was a boy.

Euan will look after you all and I know that somehow we will be together again, some years hence.

Though an ocean separates us, I will endeavour to see you all again and will write at the earliest opportunity. Pray for me.

Your brother,

Johnnie"

"Father, Father." Euan took the letter over to his bed at the back of the den. "Johnnie's going to be alright, he's been transported."

"Johnnie?" His father stared at him with blank eyes.

Uncle Munro tutted and Uncle John nodded his head in sympathy.

Alais signed as tears fell, "He ... didna ... mention ... my ... name ... and ... he ... is ... everything ... to ... me."

Euan was grateful when Morag put her arm round Alais' waist and they went off to seek the children together and tell them.

Later that evening, when the children were asleep, they sat round the fire. Uncle Munro mentioned an Act of Parliament that would come into being the following year.

Euan tensed sensing trouble ahead. *What now?*

"To be forewarned is to be er ... forearmed." Uncle Munro sniffed, tapping the side of his purple veined nose. They listened, as he pulled out another page of parchment, and summarised the contents. "Your chiefs will lose their judicial rights and become proprietors of the clan-lands. Highlanders willna be allowed to bear arms, or wear tartan, you know this already, play the pipes or speak Gaelic."

"What?" Euan sprang up.

"Let me finish, Nephew. Finally, a great many estates are to be escheated and their rent used for agricultural purposes."

"My God," said Euan, "Highlanders will be no more. A clansman willna have right of tenure of the land and no reason to follow his chief. Our culture, language, our very being will be stripped from us with all the force of British law."

"This is worse than being keel hauled." Uncle John looked worried.

"Yes it will be very bad and er ... as the years pass it will only get worse," added Uncle Munro. "You need to look to the er ... future for you, your family and what's left of the clan and decide what to do for the best." He sniffed and dabbed at his nose with his handkerchief. "Now show me a bed, for I'm an old man and in need of er... sleep."

"It canna be borne," said Morag. "We need to do something."

Euan turned to her with dead eyes. "Whatever we do they mean to annihilate us."

CHAPTER Sixty-six

Alais and the children slept and breathed in unison. Morag turned on her heather bed. The fire spat gleaming sparks onto the den floor and illuminated the faces of the men talking in low voices round it.

In the light of the glowing flames, Uncle John spoke of the Stewart's ships. It seemed to Morag as she watched that Euan's back straightened as if his uncle had given him some hope.

As she fell asleep she wondered how Uncle Munro and Rob could be on the side of a government so merciless in victory. Her last thought: poor Johnnie chained in a ship's hold on his way to the Americas.

The next morning the air filled with the stench of burnt broth. "Well, that's the last of the barley." Morag sighed. Her mind had been on other things. *What will we eat now?*

The sound of hooves and jangling harness made their eyes swivel towards Jamie Moffat leading two riders towards them. Everyone tensed until they recognised Rob wearing a white shirt, black waistcoat, jacket and black breeches.

He brought his horse to a halt and sniffed the air saying, "Thought it better to visit in civilian clothing. Have you so much food you can afford to burn it? I suppose this means you're no' interested in the provisions I've brought courtesy of the British government?" Dismounting with a wide grin, he presented them with two sacks. "Uncles, I didna expect to see you here."

"Rob, you're a sight for sore eyes." Euan and his uncles shook Rob's hand whilst the women fell on the food.

"We haven't seen bread, flour or ... soap for months. You're a wonderful, wonderful man, Rob Stewart." Morag raced to kiss him on the cheek making him turn to the smiling woman on the horse and shrug. The children put their hands over their mouths.

"It's really someone else you have to thank for the soap." He indicated the young woman assessing Morag with curious eyes.

"I thank you." *The woman didna like that kiss. How silly. Does Rob mean something more to her?* The woman seemed familiar and very beautiful. Morag experienced a spurt of recognition. "Lady Anne Kerr."

"She was." Rob smiled.

"Was?" Morag pondered on that for a time.

Rob helped Lady Anne dismount and seemed to hold her waist a tad longer than strictly required thought Morag. *He loves her.*

"Why have you brought *her* here?" Euan demanded his hand on his sword. "When we saw her at Holyrood we heard rumours she spied for the government."

Lady Anne blanched before his attack and if it hadn't been for Rob's steadying arm, Morag thought, the woman would have fallen. The Stewarts gave shocked cries.

Morag remembered Lady Anne's arrival at the ball in Holyrood, the sneers and whispers.

"Take that back, Euan," said Rob. Lady Anne touched his arm.

To pull him from the brink?

"She could betray us." Euan's eyes were alight with concern. "Jamie, go back down the trail and look for any patrols." Jamie raced off.

"There's no need." Rob stopped him. "She'd never betray you. You have my word on it."

Morag studied Lady Anne. "Did redcoats no' tie you to a cart on the Inverness road?"

"How did you ...?" The woman began, then smiled and took Morag's hands. "You gave me food and water. I recognise you now. Thank you for your kindness."

"She's no government spy." Morag elbowed Euan in the ribs. "The redcoats made her walk all the way to Inverness. She's a Jacobite."

A muscle worked in Rob's cheek. "She was involved in secret work for The Cause."

Morag grinned at Lady Anne who smiled back at her and Morag recognised something of herself in the other woman, a strong will perhaps?

A groan came from the corner of the den where the laird lay.

"I want to see Father." Rob led Lady Anne by the hand. "It's Rob. I've brought my wife to see you. We want your blessing."

Audible gasps came from everyone watching. "Wife."

Father's slight figure lay on a bed of plaids.

Didn't Rob jilt Anne Kerr before he disappeared? Morag could tell from their glances they loved each other.

The laird stirred as the woman curtsied.

"Father, may I present Lady Anne of Kerbilly," Rob said as she curtsied.

The laird struggled to sit up. "Rob, your brothers ... told me ... what you ... did for them. You ... were always ... a good lad." His voice was weak, "Your wife you say? Didna I ... pick her ... out for ... you? You have ... my ... blessing." They knelt as he placed his hand on their heads. Then he sank back and closed his eyes.

Rob turned to the waiting figures. "May I introduce my wife."

Euan knelt on one leg before Lady Anne. "I'm sorry for my harsh words. I promise to defend your name with my life's blood and I welcome you into our family and clan."

"Thank you." She smiled and curtsied

"This is my brother, Euan." Rob waved a hand at him. "You'll have noticed my brains and good looks dinna run in the family, on the other hand we've superb taste in beautiful women and Morag is Euan's wife."

They curtsied to each other.

Morag thought a look of relief flitted across Lady Anne's face.

Euan introduced Alais, Comrie and Neill. Alais curtsied, Comrie jigged up and down and Neill attempted a bow. "Alais doesna speak," he continued, 'redcoats burnt out her farm and ..." He looked at Rob ... "Well ..." He rubbed his brow.

"Sorry *Braedrumie House* will remain with Tolbain. I did warn you. The government isna sympathetic to Jacobites."

"Have you heard about Johnnie being captured?" said Euan.

Rob stared at Euan in horror.

"He's been transported. There's a letter, Alais let Rob see."

Rob read and reread the parchment. "At least he's alive." He handed the letter back to Alais. "Uncle John can you do ought for him?"

"I've put word out to the captains of our ships, dinna worry. He'll have friends in the Americas. Now, are you going to introduce your poor uncles to this lovely lady?"

"Uncle John and Uncle Munro, may I present my wife."

Uncle Munro kissed her hand followed by Uncle John.

Delighted to meet you, my dear," said Uncle Munro.

"Likewise I'm sure," said Uncle John.

"I canna thank you enough for all you've done for Johnnie." Euan shook his uncles' hands. "Please sit and eat. There's something important I need to discuss with you and Rob."

Morag took Lady Anne under her wing. They listened to the soft rise and fall of the men's voices becoming loud and argumentative. Morag raised an eyebrow at the women as they fed the children. "The men will agree in the end, whatever it's about."

***

Their visitors stayed till late the following afternoon when Morag saw Euan note the gathering dusk and lengthening shadows.

He said, "I think it would be safer for you if you left now. Redcoat patrols are always a danger."

"Of course my boy." Uncle Munro heaved himself up. "Understand, don't we, John? Our thanks." He put a hand on Euan's shoulder and shook Rob's hand. "We were about to saddle up."

"Rob, this family owes you a lot and more than it can ever repay. There was never any hope for The Cause, I see it now," said Euan.

Morag winced. *All those men dead and for what?*

"And you're laird now, in all but name, who'd have thought it?" said Rob. "I'm sorry."

"There's no need." Euan put his arm round Morag's waist.

"We all make errors of judgement, me more than most." Rob looked at Morag. "Now I've found Anne, I understand how it is between you and Euan." He kissed her cheek and turned to Euan. "Till we meet again," he said and shook Euan's hand. "I hope all goes well for you and yours. I'll pray for you."

"And I for you."

Anne hugged everyone before Rob helped her mount. They trotted off, waved a final goodbye and disappeared into the pine forest below.

Euan brought his uncles' ponies whilst Uncle John hugged and Uncle Munro kissed everyone before they mounted. Uncle Munro had only gone a few yards when Morag heard him say, "Damnation, I've forgotten something." He turned back, summoned Alais, leant down from his saddle and whispered in her ear. Morag thought she heard Johnnie's name. She watched her friend's face crease into a broad smile. Then the uncles were off and with one final wave from the top of the hillside they disappeared from view.

CHAPTER Sixty-seven

Spring arrived in March, 1747, it had been the one of the worst winters Morag could remember and the waiting had been hard. They'd struggled with ice, snow and little food.

Only the odd redcoat patrol had dared venture out from Fort William towards Braedrumie. The cold wind shrieking through the mountain passes and huge falls of snow, had kept all, but the most hardy and desperate indoors.

She knew Euan would act now when waters gushed, birds sang and heather and gorse dusted the hills. Morag thought Braedrumie had never looked so lovely.

Was it October when Euan argued with Rob and browbeat him? Euan wouldna have been able to do that when his brother was heir, but Rob had finally agreed to the clan's 'last mad act' as he'd called it.

It was a cold night, the moon flitting between restless sea-clouds. Morag knew Euan missed the support of his brothers and Dougie as he told the clan of their decision. They'd gathered on the cliff above Braedrumie, where they'd burned the cross in 1745. The families wept and wailed as they hugged each other.

Just after midnight Morag and Euan slipped undetected into *Braedrumie House*. Morag watched as Kirsty woke with a dirk at her throat and Euan's hand over her mouth. "Don't scream."

Loose words in several inns had sent Tolbain and his retainers riding east, thinking to catch Euan Stewart. The duke would be ambushed and dead before dawn. His sentries had already been killed and the servants had crept away in the night.

"Dinna kill me, I saved Johnnie remember." Kirsty pleaded.

Morag caught a movement out of the corner of her eye and raised her dirk.

"He's new born, an innocent." Kirsty put herself between Morag and the soft mewing sound.

Of course, Morag could smell milk and see wet spots on Kirsty's nightdress, where her breasts responded to the faint sounds of her baby. Morag's heart lurched and womb tightened. She lowered the blade. "Cover yourself." She couldn't take her eyes from the babe. She passed a shawl to his mother.

Kirsty wrapped it round herself. "He's only a few hours old - he's Johnnie's."

"No." said Euan.

"No." echoed Morag. "Sweet Jesu, he couldna be. Johnnie wouldna have looked at you after what you did to him."

"On my life, he's his."

"Dinna worry Stewarts don't murder women and children, unlike your fine husband. Get what you need for a journey," said Euan.

Kirsty wrapped the babe in several plaids. He began to cry.

"Sssh, sweetheart, sssh," said Kirsty and kissed his forehead. He quietened.

Morag and Euan led Kirsty and her babe on horseback up to the deserted den. They dumped her belongings on the ground.

"What are you going to do?" Kirsty asked as she rocked the sleeping child in her arms.

"You'll find out soon enough," Euan said. "You need to thank God, Kirsty Tolbain, we've given you your life and your babe's; that you've a roof over your head and the means to cook and warm yourself." He pointed at the battered cauldron hanging over the dead fire. "That's more than the redcoats and your husband did for those they murdered." Then they left her.

She shrieked after them, "You know nothing. You'll rue this day. Johnnie'll never forgive you."

Morag felt Kirsty's eyes burning into her back as they rode away.

By the time Euan and Morag returned the preparations were complete. The clan lit torches which they held high for all to see. They bathed the scene in a whirlpool of glimmering light producing a roar from everyone. Men yelling Gaelic war cries set light to *Braedrumie House's* empty stables. The flames licked the timbers and as the fire took hold, red sparks flew into the sable night.

Morag watched with hollow eyes as Euan and his men ran to the cellar which had been packed with stolen redcoat gunpowder. They lit the fuses and raced back out into the darkness. Throwing themselves over the stone wall beside her, they peered over the top.

Euan wrapped his arms round her. A deafening explosion and flash of bright light followed seconds later. The ground trembled and broke apart beneath her knees as the blast made the house heave up and out and down as if torn from its foundations. She stared as broken timbers, roof tiles, stones and millions of splinters of glass soared into the air and then rained down on them like missiles. Great belches of purple-black smoke rose into the sky and ochre, cerulean and vermilion flames shot out of windows, doors and roof. Her nostrils filled with the acrid stench of gunpowder, burning timber and rubble making it difficult to breathe as the watching crowd roared again and their torches swirled. *Braedrumie House* was ablaze.

Behind them, dark clouds gathered on the hills and the mountains. Ahead, the dying moon lit a thin silvery strip of water leading from Loch Linnhe to the Atlantic Ocean. A deathly hush descended as they turned their backs on the place they'd called home for all of their lives. Jamie Moffat's strong voice started a lament and it was taken up by all of them:

We're leaving our birth place now,
This precious plot tended by our hands.
We'll follow the gulls' way and the whales' way,
Towards the west and a new land...

The first light of dawn gilded a single standing stone. It stood on the hills overlooking Braedrumie and had the words: *THE STEWARTS, THEIR LAND* chiselled into it.

Morag thought about Duncan and Dougie and all the other men, how their lives had been cut short because they'd trusted the word of a prince. She thought of Johnnie and the dreams she and Euan had shared; of the house he was going to build and the life they'd planned to lead. All so much dust now.

But their love had held through fire and sword. They'd been seared in the furnace of war, and forged into finer steel. They'd build a home, but not in this place. Golden rays lit their faces as they set off, carrying their laird to Port Lachlan, one of their ships and the Americas.

Morag wouldn't tell Euan about Tolbain's assault on her until they'd sailed away from Braedrumie. First she'd share her news with him. Her hand went to the slight rise of her womb and she smiled to herself.

The End

The Jacobite's Daughter

Bibliography

Ashley, Mike (2002). *British Kings*, London, Robinson.

Allison, Hugh (2007). *Culloden Tales*, Edinburgh and London, Mainstream Publishing.

Craig, Maggie (1997). *Damn' Rebel Bitches*, Edinburgh, Mainstream Publishing.

Devine, T.M. (2004). *Scotland's Empire 1600-1815*, London, Penguin Books Ltd.

Duffy, Christopher (2003). *The '45, Bonnie Prince Charlie and the Untold Story of the Jacobite Rising*, London, Cassell.

Forbes, Robert (1747-1775).

Henderson, Jan-Andrew (2008). *The Town Below Ground*, Great Britain, CPI Cox and Wyman.

Herman, Arthur (2001). *The Scottish Enlightenment, The Scot's Invention of the Modern World, London*, Fourth Estate a Division of Harper Collins Publishers.

Hunter, James (2001). *Culloden and the Last Clansman*, Edinburgh, Mainstream Publishing Company Ltd.

Lanman, Bruce (1980). *The Jacobite Risings in Britain 1689-1746*, Edinburgh, Scottish Cultural Press.

Magnusson, Magnus (2001). *The Story of a Nation*, Edinburgh and London, Scotland, Harper Collins.

Paton H. *The Lyon in Mourning*, Scottish History Society. (1895)

Printed in Great Britain
by Amazon